THE QUEEN'S COMMAND

THE QUEEN'S COMMAND

MAGGIE OSBORNE

MADISON
PARK
PRESS™

NEW YORK

Originally published by William Morrow & Company in 1987 as *Chase the Heart*.

Published by Madison Park Press, 15 East 26th Street, New York, NY 10010. Madison Park Press is a trademark of Bookspan.

Book design by Christos Peterson

ISBN: 978-1-58288-264-2

Printed in the United States of America

To George and Zane

CHAPTER

1

*F*or those with wit and political dexterity, the Tudor court was the most exciting court in the world. Each day opened with a fresh contest combining elements of frivolity, intrigue, and crisis. Long ago Nell had decided there was no better place to be.

Until the crisis became personal.

But Lady Nellanor Amesly didn't want to think about that now. Instead, she stroked the merlin perched on her left wrist and let her gaze drift across the field. Since the victory the court had swollen, attended by more lords and ladies than Nell could remember. Even those who had not participated in the battle had braved the muddy autumn roads to journey to London and share in the celebrations.

It was an exhilarating time to be English and to be at court. Every day was crowded by tilts or hunts, excursions or city progresses; nights were filled with banquets and dancing, card games and fireworks. There were moments when Nell forgot she was in mourning.

Biting her lip, she ducked her cheek near the merlin's dun-colored plumage. She wished her guardian, Robert Dudley, Earl of Leicester, had been here to participate in the glory of England's triumph over the Spanish Armada. He would have loved being at the center of it. He would have strutted about the hawking field today, resplendent in plumes and silver thread, bowing and smiling and making the queen laugh. Quick tears glittered and her throat ached. Robert's death had diminished the court. A spark of grandeur and, yes, innocence had gone forever.

"What am I going to do?"

Her whisper was lost in the shouts and laughter rising around her. The court and its servants spread across the stubble, dogs yelped and strained at leashes, a dozen or more tiercels shot upward and hovered against a crisp clear sky.

"That's a fine bird, my dear. A merlin, isn't it?"

Nell started then her mouth relaxed into a smile of pleasure as William Cecil, the queen's high treasurer and confidant, moved to stand by her side. Cecil was one of her favorites and had been from the time she had first arrived at court nine years ago. Gossips said he hadn't been attractive even in his youth, but hidden behind the folds overhanging Cecil's eyes sparkled a brilliance few could aspire to. And kindness.

"I'm hunting larks today," Nell said. Merlins were among the smallest of the hunting birds, but boldly aggressive. She untied the merlin's jesses and smoothed the tangles from its vervel before slipping the leather hood. The hawk blinked and tightened its talons on her gauntlet.

Nell raised her arm and the bird soared up and up, hanging against the sky. Free and alone. "You're not hawking?"

Cecil shook his head. It was far more profitable to circulate among the pleasure-seekers. A word here, a whisper there—much business could be transacted. "My condolences for your recent loss," he murmured, glancing at her dark hat and black velvet. "Lord Leicester will be missed."

Jesu, was she wearing her heart on her sleeve now? She who prided herself on concealing her emotions? Nell blinked rapidly as the merlin swooped toward the ground. A faint tinkling of leg bells carried on the breeze.

"Thank you, Cecil. Robert was like a father to me."

Guardian, father, protector—he had been all that and more. He had lifted her out of obscurity by purchasing her wardship from the Master of the Wards and had given her a life many envied. Because of Robert Dudley, Nell had enjoyed an education equal to that of any man; she had lived in the midst of court and history. His dower had financed a brilliant marriage and had gained her a title. Whatever she was she owed to him. Had he truly been her father, she could not have loved him more. God forgive her, but the pain of Robert's death affected her more deeply than had the loss of Edward, her husband.

Cecil flipped out his cloak and clasped his hands behind his back, watching the falcons circling overhead. The field was noisy; dogs barked joyously, birds screamed, the lords and ladies chattered and shouted. Such an atmosphere was ideal for business.

"Your success in the Papist Affair is deeply appreciated," he said quietly. "I regret your accomplishments cannot be made public or the acclaim and honors you so richly merit be bestowed."

Shading her eyes, Nell looked upward. She thought she identified her merlin but she couldn't be certain. "It would be unfortunate politically if the plot were known."

Cecil smiled. "If I've given offense by stating the obvious, I beg pardon." He pressed her arm. Despite her youth, Lady Nellanor possessed a rare gift for intrigue. The deeper implications of the plot would not have escaped her notice. But one couldn't be too cautious.

"I understand the gentlemen involved will go before the Star Chamber on Monday a week."

"For treason, but not for insurrection thanks to the information you supplied." Such information was not easily acquired as he well understood. But to have charged the Catholic lords with instigating an uprising would have called attention to a faction he and the queen wished hidden from general view. In the wake of the armada, patriotism ran high. For the first time in living memory, England's lords had set aside personal animosity and had united behind the queen against Spain. This precious unity was to be preserved at all costs. The illusion would have unraveled had it not been for Lady Nellanor Amesly.

She had uncovered a plot by English papists to raise an army in support of the Spanish. Once the armada had landed and the invasion had begun, the Catholic lords pledged to strike from within. They had vowed to assassinate the queen and aid Philip of Spain in placing a Catholic monarch on England's throne. Nellanor's skillful counterplot pitted one lord against another and had ended with each rushing to denounce the other. It had been a superlative piece of business, capped by information guaranteeing the plotters would go to the block but the plot would not be publicly exposed.

"It might be said you saved the queen's life," Cecil observed. "The crown owes you a debt of gratitude."

Nell was too politically astute to disclaim Cecil's words. But in truth she had not acted in expectation of reward. She had acted instinctively, propelled by a love of England and, more urgently, by a deep abiding loyalty to Elizabeth.

Her gaze strayed to the queen's party and she watched Elizabeth bending to the pile of partridge at her feet. As always, conflicting emotions constricted Nell's chest. Few queens had inspired such devotion in their subjects—and such teeth-gnashing exasperation. Elizabeth Tudor was loved, but she was not an easy woman to like. Or to understand. Perhaps Robert Dudley had understood the queen, but few others could make that claim.

Least of all Nell. Her relationship with Elizabeth defied definition. Robert had presented her at court when Nell was thirteen; she would never forget the moment she first saw the queen of England. Elizabeth had seemed the most glitteringly majestic creature imaginable. She was beyond the mortal pale, timeless and mythical. Speechless, Nell had gazed at her with awe and adoration. Now, with the passage of years, the awe remained but the adoration had altered to wary regard. The queen was all too human, all too quick to follow a pet with a slap.

"My Liza is not like other women," Robert Dudley had said. But Nell didn't find the queen's capriciousness as charming as Uncle Robert had. There were moments when Nell basked in the warmth of Elizabeth's approval, moments when the queen smiled at her with pride. Such moments had been high points in Nell's life. But each had been followed by periods of unexplained coldness. For every compliment there was a cut, for every favor an obvious repugnance. Even now, Nell could not have said with certainty whether the queen admired her or loathed her.

At present she appeared to be in disfavor, although she couldn't think why. By rights, it should have been Elizabeth instead of Cecil who applauded Nell's triumph in the Papist Affair. As she had done countless times before, Nell searched her memory for an offense, real or imagined, that she might have committed against the queen. She could recall nothing. Unless Uncle Robert's death had made her persona non grata. This was a distinct possibility.

On her own she had no family or influential connections; Robert Dudley's backing had secured her position. Now that Robert was dead, a wait-and-see distance had developed between herself and those whom she had considered friends. The breach was not yet complete, nor would it be until the queen's attitude was known, but a withdrawal had begun. It shouldn't have hurt, but it did.

Nell glanced across the field then lifted gray eyes to Cecil. No, she had not acted in hope of reward, but she would be a fool to refuse if one were offered. "It would please me to remain at court," she said.

The pity in his eyes told her Robert's death had ended her tenure at court. "Perhaps when the Papist Affair is behind us . . ."

Or perhaps never. "I see," Nell said quietly. Until this moment she hadn't realized the full extent of her desperation, hadn't realized how heavily she had secretly depended upon Elizabeth as the solution to her future. This, then, was why Cecil had appeared at her side. To open a chasm at her feet. Suddenly the mild autumn sun turned chill and she drew her cloak to her throat, watching the falcons flirting with heaven. "Why is she punishing me?"

William Cecil didn't know. Others who had contributed far less were being feted and honored. But the queen had rejected his suggestion that Lady Nellanor be awarded a permanent court position and a stipend. It was his business to know everything and he was aware of Lady Nellanor's troubles. Her husband, an ineffective and limited man in Cecil's opinion, had died bankrupt, and Dudley's will had not provided for her. What would happen to her, he didn't know. But he would miss her. There were not many women whose company Cecil enjoyed, but this was one.

"First, you are to go to Kenilworth and assist Lady Leicester with the inventory. Then"—he shrugged and added gently— "Lord Marshton will see to your future."

"Lord Marshton." Nell met his eyes and smiled. It had long been a jest between them that one day she would pass into Lord Marshton's protection. By law her brother-in-law had become responsible for her when Edward died. To her relief and his, Lord Marshton had evaded his obligation for two years, leaving Nell to Robert Dudley. Now Robert too was gone and she was adrift once more. As she had been so often during her life.

"The honorable Lord Marshton."

"The esteemed Lord Marshton," Nell said. She tilted her head and smiled. "And his wife, the formidable Lady Marshton."

Cecil effected an elaborate shudder which coaxed a laugh from her. He patted her shoulder and genuinely wished her well. She reminded him of someone, but he could never quite remember who. Glancing across the stubbled field, he caught the queen's eye and nodded slightly, waiting for her to signal if she would receive the girl or not. Pleased, he returned his attention to Lady Nellanor.

"Everything will work out," he said, hoping it was true. She bent to take a lark from the dog's mouth and he indulged an old man's pleasure by smiling at the wisps of reddish-gold hair teased by the breeze from her hat. She had warm strawberries-and-cream coloring balanced by cool gray eyes. And a quick incisive mind, so surprising and so seductive in a woman. "Now run along and say hello to the queen. She's expecting you."

"She is?" Nell straightened and resisted an urge to embrace him, knowing to do so would embarrass them both.

"She is. Her Majesty is well pleased with you."

For once it seemed to be so. When Nell presented herself, Elizabeth beamed and drew her forward, showing her such favor that Nell felt lightheaded. Within moments a rosy glow replaced the pallor in her cheeks; her eyes danced and sparkled. This was what Nell loved most, the wit and repartee that pulsed through the Tudor court, and never was it more evident than in Elizabeth's presence.

Enjoying herself, she exchanged witticisms with Francis Drake, recently knighted, and cast a dancing glance toward aging Lord Howard. They were the true heroes of the day, having routed the armada. And she was standing between them laughing with the queen of England. It was a moment to treasure.

"Come now, Sir Francis, tell us—was there a woman aboard your ship as rumors claim?" Elizabeth winked at Nell and Lord Howard.

Francis Drake grinned slyly and tugged the point of his beard. "If so, she wasn't as lovely as present company." He glanced from Nell's sparkling eyes to Elizabeth's flirtatious gaze. "Look at them, Howard, the two most beautiful women at court. And enough alike to be sisters."

"No man could disagree," Lord Howard said, smiling.

Nell's heart sank as the queen removed her fingertips from Nell's wrist. She felt Elizabeth stiffen and watched a flinty stare replace the flirtatiousness. And it didn't make sense. No one loved flattery more than Elizabeth Tudor.

Drake and Howard exchanged a hasty glance and Nell guessed they were as taken aback as she. She slid a quick look toward the queen and discovered Elizabeth's narrowed eyes focused on her.

"Do you think we resemble sisters?" the queen demanded.

Their age difference made the question ridiculous. "I would be honored to think so, Your Majesty." Nell inclined her head prettily but glared at Drake from beneath her lashes. He gave her a tiny bemused shrug.

"Would you really?" The queen's eyes seemed like cold slate beneath her violently red wig. "We see no similarity ourselves." Her expression indicated any similarity would be repugnant.

A rush of embarrassed color flooded Nell's cheeks during the awkward pause that followed. She heard Lord Howard's stomach rumble, then breathed a silent sigh of relief as he cleared his throat and arranged his expression into one of sorrow. "Dudley will be missed, Lady Nellanor. We all share your loss."

"Thank you." If Robert had been here, he would have teased the queen out of her sudden unexplained ill humor, employing the odd combination of irreverence and intimacy that only he had been allowed.

For an instant Nell felt Robert Dudley's loss like the swift, sharp thrust of a dagger. When she opened her eyes and met Elizabeth's stare, she saw there a grief as startlingly savage as her own. For a moment their gaze held and Nell experienced a quick compelling need to comfort the queen and to be comforted by her. Eyes brimming, she impulsively reached a hand toward Elizabeth's jeweled fingers, and for the span of a heartbeat she believed the queen also reached out to her.

But Elizabeth's hand continued upward to press against her jaw. "We're thirsty," she said abruptly, continuing to look at Nell. "Someone fetch the bloody ale."

Later Nell remembered the strange moment as she was lying in her bed exhausted from hawking, banqueting, and the masque that had followed. At court nothing was ever what it seemed. Layers stacked upon murky layers. On the surface it seemed she was deserving of reward for her role in the Papist Affair. Instead she found herself essentially banished. Usually she could guess the layers beneath, but this time she could not. It was as much an enigma as the rejection she'd read in the queen's eyes. As much a mystery as her own uncertain future.

Nell stared at the dark rafters overhead. She had no fortune, no prospects, no place to go. A tiny smile touched her lips. She who had saved the queen's life and resolved the Papist Affair was unable to save herself.

Jesu, what would become of her?

At age fifty-five Elizabeth Tudor felt the evening damp as she hadn't in her youth. Once she had thought the night air invigorating; now it seeped into her bones and carved a chill. The realization added to a weight of depression.

After dismissing her ladies for the night, she leaned to her glass and regarded her image without pity, then she drew back and pressed her fingertips to her eyelids. Without her wig, without her powder and paint, and without her dearest Robert to pay her extravagant compliments and make her believe them, she was old. She looked like any other woman her age. And she despised it. She loathed the fine wrinkles fanning her eyes and framing her mouth, hated the gray that dulled her thinning hair. She detested missing or blackened teeth, resented the vague aches and pains that signaled her mortality. With one swift motion she swept the mirror crashing to the floor. What had once been her friend was now her enemy.

Tilting her head backward, she stared unseeing at the gilt ceiling of her bedchamber. No, she was not the weary woman who stared out of her glass. Never. She was ageless, beyond time. She was the Sun Queen, Gloriana, shining in splendor and eternal virginal youth.

Standing abruptly, she deliberately ground a shard of glass beneath her slipper's heel and a curse of impotence scraped her throat. If only she could have the years again; if she could spin the clock backward . . .

"Oh Robert. My dearest Robin."

She dug her fingers into her hair and tried not to think about him. The Spaniards—she would think about her victory over Philip. What anguish Philip must be suffering now, what delicious humiliation. She needed to think how he would retaliate, for she had no doubt that he would. The king of Spain would not easily accept defeat; he would lash out at her. In his place, she would be plotting revenge. Not another armada, but something. Something subtle and lethal.

What Philip didn't know was that she suffered an anguish as devastating as his own. The roust of Philip's mighty armada paled beside Robert Dudley's death. Robert's death overlay everything.

She paced beside her bed, sucking on the tooth that pained her. Robert, Robert. His image floated behind her lids and her hands curled into fists. All the glory and might of England, all the power and prestige of its queen, had not been able to save one man from one fever. The knowledge ravaged her.

He was gone. He who should have led the victory celebrations was not here to share them. Pressing her fists to her temples, she bowed her head and bit hard on the bad tooth. Tears scalded her eyes and in the privacy of her chamber she let them fall unchecked.

How could she face the days ahead? For whom would she adorn herself and paint her face? Who would notice if her gown was new or old? Who was left to look at her and see beyond the fan of wrinkles? For thirty years Robert Dudley had been her anchor, her rock, her friend—and now he was dead. At the same age as herself.

Angrily she kicked aside her fur-edged hem and extended her hands over a perfumed brazier, rubbing them in the smoky heat. Her hands at least were not old but remained as elegant as ever, as white and smooth as whalebone. She was as slender as a maid and her health was good. She would live forever; she would never die.

Fresh tears welled in her eyes and she dashed them with the back of her hand. Jesu, but she missed him. Where might destiny have led had God cast her as a commoner or invested Robert Dudley with royal blood? Would she have wed him then? Would she have submitted her will and her body?

The questions were as foolish now as ever they had been. She was who she was, the daughter of kings, the Queen of England. She would not have altered destiny for any man. England was her husband, all the husband she had ever needed or wanted.

But—Robert Dudley. There had been Robert Dudley.

Through all the years he had remained steadfast by her side. Through all the plots and deceits. Through the fevered urgings that she marry and produce an heir. Through all the triumphs and all the despairs, Robert had been there. Sweet, patient Robert, flawed but constant, her foolish, proud Robin. Her weakness and her strength.

She saw him now in her inner mind, shining in gilded armor, off to war in her name. And she saw his face above hers, his clear eyes soft and loving. They had shared the best. And now he was gone. Forever. And Lettice Knollys, the sultry whore he had married, Lettice would wear the widow's weeds while she, Elizabeth the Queen, was denied them.

She sank to the edge of her great bed and wept.

CHAPTER 2

Kenilworth was the nearest thing to a home Nell had ever known. Dimly she recalled Uncle Robert bringing her here when she was three. Or did she only remember a story he'd liked to tell? Whether or not she had appropriated his memory as her own, her love for Kenilworth had been as instantaneous as her love for Robert Dudley. She had fastened on it immediately as her own.

But of course it was not. As Lettice Dudley, Lady Leicester, took pains to remind her, Nell had nothing of her own. Except for the brief span of her marriage, she had lived on Leicester charity. But she had dreamed.

Nell glanced at Lord Marshton then paused on the path beside the mere, letting her mind drift from the monotonous drone of her brother-in-law's voice.

Nowhere were the seasons as vivid as at Kenilworth. Harvest stubble flowed like gold toward emerald parklands then swung toward the forest rim. Beech and oak erupted in showy displays of gold and orange and, here and there, columns of flaming scarlet. Breathing deeply of the cool clean air, Nell bent to pluck one of the last brave violets sprinkled along the water's bank. Soon the bright colors and autumn flowers would fade to winter's bite. The swans gliding across the mere's surface would disappear. Idly, she wondered where the swans went when the snows came.

Closing her eyes, she crushed the violet to her lips. Next year she wouldn't be here to watch Kenilworth blossom into spring or to witness the return of the swans.

"Nellanor, are you listening? It's your future we're discussing."

"I'm listening, John."

Certainly she heard his reluctance. With no family and, now that Robert was dead, no connections, Nell had become a liability. The time had come to "do" something with her. No one had suggested John, Lord Marshton, possessed tact, Nell thought as she gazed across the mere. Perversely enjoying his discomfort, she watched from the corner of her eye as he cleared his throat and rubbed his boot across the gravel stones.

"Is there any possibility Lady Leicester will keep you in her household?"

"It's doubtful." Lettice had never shared her husband's affection for Nell. If the truth were known, Nell guessed Lady Leicester felt little genuine affection for anyone but herself.

"I see." Lord Marshton puffed out his cheeks and frowned at the sunlit waters, his profile reminding Nell of Edward. John was stouter and more florid of feature, but the brothers had shared a bluntness of profile. And the same plodding approach to matters. When John looked at her, Nell saw Edward's eyes, eyes that carried a hint of permanent bewilderment. "Is there any possibility of remarriage, Nellanor?"

"The possibility is slim."

Which was to say nonexistent. To retire Edward's debts, Nell had been forced to sell the London house and all its furnishings, her coach and equipage, what jewels she'd owned. Uncle Robert had paid the remaining balance. Three years of marriage had gained her nothing but a small wardrobe and an empty title. Worse, she had not borne Edward an heir, thus failing in her duty as a wife. A man would be a fool to pursue her; she had nothing to offer.

Lord Marshton ran stubby fingers through his hair and cursed beneath his breath. Had Edward exercised even modest caution, his widow would not now be weighing heavy on John's hands. With even a small allowance, he could have found her a husband. There were men willing to accept a barren wife if she came with an attractive dower. Not a man of rank or influence, but someone.

He kicked a stone into the mere waters and turned a heavy frown on his sister-in-law. Sunlight struck red-gold from her hair and made her gray eyes appear translucent. A light breeze fluttered her cloak and he glimpsed soft breasts curving above her bodice.

Another man might have thought her achingly lovely, but he mistrusted intelligent women. The cool quickness in her gaze unnerved him. Not for the first time he wondered if it had been she who had embroiled his brother in the muck of political intrigue. Or if, as some said, it was Nellanor who had continually rescued Edward from his follies. No less a personage than the Duke of Bedford had acidly remarked that Edward was but a pale shadow of the skirt he had married. Bedford had also ventured that Edward would have ruined himself two years earlier had it not been for his wife's wit. Family honor prompted John to disagree. Fair or not, he laid Nell's troubles at her own door.

"I would offer you the hospitality of Marshton Manor, but . . ."

Nell smiled at the color infusing his cheeks. "I'd not think of intruding." Nor would Lady Marshton permit it, she thought. Lady Marshton had often expressed her disapproval of educated women who had been to court and accorded themselves "airs."

They were gradually eliminating alternatives. After brushing the leaves from a bench near the curve in the path, Nell seated herself and gazed longingly at Kenilworth's cornelian colored towers and walls. As foolish as it sounded, she had never considered that she would lose Kenilworth too. She had mistakenly focused on Kenilworth as providing the permanence she had sought all her life.

Pressing her lips together, she touched her fingers to her forehead. More than anything she wanted a home of her own. And children to fill it. From the moment she'd fully comprehended that she was homeless and without family, she'd craved a home of her own. And lacking a mother's love, she yearned to give it. An untapped bounty of love lay within her breast seeking stability and focus.

"You leave me no choice, Nellanor."

"There are always choices," she responded lightly.

"I've considered carefully, and I've concluded you have a vocation for the Church."

So that's how it would end. Keeping her expression carefully blank, Nell gazed at him. "I didn't realize Protestant convents existed."

"Not a convent, a retreat. In Wales." At least he possessed the grace to appear uncomfortable. "I'm told it's restful there, very peaceful and quiet. The ladies occupy themselves with good works; a profitable life, wouldn't you agree?"

Nell suspected the "profitable life" had been suggested by Lady Marshton. "A retreat," she repeated softly. She might have guessed. Men would always create institutions in which to dispose of unwanted females. She drew a long breath. "Thank you, John, for holding my interests upper-most." If he noticed her sarcasm, nothing in his expression revealed it. "A retreat is, of course, a suitable discharge of your obligations."

"Then you agree?" Relief flooded his broad features.

That wasn't what she had said. "What choice have I? My fate is in your hands." Though she railed against the law, she was bound by it.

"Of course. I'll make the arrangements immediately."

Not if she could prevent it. Never. "There's no need for haste, is there?" She rose smoothly to her feet and gave him a dazzling smile, amused by the suspicion that leaped to his eyes. "I can't leave Kenilworth until the inventory is complete. Surely you wouldn't insist I abandon dear Lettice in her time of grief . . . ?"

Lord Marshton's transparency would not have stood him well at court. Nell easily read his dismay. "How long will the inventory require?" he asked, falling into step beside her.

"I should think—perhaps six weeks."

"Six weeks."

Given six weeks, she would uncover a way to circumvent the retreat. There had to be an alternative. At twenty-two, Nell was too young to bury herself in a forgotten refuge. For a terrible instant she envisioned the future John had arranged—she saw herself as dry, juiceless, her eyes dulled by the company of discarded women, her back bent by a lifetime of good works. Immediately Nell's shoulders contracted and her teeth set. There had to be a place for her other than Wales.

When John had departed, she stood at the gatehouse watching as his horse skirted the fields and turned onto the road to Warwick. Seeing him had reminded her of Edward. Although she'd been fond of Edward, his primary attraction had been the stability he offered. And the promise of a home and family. What she had failed to grasp was that Edward's stability had been but lack of opportunity. With her dower in hand and Robert's court connections, Edward had found himself catapulted into new and heady possibilities. Unable to resist, he'd plunged headlong into court politics. With disastrous results.

The leechers had told her Edward had died of black humors, but Nell knew he'd died of broken ambitions. Her gentle husband had lacked the ruthlessness to succeed. He hadn't the skills to dissemble or to extricate himself when others sought a scapegoat. He'd paid too much for pomp and not enough in bribes. In the end, not even Robert Dudley could save Edward from ruin.

Nell gave herself a shake. There was no profit in worrying the past. She needed to apply herself to the future. She cast a last glance at Kenilworth's reflection shimmering over the mere, then crossed the bridge leading to the inner courtyard, a frown of concentration drawing her brow.

The obvious solution was to induce Lettice to offer the hospitality of her household. Life with Robert's widow would not be easy, but it was preferable to a retreat. The prospect of swallowing her pride and begging Lettice's charity galled her, but at the moment she could conceive of no alternative.

At the entrance to the great hall, Nell paused to smooth her hair and run her hands over the dark skirts she wore. She would rather have emptied chamber pots for a year than crawl to Lettice. But a retreat. For all she knew emptying chamber pots counted among the ladies' good works.

Grinding her teeth, she pressed the latch and strode boldly into the hall, nearly colliding with a man and woman whispering near the doorway.

"Forgive me," Nell murmured hastily, stepping backward, "I didn't realize we had visitors." The couple was unknown to her, an oddity that piqued her curiosity. It meant they were likely from Wales, Scotland, or the borderlands. While there were few nobles whose names she would not have recognized, many of the border lords visited court so seldom, not many were recognized in person. When the woman asked for Lettice, Nell listened for an accent, but heard none.

The man, however, bore a certain resemblance to the March family, which, if true, was intriguing, as Lettice cherished no love for the Marches.

She was about to introduce herself when Lady Leicester spoke from the end of the hall, sweeping forward with regal assurance. "Lady Nellanor, there you are. Aren't you supposed to be helping in the west tower?"

As usual, Lettice drew all eyes. Nell noticed Lady Leicester's concession to mourning was minimal. She wore dove-gray silk trimmed in a flattering shade of blue, blue embroidery, a blue lace ruff, and sapphires at her throat and ears. When she reached the group near the arch, she waved a graceful hand. "May I present my late husband's ward, Nellanor, Lady Amesly."

"I'm honored, my lady." The man bent over Nell's hand, his blond beard brushing her fingertips. The woman's shrewd eyes swept Nell, then she turned away to face Lettice.

It was not until Nell had withdrawn that she realized Lettice had failed to present the visitors. The slight did not augur well for Nell's future. Throughout the day, she considered possible explanations of a less ominous nature, finally concluding the strangers' presence had proved a blessing in disguise, as they had prevented her from approaching Lettice too hastily.

Entering her chamber, Nell washed the ink from her fingers at the wall laver then ordered a supper tray in her room. Her room. It wouldn't be so much longer.

Standing beside the bed curtains, she slowly gazed about the chamber. What actually belonged to her would scarcely fill one cart. The embroidered pillows were hers, and her clothing and cosmetic pots. What else?

She had Robert Dudley's old signet ring. Turning it on her finger, she gazed down at the chipped surface. He'd given her so much throughout the years, but this was the most precious because it had been his. Not something she needed, but something he had wanted her to have. This thought reminded her of the silver casket and she made a mental note to remind Lettice.

What else? Her fingers strayed to the gold locket beneath her ruff. The locket was more precious even than Robert's signet ring.

Sinking to a stool near the window, Nell withdrew the locket from her bodice and cupped it in her palm. Over the years handling had worn the corners smooth, so the shape was now more rounded than square. She held the locket to the waning light and traced the initials etched on the surface: *A.B.* Her mother.

Nell closed her eyes as her fingers curled around the locket. Who had A.B. been? A woman in disgrace? A woman with too many children already? Or had she died? Not even Cecil, who knew everything, had been able to answer Nell's questions. He knew no more than Robert or Nell herself. A.B. had been a lady of nobility, else her babe would not have ended with the master of the wards, and she had cared enough to tuck the locket within the folds of swaddling.

Pressing the tiny latch, Nell opened the locket and stared at the miniature within, examining it as if this time the answers would appear. Over the years the paint had altered and now her mother's eyes looked pale blue rather than gray like Nell's. But she shared the same strong forehead and chin as the woman in the miniature. Nell examined the line of hair showing beneath a lace cap at temples and forehead. Here too the paint had decayed. Instead of the shining reddish gold Nell remembered, the paint had darkened to a muddy brown. Still, the woman in the miniature was a beauty. There was warmth and intelligence in her laughing eyes.

"I've needed you so much," Nell whispered, staring at the portrait.

When the light faded, she snapped shut the locket and dropped it around her neck, settling the square against her heart. If ever she had children of her own, she would love them and cherish them. She would be there for the scraped knees and the night terrors. Her daughters would not begin the bleeding alone and terrified. Her sons would know the permanence of a home.

Nell dropped her head into her hands. Dreams—only dreams. Reality was a retreat in Wales. Unless she could persuade Lettice to offer assistance.

The items to be sold were crated and stacked in the great hall. Items Lettice Dudley believed no one would miss ended in the barrels marked for her London house, claimed as personal belongings or part of her widow's third.

"This is mine," she said, removing a jeweled frame from the dining-room cupboard. "You needn't list it." She glanced at Nell seated at the table before an inkhorn and a pot of sand.

Without comment, Nell watched Lettice wrap the frame in an ell of silk then push it into the barrel. The estate sale ordered by the queen would not yield much to repay Robert's debt to the crown, not if Lettice could prevent it.

If rumors could be credited, Lettice planned to make Sir Christopher Blount her next husband. Sir Christopher had been Uncle Robert's Master of the Horse and was half Lettice's age. Though Nell's heart ached on behalf of Uncle Robert, she wasn't surprised. Lettice looked younger than her mid-forties; she possessed the ripe figure of a maid. Additionally, Lady Leicester projected a lush sensuality that drew men like bears to honey. Nevertheless, Nell didn't comprehend Lettice's appeal. A hard kernel of avarice lay beneath her seductive smiles, revenge for petty slights occupied her conversation. Why Uncle Robert had married such a viper mystified Nell.

"Shall I note the plate, Aunt Lettice?" After careful thought, she had decided the word *aunt* would test the waters.

Lettice cast Nell a glance from beneath hooded lids. She turned a silver tray between gem-studded fingers before wrapping it within a length of priceless tapestry. "No, this too is mine," she said, fitting the plate into the barrel. "I'm not your aunt, you know," she added after a pause. When Nell didn't respond, she said, "I shall miss you, my dear. Have you decided yet where you will go?"

The waters were cold, as unyielding as ice. Nell swallowed the brackish taste of pride and made herself speak plainly. "I have nowhere to go," she said quietly. "I had hoped to remain with you." If Lettice possessed a thimbleful of compassion, she would now extend an invitation.

"My dear, I'm afraid that isn't possible. Not in my current financial straits." Lettice shrugged prettily, but the rejection was complete. "But when you're settled, you must visit me." Her voice purred. "Not too often, of course, lest people think the worst of you. People of my rank are so often exploited, don't you agree? After all, my grandmother was Mary Boleyn, sister to Queen Anne. One can't forget."

Nell held her head rigidly high. "No," she said finally. "One can't forget." What would she do next? Where would she go? "Are the chairs to be kept or sold?" Chairs were rare; they would fetch a goodly price.

Immediately Lettice's face twisted from satisfaction to loathing. "Sold," she said bitterly. "The bitch wants every shilling due her!"

Nell stared then hastily glanced over her shoulder. "Lettice," she whispered, "the walls have ears."

"Then let the walls tell my niggardly cousin what I think of her latest affront!" Lettice tossed dark hair and her eyes blazed. "Elizabeth could have canceled Robert's debt to the crown, she could have eased my bereavement. But no. She takes pleasure in forcing me to auction Robert's belongings in the street. How very like a Tudor to be so petty and grasping!"

"Lettice, I beg you. You're speaking of the queen!" Ink dripped from Nell's quill and smeared the words she had just written.

Shrill laughter issued from Lettice's lips. "What has my cousin the queen ever given me that I should bow my head to her? She's humiliated me by keeping my husband from me whenever she could. She's banned me from court. She intends to diminish my inheritance. And now she's taken my son, Lord Essex, and told him lies about me and ensnared him to her side!" Droplets of spittle sprayed from her lips and her hands flew outward. "And why does she plague me so? Because she's consumed by jealousy, that's why. Her precious Robert chose me!" Her rings caught the handle of a vase and sent it crashing to the reeds. "Well, I fixed her; you'll see. The whole world will know her for the deceitful fraud she is." Triumph thinned Lettice's smile into something ugly. "She'll rue the day she told me to get out of her sight!"

Nell was as amazed at Lettice's loss of control as she was by the treasonous words. Speaking quietly, she asked, "Lettice, what have you done?"

The question caught Lettice up short. She blinked at Nell then glanced at the pieces of vase at her hem. Instantly her expression altered. "Never mind." A long breath moved the sapphires on her breast as she met Nell's steady gaze. "You know the slights Elizabeth has dealt me," she said in a calmer tone. "And naturally, I'm hurt. But of course I would never do anything to injure the queen."

"Of course."

Nell didn't believe it for a moment. And she was thankful that it didn't concern her. But she recognized it was not in her best interests to remain with Lady Leicester. One reaped what one sowed and Lettice was sowing dangerous seeds. She gazed at Lettice thoughtfully and decided it would be interesting to know the nature of those seeds. The intrigue piqued her curiosity. When the time was right, she would ask a few discreet questions.

They worked in silence until Nell remembered the casket she'd been promised. "Lettice, where is Robert's silver casket?"

Lettice's dark head snapped up and she gave Nell a hard stare. "What casket?"

"The scrolled silver. About this big." Nell held her hands a foot apart. "Robert promised I was to have it if anything . . ." Quick tears threatened behind her eyes. She still couldn't believe he was gone, that he would never again stride into a room and make it his.

"Robert never said anything about you having that casket."

Now it was Nell's turn to stare. "You know he did," she said slowly. "Lettice, he mentioned it several times. Before he sailed to Flanders and again recently just before the Spanish threat. You must remember—you were there when he showed me the key and . . ."

"I don't know what you're talking about." Lettice bent to the barrel and poked about the contents. "There was no mention of a casket in Robert's will."

"Probably because he'd already mentioned it to us both. Lettice, he wanted me to have it."

"That's a lie. If he'd wanted you to have it, he would have said so to me or in his will."

Trembling with anger, Nell stood from the table and clenched her hands at her sides. "The silver casket is mine, Lettice, and I insist that you give it to me."

The two women faced each other across the dining room and now the hatred Nell had long suspected flared in Lettice's eyes. "You grasping little nothing! How dare you insist on anything? Robert took you in when no one else would and gave you everything! Nothing was too good for 'my Nellie.' And what did you do? You threw everything away on that stupid Edward. And where did you come running then? Back to Robert and Robert's largess. Well, it's finished now. You won't get another shilling that should rightfully be mine!"

The blood rushed from Nell's face and she steadied herself against the table. "At least I loved him," she whispered.

"You loved what he could give you! A place at court, money, a marriage above yourself. But it wasn't enough, was it? You want more, you want to pick over his corpse before he's cold in his tomb!"

"No! That is a lie!" Steady, Nell told herself, breathe calmly; you know how vicious Lettice can be, how she can twist the most innocent words. With great effort she checked the shock and anger shaking her voice. "I only want what was promised to me. That's all."

"Nothing was promised you," Lettice hissed.

Both women straightened abruptly as the steward entered the

room. He paused, looking uneasily from one to the other, then cleared his throat and extended a silver salver to Nell.

With shaking hands she removed the letter and looked at the queen's seal. Then she unrolled the parchment and read it through. "I've been recalled to London," she said in response to Lettice's impatient question. "I'm summoned immediately."

"Good."

Nell looked into Lettice's narrowed eyes and saw the intractability there. And she knew the silver casket was lost to her. Defeat stiffened her shoulders. "Will you please tell me what the casket contained? What was it Robert wanted me to have?"

"I don't know." The words rang true, but the preceding hesitation told Nell that Lettice had guessed the casket's contents.

An uncharacteristic pleading filled Nell's eyes. "Could you at least tell me what you believe is in the casket?"

"It doesn't concern you, of that I'm certain."

Nell watched Lettice's skirt billow as Lady Leicester turned on her heel and left the hall. Slowly, she sank to the stool and closed her eyes. She would wager all she owned that Lettice had left to fetch the casket and open it.

What was inside? Jewels? Money? Robert's will had indicated that Nell would be taken care of. Had he meant the casket and its contents? Due to Lettice's avarice, she would never know.

She struck the table with her fist. "Robert wanted me to have it!" He'd made a point of showing her the casket, had told her it was his legacy to her, to do with as she deemed best.

Tears of frustration sparkled in her lashes. She could visualize the casket as clearly as if it sat before her. Etched silver. Two dots of blue wax on either side of the lock stamped with Robert's signet. Large enough to hold the deed to a house or a modest fortune in crowns or perhaps jewels that could be sold.

"God's bones!" It was a terrible, terrible thing to be helpless, to be utterly without power or recourse. All her life Nell had been at the mercy of the whims and pleasures of others. She went where she was told, did as she was told, accepted what was given or what was withheld. And she did so without protest because she had no voice of her own; she was helpless.

Somehow, someway, she was going to change that. She would not, by heaven, live the rest of her life as she had lived the beginning. She would find a way. Others would dance to her tune. She would make the decisions.

Pressing her lips into a grim line, she smoothed out the queen's summons on the table before her.

Perhaps Elizabeth had reconsidered and was prepared to offer her a court position. Or perhaps she was to be punished for some forgotten infraction. One never knew with Elizabeth.

At least she had a place to go.

CHAPTER

3

*T*he victory celebrations continued unabated offering daily hunts and bonfires, masques and mummeries, banquets and lists.

Before he lowered his visor and positioned his lance, William Steele, Duke of Brampton, smiled toward the gallery overhanging the tiltyard. From this distance the old queen looked as fresh and radiant as she must have looked twenty years ago. He was pleased to be wearing her black and white silk on his helmet.

He suspected the mark of the queen's favor enraged his opponent and perchance others as well, and he didn't give a damn. Worse things could happen to a man than to enjoy the favor of his queen. One of the worse things was residing at court. The pleasure had begun to pall as it always did rather sooner than later.

As he waited impatiently for the joust to begin, Will concluded it was time to go home. Long past time. The silken peacocks squabbling about Whitehall's corridors had ceased to amuse; the chaotic comings and goings reminded him of a hen yard. Other than one or two of the northern lords, he'd yet to meet a man he would choose to drink with. He doubted many had visited their estates within easy memory or would know how to manage them if they did. An expression of disgust sent knots up his jawline. Aside from the women, court was an utter waste of time.

As the page adjusted the armor over his thighs, Will's gaze settled on the plump little morsel standing in the queen's shadow. He'd learned her name was Lady Bledsoe. She'd been playing mouse to his cat throughout the long weeks of his sojourn at court. He meant to sample her charms before he departed for the border and home. And if the look in her beckoning eyes meant what he hoped, she was willing to be sampled. His stomach muscles tightened pleasantly at the prospect.

"Lord Essex leans to the right, Sir," the page shouted up at him. The boy looked over his shoulder then lowered his voice. "A word to the wise, m'lord." Will grinned at him. "Lord Essex is a great favorite of the queen, if you know what I mean, him being the stepson of Lord Leicester and all."

"What are you saying, boy?"

The page squinted and winked slyly. "I wouldn't want no favorite angry at me, m'lord, if you know what I mean."

Will scowled and boxed the boy's ears. "Will Steele yields to no man, favorite or not. If you know what I mean."

The page's eyes widened. "You're Will Steele? The Fighting Duke?" His mouth rounded.

"That I am, lad, that I am." Laughing, he snapped shut his visor and guided his horse into position at the end of the track, testing the weight and balance of the blunted lance resting in the crook of his arm. Young Essex looked impressive, Will gave him that. Instead of the battered and battle-scarred armor Will wore, Essex was fitted out in a gilded suit as smooth and pretty as a baby's behind. Stripes of metallic gold and burnished copper ran the length of Essex's breastplate and helmet. If Essex's armor had seen a day of battle, Will vowed to retire his sword. What finally caught his eye, however, was the scrap of black and white fluttering from Essex's hilt.

So that was the game. He glanced toward the queen's gallery and his grin widened. The wily old girl had given her favor to them both. She couldn't lose. Now he understood why the stands twittered and pointed. "What are the odds, lad?"

"Ten to one against you, m'lord."

The oddsmakers thought he'd yield to the queen's favorite, did they? Will smiled at the flags cracking briskly in the breeze, studied the sunlight flashing off Essex's gilded armor. It was a glorious day. A good day for a fight. "Put everything you own on Will Steele," he advised cheerfully. "I'm going to dump that pretty bastard in the dirt."

Finally the tilt master shouted, "Attend!" and an expectant hush rolled over the stands. Will nudged his horse past the dropped ropes and both men shifted their lances and stared down the length of the track. The tilt master shaded his eyes against the sun, watching as Elizabeth raised her arm. When she dropped her glove, he shouted: "Charge!"

Will tensed at the surge of power beneath his thighs as his charger thundered forward, gouging great clods of earth from the track. Deliberately, he carried his lance high and to the outside, all the while observing that Essex leaned to the right as the boy had said. He tightened his chest instinctively as Essex's lance glanced harmlessly off his armor and his own blunted lance shattered against Essex's thigh. The young favorite would be limping for a day or two unless he missed his guess.

He wheeled the charger at the end of the track and accepted a fresh lance handed up by the page. The first pass was seldom decisive, merely a measuring device. The next pass was a different matter. Will watched Essex bowing toward the gallery and to the stands, then he swallowed the ale handed up by the page. When Essex finished preening himself before his audience and finally pronounced himself ready, Will saluted the queen, snapped down his visor, and positioned the charger.

"Attend—charge!"

This time Will carried the lance low as if the weight bothered him. Low and inside as beginners were wont to do. But he was no beginner. Hunching his shoulder to deflect Essex's blow, he waited until the last possible second before he swung the lance up and out, catching Essex in the armpit. The metallic gold and burnished copper pinwheeled up and off the palfrey. When Will spun at the end of the track, Essex's men were running forward to where the young lord lay sprawled in the dust.

Will smiled. Ordinarily he would have given Essex the courtesy of a third pass, but Essex annoyed him. Essex possessed the same cloying vanity as had his stepfather, Robert Dudley. Will had always thought vanity a petty quality in a man. He raised his visor, wiped the sweat from his eyes, then saluted his queen with his shattered lance.

Elizabeth smiled and raised her hands to applaud him as did her ladies, including the delectable Lady Bledsoe. The queen didn't glance at Essex as his men pulled him to his feet. At her gesture, the Captain of the Queen's Guard presented Will with a gem-studded sword which he raised to his forehead amid boisterous cheers. Then he wheeled about smartly and trotted to the changing tent. His shoulder ached where he'd taken the brunt of Essex's lance, but he would have suffered far greater discomfort before admitting it. He supposed he had his own small vanities.

The sartorial excess at court was enough to deplete a man's purse and patience. In the past weeks, Will had kept two tailors working from dawn to dusk and his wardrobe was still modestly limited when compared to puffs like Essex and others of his ilk. Once the queen gave him leave to depart, he would consign his new elegance to his master of the wardrobe, along with the fervent hope that he would never again have to wear it. One didn't require velvet breeches stuffed with sawdust or sleeves padded with horsehair to fight the thieving Scots.

Who were no doubt plundering his sheep, his storehouses, and his villages while he sat here pretending to enjoy an allegory that was putting him to sleep. He moved on the bench and looked past heads and shoulders toward a dais where three garishly clad ladies of the court pranced about purporting to represent faith, hope, and charity. Somehow this was intended to relate to the victory, although Will hadn't yet grasped how.

If he'd produced the allegory, he would have named the ladies luck, luckier, and luckiest, as that would more accurately describe the victory. Weather had beaten the Spaniards, not the English. The English had bungled the job from start to finish. The English navy had ceded to the sea dogs, and the sea dogs, a collection of privateers and near-pirates, had appeared more interested in plunder than patriotism. So the stories ran. Had a storm not scattered the armada and wrecked it along the coasts of the North Sea, God only knew what the outcome might have been.

As for England's land defenses, Will knew about that firsthand. When the call to arms went out, he'd mustered six hundred archers and two hundred harquebusiers and had marched them south where he placed them and himself in the service of Robert Dudley, whom the queen had named Supreme Commander. His mouth twisted at the memory of the appalling conditions he'd discovered upon his arrival at Dudley's camp on the Thames.

Inefficiency and disorganization marked the campaign from the beginning. Leicester had erected silk tents and kitchens to rival Whitehall; he had a platoon of men working diligently to polish the lords' armor to a gloss high enough to blind a man. But he'd overlooked such unglamorous items as food for his army and fresh water and sanitary facilities. The camp reeked and the men foraged nearby villages to fill their bellies. Before long, the men were grimly predicting the Spaniards' armada could sail up the Thames unmolested as Dudley's commanders wouldn't notice them; the lords would be in the silk tent arguing about who held precedence over whom and how the spoils were to be divided.

When the army was finally disbanded, Will seethed with frustration, wanting nothing so badly as to ride for the border and knock a few Scottish heads, something to take the bad taste from his mouth and restore his sense of honor. His disappointment had been acute.

He'd hoped to distinguish himself in the field and perhaps earn a benefice. With more land and thus more men, he might have put an end to the blasted Scots, damn their eyes. They were probably stealing his sheep this very minute; he could feel it in his bones. For certain they would sweep out of the hills for a major raid before snow clogged the roads and passes. If he were home, he would retaliate and give their black souls something to ponder during the long winter nights.

But he wasn't home and it was beginning to appear the queen would never give him leave to depart. He could understand why she wanted the navy heroes in London for the celebrations. But he did not comprehend why she also retained the lords who had served with Dudley, those who hadn't caught a glimpse of a Spaniard or bloodied a single sword.

Scowling, he turned from the dais and glared at the man seated beside him. "A man wasn't intended to wear ruffles around his bloody neck," he muttered.

"Beg pardon?"

Will stared at a head that appeared disembodied. A face and perfumed beard sat upon a white platter as wide as a wheel. He could see a line chafed red by the starched edges of the man's ruff. Will made a sound of disgust and tugged his own idiotic ruff away from his jawline. God's blood but he hated it here, hated being tricked out like a fancy man, hated the sooty air and noisy crowds. All of it.

Relief brightened his face when the allegory ended and those around him stood. Chatter rose in waves, a bench overturned, shoulders brushed his. And a note appeared in his hand. Across the room he saw Lady Bledsoe watching him, her eyes filled with darkling promise.

Turning aside, he smoothed the scrap against his palm: *Midnight. Fifth door on the left.*

Will grinned and met Lady Bledsoe's eyes. As long as he had to be here, he might as well enjoy himself.

The palace was dark and quiet. A solitary torch at the end of the corridor cast a smoky glow a few feet in either direction, leaving the greater length of the hallway in blackness.

Having removed his sword and spurs in his chamber, Will moved silently along the corridor. Bribing the sentry had divested him of jingling coins; he'd removed the chains from his doublet. Counting beneath his breath, he passed four arched doorways then paused before the fifth, Lady Bledsoe's chamber. He glanced over his shoulder then depressed the latch soundlessly and stepped inside.

The darkness within surprised him. He'd expected the welcome of warm candlelight and Lady Bledsoe's small plump body immediately pressed to his. Standing by the door, he waited for his eyes to adjust to the faint light admitted by a window recessed near the rafters. Gradually he discerned a small room sparsely furnished and more orderly than he'd expected. Finally, he saw a frilled nightcap peeping above the blankets strewn across a narrow trundle bed. Will stared at the cap and frowned. This wasn't the eager reception he'd anticipated.

Lady Bledsoe's note had said midnight, and he'd heard the midwatch call but minutes ago. He'd counted five doors beneath his fingertips. He was in the right place at the right time.

A small sound murmured from the bed as she shifted and pushed the counterpane from her breast.

Ah, now he understood. She was playing coy. As a rule, Will didn't care for love games, but his experience of court was extensive enough to comprehend the jaded nature of its occupants. Here the game was often considered more satisfying than the actual conquest. Not to him but to some. If Lady Bledsoe wished to pretend she was dreaming, so be it. He'd play along.

He stepped forward, inhaling the dusty scent of costmary and dried lavender that wafted from the rushes underfoot. At the side of the bed he gazed down at the lace cap shadowing her face. He glimpsed a fringe of heavy lashes against her cheek. "Mary?" She didn't respond, but he noticed movement beneath her lids.

Will wasn't at all certain what he was expected to do next. This was the strangest damned tryst since the Flemish lass with the gold spurs. For an instant he considered departing as silently as he'd arrived. But she'd given him the note, and she had pushed the counterpane away to expose her breast, and she was a desirable little thing. He looked at her and hoped she didn't intend to feign sleep from start to finish. That game didn't appeal.

Again she moved slightly, tilting the curve of one satiny breast to the shadowy light. Will smiled and felt his groin tighten. Watching her, he dropped his doublet to the rushes and opened his shirt. He thought her eyes flickered when he dropped his breeches, but the darkness was too deep to be certain.

When he bent to remove his shoes, he paused, and decided not to take off his hose just yet. The stones were icy beneath the rushes. Carefully he eased his weight onto the bed and slipped the counterpane to her waist, wishing she hadn't worn a nightdress. A scent of roses and honey became stronger as he leaned to nuzzle her neck then cupped her breast, feeling the nipple rise like a small bud against his palm.

Immediately Will knew he had blundered. Whereas Lady Bledsoe had breasts the size of ripe melons, the breast in his hand comfortably filled his palm but could not be said to approach the size of a ripe melon. He stared at the woman as she brushed his hand away and struggled sleepily to sit upright.

"My mistake," he murmured hastily. "I most humbly beg your pardon. Now if you'll excuse me, I'll just be on my way." He fervently hoped it would be that easy.

"What? Who . . . ?" She sat up and blinked at him and then at her disarranged nightdress. Instantly the sleep flashed from her eyes and she opened her lips to scream.

It was not going to be that easy. God's teeth. Will clapped his hand over her mouth and caught the wrists coming toward his face with his free hand. "Shhh, I'm not going to hurt you. There's nothing to fear." In truth, she didn't look frightened, she looked furious. Blazing eyes raked his face then followed his naked chest down to his thighs. When her gaze returned to his, he read her contempt and wished to Christ he had either kept his clothes on or had taken his hose off. Having his legs covered made the rest of him feel doubly naked.

"What we have here, m'love, is a simple case of mistaken identity. The wrong chamber." He spoke in a pleasant conversational tone while feeling more foolish than he'd felt in years. It occurred to him that a naked man was as vulnerable as a babe. The contempt staring out at him above his hand underscored the point. Irritation rose in his own eyes. Women had looked at him in many ways, but he'd never before sat on a woman's bed and experienced the sting of contempt. A grim smile twitched the corners of his lips. And he'd thought Essex vain?

"There's no need for alarm, no need to raise a scandal." Now he could see the curls spilling from her cap were reddish gold. While not melon-sized, her breasts were firm and taut against her gown, rising and falling with each rapid breath. Soft lips pressed against his palm. He suspected she was a beauty and wondered why he hadn't noticed her before. He gazed into pupils so large her eyes appeared black. Icy black. "If I take my hand away, do you promise not to scream?"

Refusing assent, she continued to stare at him while struggling to free her hands. Above his mounting annoyance, Will experienced a grudging admiration that she refused a promise she wouldn't keep.

And he wondered what in hell he should do next. The instant he dropped his hand, she would scream; the corridor would fill with the queen's ladies, guards would arrive in short order, and he would end in the Tower trying to explain to a virgin queen what he was doing in her ladies' chambers. The queen was notably unforgiving of such escapades. Jesu, women would be the death of him.

Well, there was nothing for it but to run and take his chances. But first . . . In one fluid motion, he dropped his hand and immediately smothered her scream by covering her lips with his own. Even though she clawed his naked back, he would never have forgiven himself if he'd departed without stealing at least one kiss. She tasted of mint leaves and sweetness and the kiss was worth the stripes of heat running down his back.

The instant he released her, she jerked violently backward. The motion pitched her toward the wall, and, tangled in her bed dress, she was unable to pull back. Her head struck the stones; she blinked once then crumpled across the bed.

He stared at her, unable to believe his good luck. Masses of reddish gold poured from her cap and he carefully felt among the silky strands for blood. There was none, but already he could feel the beginnings of a welt. When she woke, she was going to have a headache that would stall an ox.

After smoothing back her hair, he noticed her gown had slipped until it hung from the tip of one breast. And heaven help him but he wanted her with an intensity few women had aroused. But he wanted her awake and moving beneath him; he wanted to stare into her wide eyes and watch the contempt flame into passion.

While he had the willpower to do it, he rose from the bed and hastily dressed. Then he stood over her, studying her loveliness in the dim starlight. It was a face and a body he wouldn't soon forget.

"Sleep well, m'love." After dropping a brief kiss on her forehead, he flexed his shoulders against the rub of material across the scratches she'd left, then he laughed softly and let himself into the silent corridor.

CHAPTER 4

ell's head was throbbing when she entered the queen's
Privy Chamber for her audience, and there were faint
purplish circles under her eyes. Last night's encounter
continued to infuriate her. When she'd wakened to find her naked
intruder gone, her immediate impulse had been to rouse the
guards. But she'd halted with her hand on the chamber latch, realizing little would be served except to tarnish her own honor. Nell
had passed too many years at court not to anticipate what gossips
would make of the incident. An intrusion would become a tryst; a
kiss would transform to a seduction; calling the guards would indicate a lovers' quarrel.

So, the intruder had escaped unscathed. Seething with impotence, Nell had pressed a cold cloth to her head and returned to
bed where she passed an angry sleepless night.

Now she stood in the queen's chambers, her head pounding,
feeling dull-witted with fatigue. Here was an opportunity, however uncertain, to wrest a future for herself, but what she felt
most like doing was taking a headache draught and falling into
bed. Resisting an urge to touch the bump under her hair, Nell
raised her skirts and sank into a deep curtsy before the queen.

"Welcome back to Whitehall, Lady Nellanor." Elizabeth extended her fingers for Nell's kiss.

When Nell straightened, she looked for hints of welcome in

the queen's expression. The smile was correct, but something in the queen's eyes made Nell feel she had been examined and found wanting. At the same time there was a shadow of something else. Admiration? Envy? The notion was ludicrous. Nell had no idea what the queen was thinking; she knew only that Elizabeth's silent scrutiny stripped her bare and left her feeling five years old again, alone and unwanted.

"Did you sleep well?"

From anyone else the question would have seemed straightforward. But Elizabeth was the master of innuendo and layered meanings. The question could hint that Elizabeth had learned of Nell's intruder. Or it could subtly refer to the fact that Nell had arrived without furnishings and had been forced to appeal to the almoner for bed and blankets. Or it might be intended to call attention to the circles beneath her eyes. Or the inquiry might combine all the above plus additional possibilities Nell had overlooked.

"As well as can be expected," Nell responded. The reply covered everything and committed her to nothing.

"Be seated."

As there was only one chair in the chamber, Nell collapsed her farthingale and sank to one of the brocade cushions arranged on top of freshly swept reed mats. Occasionally Elizabeth joined her favorites on the cushions, but today she chose the chair, which forced Nell to look up at her.

This, of course, provided Elizabeth a distinct advantage, a tactic not lost on Nell and one that sharpened her wits. Any encounter with Elizabeth was a contest. What made it intriguing was that the stakes and rules were known only to the queen.

And today there was no question that it was a queen sitting before her. Elizabeth had chosen to appear at her most regal. Dozens of pearls adorned her bright wig, ropes of jewels hung down a bodice stiffened by gold and silver embroidery. She wore a wide burgundy skirt over a kirtle made from cloth of gold, and her face had been painted with meticulous care.

In the shadow of such magnificence, Nell felt very young and momentarily insignificant, as she suspected she was intended to feel. Unlike Elizabeth's elaborately curled wig, Nell's coiffure was elegant but simple. She'd parted her hair in the center and pinned it in a heavy twist at her neck, covering the arrangement with a silk net. She'd worn her best black velvet and her bodice with the seed-pearl trim. But she couldn't hope to compete with the queen—a contest impossible to win. Still, there was much to be said for the beauty of simplicity. If the queen sought to overwhelm her with jewels and embroidery, the ploy had failed. She was young, yes, but she refused to feel insignificant.

Elizabeth tented her fingers beneath her chin, a trick used to display long jeweled hands. "We shall dispense with chat, Lady Nellanor, and speak of weightier matters. We would know your ambitions."

Though nothing showed in her expression, Nell couldn't have been more surprised if the queen had calmly asked if she could sprout wings and fly. Plus, the directness of the question was astonishing. Ordinarily Elizabeth did not cast so obvious a net. "I have no ambitions, Your Majesty, except to serve you however I may."

An impatient flutter of fingers dismissed her reply. "Everyone has ambitions. We wish to learn yours."

But for what purpose? And how much truth could safely be revealed? Nell smiled cautiously. "My wants are too small to be considered ambitions, Your Majesty."

"We would hear them nonetheless."

So the question was not to be avoided. Nell's mind raced, looking for traps and finding a dozen. On the other hand, she also saw opportunity. Perhaps . . . perhaps she was being asked to name her reward for the Papist Affair. It was a possibility not to be overlooked, an opportunity worth the risk of pursuing. "I wish for a small degree of independence, Your Majesty. A future with hope of permanence." Did she dare risk it? Maybe she would not have another chance. "Perhaps a position at court . . ." Nell looked for a hint of acquiescence in the queen's eyes and found a careful blankness.

"That is all?"

In for a pence, in for a pound. "If I were granted my fondest dream, I would like a home of my own and children."

The queen gazed down at her. "It was our understanding that you bore Lord Amesly no children."

The reminder of her failure raised a flush to Nell's skin. In this particular contest, she sensed Elizabeth had scored. "It appears I'm barren, Majesty." Why this should make the queen smile, Nell had no idea. "But I've heard of barren women who have borne children for later husbands."

"We've learned of such oddities ourselves. Why do you not request permission to marry then, if that is your ambition?"

The contest became clearer by the moment, but no more comprehensible. It appeared the opening challenge was to circle around the obvious, for Elizabeth certainly knew Nell was not marriageable. The queen knew her court like she knew the jewels around her neck. Each had a special brilliance and a specified place on the chain, each had qualities to admire and flaws to bemoan. Elizabeth knew more about her courtiers than they often knew about themselves. It was inconceivable that she was unaware of Nell's situation.

"I've had no offers," Nell said, seeing no alternative but the truth. "Nor is it likely I'll receive any."

"You have no fortune?"

The queen knew she did not. "None." Each step of the conversation was being carefully staged, a thought that gave Nell no comfort as she could not discern the design behind it.

"Robert did not provide for you?" One painted eyebrow rose.

Nell wished to heaven that her head wasn't throbbing like a mummer's drum. Elizabeth knew Robert Dudley's will better than she, thus the inquiry had deeper significance than Nell could immediately identify. "Lord Leicester provided generously for me during his lifetime," she answered carefully. "His will mentioned the expectation that I would continue to be provided for, but it did not offer particulars."

"We must assume Robert referred to a second match."

"Perhaps," Nell said, hiding her surprise at this turn to the conversation. "But I would suggest it as unlikely as Robert knew of my financial straits and of my failure to provide Edward an heir."

"Such obstacles can be surmounted."

So. The purpose behind her summons was to discuss a match. Quickly Nell turned the idea in her mind. It went without saying that the match would be beneficial in some way to Elizabeth. Nell knew she was but a pawn in a greater game, one she didn't possess enough information to recognize. The question was: Would the match be beneficial to her? And would she be allowed the right of refusal?

Elizabeth examined her curiously then asked, "Is marriage disagreeable to you?"

It was a thousand times better than a retreat in Wales. But Nell remembered Edward and the helplessness of standing aside while he rushed toward ruin. She recalled the evenings she'd wished to go out but he'd refused permission. The nights when he had claimed his marital rights. In these instances, Nell agreed with the queen's well-known repugnance for marriage. But there were balancing arguments. A husband's protection greased the wheels of everyday commerce. When Edward was alive, merchants had delivered goods promptly, her carriage and horses were impeccably serviced, she'd had coins in her purse, and her life ran smoothly. Most important, for a time she had been mistress of her own home.

"Marriage is not disagreeable to me," Nell answered cautiously.

"But we sense hesitation. What *do* you find disagreeable, Lady Nellanor?"

Here she was on safe ground as her opinions aligned with those voiced by Elizabeth herself. Still, she proceeded slowly, watching the queen's face for hints of disapproval. "I resent bowing to a husband's will simply because he is a man and I am not. I dislike keeping silence in the face of stupidity." She spread her hands. "I would like nothing better than to have the benefits of marriage—a home and wealth to support it and children to fill it. But I hesitate to again become a man's chattel."

The intensity of her emotion charged the chamber, dissipating slowly. As it did, embarrassment flamed in Nell's cheeks. She'd spoken intimately and with unseemly directness. She had laid herself bare, which was never wise. Worse, it was possible she had just thrown aside a beneficial match and sealed her fate in Wales. Silently Nell cursed the naked lout who had ruined her sleep and given her this aching head. She called God's wrath down on his miserable soul; if this turned out badly, he was to blame.

"Possibly we can resolve this dilemma," Elizabeth offered smoothly as if the thought had just occurred to her. "Are you acquainted with Lord Thomas, the Earl of Mendenshire?"

Nell had heard of him. Lord Thomas was ancient, a living fossil some said, a man confined to bed and seldom seen in society. He'd outlived three wives and all his sons. "I've not had the pleasure," she said warily. A silent alarm warned that the preceding conversation had been but a preamble to what would now follow.

Elizabeth wound her long fingers through the ropes of jewels. "Lord Thomas approaches his seventieth year. We're told he may see spring, but summer is doubtful. If he were to marry, the widow's third would amount to a fortune."

"Lord Thomas?" It was an effort not to reveal her dismay. "Your Majesty, my fondest hope is to bear children. Can Lord Thomas . . . ?" A rush of revulsion thinned her lips. "Is he able to . . . ?"

"To raise his sword?" Elizabeth chuckled, then returned to the business at hand. "If a match were arranged between yourself and Lord Thomas—of brief duration we would imagine—it could also be arranged that any child conceived during the marriage would be recognized as Lord Thomas's heir." Elizabeth's canny gaze remained expressionless. "The parentage of your child would not be questioned."

The implication was unthinkable; coming from Elizabeth it was beyond imagining. Nell stared. "I'm not certain I grasp your meaning, Majesty."

"We think you do."

So she'd made no mistake. The queen advised her to cuckold

Lord Thomas and promised any resulting child would be recognized as legitimate. Her prayers had been answered; the retreat in Wales circumvented. By agreeing to this marriage Nell would soon have a vast fortune to purchase a home and the permanence she craved. And possibly a child. And all this, her most cherished dreams, without the burden of a husband.

"Such an arrangement," she said when her breath steadied, "would be agreeable to me." Why it would be agreeable to Lord Thomas mystified her. But she had no doubt Elizabeth would deliver what she had promised and further, that Elizabeth would somehow gain from it.

Elizabeth waved Nell up and toward a decanter of watered wine. "We'll drink to it, Lady Nellanor. From this moment you may consider yourself betrothed. Cecil will have the documents for you this afternoon."

Nell held a sip of wine upon her tongue and swiftly reviewed the conversation. It was tempting to think the queen's largess resulted as gratitude for Nell's role in the Papist Affair. But no such hint had been offered. Therefore—as the Papist Affair had not been mentioned, and as gratitude was not one of the queen's more prominent qualities—price was yet to be discussed. It was Elizabeth's way to dangle favors then extract a price, the hint being that the favor would be snatched away lest the price was paid.

"From the bottom of my heart, I thank you for providing so generously for my welfare." Nell regarded Elizabeth's pleased smile from beneath her lashes then posed the crucial question. "How may I repay your kindness?"

Elizabeth waved Nell back to the cushions and gave her a small nod of approval. The game proceeded smoothly when the players understood the rules. And few played the game any better than Lady Nellanor. "There is a task we would ask of you."

"I would be honored to serve in whatever small capacity I can."

"My spies inform me that Philip has not accepted defeat gracefully. It seems he seeks to wound England and ourself in retaliation for his humiliation at the hands of our navy."

Elizabeth had embarrassed Philip in front of the world and

she had enjoyed it enormously. She'd lost no time in informing the courts of Europe that Elizabeth Tudor had utterly smashed her former brother-in-law and his Catholic armada. She, who had secretly feared Spain for years, had sent it packing like a dog with its tail between its legs.

Not for one moment did she expect Philip to accept defeat meekly. But she had not anticipated so swift a strike, nor from this quarter. Staring at the girl before her, she suddenly saw Robert Dudley instead. Her dear, sweet Robin, reaching out from the grave to plague her. Vain, foolish Robin Dudley, who would never obey but who twisted her commands to suit his own aims. This time he was not here to plead her forgiveness, nor was she certain she could have forgiven him. Not for this.

Elizabeth touched her fingertips to her jaw and pushed her tongue against the bad tooth. A sharp pain shot up behind her eyes and she cursed solidly and steadily until the ache receded. Then she brought Nell's blanked expression into focus.

"Lady Leicester," Elizabeth said, the words a long hiss of hatred, "has sold Philip's agents documents that could be damaging to England and to us."

"Lettice sold . . . ?"

"We're told you saw the Spaniards and spoke to them. Is that correct?"

"I saw the Spaniards?" Nell was astonished.

"At Kenilworth."

"Spaniards at *Kenilworth*?" Surely the queen was mistaken. It was unthinkable.

Elizabeth fluttered impatient fingers. "A fair man and a dark woman. Our spies tell us neither looks nor sounds foreign. Did you or did you not speak to them?"

If the welt beneath her hair hadn't felt like a large, hot walnut, Nell might have grasped the connection immediately. As it was, she hastily shuffled the visitors to Kenilworth through her mind until she recalled the blond man resembling Lord March and his dark-haired companion.

Comprehension dawned in her eyes. No wonder Lettice had chosen not to make introductions.

"Aye," she admitted slowly. "I did speak to them."

"And you would recognize them again?"

"Aye." The fabric beneath the pattern was beginning to emerge. Other than Lettice, Nell was the only person who could identify Philip's agents, agents who didn't resemble Spaniards.

"Lettice Knollys, that stinking harlot, sold Philip politically damaging documents for the sum of twenty thousand crowns."

"Treason!" Lettice would go to the block.

Elizabeth cut her off with a sharp downward motion. "We'd like nothing better than to see her Ladyship's head in the dirt, but to bring charges requires evidence." Evidence Elizabeth would never allow anyone to see.

Was Nell being asked to testify? She would do so and gladly. She said so but the queen waved the offer aside.

"The whore sold private letters we wrote to Robert Dudley." She stared at Nellanor. "We want them back."

This then had been Lettice's revenge. Something in those letters would "fix" Elizabeth and expose her as a fraud. Nell dropped her eyes and pressed her palms together. Never in her wildest imagination had she suspected Lettice of treason.

"We want you to fetch the letters for us."

"Me?" Nell's cool exterior dropped away and astonishment drained the color from her face. She gazed at the queen like an utter fling-brain.

"You can recognize the Spaniards and you are certainly capable of outwitting them. In that regard we have no doubt." Elizabeth examined her with hard eyes. "If the letters are exposed, Robert's honor will be besmirched. You have said you owe him much. You can repay that debt by salvaging his honor."

Nell raised a hand to her forehead. There was more here than appeared on the surface, much more, layers she would most likely never uncover. That didn't concern her as much as the astounding fact that Elizabeth expected her to retrieve the letters. Naturally, she was flattered, but she was also bewildered. She could think of a dozen people—men—better qualified than she to chase down the Spaniards.

But they couldn't recognize the Spanish agents. For that, Elizabeth needed Nell. The last pieces of the puzzle fell into place.

"I'll try, of course," she promised. But Wales rose before her vision, not as safely distant as she had supposed. The challenge intrigued Nell, but at the moment she had no idea where to begin.

"We expect you to succeed." Elizabeth tasted her wine and wiped her lips. "William Steele, Lord Brampton, will accompany you. Steele is arrogant, rough-edged, and opinionated. Should a difference of opinion arise between you—your decision shall prevail. What you must remember is that Steele is also courageous and loyal. We would trust few others with this matter."

"Is Lord Brampton aware my opinion prevails in the event of a dispute?" Retaining her composure was becoming increasingly difficult. One astounding revelation followed quickly upon another, leaving scant time for assimilation.

"He will accept such terms." Elizabeth leaned forward and her gaze held Nell's eyes. "The letters are in a silver casket of about this size." Her hands defined a box a foot long and perhaps three inches tall. "A locked casket sealed on both sides with Robert's wax and crest."

"The silver casket!"

Instantly, the queen's eyes narrowed. "What do you know of it?" she asked sharply.

"It's mine," Nell blurted. "Robert promised it to me. He said I was to have it if . . ." she halted, stunned by the shock and fury drawing Elizabeth's expression.

"He had no right! Years ago we commanded Robert to burn those letters and we believed he had. Those letters are ours!" With effort Elizabeth regained control. Her gaze was iced and unyielding. "The casket is to be returned to us. Unopened. The seals intact. Do you understand?"

Nell did not understand, not for a moment. The casket had been promised to her. Robert Dudley had embraced her and had told her the casket was her legacy. Why he had wanted her to have the queen's letters she couldn't guess, but he had. By rights, they were now hers.

Something of this thought must have shown in her eyes because she met the queen's stare and for a moment they were equals. The majesty dropped from Elizabeth's demeanor and she faced Nell as a woman. Betrayal was in her stare and defiance in Nell's. For one terrible moment they saw each other as rivals.

Nell was first to look aside. Holding her head stiffly erect, she said, "I understand the reward for success. But if Lord Brampton and I fail to recover my—your—casket . . . ?"

"In the event of failure we shall seal you in the Tower and forget you exist. You shall die in obscurity." Elizabeth's gaze traveled slowly across Nell's flushed face, her slim body. "Make no mistake—if the casket is opened, the failure is as great as if the casket had not been recovered."

"I understand." She would never learn what Uncle Robert had wished her to know. First Lettice and now Elizabeth had stolen her legacy. Nell's mouth pressed in a bitter line. So be it. She could not fight the queen of England. She would concentrate on what could be salvaged, not on what had been lost. Once again, she was powerless to assert her own rights. But she would succeed in this dangerous game. At the finish she would have a home and a child.

But she could not deny that what had first been a patriotic mission was now deeply personal.

"You will meet Lord Brampton at supper tonight," Elizabeth said, standing.

It was clearly a dismissal and Nell sank into a deep curtsy. But Elizabeth stopped her before she reached the chamber door.

"Do you miss him?" she asked in a low voice, looking at Nell's black velvet.

"Every day," Nell answered simply. Unconsciously, she turned Robert Dudley's signet ring around her finger. "I loved him."

Elizabeth stared at her. "You're a fling-brain to want children, you know that, don't you?" She drained her wine and dropped the cup upon the cushions. "You'll rue the day you whelp a pup. It will grow to snap and bite at your heels."

"With respect, Your Majesty, I disagree." This singular con-

versation had bumped from subject to topic. Nell glanced at the
wine cup from the corner of her eye.

"If your parents were alive, you would be at their throats
even now, taking what was theirs."

"Never!" Nell's hand rose to the locket beneath her bodice.
"I've missed my mother every day of my life. Had I known her I
would have worshiped her." She was shocked by the vehemence
in Elizabeth's face and tone. Had the queen forgotten what it was
like to grow up without a mother? She would have thought Elizabeth would have understood.

"Worshiped her? You would have devoured her. The sunrise
has no regard for the sunset. You would have devoted your life to
eclipsing her!"

"No."

The queen dismissed her with an impatient flick of her fingertips. "Get out of our sight. We don't wish to gaze upon you
again until you have our casket for us. Intact."

Head spinning, Nell gathered her skirts and retreated. It
didn't surprise her to discover she was perspiring freely though
the morning was chill.

Will Steele followed the lords and ladies toward the gardens,
glad for the fresh cold air after the smoky closeness of the banqueting hall. He was in a vile temper. All morning he had pursued Lady Bledsoe in hopes of explaining his failure to appear
in her chamber as invited. But Lady Bledsoe, certain she'd been
jilted, cast him poisonous glares and wouldn't speak to him. Instead she whispered to small clutches of ladies who turned to
look at him with the same murderous stares. He rightly suspected
those melon-sized breasts were lost to him forever. A tragic
damned pity.

Scowling at the path, Will fell into step with the swaggering
lords trailing the queen's ladies. He observed ruffs larger than his
own and gem-encrusted doublets the sale of which would have
armed and clothed a respectable army. He had half a mind to
bump the perfumed and jeweled dandy strolling next to him for
the sole purpose of provoking a challenge. What he needed was a

good rollicking fight, something bluntly physical with a dash of good-natured loathing. He would have traded his new Spanish boots for a Scotsman right now.

Two events saved the dandy from ending sprawled in the box hedge. First, Will exchanged bows with Lord Essex, who looked in fouler temper than he and who was limping noticeably and favoring his right arm. Second, the queen invited Will forward to walk at her side and she waved the others back out of earshot. She also allowed him the favor of kissing her hand.

"So, Lord Brampton. Are you enjoying your stay at court?"

He hoped Essex noticed and brooded that the queen rested her fingertips upon Will's sleeve and leaned slightly against him as they followed the graveled path. "I am indeed," he lied. "I thank Your Majesty for including me in the celebrations." A satisfying envy thickened the air behind him.

"Liar," Elizabeth smiled. "If you enjoyed court you'd appear more often. We suspect our Fighting Duke would rather match swords than wits."

"Not at all," he managed gallantly. "What greater joy can life offer than to walk in the perfumed shadow of Your Majesty's grace?"

"Well done," Elizabeth laughed. She pressed his arm. "So tell us, Will, how goes the war?"

"It would go much better if Your Majesty would join me." He smiled, pleased that he'd made her laugh, though it was no laughing matter. What the queen referred to as "Steele's private war" was in fact England's war. The sooner England took arms against Scotland the better. He'd believed when Elizabeth beheaded Mary, Queen of Scots, that both sides would issue a call to arms and the border would be settled once and for good. But it hadn't happened. Mary's cowardly son had let his mother be beheaded without a squeak, and that being the case, Elizabeth had withdrawn the troops she'd placed on readiness. Royalty looked the other direction while the border raids continued with unabated ferocity.

"We're honored that you delayed your war long enough to join ours," she said, teasing him.

"The honor was mine." And the cost, he thought ruefully, thinking of the pound sterling he'd spent to arm and outfit his men, not to mention himself.

While the queen jested with him, he smiled into her eyes, noticing they were not black as he'd imagined but gray. The large pupils of shortsightedness had provoked his error. Gazing into her keen gaze and radiant smile, he forgot she was twice his age. Despite the scalding red wig she wore and the rice powder so white her teeth were yellowish in contrast, she was still a winsome woman, one who could charm a man with wit and grace. She was slender as a maid, elegant, and stunningly majestic. Strolling beside her, he forgot Lady Bledsoe.

Elizabeth tilted her curls and gave him a coquettish glance. "Are you as skilled with your sword as you are in the tiltyard?" she purred.

God's blood, she was flirting with him, teasing him with bawdy references. And he was returning her warm glances and intimate touches. Once again Will felt himself slipping under her spell, seduced by a teasing word, a challenging flash within those fine eyes. Long ago it had ceased to surprise him that men were willing to lay down their lives for her. Each time he found himself in her presence, he also discovered himself yearning for a chivalrous deed to perform in her honor, even though he recognized he was being outrageously manipulated to that very thought.

"We wonder . . ." She gazed up at him through darkened lashes, a coy look on her powdered face. "Were you aware Baywick Castle has reverted to the crown?"

Baywick. Will narrowed his eyes. He was not innocent enough to think the queen made idle chat. And she knew he'd lusted after Baywick for years. His mouth watered at the thought.

"We own it now."

Abruptly Will halted on the path and stared down at her. Baywick. He'd ridden there uncountable times. Baywick Castle commanded the mouth of Weyley Valley; the man who owned Baywick and its villages could blockade Weyley Valley and cut off the Scots like turning the tap on a wine butt. "I'd like to have it," he said bluntly.

Elizabeth laughed and gazed at him from dancing eyes. "You're a rogue, Will Steele, but an innocent all the same." She laughed again as his shoulders stiffened in protest. "May we assume if Baywick were offered, you would accept?"

"I would single-handedly fight every thieving Scots in Edinburgh to own Baywick." His eyes flickered. "What must I do to earn it?"

"Ah, perhaps not so innocent." Elizabeth smiled engagingly and rested her fingertips on his wrist. "There is a small price. One we think you'll not find too unpleasant."

The day had brightened immeasurably. A sudden grin eased the lines framing Will's mouth and he laughed out loud. Whatever the old girl wanted from him, the reward would cost her nothing as Baywick had only recently come into her demesne. But to him—it was everything. With Baywick he would be one of the largest landholders in the North. The bloody Scots would rue this fine day.

"You're a bewitching chit of a girl," he said, grasping her by the waist and swinging her high in a circle. The lords and ladies behind them gasped, but Elizabeth's laugh told him he had not overstepped. Another time, another day, she might clap him in the White Tower for daring to touch her person. But not today. Today he was her favorite—and she wanted something.

"Put us down, you fool," she said, her laughter as light and pleased as a girl's, her hands intimate on his shoulders.

After placing her on her feet, he lifted her chin with his fingertip. "And now, m'love, what must I do?" At this moment he would have marched against dragons for her.

She smoothed her skirts and patted her hair. Then her gaze sobered into an implacable hatred. "Lady Leicester has dared sell that which did not belong to her."

There was no mistaking the rage thinning her lips, but Will mistook its purpose. "You wish me to arrest Lady Leicester?"

"No," she said with obvious reluctance. "Imprisonment would require explanations, even for a queen."

He waited. And listened as she spoke of Spaniards and Philip's malicious designs and a silver casket and letters she'd written to Robert Dudley long ago, letters she hinted were of delicate political importance.

When she finished, Will suppressed a smile. Baywick was as good as his. "I accept the charge, my queen. I'll place your letters in your hands within a fortnight."

"No. Not the letters—the casket. Unopened. We must have it locked and bearing the original seals. Intact."

Will regarded her curiously. The life had bled from her eyes as she spoke of the letters. Beneath the rouge and rice powder her face had paled. She looked old and pinched. And he comprehended the letters were far, far more important than she had admitted.

"Two Spaniards are no match for an Englishman," he said gently. "You'll have your casket."

Elizabeth leaned heavily on his padded arm. "Our astrologer predicts the day after tomorrow as the most fortuitous time to begin the recovery."

Frustration knotted his jaw. Will set small store by figure-finders as they dealt in magic and conjecture, both of which he scorned. Already the Spaniards had a four-day advantage; the trail had begun to cool. But he recognized the intractability in her expression. "As you wish," he conceded finally.

"As we command," the queen softly corrected. "And you shall have a companion."

"I require no assistance."

"A woman." Elizabeth smiled as his handsome face darkened at the insult. She raised a slim hand to halt his flow of impassioned protest. "One of the Spaniards is a woman. Not even Will Steele can outguess a woman. No man can. Therefore, to even our odds, we shall have a woman too." The glint of amusement left her gaze. "And Will—in the event of a dispute, Lady Nellanor's opinion shall prevail."

Anger and astonishment clouded his expression. "I'll travel faster and further unencumbered by a skirt. To place me at a woman's command is sheer idiocy."

Elizabeth's gaze cooled. "Remember to whom you speak, Lord Brampton."

"But a woman's judgment is . . ."

"Aye?"

The icy sharpness of her tone brought him to his senses. He stared into the face of the woman who had ruled England for thirty years, who had stood firm at the helm and guided the ship of State through three decades of choppy water. There was nothing more to say. Clenching his jaw, he inclined his head. "As you command."

"Indeed." She challenged his scowl. "There is one final condition."

God's teeth. Claiming Baywick was not the child's task he had originally believed.

"If the casket is opened, if the letters are read—by anyone including yourself or Lady Nellanor—you are to kill Lady Nellanor at once. That is a direct command. Do you understand?"

Will Steele stared at her.

"Do you scruple to kill a woman, Lord Brampton?"

"No," he said slowly. To refuse would constitute treason. "I'm sure there's good cause for this command."

The queen's smile did not touch her eyes. "Princes don't justify or explain." Subtly leading, she turned along the path toward the gate. "You will meet Lady Nellanor tonight at supper."

"I anticipate the meeting with pleasure," he said through his teeth. He hoped to Christ Lady Nellanor was as ugly as a Scot's toad and not of a type a man might grow fond of. Baywick's price had risen considerably since the conversation had begun.

"When you succeed," Elizabeth said before they rejoined the court, "Baywick and its surrounds will be yours." He nodded, wondering who would kill him if the letters were read. The answer was forthcoming. "But if you fail—we will hang you. You will not be beheaded as fitting your rank; you will be hanged for treason. Then disemboweled before your eyes. And drawn and quartered." Briefly Elizabeth touched his dark moustache and laid her palm against his cheek.

Sun-bronzed lines creased around Will's eyes and speculation flickered in their depths. "You must have loved Dudley very much." Her hand was warm and light against his skin.

Elizabeth's lashes flared then narrowed. "You're not innocent at all, are you, Will Steele? You're an insolent dog."

Before she could turn away, he caught her hand and brought it to his lips. "You'll not put this head in a noose, my queen."

"We will if you fail. No place on earth will be safe for you." She gazed at breeze-tumbled dark curls and teasing eyes and released a small sigh as his lips caressed her palm. "We hope you don't fail," she said gently.

At the arched doorway to the banqueting hall Nell stifled a yawn and chastised herself for not stealing away for a nap. But she hadn't wanted to miss a moment. There were friends eager to exchange news, gossip to enjoy, shifts in the power structure even during the brief span of her absence. As tired as she was, she glanced over the hall with interest stimulated by the noise and the undercurrents.

Lord Bennington and the Duke of Bedford sat near the cauldrons of beer suspended over the fire, their heads together. She couldn't mark their expressions for the smoky haze overhanging the tables, but it was an odd political alliance to say the least. And unless she was mistaken, Mary, Lady Norburton, had just passed a note to the Earl of Kent.

Nell smiled, glad to be back. She watched the dogs racing between and under long carpeted trestle tables, watched servants bearing great platters upon their shoulders, inhaled the scents of food and perfume and intrigue. Laughter shouted back and forth across the hall; musicians doggedly sawed a madrigal into the noise. There was no place she would rather have been.

After giving her name to a harried steward, she lifted her skirts above the greasy rushes and followed past those who ate off rounds of day-old bread, past those who merited wooden trenchers, to the tapestry-covered tables nearest the dais where rank entitled the diners to pewter platters.

Once seated upon the bench, Nell removed her dinner knife from the tiny embroidered sheath at her waist and tucked her napery into the top of her bodice to protect her gown. She waved at a table of friends where she would have preferred to be, then waited politely for a gentleman to serve her and share his cup. Lord Kritterton was occupied with his lady and the space to her right was vacant. Nell eyed the bowls marching down the carpet, then folded her hands in her lap and waited, annoyed at Lord Brampton's lack of promptness though she might have expected as much.

The northern lords generally had the manners of swine. Elizabeth might call them her diamonds in the rough, but to Nell they were just rough. Distaste tugged at her lips. The border lords were nine parts pride and one part treachery. Their loyalties wavered to suit self-interest. On the other hand, Elizabeth wouldn't have chosen a fool for so delicate a mission. After considering a moment, Nell decided to set aside her prejudice and overlook Lord Brampton's failings. Their association would be brief, after all. And—in the event of disagreement, her word would prevail.

"Lady Nellanor?"

Nell turned to the man sliding into the seat next to her, his thigh a sudden explosion of heat next to her own. She gazed into laughing eyes as black as coal, into a craggy sun-burned face and teeth as white as bone. That face was seared in her mind.

"You!" Her fingers flew to the bump on her head.

"Will Steele at your service, m'love."

CHAPTER
5

Crimson heat fired Nell's cheeks. A murderous urge to grip her chalice and knock him over the head raised a tremble to her hands. Instead she rose abruptly and stiffly and without a word strode out of the banqueting hall and into the courtyard. She inhaled deeply, holding the damp cold air inside, and she stared at the first stars appearing above the final glow of sunset.

All day she had conducted an inner harangue against the intruder. She had rehearsed what she would say if she encountered him again. Outrage and fury had played large roles in her rehearsal.

"I did apologize, you know." Will Steele appeared at her side and Nell turned her back to him.

The patience in his tone enraged her. He seemed mildly surprised that she was angry, that she resented the intrusion of a naked man disturbing her rest and causing the worst headache of her life, traces of which still remained. Not trusting herself to speak, Nell clasped her mantle beneath her chin and glared at three cup-shotten courtiers emerging from a coach. Laughing, they staggered toward a servant who ran forward to light them inside. The coach rattled into the deepening darkness.

"It was a simple error—I had the wrong chamber." Moving in front of her, Will framed her face between his hands and gently touched the lump on her head. "I'm sorry you did this to yourself."

"*I* did this . . . ?" Sputtering, Nell jerked backward and her eyes blazed. "Don't touch me! Not ever again, do you hear?" Torchlight illuminated his eyes, eyes dancing with infuriating amusement. In defiance of fashion he wore no beard, but a moustache followed the curve of his smile. His clothing was elegantly cut though he'd chosen for practicality as well as fashion—a cloak of dark warm wool, boots of heavy Spanish leather. The ruff about his throat was of good Dutch linen, but the smallest Nell had seen.

"I apologize for my part in last night's incident."

Nell was speechless. Open-mouthed she watched him flourish his hat and lean into a bow. "Your part was the only part," she said when she found her voice.

"We can argue fault, m'love, or we can each forgive and forget and discuss our mutual endeavor."

He was beyond comprehension, a creature the likes of which she'd seldom seen. "*We?*" she gasped. "*We* can forgive and forget?"

"Do you always repeat things? Not that it isn't charming, but I can't help wondering if such a habit wouldn't grow wearisome." Jesu, she was lovely, a living blaze. Torchlight leaped in her eyes and transformed her hair to flame. Languid types left him indifferent, but a woman like this . . . She was for damned certain no Scottish toad. This was a woman to heat a man's blood and bed.

Nell snatched her cloak over her breasts when she saw his gaze stray to her bodice. Then she drew a long breath and gathered her wits. Setting her expression in icy hauteur she reminded herself that Will Steele was a coarse lout unworthy of her temper.

In a level voice she said, "First, we will never speak of last night's affront again. Secondly, you are not to call me 'm'love.' My name is Nellanor Amesly. Lady Amesly to you. Is that understood, Lord Brampton?"

"As you wish," he said cheerfully.

"Aye. As I wish. My opinion prevails." Happily, his smile vanished, replaced by a satisfactory scowl. A tiny smile touched her own mouth. "Now, we'll make plans." Moving to combat the evening chill, she followed the curve of the wall toward the gate.

"Something you need to understand, Nellie love, is that I don't take orders from a woman." Will spoke pleasantly, his cloak swinging against hers. "Not now. Not ever."

The *Nellie love* made her furious. Nell clenched her teeth and struggled to do the sensible thing, which was to ignore his familiarity and focus on what was important. She tilted her head back to meet his eyes. "In this case you do. Or perhaps you'd like to explain your reasoning to the queen?"

His shadow loomed over her as he stopped and fisted his hands on his hips. "Nellie love," he said in a dangerously soft tone. "I don't know what you stand to gain or lose, but Baywick Castle is mine if we succeed. I want Baywick." Torchlight glittered in his black eyes. "If we fail, I'll hang, simple as that. No slip of a wench is going to put this neck in a noose. Your opinion shall prevail, m'love, only if it agrees with mine."

"I see. Well, I'm not going to risk rotting in the Tower by depending on a man who can't even find the right chamber!" Her chin rose boldly and she didn't yield an inch. "I've been the victim of one man's poor judgment; I'll not be again!"

"Dammit, I was told five doors and I counted five doors."

"You counted four doors." Five doors meant—Lady Mary Bledsoe. Nell might have known. Mary Bledsoe with the stuffed bodice and the empty head would tryst with a goat.

"It was black as ink."

"There was a torch at the end of the corridor. Did you fail to notice that too?"

"God's teeth, woman! I thought we weren't going to discuss this." They glared at each other across a patch of shadowy starlight. "What do you gain if we succeed?" Will asked, abruptly changing the subject. In truth, he was humiliated that he'd miscounted. And damned uncomfortable that this particular woman knew it.

"That is none of your concern."

He strove mightily for patience. "Would it be fair to assume the reward is ample?" Staring at the stubborn set of her chin, he tried to decide if he wished more to shake her or kiss her. Starlight made her skin luminous; he recalled the warmth of her breast in his palm.

"Aye."

"Then it follows that we each have much to gain and much to lose," Will said. She'd mentioned the Tower, but she had more to fear from him. He gazed at her flashing eyes and thought of the slim body beneath her velvets and he wished to hell Lady Nellanor had been anyone but this woman. "Our best approach is compromise. You give a little and," he frowned, the promise coming hard, "and I'll give a little."

What did a man know of compromise? Nell almost laughed. If they failed, he died; a few moments of agony then done. But she would die by inches, confined to the blackness of a cell with no hope but the threat of Wales if she secured release. And if they succeeded? Then she had a life while all he had was more land, land she doubted he needed.

"You hang if we fail?" Hanging meant treason and that meant disembowelment and quartering.

"Aye."

The thought made her feel better. "Very well. We're agreed on compromise." In her heart she'd known no man worth the name would fully cede to a woman's judgment. Under the circumstances she supposed he'd bent more than most, particularly for a northern lord. "But. If we disagree and if you ignore the queen's command and if we fail in consequence—I will inform the queen we failed because of you."

Will shrugged and laughed. "The old girl can only hang me once, Nellie love." Leaning against the stone wall, he crossed his arms over his chest and studied her until she ducked her head and frowned in irritation. "By now the Spaniards are across the Channel. We can't leave until the day after tomorrow according to the queen's figure-finder, so the Spaniards will have hundreds of miles head start. We'll have to travel hard and fast."

"What convinces you they're already across the Channel?"

Until now she'd seemed almost reasonable. It surprised Will that she'd ask a fling-brained question. She wasn't a stupid woman. "They had a job to do—they did it. Of course they're across the Channel. Probably halfway to Spain by now."

Nell resented his tone and answered sharply. "I don't think so. I've been considering this . . ."

"And?"

The amused indulgence in his voice brought a rush of angry pink to Nell's cheeks. "And I've concluded the Spaniards are very likely here in London. Or at worst, only a day or so ahead."

Will raised his eyebrows and stifled a sigh. Women had no mind for the tasks of men. This was going to be a tedious association if he had to explain every elementary item. He wondered fleetingly if he'd overestimated the intelligence in her clear gray eyes. "Spain and England are at war."

"I know that," she snapped.

"Good. That is a good starting point." He waved toward the celebration bonfires flickering in the distant city. "Because we are at war, strangers are suspicious. Londoners are rousting every foreigner they encounter. Yet you think two Spaniards—Spaniards for sweet heaven's sake—are going to boldly set up residence without anyone noticing?"

"Don't patronize me! These two Spaniards look more English than you do."

"And like me, they are emissaries for their sovereign. This means they are not going to dally. In their place I'd be sitting in Madrid right now tipping cups with the king of Spain."

"Would you really?" The hem of her mantle brushed the frosty stones as Nell thrust her hands into her sleeves and strolled forward, making him follow. "Particularly if you had no reason to suspect anyone was chasing you? I don't think so. I think, feeling safe and successful, you'd enjoy London for a few days. After a village like Madrid, London must be a fascinating curiosity." There was a woman on the opposing team, a woman who would be interested in English fashion, in the marketplaces and the shops on the bridge. Perhaps she would wish mementos of her journey.

Will glanced at the reddish wisps escaping her hood and tried not to think of reddish gold spilling into the darkness, filling his hands with silk.

"Well?" Nell asked.

Grudgingly, he pretended to consider her suggestion. "All right," he said finally, conceding the one valid point she'd scored. "They don't know they're being chased." The rest was unimaginable. If the Spaniards weren't in Spain, they were certainly in France.

"I think they'll want to tour the shops, inspect the fortifications, and . . . and so forth."

The word *fortifications* caught him up short. From that position, she was probably correct, though it irked him to admit it. It was, in fact, distinctly possible that spying was part of the Spaniards' mission. It made sense. He gazed at Nell thoughtfully. "I spent most of today asking questions at the docks. No Spaniards have booked passage."

It was her turn to summon patience. "I told you—they don't look Spanish or sound Spanish or chant a rosary every five minutes." They turned at the corner, following the courtyard wall and carefully not touching. "The man is fair, not as tall as you, and he wears a pointed beard and long moustache. Both are dressed richly and speak flawless English." She cast him a sidelong glance. "You'll enjoy meeting the woman. She's dark-haired—much like Lady Bledsoe—and very beautiful."

"Spaniards are like Scots, m'love. Even the women will cut your throat given half a chance. Our job is to do it first."

"Our job is to retrieve the queen's casket." Which was actually hers.

"We have to find it first." From the repugnance on her face he sensed she shied from killing. What did she think they were going to do? Politely ask the Spaniards to return the casket?

"We'll begin by searching London." Nell was tall for a woman, but Steele's height made her feel uncomfortably diminutive. She didn't like it.

"Jesu. Search London in one day? It's a waste of time," Will said flatly. "Like seeking two spotted minnows in the Atlantic."

"The alternative is to waste the day some other way." Already

Nell realized every small victory would be hard won. The idea of spending time with this maddening man depressed her to contemplate. She gazed into his dark eyes. "You may do as you like. I'm going to search London. All I have to do is find evidence they've been here. Then we'll have an idea of how far ahead they are."

"You're going to inquire at inns and hostels?"

"Aye."

"There are over a hundred inns in London, more in Southwark."

"Aye."

"You can't possibly stop at them all."

"I know that."

"But you're going anyway." The stubborn set of her jaw told him argument was useless. She was going to be a hindrance, a burr under his skin. After running his hand through his hair, Will cursed beneath his breath then glared down at her. "All right. As you well know, I can't allow you to ride about London unescorted."

"You can't allow me?"

"You're repeating things again. An unbecoming habit, m'love."

"I am not asking your permission, nor are you in a position to grant it!"

He ignored her. "I'll put ten men in Southwark and another ten in the city."

"You may do as you like," Nell snapped. Then added, "No lady would stay in Southwark." That's where the bearbaiting and cock-fighting rings were, and most of the whores and cutpurses.

"No man would sleep in London." Will's tone was as sharp as hers. "Even if he doesn't know he's being chased, the Spaniard won't box himself in. Once the city chains are locked for the night, he'd be trapped. He'll stay in Southwark. If he stayed at all," he added grimly.

"Put your men in Southwark if you must," Nell said between her teeth. "But I'm going to ask about London just the same."

"*We* will ask about London." And waste a day they might have spent more pleasantly hunting or hawking.

They walked in stiff silence toward the banqueting hall then regarded each other warily in the light of the torches flanking the entrance. "Regardless what happens tomorrow, Nellie love, we sail the day after."

"How utterly stupid," she replied evenly, watching the anger rise in his eyes. "We haven't an idea of where to sail. You said yourself there is no evidence the Spaniards booked passage. We don't know if they'll travel overland or by sea. Is this plan based on the same method you used last night? Sail into any handy port and hope for the best?"

Had she been a man Will would have challenged her on the spot. He gripped the hilt of his sword and his mouth thinned. "I'm going to explain this and hope you have the wit to comprehend, though it appears doubtful." A flush spread upward from her ruff. "If the worst happens and we don't catch the Spaniards, all we have to do is sail to the mouth of the Tagus River and wait there. Sooner or later the Spaniards will appear. Because if they travel overland as I think they will, it's likely they won't attempt to cross the Pyrenees in winter. Once they get that far, they'll book ship to Lisbon and continue from there up the Tagus. Is that clear enough for you?"

The flinty depth of his stare was meant to intimidate, and if Nell hadn't thought of all she had to gain, and all she had to lose, it might have done so. Instead, her own eyes turned a granite shade. "Perhaps I'm too witless to grasp the obvious, but why travel overland when a ship is faster?"

"Because ships sink, Nellie love. Especially this time of year. I believe it's safe to conclude the purpose is to deliver the letters intact to the Spanish king. The safest way would be to travel through France."

What he wanted now was a steaming tankard of ale and the company of steady, predictable men. She was full of fire and undoubtedly intelligent. But she was a woman. And she didn't know the first bloody thing about this. Briefly he wondered what the queen would do if he simply left Lady Nellanor behind and retrieved the letters himself. He stared down at her and decided the stiff straight line of her bodice didn't hint at the breast he'd held in his hand.

Nell spun on her heel. "Be here at first light," she said over her shoulder. At least they'd end this miserable charade on her command. Raising her skirts, she mounted the steps and turned toward the ladies' chambers. She didn't feel up to attending tonight's masque after all. In two minutes she would be asleep.

"Nellie love?"

She halted, drew a long breath, then turned in a whisper of velvet to see him leaning against the archway, arms folded over his chest, his ankles crossed. He looked like a man without a care in the world. That and his bemused smile struck a chord of irritation. "Well? What is it?"

"I thought I'd mention you need a new nightdress. There's a tear over your right breast."

Nell gasped. She knew he was seizing the command she'd so smugly thought she held. Suddenly she saw him sitting on her bed, naked muscles swelling on his arms and thighs. She remembered sweeping her gaze from the dark hair on his chest down to . . .

Her farthingale swung in an awkward arc as she spun and marched down the corridor, her head high, her fists clenched at her sides. And she seethed as his low chuckle reached her before she turned the corner.

Dona Catlina Valencia, daughter of Don Reynaldo Monterez and niece of Cardinal Adolfo Reggia, wrapped her cloak tightly around her body and sidestepped a dead cat clogging the drainage gutter. Unlike Rome or her beloved Venice, this filthy town had no street lighting, only a torch at the watch boxes which were so widely dispersed a person could murder another with impunity. The English were barbarians, as cultured as an olive pit. And Southwark had given her a view of the worst of them.

Between the buildings leaning out over the lane, she could glimpse sight of London Town across the river. She would have preferred to stop in London, but Fernando had proved intractable. Her usual manipulations had failed. Not that London Town was much better, she suspected, but neither did it appear to be the sinkhole that Southwark seemed to pride itself on being.

"What can one expect of pagan heretics?" she said when they had returned safely to their inn. At least the witless serving wench had troubled herself to light the fire and leave them a salver of cheese and bread. Coarse English bread. She sniffed and turned up her nose.

Don Fernando Valencia draped himself across the bed and crossed his arms behind his head, smiling as his wife fumed. She was a classic Castilian beauty, a fact of which she was well aware and had used to the advantage of them both. No one fumed more elegantly than a Castilian. Watching her, he decided Catlina managed scorn as effectively as anyone he'd observed. She could dismiss the largest city in the world with a twist of her full lips.

"Bearbaiting!" After peering into a square of mirror, she began pulling the pins from her hair, scattering them across the tabletop. "And cock fighting."

"Your uncle the cardinal has been known to wager a ducat or two at the ring," he commented mildly.

She flashed a glance at him over her shoulder. "Don't be a fool. The cardinal would never stoop to barbarism."

"I suppose the nobility indulges more cultural amusements, my dear." He smiled. "I doubt we'll be invited to participate." A crusted pot of turnip butter sat beside the salver and he pushed it aside with a grimace of distaste then cut a wedge of cheese and returned to the bed. He watched her hair cascade to her waist and wondered absently how many men had run their hands through those dark masses. The thought aroused him.

"Can you name an English playwright? A poet? An artist?" Her lip curled from her teeth and she pulled the brush through her hair with an impatient gesture.

"No."

"Of course not. There are none." As she had known he would, Fernando moved to stand behind her and took the brush from her fingers. She felt the heat of him pressing against her back. "England stinks of louts and heretics. I've completed my shopping, it's time to go home."

"In the morning, my sweet."

Closing her eyes, Catlina surrendered to the sensual tug against her scalp. She had married beneath herself, everyone said so, but Fernando had his uses. "Think of it, Nando," she said dreamily. "A viceroyship. In New Spain." They would live in a palace to rival anything yet seen, and the wives of lesser men would bow their heads to her. She would establish the fashion; she would be the standard by which other women would measure themselves. A slow smile of pleasure ripened at the thought. There would be gilded coaches and crimson livery. Servants hastening at the flick of a finger. And riches beyond imagining for the man with a clever wife.

"Opportunities we haven't yet dreamed of," Fernando murmured. He wet his lips and looked at the long ivory expanse of her throat. His hands tightened in the silken tresses flowing down her back.

"Finally." New Spain, and more importantly the coveted viceroyship, was the culmination of her ambitions. The scheming and plotting had reached fruition in a manner not even she had dared to hope. "At last you will be adequately rewarded. The piazza in Venice will be as nothing to the kingdom that awaits us in New Spain."

"I could not have managed it without you, my sweet."

"Nonsense," she lied. Fernando Valencia was perhaps the best swordsman in Spain and Italy and certainly the best lover. But he was not the best politician or the most clever diplomat. For that, he needed her. And she needed him, though it was wiser he didn't know that. He was the voice through which she spoke, the sword through which she did battle.

When he bent to kiss her throat, she glided away. Indifference inflamed him. Standing at the window, she gazed toward the bonfires flickering across the river. She refused to recognize the fires as celebrations; instead she preferred to think the English sought warmth. They needed it. The damp rose from the river and invaded her; she did not find it invigorating. She far preferred the languid heat of—New Spain, she thought with a smile.

She'd been told lace could be worn there all year. And the streets were cobbled in gold. Even shopkeepers ate from silver plate. This was an exaggeration, of course; she was no fool. Nor would she wish to live in a place where shopkeepers dined like their betters. But where there was rumor there was often a grain of fact. And if shopkeepers were said to dine from silver plate— then how did the aristocracy dine? From golden platters? From gem-encrusted bowls? Her eyes glittered with a deep fire.

It had all been so easy. So ridiculously easy.

"Nando, what do you suppose is in that casket?"

He smiled. He knew her so well. "It excites you, doesn't it, my sweet?" Reaching inside his doublet, he withdrew a satin pouch and shook the casket onto the bed. It caught the candle-light and drew it into glossy depths.

Catlina stroked the key she wore suspended from a chain around her neck. Sitting on the edge of the bed, she leaned forward and fitted the key into the casket's lock. It would require but a quick twist and the casket's secrets would be known.

"Wicked girl," Nando said, smiling. He pulled the key from the lock and laid it against her breast. "Remember what the king said. It must be locked and sealed."

She kicked her feet up onto the bed and crossed her ankles prettily. Running her finger the length of the lid, she looked at him. "What is worth twenty thousand crowns to a king who counts quills and tiles? What is worth a kingdom in New Spain?"

"Lady Leicester mentioned letters."

So he had noticed too. "Letters worth twenty thousand crowns?" He stroked the casket down the length of her throat and she shuddered with pleasure as the cool silver met the heat of her breasts. "Important letters."

He buried the casket in her hair and slipped her gown from her shoulders. "What does it matter?" he murmured huskily. "They will buy us a kingdom."

"A kingdom," she whispered, her lips caressing the word. With skilled fingers, she opened his doublet and then his shirt, pulling her nails lightly across his chest. He moaned and tore at her skirts and because she was thinking of kingdoms, she abandoned any pretense of indifference and returned his passion with an eagerness that drove him to new heights. And through it all, she held the casket to her skin until it caught her heat and gleamed as brightly as her eyes.

Though Nell seemed to devote her full attention to the people and events around her, this was often not the case. Occasionally an essential part of herself detached and viewed the scene not as a participant but as an observer. For most of her life Nell had sought to unite these two pieces of herself, but the unifying link was missing. That link was her history, that vast unknown body of information others possessed but she did not.

Now, nudging her horse through the crowded lanes of London Town, she let her hand drift to her breast and pressed against the familiar shape beneath her bodice. The locket absorbed her warmth and, though she was always aware of it next to her heart, she drew assurance from touching it.

She was cognizant of the hawkers pulling on her skirts to call attention to their wares, and wary of the red-faced women calling "Slops below" before they hurled night water into the streets from upper stories. She saw the beggars and the grand lords and the cutpurses dodging stones in the stocks and smelled the oyster carts and roasting chestnuts and cider fresh from the press. Boys darted between coaches and horses, shouts and curses lifted around her. She saw and heard and smelled it all while at the same time that other self searched the throngs for ghosts.

Had her mother ridden through these same streets? Had she paused before that shop window, lingered at the goldsmith's door? Would the beadle in his fine robes have recognized A.B. if she had been here now? Or the lady peering from her coach window, would she have called out a greeting to the woman in Nell's locket?

Nell searched the crowd and A.B. was not there. She was never there. But elusive hints appeared with tantalizing frequency. A profile here; a smile there. Perhaps a cousin with the family chin? Or an aunt beginning to thicken in the middle?

Nell gazed about and wondered where all these people came from and where they went at night. To homes and families. To a solid history of receding hairlines or gouty legs. The daughter looked at the mother and saw herself in twenty years. The sons exchanged remembered jests with fathers. They did not divide within their mind and ask with anguish: Who am I? Where do I belong?

A.B. was dead. In her heart, Nell knew this. Had her mother been alive, she would have sought Nell out. This she had to believe. Even if it meant she would always be divided and could never be whole. Divided because she didn't *know*.

Lifting her hand, she stretched her neck against her fingers and flexed her shoulders, feeling the stiffness of spending most of the day in the saddle. At least the day had been mild and sunny, one of those rare autumn days that danced with the shade of summer, unwilling to let go. At some point she had tossed her cloak over her shoulders and Will Steele had discarded his altogether.

Now as the late afternoon sun dipped and glowed orange through the thin haze overhanging the city, Nell caught the ribbons at her throat and tied them, pulling her cloak around her body.

She had been so certain the Spaniards would remain in London. Disappointment made her clumsy with the ribbons and she made a sound of exasperation before reining behind the traffic jamming the entrance to the bridge. She passed a hand across her brow then glanced at Will, waiting for him to gloat.

Satisfaction overlay his expression as he swiveled atop his horse to look back at her. "We've ridden from the Strand to the Tower and back again. We've scoured Cheapside and Leadenhall; we've tried the Exchange and Mooresfields—no trace of any Spaniards."

She had told him a hundred times that the Spaniards did not look like Spaniards, but he persisted in inquiring after Spaniards. With a wink and a nod toward her. She grimaced at the memory of the responses they'd received. Wild tales of blood-crazed Spaniards hiding in the next alleyway. Or uproarious laughter. Or threats detailing what would happen to any Spanish Catholics suicidal enough to stroll the lanes of London Town. She gave him a long thoughtful look and decided Will Steele would be an easy man to loathe.

He nodded toward the bridge, shouting to be heard. "Shall we try Southwark, Nellie love? Or trust to my men's efforts?"

Very easy to loathe. The process had already begun. It was difficult to isolate what she despised most as there was so much to choose from. Perhaps the proud swagger in his stance, evident even on horseback, though she admitted this was impossible. Or his relentless cheer. Or the way he treated her with elaborate politeness as if this were a game and he alone were privy to the rules. No, what she hated most was his familiarity. His "Nellie love." The phrase set her teeth on edge.

"Very well," she said, her mouth pinched with defeat. "I surrender." A wide smile lit his face and she narrowed her eyes before she jerked the reins and turned from the congestion clogging the entrance to the bridge. "I'll meet you at the Sign of the Oyster."

The noise was too overpowering to be certain, but she thought he had said "Thank God" before he was lost among the coaches and carts and shouting horsemen. If she was fortunate, he would be swallowed by them and she would never see him again.

"Not likely," she muttered, urging her horse against the flow of traffic. The Sign of the Oyster was near the docks where the wherries put in, not a place for ladies of quality, but that was where Steele had arranged to meet his man.

The stench of laystalls assaulted her nostrils as she turned into the narrow twisting lane running parallel to the river. The stink of a nearby tannery added to the rancid odors of a soap factory made her stomach cramp. Nell fumbled in the bag hanging from her saddle until she found her "necessity," the pomander ball, and pressed it to her nose.

Once the letters were recovered and she'd earned her reward,

she'd build a home in Giles Field. Giles Field was not as fashionable as the Strand, but it was far enough removed to escape the
evil smells of the city, yet near enough to shop the city markets
and to enjoy court. Her son or daughter would grow up in a tim-
bered house with mullioned windows and reed mats on the floor.
Flemish tapestries and arras would warm the walls and Turkey
carpets would cover her tables. The house would be hers, not
borrowed or given in charity, but honestly earned and hers. For
herself and her child.

It would be earned by giving Elizabeth what rightfully belonged to Nell. The thought troubled her deeply. Robert Dudley
had intended those letters to be hers. However many times she
examined the situation, she continually returned to that thought.
The casket and its contents were hers.

"Stop this," she muttered, reining before the Sign of the Oyster. Quickly she ran through the reasons to put the ownership of
the casket out of her mind. First, at the moment the whereabouts
of the casket were unknown. Second, there was a faint possibility
the Spaniards would escape with the casket. Third, the queen of
England claimed ownership. Fourth, if Nell took what was hers,
she would end in prison. All very good reasons to ignore Uncle
Robert's wishes. Still . . .

She gave herself a shake and looked at the sign over the tavern gate—a flaked painting of something disgusting in a shell.
Drifts of smoke curled from the tavern door bringing with it
shouts of raucous laughter. Beyond the gate where she waited,
Nell could see a tiny courtyard crowded against the river wall, littered with broken tiles, weeds, and scraps of food which two yel-
low dogs snarled and fought for. She would have ridden away
had not Will Steele appeared.

"Apologies, m'love, I didn't realize what a hole Mr. Killian fre-
quented." He reined near enough that Nell could feel the heat of
his body. "Come here, boy. Have you grown to the ground? Take
these horses and fetch ale and stools to sit on." A surly boy
hitched from the tavern wall and slouched forward as Will raised
his arms to Nell.

"I can manage myself." But his large hands circled her waist and he swung her to the ground as effortlessly as if she weighed no more than the brown leaves fluttering over the tavern courtyard. "Who is Mr. Killian?" She continued to feel his hands around her waist, an oddly disturbing sensation.

"Mr. Killian is a finder." Will's gaze swept the crumbling river wall and the greasy smoke wafting from the tavern doorway. "For enough money, Mr. Killian will find and provide whatever a man wants."

Nell considered, then decided she didn't want to know more. Raising her skirts from the broken stones, she stepped into the courtyard and waited while the boy rolled forward empty wine kegs for them to sit on. She settled herself in a wedge of sunlight. "Go ahead. Say it."

"Say what?"

"That you were right and I was wrong. The Spaniards aren't in London."

Smiling, Will drained his tankard and shouted for more ale. "I was right and you were wrong."

Nell ground her teeth. "When will Mr. Killian arrive?"

The question had not left her tongue before the gate banged and the ugliest man she'd ever seen entered the courtyard and bowed to Will. His cheeks were seamed with purple scars; the tip of his nose was a raw open wound. Tiny weasel eyes flicked over Nell and made her skin crawl. She edged nearer to Will.

The man thrust out a dirty palm. "I'll take me money now, Lordship." He took Will's purse, weighed it in his palm, then nodded and pushed it inside a doublet of undeterminate color.

"Well?" Will placed his boot on the keg and leaned an elbow on his knee. "Did you or your men discover anything?"

"Aye. Them thieving Spaniards was here all right."

Nell straightened. "Are they here now?"

"They sailed this very morn. At first light."

"God's teeth!" Will slapped his hat against his thigh then pushed his fingers through his hair and looked at Nell. "Seems you were right, m'love."

"I don't think I heard you," she said sweetly.

His reluctant grin exposed strong white teeth. "You were right, Nellie love, and I was wrong. They stayed in London."

"Not London, Lordship. Southwark." Will gave Nell a triumphant smile and she shrugged.

"At an inn not a stone's throw from the bridge it was."

"You're sure it was them?"

"They fit how you says they was. Middling-size fair man, foppish moustache and pointy beard. A good-looking skirt. Rich dressed." Mr. Killian smiled, exposing black and missing teeth. "And—the chamber wench heared 'em speaking tongues, says she knows it were Spain talk cause she gots a cousin what talks it."

Nell raised an eyebrow and studied Will Steele. He may have toyed with her all day, but he'd given his men in Southwark an accurate description. She didn't understand him at all.

"Did they say where they were going?" she asked.

"Claimed they was Flemish, Ladyship; claimed they was sailing home to Flanders. But Johnny Rumm, he found a fish wench on the dock what says them Spaniards sailed for Calais."

"Mr. Killian . . ." The name stuck to the roof of Nell's mouth. "Did anyone at the inn notice a silver casket? About this big?"

His eyes gleamed with interest. "Ain't none what said so."

It wasn't to be expected they would flaunt the casket. Nor would they have sailed without it.

"They're only a day ahead." Will bounced the tankard on his upraised knee. "Well now, that changes the odds a bit, doesn't it?"

They didn't speak again until they'd reached Whitehall. In the palace courtyard Will Steele again disregarded Nell's protests and swung her off her horse, then handed the reins to the boy running forward with a torch. Nell swiftly stepped from his large warm hands and concealed the annoying flush of heat in her cheeks by lowering her head and brushing out her riding skirt.

Before she understood what he was about to do, Will lifted her chin and gazed down into her eyes. "Travel lightly, Nellie love. This is a chase, not a parade."

Their eyes held and for one endless moment Nell thought he would kiss her. Then she slapped his hand away and hastily stepped backward.

"We need to settle a few items, Lord Brampton, as it appears our association will be lengthier than I'd hoped." Sunset bathed his face in tones of gold and fading blue. It was a strong face, bold and handsome, the face of a man confident and easy with himself. When she saw he was staring at her mouth, Nell frowned and flipped the edge of her cloak. "Are you listening?"

"Is your mouth as soft as it looks?"

Nell made a strangled sound.

"Sunset turns your hair to flame."

"Enough!" She pulled to her full willowy height. "These remarks are insulting and offensive. You are to stop this at once. Further, I expect your behavior to be exemplary throughout our journey." At this moment she couldn't bear to think about what lay ahead. Steele brought out the worst in her, brought her emotions surging to the surface.

Will smiled. She was a difficult woman and one he shouldn't enjoy. But he had never shied from a challenge. He bowed before her. "It's been said that Will Steele is the embodiment of exemplary behavior. In fact . . ."

"Stop that." When Nell could speak calmly, she continued. "Whatever charm you possess is wasted on me. I have no interest in you whatsoever beyond the limits of our charge." Subtlety was lost on him; she was forced to speak more directly than she was comfortable doing.

"I understand perfectly. You have no interest in me."

She contained her temper with effort. "That is correct. Therefore you are to cease immediately touching me at your pleasure."

"Nellie love, did you know there are green flecks in your eyes?"

It was hopeless. She squared her shoulders and made one final attempt, spacing her words between angry lapses. "I am not your 'Nellie love.' I am, in fact, betrothed and will marry when we return."

He fell into step beside her, his long stride easily matching her furious pace. "May I inquire who this fortunate gentleman might be?"

"Lord Thomas," she snapped. "The Earl of Mendenshire. Not that it's any of your concern."

He stopped short and so did she when she heard his burst of laughter. "My father was the earl's son by his second wife. If you marry Lord Thomas . . ."

Nell stared at him, her heart skipping a beat.

"Grandmother!" Will Steele grinned at her. Then he doubled over in helpless laughter.

Mortified, Nell lifted her flaming cheeks high and swept past him into the hall.

CHAPTER 6

Without pausing to quench her thirst or to brush the dust from her riding skirts, Nell hastened directly to William Cecil's chambers and requested—nay, demanded—an audience.

"Forgive me for appearing at the supper hour," she apologized when she'd been shown into Cecil's study. The chamber was paneled in dark oak, lined with books and ledgers. "I need to speak to you." If she didn't speak to someone, she would explode. The feather trimming her hat trembled with indignation, her cheeks glowed bright pink.

Cecil waved toward the stool before his desk. "Be seated, child." Mild curiosity appeared beneath his brows. After ordering Vernage, he leaned backward from the papers covering his desk and turned the wine between his fingers. "How may I serve you?"

The Vernage steadied Nell's thoughts and she thanked heaven it did. Mayhaps she erred in approaching Cecil so impulsively. With unnerving abruptness, it occurred to her that possibly the queen wished the Steele-Mendenshire alliance to remain undiscovered. If so, it was foolhardy to pursue the issue. For, as she'd learned from past advantage, words spoken in Cecil's chambers eventually found the ear of the queen.

Regretting her hasty appearance, Nell smoothed the anxiety from her brow and summoned a smile of caution and dissem-

bling brightness. "As you know, my dear Cecil, I depart tomorrow on the queen's business. I couldn't leave without bidding you
farewell."

Cecil smiled into his wine. "And before you sail, you wish to
learn more about your esteemed betrothed, Lord Thomas, the
Earl of Mendenshire," he suggested softly.

So, she was intended to know. The knowledge eased her
mind somewhat. "I've had many matters to occupy my attention
of late—I've scarcely spared Lord Thomas a thought. However, as
you've raised the issue, dear Cecil, if you wish to gratify a bride's
curiosity . . ."

"Lord Mendenshire's wealth is legendary. You've contracted a
brilliant match, my small friend. Especially with the, ah, private
agreement."

She colored prettily. "Naturally it is my hope to fulfill my
duty to Lord Mendenshire by bearing his heir." Nell glanced at
him through her lashes. "I wonder—am I correct to assume Lord
Thomas has no living heirs?"

"None that need concern you. Your widow's third shall pass
unchallenged. And," he added after a pause, "If you should discover yourself in the happy condition of breeding, Lord Thomas's
son or daughter will naturally take precedence over a grandson
whose claim may be clouded."

God's teeth. "A grandson?" Dots of color pinked her cheeks
as she recalled Will Steele's burst of laughter. She had prayed it
wasn't true, that he was no kin to Lord Mendenshire.

"Aye. Lord Brampton."

"Will Steele? What an amusing coincidence." By supreme effort, she contrived to mold her lips into a pleasant curve, but her
voice sounded strangled.

"Indeed. An amusing coincidence." Cecil returned her smile.
Elizabeth would be pleased to learn the girl was as keen as Cecil
had promised. The queen had adopted many of her father's poli-
cies; it was therefore essential that Nellanor be made aware of
Steele's interest in her affairs. Old Harry, and now his daughter,
protected the crown's interests by prudently dispatching two
couriers in place of one. For best results the two should be ene-

mies or made to be so. This prevented any unfortunate collusion and ensured that each would police the other. Directed properly, fear and hatred were useful tools.

Nell wet her lips and folded her hands tightly in her lap. "I believe you mentioned Steele's claim is doubtful?"

"Aye. It's rather an interesting tale. If you have leisure to hear it?"

"You're certain I'm not delaying your supper?" Nell pretended hesitation. It gained no profit to appear anxious or to betray more than casual interest. In Elizabeth's court one was wise to keep private counsel. "Well, then . . ."

"Lord Thomas's only son, young Tom, was a rebellious and willful young nobleman. In defiance of duty and against his father's wishes, he contracted an unsuitable match with the daughter of an Irish lord. It was love, you see." Cecil shook his head and cocked an eyebrow. "The young woman came without dower, lands, or position. Naturally Lord Thomas disinherited Tom."

"Naturally," Nell agreed. No responsible father could do otherwise.

"Young Tom became Lord Brampton's father. Tom retired north on estates inherited through his mother's kin. Being in disgrace, whatever social and career ambitions he may have aspired to were lost to him. And, of course, there was the Irishwoman . . ."

"Was? Lord Brampton's parents are dead, then?" When Cecil nodded, Nell leaned slightly forward. "Is Lord Brampton also disinherited? As was his father?"

"Lord Thomas's heirs have all expired except Will Steele, which complicates matters." Cecil regarded her over his tented fingers. "If Lord Thomas died tomorrow, I doubt there is a court in the realm to deny Lord Brampton's claim. He would most certainly inherit his grandfather's titles and fortune. But if Lord Thomas remarries . . ."

Nell nodded slowly. When she wed Lord Thomas, Steele would forfeit a third of his grandfather's estate. And if she birthed a child recognized as Lord Thomas's heir—Steele would lose everything. "I see."

"And, of course, Lord Mendenshire will remarry." Cecil drove home the final peg. "As soon as you return." The flicker of unease at the back of her gaze assured him the process was now in place. Lord Brampton and Lady Amesly were contenders for the same fortune. Enemies. "But let us speak of you, Nellanor. Your future is bright and full." He gazed at her fondly, hopeful she would win the prize she had been promised. "Have you viewed Lord Mendenshire's manse in Saint Giles Field?"

"In Giles Field?"

"I think you'll find it impressive."

"I've dreamed of a home there," she responded absently. Her thoughts were elsewhere.

Thin pockets of fog clung in the low areas, dipping the lanes skirting London Town. Raising the window flap, Nell gazed moodily into the milky darkness. The city gates wouldn't drop their chains until first light, so her coach followed the outer walls to reach the docks. As the coach sped past Ludgate, she heard a disembodied voice call, "Half past four." The voice melted into the fog, leaving the eerie monotony of muffled harness and mist-damp wheels. She nibbled the fingertip of her glove and wished she were tucked into a safe, warm bed instead of jolting toward Will Steele.

Now Nell understood Elizabeth's confidence that she could influence Lord Thomas to recognize Nell's child or children. Cecil had hinted that Lord Thomas would rather scatter his fortune in the streets than have it benefit the whelp of an Irish whore.

A humorless smile paled Nell's lips. She was not unaware of Elizabeth's penchant for pitting adversaries one against the other or for creating ill will where amiability had previously existed. While Nell could hardly view her acquaintance with Will Steele as amiable, the queen had ensured it couldn't be by placing Lord Thomas's vast fortune between them.

As the coach rattled through the foggy lanes, jolting Nell from one side of the upholstered seat to the other, she pondered the situation as she had throughout the short night, attempting to perceive it from Steele's perspective.

Should Will Steele inherit Lord Thomas's fortune, he could finance his famed war against the Scots with ease. He could, in fact, raise a formidable army. From what Nell had learned of him, it was reasonable to assume this as Steele's eventual plan. Unless his grandfather married again.

But. Unless they failed to retrieve the silver casket, Lord Thomas would indeed remarry. Therefore, a successful mission threatened Will Steele's inheritance. He would benefit if they failed to fetch back the casket.

However, if they failed to retrieve the queen's letters, Will Steele would hang.

Frowning, Nell tapped a finger against her chin, leaning as the coach swayed into a turn. Could Steele conceivably believe he might escape the hangman's noose? She recalled the purpose hardening the queen's gaze and thought not. Elizabeth would make good her threats and promises.

Concentrating, Nell attempted to project herself into Will Steele's thoughts. How could he resolve the dilemma in such a manner as to gain both his life and his grandfather's fortune?

Almost immediately she grasped the answer to Steele's problem. The queen's mission had to succeed—but Nell had to die. If Will returned with the queen's letters, but without Nell, he profited everything; his precious Baywick plus Lord Thomas's fortune and titles.

"God's teeth!" Nell blinked. She was racing through the early morning fog to her eventual death. The question was merely when. If the queen's business failed, she'd end her days in a Tower dungeon. If the mission succeeded, Steele would put her to the sword. This was as obvious as the rosebuds adorning her gloves. Nell pressed a hand to her heart and squeezed her eyes shut.

"Think," she muttered between her teeth. "There is no problem without a solution."

Very well. If she was to preserve her life, she must strike first. Opening her fists, Nell pressed her palms flat against her traveling skirts. Clearly, she had to dispose of Steele before he disposed of her. Years at court had taught that successful plots must be timed precisely; her strike must occur when Steele was no longer useful to her but before she ceased to be of use to him.

And when might that be? Most likely, she reasoned, Steele would delay until they had recovered the letters. Until then, Nell did not become a genuine threat. But once they took possession of the casket, her life wouldn't be worth a brass shilling. She would have to act and swiftly.

Unfortunately, she had no clear notion of how to dispatch Will Steele. There would be no leisure for subtle entrapments, no discernable method by which to maneuver him into tying the noose around his own neck. And Nell could not visualize herself murdering him by more direct methods. The entire wicked business made her skin crawl.

She passed a hand over her eyes. Everything she had just deciphered was surely known to Elizabeth. The queen would be aware that only one of her couriers could return. Was the second layer to the business merely a game staged for the queen's amusement? Jesu, had Elizabeth and Cecil placed wagers on who would return?

Nell sighed. Elizabeth continued to confound her. What had she done to incur the queen's displeasure this time? Why could she never please? There was no one Nell admired more than Elizabeth Tudor. From the first she had adopted Elizabeth as her pattern, secretly bonding to another who had also been motherless. She had sought approval by developing her mind through reading and study; she had honed court skills by studying Elizabeth as example. She had spent years chasing the queen's approbation.

And what had she received for a lifetime of effort? A baffling ambivalence. Terse words of praise. A few favors scattered here and there. And pointed indifference. An attitude almost of suspicion, mounting as the years passed. Nell thought of all the small traps Elizabeth had baited throughout the last decade, and the strange mixture of pride and irritation when Nell had sidestepped them. At times Nell thought with frustration that Elizabeth wished her to succeed but became alarmed when she did. It was a game Nell couldn't win.

Now the queen had sprung a trap from which Nell could not easily extricate herself. The game was life or death.

Layers upon layers. She could try to second-guess Elizabeth until her head split and still arrive no nearer the truth than anyone ever had. Elizabeth Tudor remained an enigma; that was what she wished to be.

Nell opened her eyes and stared unseeing into the drifts of fog. Whatever the queen's plan, Nellanor Amesly would, by God, emerge alive and with the silver casket in hand. She had eluded Elizabeth's traps before and she would again. Nothing would deny her the home she craved and the chance to bear a child. If the choice was kill or be killed, she knew what she would choose.

After fumbling within the folds of her skirt, she found the chain clasping her small dinner knife. As a weapon, it was admittedly feeble. But gripping it made her feel better.

Will Steele leaned on the ship's oak railing and watched Nell's wherry approach through the blue-gray shadows of dawn. He nodded to the master and immediately a shout rolled over the decks, "Leadsman, sound the depth!"

The chase was on. Finally Will was freed from the stifling boredom of court and the world looked brighter than it had a week past. With the Spaniards but a day ahead, Baywick was practically his. With luck he could be home in Carlisle before the first snow packed Weyley Valley and blocked it until the spring thaw. He might have time for one last lightning raid to fill his winter larder with Scottish mutton, the best in the world considering most of it came from his own fields. The thieving bastards.

When the wherry bumped the hull, he leaned to assist Nell from the rope ladder onto the ship's deck. Then he frowned as first one then two heavy leather chests followed her over the side.

"And what, pray tell, is all this?" The cheering thoughts of Scottish plunder faded to a scowl as yet another chest appeared on deck.

"It's my luggage. As any dolt can see." Nell stepped backward as bare feet pounded past her, racing the length of the deck. Men swarmed up the ratlines, crawled out on the yards. At the first mate's shout, the anchor winched upward and broke from the waves trailing weed and water.

"Good God, woman! What do you have in there?"

Absently, Nell ticked off her list, her thoughts on the excitement of getting underway. "The bare essentials. Three corsets, three chemises, four pair of sleeves, a traveling bodice, riding bodice, and dress bodice, four skirts, a warm cloak, a dress cape, a dozen ruffs, six hats." She hadn't packed additional farthingales as the hoops required too much space. She'd make do with the one she was wearing. "Six pair of gloves, two pair of boots, a pair of dress shoes, perfumes and cosmetics, extra tooth cloths, various toiletries, my jewelry." She didn't think she'd forgotten anything important.

Will stared at her. "May I inquire how you intend to pack three chests on the back of a horse?"

Subtleties simply bypassed him, Nell thought. Everyone else in her acquaintance would have immediately grasped that travel by horseback was not an issue. It was out of the question. Though it pained her to explain the obvious, she ceded to necessity.

"We're to conduct this pursuit by *coach*?" Will asked, incredulous.

Nell caught a quick breath as sheets of sail spilled from the yards. Pouring canvas billowed above them catching the wind with sharp cracks as crisp as musket shot. Shouts rang from stem to stern and, as the sail cupped, the ship slowly swung toward the deeper swift currents in the river's center.

"Of course." The only way to communicate with a northern lord was to do so in the manner of instructing a child. Patiently. In simple terms. "First, there's the matter of our luggage . . ."

"I brought seven shirts and seven pair of hose. All of which will comfortably fit into a sling-sack."

"Then, there is the probable fact that the Spaniards are traveling by coach."

"It's fling-brained to send a coach to catch a coach. We'll travel faster by horse. Surely you can grasp that."

Nell turned away from him. Dawn tipped the sails with pink as London's chimney pots and steeples slid past on the left. She cast a last lingering look toward Whitehall before devoting her full attention to Steele's annoying questions. But first she dropped her gaze down his length, disapproving of his dress. Either he'd worn no doublet or had cast it aside. He stood before her in an embroidered waistcoat and a cambric shirt. His wide sleeves caught the breeze and fluttered. Instead of a ruff, he wore a falling collar of the same material as his shirt. And no hat. Nell thought it disgraceful for a lord of the realm to appear in such a state of undress.

"Traveling by horseback is not a consideration," she announced coolly. "I shouldn't think it necessary to remind you a lady of quality does not embark on an overnight journey without luggage." He might choose to abandon standards, but she would not.

Will glared at her. By God she tried a man's patience. "Listen carefully, Grandmother." Her gray eyes flared and she looked as if the tilt master had just shouted, "Attend!" Her eyes hardened like stones and her glove dropped to the dinner knife on her waist chain. "We're not embarking on a leisurely pleasure progress. May I remind you we are charged with the queen's business? And the queen's business necessitates haste. Which indicates horses rather than fancy coaches." He gestured impatiently toward her chests. "Which in turn means you are to pare that down to what will fit in a sling-sack."

The smile she gave him didn't warm her eyes. "You may proceed as you wish. *I* am traveling by coach." The issue settled, she commandeered two tars, setting them the task of taking her chests to her cabin. A third she dispatched to fetch a tankard of warm ale and a biscuit fried in hot grease. When she again looked toward Will, her gaze was unyielding.

Knots rose along his jaw. He fisted his hands on his hips and stared at the white plume ornamenting her hat. It was a damned pity that such beauty was wasted on a shrewish nature. He wondered if she had any Scots blood in her. If so, it would explain a great deal. On the other hand, mayhaps it was just as well that she stood beyond the logic of a reasonable man. He didn't ken to killing women. Although there were moments when he looked at this one and thought the task might not be all that repugnant.

"I'm growing a bit weary of you, Grandmother," he said, his eyes narrowed. "I'd advise you to remember which of us holds expertise in these matters and which of us is all theory and blather."

She regarded him above the rim of her tankard. "And I'll thank you to recall which of us holds command."

"The queen did not grant you command, m'love; she vested your authority in the event of dispute."

"Then kindly notice this is a dispute and I am exercising that authority. We travel by coach."

God save him from a general in skirts. Will turned his face into the wind and ground his teeth. Short of throwing her over a horse's back and tying her down like a sack of grain, he didn't perceive how he would get her out of the bloody coach and onto the back of a horse. And she well knew he wasn't going to abandon her and proceed alone as much as he would like to. What he needed was a persuasive argument powerful enough to penetrate a mind shuttered to logic. The challenge defeated him. Women were absolutely the most contrary creatures inhabiting God's fine earth. They were born knowing how to twist men's reason.

If he required proof, and he did not, he had only to admit Lady Nellanor Amesly already manipulated him as if it were child's play. Twice she had coolly met his eyes and said, "Do as you like, but I'm doing it this way." And damned if he didn't fall into line as neatly as a carpenter's plumb. What choice did he have? He had no bloody recourse, no legal command over her, no authority of kinsmanship. She was within her rights to march off on her own, much as it galled him. And if he hoped to preserve his image as a gentleman, he had to march after her. He stared at her squared jaw and determined gaze and weighed chivalry against the queen's command. Though it would disgrace his name to eschew his duties to a woman alone, his loyalty and obligation to the crown came first.

Throughout the day he debated the wisdom of tucking Nell into a coach, tipping his cap, and galloping off on his own. He had no doubt he could retrieve the casket, and with a great deal less trouble if he did so alone. Providing a make-weight against this imminently sensible plan loomed the unpleasant possibility that he might discover the casket opened by the Spaniards. Then he would have the casket and no Lady Nellanor. He was too experienced a soldier to believe he could backtrack and expect to find her patiently awaiting his sword. Such assumptions too often led to disaster.

They spoke little during supper in Master Pettifog's cabin, ceding the conversation to Master Pettifog and to an apple-cheeked parson traveling to France to dispense cheer to beleaguered Protestants.

"God's chosen shall prevail," the parson predicted, helping himself to more pigeon pie. "France is weary of the religious wars. It's necessary only for Henri of Navarre to bide his time until the king and the Duc of Guise have devoured one another."

Master Pettifog regarded him with mild interest. "I'd not pass the collection plate just yet, Parson. At present Guise enjoys immense popularity. His position couldn't be stronger. I have it on good authority Guise will force the Valois king to abdicate in his favor."

"May his black soul rot in hell, Sir! Guise uses Catholicism to advance his political ambitions. When he's exposed for the devil he is, France will flay him alive and fall on its knees before Navarre."

"I'll wager we see Guise as king before France places a crown on a Huguenot head."

"Oh, my poor misguided friend! No, no, no. You fail to grasp the strength of the Religion. Now is the time for great forward strides! Mark my words, Guise shall never seize the throne of France."

Nell rose and smoothed her skirts. "I'm confident France shall benefit greatly by your intervention, Parson," she murmured. Before the parson could explain his plan of assistance, she smiled at the three men. "If you'll excuse me, gentlemen, I think a turn on deck will settle this excellent meal and ensure a calm night's rest."

She tied her cloak beneath her chin as she stepped onto the deck and inhaled the frosty salt air. A thin band of moonlight ribboned across waves tossing in a light chop. Sidestepping coils of rope, Nell moved to the stern and leaned on the railing, watching the luminous roll of the ship's wake. A melancholy air played on a mouth harp drifted over the decks, the tune weaving through the hissing wash of waves lapping the hull.

"Do you find French politics boring?" Will asked, settling his elbows on the rail beside her.

"To the contrary. Political machinations fascinate me." Irritated that he presumed to intrude on her solitude, Nell edged away from his warmth.

"Ah, then 'twas the company you found tedious."

The idea seemed to amuse him. Not deigning to respond, Nell watched a silvery arc lift from the water then cut downward with a splash. When the silence exceeded the limits of social comfort, she said quietly, "Suppose we've erred, Steele. What if the Spaniards didn't sail to Calais?" The question had bothered her throughout the day.

"The low countries are at war, so they won't sail to Flanders. France is Spain's ally and Calais, the nearest safe port." He shrugged. "Where else would they go?"

"How do we enter the town?"

"As soon as we reach coastal waters, Master Pettifog will exchange the Saint George for the flag of Flanders. Our passports state we're Flemish. Upon docking, I'll hire men to spread over the wharf and ask if anyone resembling the Spaniards have recently disembarked. I believe we'll learn they have. Next we question the coach depots. When we discover their route, we pursue."

Nell could discern no flaw in the plan.

"I anticipate they'll hug the coast as far as Eu then cut South. But we'll catch up to them before then."

Nell lifted her face to meet his black eyes. "What if we fail to catch them?"

"We won't fail. Especially if we proceed on horseback."

She ignored his reference to horses. "But if we don't?"

"Pettifog will wait off Calais seven days. If we don't return within that time, he'll sail to Bayonne and wait there." Will nodded toward the animal pens secured at the ship's waist, toward the hogsheads of fresh water and the kegs of biscuit the men rolled toward the hatches. "The ship is provisioned for three weeks."

"I see." She gazed toward the horizon. "What if something—happens—to one or both of us, and one or both of us fail to arrive in Bayonne?"

A thoughtful expression deepened the lines framing his mouth. "When the provisions play out, the ship returns to London and that's the end of it."

Interesting, Nell thought. They had three weeks at the outside to retrieve the casket and resolve which of them would return with it.

"The master sends a tot of rum with his compliments, Ladyship." A young lad wearing a sailor's thrum and canvas pants extended tin mugs that steamed in the cold night air.

"Thank Master Pettifog on our behalf."

Will watched Nell's slender fingers curl around the mug. The night breeze tossed back her hood and teased wisps of hair from her net. In the moonlight, her hair appeared golden. Lest he be softened by moon-gold tresses and ivory skin, he followed her glance and focused on the water.

"What do you expect to 'happen' to one or both of us?" Her statement aroused his curiosity. Was it possible she knew or had guessed the queen's command? This wasn't as remote a possibility as he had first supposed. Ordinarily when person A wanted person B dead, person B damned well knew the reason and wasn't greatly surprised.

She cast him a swift glance then dropped her lashes. "What do those letters contain do you suppose?" Nell murmured. Did Steele truly imagine she would blunder into so obvious a trap? She almost laughed.

"Who can say?" He welcomed a neutral topic they could safely discuss. Though he noticed she had avoided answering. "Did Dudley ever mention the letters?"

"Never. He spoke often of the casket—it was a treasured possession—but never of what it contained."

" 'Tis none of our affair. The letters belong to England, that's all that need concern us."

After a brief private struggle Nell nodded reluctant agreement. She continued to regard the letters as her legacy and yearned to know their content. What in the name of God Almighty had Elizabeth written to Dudley that could conceivably concern Nellanor Amesly? And if the letters did not concern her, why had Uncle Robert wished her to have them? 'Twas a bitter pill to swallow that she was unlikely to solve the mystery. "They're of a personal nature, I would think. Not political."

Politely, Will refrained from disagreeing. She didn't appear to note the effort it cost. "Have you seen the casket?"

"Aye." Nell described it from memory. "About a foot long, three inches wide, two or three inches tall with a slightly curved lid."

"Most likely the Spaniard will carry it on his person."

"So it's not a simple matter of tossing their luggage."

"No," he agreed, wanting to touch her hair. "Do you shy from bloodshed, m'love?"

Nell's head lifted quickly and her spine stiffened. "No," she stated emphatically, meeting his eyes. "Make no mistake, Steele, I can be as brim as a boar if I have to be! I'll say this directly so even you can understand. I've killed before and will again."

"Truly?" White teeth flashed around a wide grin. "Just how many men have you sent to their final reward, Grandmother?"

"Many." Nell spread her hands. "Too many to name."

"Ah, I see."

The amused arch of his eyebrow infuriated her. "You'll forget to your peril," she warned, turning on her heel.

He watched her go. She was a fey little thing. Soft as new butter and hard as coal chips. Vulnerable one minute, doggedly stubborn the next. And so filled with fire and beauty that his groin ached at sight of her.

He hoped to Christ he didn't have to kill her.

CHAPTER
7

Nell's cramped cabin provided space to accommodate a slab bed chained to the bulkhead, a stained laver, her chests of luggage, and perhaps an inch or two to spare. Necessity had been provided for; comfort had not. As the minuscule cabin reeked of lantern oil and past occupants, she chose to pass the day on deck, though as the pinnace was small, this meant she couldn't avoid Steele as she had hoped to do throughout the voyage.

From the stool master Pettifog offered her on the upper deck Nell enjoyed an unobstructed view of the ship's activities. After a time, she realized she could observe Will Steele without appearing to do so.

Long before the midday meal of scrapple and barley ale, she concluded Steele thrived in this element, surrounded by the company of men, fresh sea breezes tumbling his hair and ruffling his sleeves. Rather than remaining fashionably idle as became a lord of the realm, Steele strode about the ship issuing orders, reviewing charts, inspecting cannon. He did so with good cheer and an easy assurance that marked him a natural leader.

To her annoyance, Will Steele's confidence and comfortable authority attracted Nell in a manner she hadn't anticipated and didn't welcome. She supposed, grudgingly, that having grown up in Robert Dudley's household it became a natural consequence that energy and vitality should draw her to a man. And a keen mind for strategy. Robert had possessed these qualities, and so, she admitted with reluctance, did Steele.

Watching him, Nell eventually conceded that perhaps her contempt for his lack of subtlety might be a wee bit misplaced. Will Steele was, after all, famed as the Fighting Duke; and one could scarce expect subtlety on a field of battle. Battle commands would resemble the commands he issued now: short, direct, and framed to prevent misinterpretation. It could hardly be otherwise. And the habit once formed would be difficult to alter. Nell pondered this logic though her line of thought disturbed her, coming as it did so near to excusing Steele's lack of polish.

"Good morrow, Grandmother." Smiling, he vaulted the steps and appeared on the upper deck beside her. "I brought you hot ale and a slice of cold pie."

"Aren't there lads to fetch this sort of errand?"

"Aye. But they're never at hand when needed."

The stool placed her at a level where it was impossible to avoid noticing Steele's hose stretched over well-shaped and muscled legs; quickly, Nell slipped from the stool and stood. Her first impression when he addressed her as "Grandmother" was that of a subtle threat. However—she slid him a glance from the corner of her eye—in view of her previous insight, she wondered briefly if this were true.

Jesu, what was she thinking? Of course it was true. And the threat was not in the least subtle.

"At this moment, Lord Brampton, you have no grandmother." Only a person daft as a warthog could fail to grasp she resented the tease.

"True. But if you marry Lord Thomas, Nellie love, I'll have the youngest, most beautiful grandmother in England."

If. While watching as he drained his tankard, she considered that word. It could definitely be construed as a threat.

Rapid assessment of their situation suggested that perhaps Nell proceeded unwisely. If indeed she were correct to assume a military man, and a northern lord at that, would eschew subtlety on the field, it was also reasonable to suppose a subsequent bluntness of social intercourse. Quite possibly she had encountered that rarest and most foolish of animals, a man who spoke his mind. If so, it could work to her advantage, particularly if she could force herself to give the appearance of doing the same.

Drawing a breath, Nell acted in a manner unthinkable at court. She asked a direct question. "What are your views regarding such a match?"

"I oppose it," Will answered promptly. His dark eyes challenged. "You are not entitled to Lord Thomas's fortune. I am."

It couldn't have been phrased more succinctly. Spots of color blossomed in Nell's cheeks. "I can't think why. You already own enough land and fortune to satisfy any man."

"That's not the issue."

"Then what is?"

He studied her for a long moment. "You know, Nellie love, if you'd speak as frankly more often, a person could understand you."

If she spoke as frankly at court she would be ruined. To announce every intention and opinion would be to bare her throat in invitation to the wolves. Of which there were many. "The issue, Steele?"

"First, a man never owns too much land or has too great a fortune. With land comes landholders. Men to swell the ranks when the call to arms sounds. Wealth provides the weapons."

Nell raised a hand to shield her eyes from the bright sun bouncing off the water. "That's your objection to the match? You covet more land and wealth?"

"In part. More important, if you wed Lord Thomas his London house will end in your ownership."

"Aye." She regarded him from expressionless eyes. "I want that house." Never in her life had Nell stated anything so baldly. Discomfort stained her cheeks, but she didn't look away from him.

"So do I."

"I'm speaking of Lord Thomas's house in Saint Giles Fields, not his country estates."

"So am I."

Exasperation pursed Nell's lips. Trust a northern lord to be motivated by greed, she thought. A sound of disgust issued from the back of her throat. Not retreating, she strove for patience and listed the obvious. "You own Brampton Manor in Carlisle and a dozen other residences scattered across the North. You own a townhouse in London and if we . . . when we succeed with our mission, you'll be awarded Baywick Castle. I'd think you could spare Mendenshire House."

"And the titles? And Lord Thomas's fortune?" He smiled, then his expression sobered. "I'll survive without the titles and without the fortune, Grandmother—but I want Mendenshire House."

Nell spread her hands. "In the name of heaven—why? Do you plan to reside in London, then?"

"Hardly. It's a point of honor."

Nell's heart plummeted to her toes. For a moment she'd cherished a glimmer of hope that a solution could be found. But for the foolishly proud northern lords, a point of honor counted more heavily than land or fortune. All traces of good humor had vanished from Will's expression. His dark eyes glittered like jet and the lines had deepened around his mouth.

"My grandfather," he said, the words a snarl of loathing, "destroyed my parents. My father spent the balance of his days in disgrace. Banned from court, refused his father's house. Embittered, he turned to drink. Eventually he blamed my mother."

His intensity was painful to witness. Instinctively Nell turned aside and leaned her wrists upon the railing, gazing out to sea.

"My mother was refused acceptance regardless of her titles. She was known as the Irish Whore, a phrase bestowed by my esteemed grandfather. For the last ten years of her life, she didn't step foot beyond Willowick's ditch. In the end she was alone, refused recognition even by her husband."

Nell nodded. She could guess where the tale was leading.

"On my mother's deathbed, I promised revenge. I swore when I inherited Lord Thomas's estate, I would burn his house to the soil and in its place I would erect a stone monument to Mary Kathryn Steele. Long after London has forgotten the Earl of Mendenshire, they will remember Mary Kathryn Steele."

Nell turned toward him, noting the dark curls blowing across his forehead, his stony profile.

"I've never had a home of my own," she admitted finally, not pausing to question why she confided in him. "From the day of our vows, Edward and I traveled with the court. We didn't spend enough time in residence for our house to become a home. But that's what I most want. Before we sailed, I hired a carriage and drove past Lord Thomas's home in Giles Field. It's everything I could hope for." His granite expression hadn't altered. "You have so much, and I have nothing. Can't you build your monument somewhere else?"

"Nay, Nellie."

"There must be a way to please us both." A note of desperation sounded in her voice. Then she brightened. "I have a solution. Once I inherit Mendenshire House, I'll sell it to you. With the proceeds, I'll build a duplicate house."

Will stared. A softness he hadn't seen before overlay her features. Jesu, but he wanted to take her in his arms and seize this odd moment of intimacy. Her mouth would be tender and open under his, her body pliant and yielding.

"No," he answered gruffly. "I've informed Lord Thomas that a monument to the Irish Whore will stand where he now dwells. He'll not die thinking he thwarted me. I swore this on my sword."

"On your sword."

There would be no negotiation then. Nell stared into his hard eyes and felt dizzy and light-headed. Ordinarily she was a good sailor, but she looked into the intensity of his gaze and felt as if she were being drawn into a winter storm. Throwing out a hand, she steadied herself against his chest. The heat of his body seemed to scald her palm and radiate through her nerves. Before she snatched her hand away she looked at Steele in surprise. Beneath her fingertips she felt the firm tightness of muscle and bone and heat as if his linen shirt had melted at her touch. Hastily, mouth dry, she stepped backward and rubbed her hands together.

"We're enemies, then," she said, wetting her lips. He had sworn on his sword. Everything she had feared was true. If Will Steele was to honor his pledge, Lady Nellanor Amesly had to die.

She inhaled deeply and stiffened her spine, then spoke quietly but firmly. "Mark me, Steele. I mean to have Mendenshire House."

He watched her tongue trace the contour of her lips and the hardness evaporated from his gaze. Briefly he touched her cheek. "Let's not pluck this string until the tune requires it, m'love. At this moment we're allies in the name of the queen."

After he'd gone, Nell returned to her perch on the stool and sipped the ale he'd fetched her. Allies. She gazed uneasily at the billowing sails and saw Will Steele's sun-bronzed face stamped on the canvas sheets. Allies. But for how long?

Lifting a hand, she absently touched the locket beneath her bodice. She would have submitted to torture before admitting it aloud, but she experienced a rush of admiration for Steele. He had made a promise to his mother, one he meant to honor. In his place she would have done the same. Nothing would have stood in her way.

When she comprehended she was searching for him among the men swarming over the ropes, listening for his shout, she turned away in disgust and scrubbed her palm against her skirts.

Ordinarily Catlina Valencia adored traveling. Her usual travel entourage comprised a coach for herself, a lesser coach for her lady's maid, her mistress of the wardrobe, her hairdresser, and her personal chef, and a dozen or so wagons and carts to transport her luggage and furnishings.

This journey, however, was memorable for its discomfort and inconvenience. Instead of stopping at the palatial villas of titled friends, she and Fernando had slipped in and out of common inns where she had been forced to employ the outdated and questionable talents of local maids and hairdressers. Worse in her view, sensibility demanded they attract no attention to themselves. Catlina was not accustomed to remaining in the background.

She adjusted her tassled boots against the charcoal foot warmer and pushed her gloves inside a sable muff. "The weather is barbaric."

"So you've said, my sweet." Fernando leaned across the hat boxes and patted her knee. "Think of the warmth in new Spain."

The thought of New Spain compensated somewhat for being jolted across the uncomfortable seat of the coach. But not enough as they were still several weeks from the pleasures of Madrid. Pleasures? Catlina grimaced. Madrid's pleasures were minimal at best. Why the king had built his fabled Escorial in Madrid of all places mystified everyone. Madrid was a filthy little village with dirt streets and sour huts. In summer the river dried to a trickle and in winter a chill wind whistled across the plain.

When it became apparent Philip couldn't be persuaded to establish his court along the coast, the grandees had slowly and reluctantly begun to build homes in Madrid. None were as magnificent as the grand villas in Catlina's beloved Venice. And for the most part their ballrooms remained silent as Philip would rather work and pray than establish a fashionable social court.

Recalling the reddish dust thick on Madrid sills sent a shudder down Catlina's spine. She and her mother had wept for weeks when her father moved them to Madrid. Boredom had eventually replaced the tears.

"What are you thinking, my sweet?"

"I was remembering the feast day I first met you."

She'd thought him compellingly handsome. Immediately she'd known his fair hair and beard would compliment her own dark eyes and curls. Still, she might not have advanced the matter had she not learned that the post of ambassador to Venice had become vacant and that Fernando's grandfather had once served in that position. With this in mind, she observed him throughout the festivities, learned of his skill with sword and horses.

When the plan was fully formed, she seduced Fernando, manipulated her father into agreeing to the match, then relentlessly pursued the Venice ambassadorship. Shrewdly, she delayed the marriage until the ambassadorship was granted.

She had been eighteen at the time of her marriage. In the ensuing five years, she had developed her diplomatic skills both publicly and domestically. Fernando's career had advanced by leaps and bounds. And now—her crowning glory—she had guided him to the doorstep of New Spain. And all it had cost was a few weeks of discomfort and inconvenience. A smile curved her lips.

Dust rose in clouds outside the windows. The coach veered sharply and skidded to a lurching halt. Before Catlina could push her hat back off her forehead the door flew open and a masked man squinted at them above the long barrel of a harquebus.

"Outside," he ordered.

When they were standing beside the road, Fernando swore bitterly and surrendered his sword and dagger to the brigands. There were three. Masked and rough-looking.

The tallest stroked a hand across Catlina's white cheek as he stripped her earrings and ruby necklace. The stout one thrust a dagger against Fernando's throat and patted down his waistcoat.

"Aha, what have we here!" The stout brigand flourished the silver casket, drawing the attention of the others. "A prize!"

Catlina gasped. New Spain flickered and faded behind her eyes. "Do something," she hissed to Fernando.

But there were three brigands and Fernando was unarmed.

The Tour du Guet was first to appear, then the citadel and the French flag snapping at its top. A shamed silence descended over the ship and hung like a pall. For two hundred years Calais had been English, a toehold on the continent, a bold taunt and proud holding. But thirty years past, the French had taken Calais and driven the English into the sea amid wild cries of jubilation. Mary Tudor had sighed on her deathbed that she died with Calais written on her heart. As well she might. There were Englishmen alive today who would gladly have written the word in her flesh with a hot poker.

Following a string of muttered oaths, master Pettifog raised his glass to his eye and examined the harbor. "A Spanish merchantman, two French galleys, a Dutch trader, and what looks to be a galleon. Italian, I'd wager." He extended the glass to Will.

Will focused on the Spanish merchantman, running the glass along the waterline. Weed, barnacles, and evidence of worm damage ran in a solid line about two feet off the water. The altered ballast line suggested she had recently been off-loaded.

"The merchantman is just in. She won't depart soon; she needs hauling and repairs." If she'd been trim and ready, he would have suspected the merchantman waited for the Spaniards.

"The customs tender is approaching," Pettifog warned. "I hope to Christ these passports meet muster."

They did. After a congenial exchange of documents, Will bowed to the officials and swung down into the boat that would row them to Calais. He lifted his arms for Nell then sat beside her, glaring at the leather chests then at her. "We need to discuss your luggage, m'love."

She held her hat against the salt spray and harbor breezes. When they had pulled well away from the ship and the oarsmen were occupied, she murmured, "Did my ears mistake me or did the harbor master address us as Herr and Frau Gutland?"

Will tilted a heavy brow and grinned, his humor somewhat restored by her grim expression. "A married couple will draw less notice." His grin widened beneath innocent eyes. "Actually, I'm a mite surprised you didn't think of this yourself."

Nell bit the inside of her cheek and cast him a poisonous glance. "You overstep, m'lord, if you imagine we'll pose as wed in all manner."

"I wouldn't dream of such impropriety." But he had, of course. He had only to gaze at her haughty aristocratic profile to recall the contrast of her warm breast cradled in his palm. It aroused him to imagine a woman's softness waiting beneath her stiff embroidery and cool demeanor. He wondered if any man had roused passion in her fine gray eyes or had made her abandon that careful control.

"Why are you looking at me like that?" she demanded, frowning.

"Like what?"

Her shoulders squared and her neck stiffened. When she spoke her tone was brisk and firmly in hand. "What do we do next? We've almost reached the wharf. Shouldn't we formulate a plan?"

"We have a plan. We install you in a hostel, then I'll hire men to inquire at the docks. When we confirm the Spaniards have arrived in Calais, I'll discover if they hired a coach. By nightfall we'll know if the Spaniards are in Calais or on the road."

Reserving comment, Nell tilted her head and studied the approaching town. Compared to London, it was minuscule. A sleepy fishing village. Two-story houses fashioned in the Flemish style encroached on the wharf area which was crowded with the usual dockside stalls and shops, many of which offered for sale the exquisite local lace.

When she glanced along the shore, Nell saw the burned-out hulks of the fireboats the English had loosed against the armada. The Spanish fleet had cut cable and scattered to escape the fireboats and that had proved the beginning of the English victory. The memory made her smile. It was a good omen. Very soon two Englishmen would again vanquish Spaniards on this site.

When they stood amidst the bustle and commotion crowding Wharf Street, she announced firmly, "While you're checking the docks, I'll inquire at the stage depot and the stables."

Will turned from the cart he had hired to transport her luggage to the nearest hostel. "That's beyond the realm of consideration. I want you at the inn where I know you're safe."

"It will take twice as long if you do everything," Nell replied reasonably. Lifting her hem, she set off after the cart. "Speed is of the essence."

"God's teeth!" An explosion erupted from Will's throat. "That's what I've been trying to tell you. But putting you on the streets is pound foolish." Exasperated, he scowled at the men pausing in their tasks to observe Nell. She'd led a protected life. She had no notion of what could happen to a woman wandering about unescorted.

"Not foolish at all," she said, pushing through an iron gate into the courtyard of a respectable-looking inn. "If the Spaniards are in Calais, we'll find them more quickly working together. And," she said over her shoulder, "if they're here, we're spared the coach-horseback debate."

Angrily, Will watched her gather her skirts and mount the

steps into the inn while he paid the carter and issued instructions for her bloody chests. He was beginning to hate the feather on her hat. It dipped to the left then curled up in an aggressive sweep. That feather sailed forward regardless of prevailing winds. It fluttered and wavered then righted itself in the same immovable position. Pushing back his cloak and frowning, he followed her into the inn's common room, arriving to find her standing beside the innkeeper wearing a suspiciously satisfied smile.

The innkeeper bowed low. "Herr Gutland. This humble house is honored to welcome you and your sister-in-law as our esteemed guests."

In less than a blink she had sidestepped what he had anticipated as an interesting situation, and in the process had somehow managed to convince the innkeeper they were personages of note traveling incognito. This was the only reasonable explanation for the innkeeper's obeisance and for the quality of the rooms they were shown.

"There's been an error," Nell observed sweetly. "My trunks were mistakenly sent to my brother-in-law's chamber. Please remove them to mine."

"A thousand pardons, Frau Gutland."

At the innkeeper's signal servants materialized to carry the leather chests to the next chamber. Watching silently, Will began to grasp how she'd managed to acquire clean, well-aired rooms unshared by other guests. Her manner was not that of a modest merchant's wife. A brisk authority belied the softness of her voice; she was accustomed to being served. And he saw now that their clothing, the cut and quality, was several degrees above that which might be expected from a prosperous merchant, as he was claiming to be.

He cursed beneath his breath then cupped Nell's elbow and firmly turned her toward the innkeeper. Two could spin this wheel. "Monsieur," he said in French that was flawed but passable for one posing as Flemish. "As you can see, my dear sister-in-law wears the weeds of mourning and is obviously fatigued from her journey." Nell's eyebrows shot toward her hairline as she stared up at him. "Fetch her your best wine and a light meal, then she will retire."

Nell glanced at the afternoon sunshine streaming past small windows at the end of the corridor. "I'm not at all weary, I . . ."

Will squeezed her elbow until she winced and a pained expression pinched her lips. "I have business in town," he continued, speaking to the innkeeper's anxious smile. "May I assume my sister-in-law will be safe in your keeping until I return?"

The innkeeper rubbed his hands against his apron and bowed low. "Indeed, Herr Gutland. Yes, indeed."

"I sincerely hope so." Will flung back his cloak so the hilt of his sword could be seen. "I would be most unhappy to learn Frau Gutland had been disturbed." Now he looked into Nell's furious face. "Or that she departed the inn for any reason."

"I understand perfectly." The innkeeper flicked a glance toward Will's sword. He wet his lips.

"Enjoy your rest, my dear."

He bowed to Nell, concealing his smile, and left her standing in the corridor, her eyes blazing. Whistling, he strode toward the docks.

The two with swords could be handled. Don Fernando Valencia focused his attention on the man with the harquebus. Above the raveled edge of his mask, small piggish eyes concentrated on the silver casket being brandished by his compatriot. Fernando also glanced at the casket glittering in the chill afternoon sun.

Whatever the casket represented to King Philip, it represented wealth and recognition to Fernando. A kingdom in New Spain. His wife's eternal gratitude. She trembled at his side, stroking her bared throat, then gazed up at him with an expectant expression.

His lips twitched, more a sneer than a smile. Three Frenchmen were no match for a Valencia. Bending swiftly, he pulled the hidden dagger from his boot and buried it in the belly of the man holding the harquebus. The man's pig eyes widened before he crumpled to the road. Seizing the moment of surprise, Fernando retrieved his sword and spun into position.

Immediately the tall man met Fernando's advance. To his plea-sure the brigand displayed a certain crude skill with the sword. Dimly Fernando heard Catlina's shouts, but he was immersed in the joy of dueling. At no time did he feel more alive than when fac-ing the possibility of death. Steel rang in his ears, the exhilarating shock of blade meeting blade traveled up his arm. Slash, cut, parry. His blood sang in his veins.

The Frenchman never had a genuine chance. Fernando toyed with him, opened a slash across the brigand's arm, his thigh, and along his jaw. Finally, with some reluctance, he delivered the fatal lunge. Placing his boot on the man's chest, he withdrew his sword and wiped it clean with the mask he ripped from the bas-tard's face.

"You fool!" Catlina raged. She screamed abuse at the white-faced coachman, then whirled on Fernando. "While you exer-cised your wrist, the French whoreson with the casket escaped!" A shaking finger pointed furiously toward a haze of dust disap-pearing down the road. "There goes our future! Our Kingdom!"

Running forward, Fernando unharnessed the lead bay from the coach traces, leaped upon its back, and dug in his spurs.

When Will returned to the inn, torches flamed in the court-yard. The common room was smoky and smelled of tallow can-dles and the greasy fat dripping from a pig turning on the spit. He saw Nell immediately.

Against his orders, the innkeeper had provided her a small private table placed near the wide hearth to catch the warmth. A servant stood behind to replenish her wine, and there wasn't a man in the inn unaware of the firelight tinting her cheeks. She glanced up and blotted her lips when he entered, then gave him a pleasant smile. It was the smile that troubled him most.

After seating himself across from her, he tucked his linen over his ruff. "I instructed you to dine in your chamber." Servants hastened to place a wooden trencher between his fists.

"The herring is excellent," she said. "I recommend it." Spark-ling eyes danced across the space between them. "Well? What news?"

"In your chamber."

"I prefer to dine in company," she responded airily, dismissing his objection as one dismissed a gnat. "Have our friends arrived?"

"Ale," he said loudly to the servant at his elbow. "The strongest in your larder." He could swear she knew what he would say before he said it. He didn't like the twinkle in her eyes. "Aye," he said finally. "They've gained on us. Our 'friends' arrived the day before yesterday. On the morrow I'll discover if they've hired a coach."

"They did. Our 'friends' departed yesterday morn. They chose the road to Eu." She leaned backward, touched her linen to her lips, and blinked wide innocent eyes. "The coach is green and gold, drawn by six bays. They're traveling with five chests. Three additional chests have been sent ahead to Don Medina Valencia in Madrid. From all indications, they're proceeding at a leisurely pace; there is no evidence of haste."

"God's teeth, woman!" Will thrust his fingers through his hair and glared at her.

"A simple 'well done' would suffice," Nell murmured. She lowered her eyes modestly and smiled at her hands.

"Innkeeper!" Will roared. A thin-lipped lad with darting eyes appeared instantly to explain that the innkeeper had unexpectedly been called away. Will ground his teeth and waved the boy away. Knots formed along his jaw as he watched Nell rise and stifle an elaborate yawn.

"Well, my dear brother-in-law," she said, enjoying his anger. "It's been a productive day, but long. I've hired a coach to arrive at first light. We'll meet then." She was well pleased with herself and with his reaction. "Sleep well, m'lord," she said pleasantly.

Long after she'd mounted the stairs, Will remained before the fire, gazing into the flames with a brooding expression. He wasn't one to shy from truth though there were moments when he would have liked to do so. This was such a moment. If Nellanor Amesly had been a man, he would have applauded her resourcefulness; he would have been damned glad for her initiative and intelligence. She'd managed to escape the innkeeper's surveillance, had avoided being accosted in the streets, and she had obtained precisely the information they required.

It irritated the hell out of him.

His temper wasn't eased to discover the walls of the inn were as thin as a blade. Lying on his cot with his hands behind his head, he could hear Nell moving about her chamber. He imagined her seated before the ewer and basin, brushing long silky hair. When next he overheard movement, he visualized her unhooking her sleeves and sliding them down creamy white arms. He could see the ivory column of her throat as her ruff fell away. And beneath her bodice and camisole, perfect round breasts tipped with rose. A slender waist. The satiny swell of hips and thighs.

"God's balls!" Turning away from the wall that separated them, he stared at the first raindrops pelting the window, and he made himself think about the thieving bastard Scots raiding his sheep and his graineries.

Catlina was waiting beside the fire the coachman had kindled when Fernando appeared out of the dusky gloom. Quickly she scanned the padding leaking from his torn doublet, his limp stocks and sagging hose. Blood streaked his clothing, had dried along a thin line crossing the back of his hand. But she could see from his glitter of triumph that he was not seriously injured.

Aroused by the thought of battle, Catlina threw herself into his arms when he dismounted. "Do you have the casket?"

"Of course."

"And my ruby necklace and earrings?"

He placed them in her hand and pushed aside her cloak to nuzzle her bare throat.

Catlina closed her eyes and inhaled the heady scent of perspiration, the coppery smell of blood. Her breath caught in her throat and her hands tightened on his shoulders. "Did he mount a great resistance?"

Fernando laughed against her breasts. "Not nearly enough." Responding to her heat, he scooped her into his arms and carried her to the carriage. Inside he threw up her skirts and, punishing her for her eagerness, teased her until she sobbed his name before he thrust into her. "Slut," he murmured against her thrashing hair. "Whore." She whimpered with pleasure.

It wasn't until the coach was again underway that she demanded to see the casket for herself. She placed the silver box upon her lap and stared at it then began to tremble violently.

"Do you recall what Philip said?" she whispered.

He recalled it well.

They regarded each other in the starry light, their expressions pale and sobered.

"If the brigands had stolen the casket, if we were forced to return empty-handed . . ."

A chill passed through his body and he placed a finger across her lips to stop the words. But she said them anyway.

"Philip would have given us to the Inquisition."

Philip's tools of retribution were too hideous to contemplate. Neither anticipated a restful sleep when they finally reached the inn.

CHAPTER
8

*R*ain thrummed on the carriage rooftop, steady and monotonous, thinning tempers and straining nerves. Twice the coach lost the high ground, skidded into boggy ruts, and wallowed to a halt, the wheels caked and clogged by heavy mud. Digging out required the passengers to disembark. Silent with frustration, Will and Nell waited beside the wet road as the coachman and footman applied their backs and shovels to freeing the wheels.

When the task was completed and the coachman had wearily pulled up to his seat, Will swung Nell into the carriage, ignoring the slaps at his hands circling her waist. Inside they shook rain from their clothing and wiped streaming faces.

"French roads are abysmal," Nell muttered, forgetting she also thought English roads an abomination. "No better than swamps." She stamped mud from her boots and wrung dirty water from her ruined hem.

"Coaches were never intended to negotiate swamps. Horses pass through them with ease."

She was heartily sick of hearing wheels compared to hooves. Grinding her teeth, Nell swallowed a sharp reply and sought for patience. "We'd be soaked to the skin before we'd traveled a mile," she pointed out, her voice betraying her snappishness. "We'd catch our death." If she died by the roadside wracked by chilblains and fever, Will Steele's fortune would be made. It wasn't going to happen. "May I remind you the Spaniards suffer the same weather? We're not lagging behind."

"We're already behind. And not making significant gains at this rate." The feather atop her hat had dampened and drooped, he noticed. The sight provided the one bright spot in an otherwise dismal day.

The next mile elapsed in silence and chill discomfort. A frosty vapor collected before Nell's lips; her damp skirts hung limp and heavy. To shield them from the driving rain, the coachman had lowered the leather window flaps. This dimmed the interior and created an intimacy not to Nell's taste. Raising a corner of the flap, she studied the wet gray day, aware that Will continued to regard her with resentment and accusation. When the silence grew as ponderous as the clouds bumping overhead, she stifled a sigh and met his gaze.

"So," she said with determined brightness. "Tell me about Carlisle and your Willowick. Is it dreadfully isolated and lonely?"

"No."

When it became evident he wouldn't elaborate, she thought what a lout he was and tried again. "I'll warrant the excitement of court was a welcome change."

"If you're suggesting Carlisle is dull—it isn't."

Nell waited expectantly and when he added nothing more, she spread her gloves and released a breath of irritation. "I'm attempting to make conversation," she said coldly. "To pass the time." They could discuss books or plays or theology or politics. Surely they could do more than cling to the straps and glare at each other.

Raindrops sparkled in the eyebrow he raised. "It doesn't impress you as wasteful to blather for the sake of blather?"

"Some regard conversation as an art," Nell answered stiffly.

He stretched his head against the back of the seat, the motion unconsciously graceful. "On the whole, Nellie love, most conversation is much foam and little cream. And nowhere is there more foam bubbling about than at court." Will's mouth turned down in disgust. "Grown men pass hours blathering over nothing more

substantial than the size of a dandy's ruff or the cut of his stocks."
He gave her a measured look, "Or chatting up a place like
Carlisle, in which at least one of the persons has no interest."

"For those with a skilled ear, m'lord, the cream is easily separated from the foam." Conversing with a northern lord was like
talking to a stone fence. "Occasionally an intriguing current
flows through the cream. The art and the pleasure lie in discovering the current and where it leads."

"In Carlisle cream is cream. With no currents, no mysteries.
A thing is what it appears. No more; no less."

"How dull," Nell murmured, losing interest. Obviously, he
didn't grasp what she was saying. On the border, politics played
in tones of black or white. The challenge of gray belonged to the
larger game at court.

"Dull? Mayhaps. But honest. The currents you speak of are
man-made, concocted from innuendo and malice."

"Occasionally," Nell snapped, her patience wearing thin. "But
none the less valid. Whether on a personal level or universal, the
game is to deflect the currents."

Conversation was hopeless; they approached the art from
widely divergent perspectives. Shifting on the seat, Nell
smoothed a glove over the book at her side and wished for
stronger light to read by. She examined the embroidery ornamenting her cuff, raised the window flap and let it drop, watched
from beneath her lashes as Will crossed and uncrossed his legs.
He tapped his fingers on the leather upholstery, clasped and unclasped the hilt of his sword. They glanced at each other and then
away.

Sighing, Nell tried to recall when last she'd suffered such dis-
advantage. Conversation appeared impossible, yet not speaking
focused her attention uncomfortably on Steele's physical presence. The rain had molded his hose to his legs, sinewy muscled
legs that made her vaguely restless to observe. The coach could
easily have accommodated six, yet Steele seemed to fill the space
himself. Most discomfiting, his hat brim shaded his eyes. She
couldn't adequately discern the direction of his gaze.

Finally, for all his protests about foam and cream, she sensed the uneasy presence of dangerous currents within Will Steele. When first they'd met, she had committed the error of dismissing him as straightforward, a man without secrets and therefore of little interest. But this wasn't true. Intuitively she grasped there was more to Will Steele than first met the eye. Swift dark currents surged behind his cautious gaze. Currents that challenged and intrigued.

The coach dipped suddenly and jolted violently to one side. Nell flung out a hand as the window flap tilted before her and her seat lifted above Will's then slapped downward. The coach seesawed wildly before striking a log buried in the mud then jarred to an abrupt halt. The coach stopped but Nell's forward motion flung her out of her seat. When the noise of creaking wood and iron wheels grating over stone ceased, she heard a stream of frustrated curses and the crack of the driver's whip. The coach strained forward then rocked back into a swampy bed of mud.

Nell dimly registered the sounds and their significance. But her own situation proved of greater immediacy. The violent pitch of the coach had thrown her to her knees in front of Will. To arrest her tumble she had reached out to him and her arms now circled his waist. The rough quilt of his doublet lay beneath her cheek.

For a moment shock rendered her immobile. Rooted in place, she waited for her heart to resume a normal cadence. Then, slowly, she became aware of Will's heat penetrating her damp clothing, aware of his thighs taut against the outer softness of her breasts. Still she did not pull away. The near accident had melted her bones; her skirts were leaden and entrapped her legs. Until Will's heat enveloped her, Nell hadn't realized how chilled she was or how her traitorous body would cling to the promise of warmth.

In the silence, his whisper seemed hoarse and over loud. "Nellie . . ."

Calluses scraped her skin as he framed her face between his hands and tilted her head upward until the frosty vapor from his whisper flowed over her lips. His gaze had darkened when her arms circled his waist and the muscles rising on his thighs tight-

ened around her, holding her against him as he studied the tremble appearing on her lips. Slowly, so slowly the journey seemed
endless, his gaze traveled to her eyes, wide and startled, as gray
and translucent as the rain dripping from the skies. Nell caught a
ragged breath, wondering wildly if the fall had paralyzed her will
as completely as it appeared to have paralyzed her body.

"Your skin is as smooth as satin," Will murmured, his tone
husky, his thumbs stroking her cheeks. "I knew it would be."

Thunder beat in her ears and her breath stopped. As God
stood witness, Nell could not move. Nor could she lift her gaze
from his mouth. Time had narrowed to this one eternal moment
and she was caught, powerless to protest, helpless to do more
than wait for what she knew must come.

Staring into her eyes, Will deliberately lowered his mouth to
hers and kissed her. What began as a gentle sampling exploded
into something more when Nell didn't resist. His tongue parted
her lips and he tasted deep of her, pulling her up to him until her
breasts crushed against his chest and a hot rigidity pressed
against her skirts.

"Monsieur? Madame? You will step outside please." The
coach door swung open to the rain and mud.

Neither of them moved. They stared into each other's eyes
until the coachman cleared his throat with a hacking cough. Will
released her then and lightly caressed her face, tracing the high
bones beneath her skin. "So lovely."

Dazed, Nell blinked rapidly then wrenched from his arms.
Stumbling, she emerged from the coach and ducked her head
against the pelting rain, gingerly following the trail of straw the
coachman had laid for her until she gained the firm ground beside the road. There she tugged the brim of her hat, hoping to
conceal the crimson pulsing in her cheeks. She turned aside
when Will joined her.

"I won't beg pardon," he said quietly.

She didn't trust her voice to answer.

"Nell, I can't stay with you." To continue sharing the intimacy of the dim coach would be to court disaster. Jesu, she
wasn't safe with him, not now. Having sampled her sweetness,

Will wanted more. His groin tightened painfully at the thought. "I'm maddened by these bloody delays. In foul temper not fit for company." His jaw corded and he examined the low hills butting the road. A farmer's rooftop rose in the distance. "I'll purchase a horse and ride on ahead." He wished to Christ she would speak instead of looking at him with that strange vulnerable expression that fairly begged him to take advantage. Jesu. At least it wasn't contempt. "Stop at the next inn and wait for me."

He had topped a low hill and vanished into the rain and mist before Nell allowed the coachman to assist her into the coach. Inside she mopped her face and unpinned her hat, waving it to dry the feather.

What in the name of God had happened? Was this Nellanor, Lady Amesly, this woman with the scalded lips and pounding heart?

It wasn't as if she were a maid who had never been kissed. She'd enjoyed her share of admirers and ardent kisses. And of course there had been Edward, her husband. But none had stirred her as Will Steele had. She had coolly regarded her lovers with degrees of amusement or boredom, occasionally irritation or dismay. But never had she stepped from a kiss feeling as if she'd been trampled by a runaway stallion.

If this was passion, then she rejected it. Passion muddled the senses, she'd observed it time and again. But she had not experienced it. She was above errors of the heart. Intellect guided her reason, not yearnings of the flesh. And this was precisely as she wished it to be. There was no place in her life for passion.

Leaning backward, she bit down on her thumbnail. How then, did she explain her reaction to Will Steele's stolen kiss? The moment his hands had cupped her face, her power to resist had evaporated like fog in the heat of the morning sun. Her body had erupted in feverish expectation; she'd been alternately hot then shivering.

Closing her lashes, Nell pressed the back of her hand to her forehead and found her skin heated and damp. Relief mingled with concern as she concluded she was catching an ague; that explained everything.

To divert her thoughts, she raised the slim volume of Sir Philip Sidney's poems near the gap of light admitted beneath the window flap. A fine spray dampened the pages. And her concentration wandered.

This time when the coach lurched and swung wildly, Nell accepted the incident as a matter of course. But alarm flared in her eyes as, instead of slowing, the coach gathered speed. Shouts and shrill cries cut through the wind and rain. Raising the flap, she shielded her face from flying mud and squinted ahead then caught a jagged breath and held it. A runaway coach was dangerous at any time; on this road it could be lethal.

Ducking inside, she curled on the seat and clung to the overhead strap, bracing herself in the corner. Later, she could not recall exactly what happened next. The headlong ride had seemed endless; the coach swung violently from side to side. Nell recalled flying from the seat and painfully banging her knees, remembered a spaceless pinwheeling sensation as the roof spun over her head then to one side. Mud gouted through the window, cold against her hands and breast. Then the coach had dropped to the roadbed and plowed to a crashing halt on its side. Nell was slammed against the coach wall. She touched her head, stared at the scarlet stain smearing her fingertips, then a veil of darkness blotted her vision.

Still later she learned she had climbed from the ruined coach and had ridden one of the horses two miles to the nearest posthouse, but she remembered none of it. Her first cogent memory was of sitting before the posthouse fire, teeth chattering uncontrollably while the postman's wife gently cleaned the gash on her forehead.

"It's not so bad as it appears, Madame."

Nodding, Nell closed her eyes and pulled a dry quilt tighter across her shoulders. Wet hair dripped into her ruff; she was bruised and battered. When the woman's daughter served hot wine, she drained it gratefully and warmed numb hands around the cup.

"Your man says the axle broke."

Sophie Marie's cloth pressed against Nell's hairline and she winced. The water in the bowl on the table had turned a muddy pink.

"Snapped clean, he says. 'Tis a marvel you weren't killed."

"Snapped clean?" Nell's eyes blinked open. Had the axle snapped—or had it been sawed through? Standing abruptly, she pushed Sophie Marie out of her path. "I want to examine that axle."

Sophie Marie's brow rose. "They're bringing the coach in now, but . . ."

Before the woman finished speaking, Nell had crossed the rushes and stepped outside. Heedless of the rain, she plunged across the yard and elbowed through the men surrounding the coach. As Sophie Marie had said, the axle break was clean three quarters of the way then ended in jagged splinters. To Nell's eye, the axle clearly had been tampered with.

A bitter oath passed her lips. She had acted the fool. Raising her head she squinted unseeing into the slanting rain. It had been no accident that the coach had earlier slid to a convenient halt before a farmer's cottage. Steele must have arranged it beforehand with the coachman. Had he returned to saw the axle while she sat inside drying her hat? Or had the deed been accomplished before they departed Calais? Whatever the case, Steele had ridden away to retrieve the casket, leaving her to die in a coach accident.

She folded her arms around her shoulders and bent away from the cold rain. But it wasn't the rain that raised a chill on her body.

Tired, hungry, and soaked to the bone, Will stopped at a hostel beyond Boulogne. Weary, he waited until his horse had been stabled and he'd inspected the feed, then he pulled himself up the stairs and out of the rain. When he'd satisfied a ravenous hunger and drained two tankards of strong local ale, Will stretched his boots to the fire and watched the steam rise from their soles.

He'd lost time in Boulogne, pausing to examine the stables for a green and gold coach, asking about the front street stalls. He'd ridden to the fortress on the hill and made discreet inquiries of the watch in the event the Spaniards were being feted as valued guests. No Spaniards. They were somewhere on the road ahead. He'd left the gates of Boulogne behind and had ridden until his horse sagged with exhaustion.

But he had gained ground. He knew this the same way he knew when he neared a tribe of Scots. Instinctively, at gut level. His hand opened and closed around the hilt of his sword and his eyes glittered darkly.

"More ale, m'lord?" A buxom serving wench bent for his tankard, exposing plump breasts reminiscent of Lady Bledsoe's melon-sized mounds. She cast him a flirtatious glance from beneath a fringe of dark lashes.

"Aye."

She trailed a teasing finger around the inside of his ruff. "Ye'll catch yer death, m'lord. Ye should put them wet clothes off."

"They're beginning to dry." The answer brought him up short. The moment called for a leer and a sly suggestion that the wench assist him in drying his clothing and himself. The disappointment drawing her mouth into a pout indicated she had expected a similar remark.

"Back in a blink with yer ale," she said, her voice soft with regret.

He watched her twitch her bottom toward the kegs in the corner, surprised that he hadn't leaped on opportunity when opportunity presented. Why hadn't he? The wench had breasts a man could weep for, wide hips and a pert bottom. It was a cold, wet night and a willing mate to warm his bed would be most welcome. He must be tired.

Jesu, he wasn't *that* tired. He was never *that* tired. But he could think of no other explanation for his peculiar lack of interest.

"Yer ale, m'lord." The wench placed his tankard near at hand, favoring him with a glimpse of truly spectacular breasts. Lifting her eyes, she gave him a long, slow look.

"Thank'ee kindly," he said, cursing himself. Angry, he glared at the fire. The timing was wrong. That was all. When he'd finished his thinking, he'd wrap the wench in his cloak and take her upstairs for a tumble. In the meantime, he had weighty matters to consider.

The problem was no longer catching the Spaniards and re-trieving the casket; Will knew he would. The problem that occu-pied his mind to the exclusion of all else was whether or not the bastard Spaniards had opened the casket. Frowning, Will con-templated the flames dancing above the logs.

He wasn't a churchgoing man, never had been, but his faith ran deep and true. Seldom did he question God's wisdom; he ac-cepted what came his way and made the best of it.

But now the time had come to strike a bargain with God.

"More ale," he shouted, pulling on his moustache. Brooding, he watched the wench's breasts fall forward as she leaned on the tap. She served him and switched her delicious little bottom be-neath his nose. He looked at the fire.

An ideal barter required that both sides gain and both sides cede. He wanted the casket unopened and the Spaniards dead. He considered this as he sipped his ale and stared into flames as reddish gold as Nellanor Amesly's hair.

For a time he wrestled the problem, seeking to have both the casket and the Spaniards' death. Eventually he understood he would have to cede one or the other if his bargain was to be valid. Very well, he conceded with great reluctance. If the casket was unopened, the seals intact, he would spare the Spaniards' worth-less lives.

The promise came hard. Not that long ago he'd been camped on the banks of the Thames drilling his men to kill Spaniards. He'd thought of little else for weeks.

But. If God gave him the casket sealed and locked—he would give God the Spaniards' lives. Not that he comprehended why God might want them. But it wasn't his task to berate God for protecting vermin like Spaniards and Scots.

Content with his bargain, he stretched and yawned and antic-ipated the comfort of his bed. He noticed the serving wench lin-gering beside the stairs, darting invitations his way. She was plump and pretty. She had breasts that weren't hidden beneath stiff embroidery and constraining corsets. There was nothing subtle about her. She had a soft tongue and had given him no cause for complaint. She resembled Nellanor Amesly as little as coal resembled diamonds. He decided she was exactly what he needed.

To his vast astonishment and vast annoyance, he tipped his cap to her and mounted the stairs alone.

He departed the hostel before first light, still irritated. During the night the rain had dwindled to a cold steady drizzle that collected in his moustache and dripped from the brim of his hat. But there was reason to hope the sky would clear by midday and by evening the roads might be firm enough to make good time.

Deciding against an inn, he halted the next night a half-day's ride from Eu. He rode until the night was black enough to fear for his horse's safety, then he turned into a stand of pine leading to the beach and spent the night with his back propped against a tree trunk. Before he slept, he remembered the buxom serving wench and cursed himself for an utter fling-brain. Then he thought about Nell and his curses doubled.

He arrived in Eu shortly after midday. The small village snuggled against the sea, bypassed by trade and industry. It was little more than a collection of thatched cottages serving as a marketplace for outlying areas. Shops and houses showing stages of neglect lined the dirt lane leading to the village center. Will noted a sagging stable, a smithy, a carter's shed, stalls of fresh fish and rows of bread, several alehouses. And one good inn.

Standing before the inn's stable was the green and gold coach, as glitteringly obvious as a jewel on a scrap heap.

Will reined sharply and smiled. The weariness washed from his shoulders and a spring returned to his step as he swung from the black and led him into the stables. After twenty minutes of spirited haggling, he traded the black for a fresh gelding and issued instructions that his horse be saddled and waiting from sunset on.

It then became a matter of patience, not his strong suit. Had he not promised God the Spaniards, he would have withdrawn his sword and taken the casket immediately. Having made his bargain however, he meant to keep it. His approach would be less bold, more cunning.

He engaged a room, feigned exhaustion, and retired to his

chamber. But not without prodding a talkative innkeeper. The innkeeper was pleased to inform Will that a fine gent and his lady occupied the room nearest his and, aye, it was their green and gold coach in front of the inn. Not one to readily accept chat, Will confirmed the innkeeper's statement by placing his ear to the wall and listening to low voices sprinkled with Spanish phrases. Impatience tensed his shoulders. Forcibly he reminded himself of his bargain with God.

When the Spaniards at last departed their chamber and descended the stairs to supper, Will felt as if he'd lain in siege for days. He flexed his muscles and loosened his body, then eased into the corridor and bent before the Spaniards' latch. As he'd suspected, his key fit their door, a not uncommon feature of French inns.

At once he saw he could toss the room without fear of discovery. Clothing was strewn about the chamber in haphazard manner. Hairpins, feathers, and various other ornaments littered the table, stockings and slippers made a hazard of the floor. The Spaniard's sword belt hung near the door; doublets and waistcoats were flung in and out of a number of opened chests. Had Will been a common thief, he could have profited handsomely by snipping the jewels from the woman's bodices and the man's waistcoats.

Thirty minutes later, he'd examined the brass-trimmed chests, each drawer, and every cubby, had squeezed down each item of clothing seeking hidden pockets, had searched the mattress and pillows. The casket was not in the chamber.

So. It would not be easy. God meant to put Will Steele's bargain to the test. "Dammit."

The casket, as Nell had described it, was thin enough to slip into one's doublet without creating an unsightly bulge. Long, narrow, slightly curved lid. A letter box. Aye, the Spaniard must carry it on his person.

Will returned to his chamber and waited. He ordered cod cakes, bread, and a berry tart served in his room. And he waited. The rain ended and a sliver of moon drifted through a break in the clouds. The inn quieted and after a time he heard no sounds from next door. He waited with a soldier's blend of impatient patience until the crier passed outside the courtyard gate singing the midnight hour.

Only then did he snuff his candle and let himself into the darkened corridor and fit his key into the Spaniards' lock. When the latch opened, he stepped soundlessly inside and paused to allow his sight to adjust to the deeper darkness.

Immediately he spotted the casket. A corner emerged from a satin pouch on the table nearest the bed curtains. He didn't see the casket's key.

Still without moving from his position by the door, Will examined the sleeping Spaniards. The man was as Nell had described, golden-haired, trim beard, and curled moustache. The lace collar on his nightdress had pulled aside to reveal a scar disappearing down his chest into the material. The Spaniard might wear lace to bed, but he was a fighter. Will noted the Spaniard had transferred his sword and dagger to the table holding the casket, placing them within easy grasp as Will would have done. He eased his own dagger from his waist sheath and gripped it comfortably.

The woman was exquisite. Will studied her with pleasure. Clouds of midnight hair spilled across her lush breast and over the pillow. In the faint light her skin appeared as smooth as ivory, her lips slightly parted. At first he supposed she wore a crucifix around her throat, then he smiled as he realized it was the key to the casket.

The casket was the focus of the mission, not the key. Elizabeth had not made it a condition that the key be returned along with the casket. She hadn't mentioned the key in fact. Wisdom suggested that Will take the casket and slip out as quietly as he had entered.

But there was pride involved. And challenge. One didn't come this far then make a halfway job of it. He'd retrieve the key too.

Cautiously, treading on the pads of his boots, he crossed the chamber and rescued the casket. Before thrusting it inside his doublet he ran a finger across Robert Dudley's seals, releasing a low breath as he discovered them unbroken. So—the Spaniards would live. That was to be regretted, but as God had kept His side of the bargain, Will Steele was bound to do no less.

Without a sound, he removed the Spaniard's sword and dagger and eased them beneath the bed. Then he rounded the curtains and drew them aside, looking down at the woman. The key rested against her breast, rising and falling with the soft whisper of her breathing.

It was a damned pity to waste such beauty on a God-cursed Spaniard. Being a connoisseur of such matters, Will judged her breasts as temptingly melon-sized. He could glimpse the darker color of the aureole through the thin material of her nightdress. Aye, a damned pity. Had she been anyone but a detestable Spaniard, she would have rated high on his list of memorable breasts. The obvious disposed of, he concentrated on the problem at hand.

The key had been threaded on a length of velvet riband long enough to drop over the woman's head. Slowly, very carefully, enjoying the challenge, Will eased the key off her skin then halted as she sighed and turned toward him. With his free hand, he lightly brushed her cheek on the far side and waited as she turned toward his touch. This did not facilitate matters as he had hoped. Reluctantly he accepted he couldn't lift the key over her head without waking her. He would have to cut it free.

The tug of his dagger against the riband was slight. But enough to wake her. As the key dropped into his palm, the woman's dark eyes snapped open and she gasped. Will clapped his hand over her lips, but not before she'd kicked out a leg to rouse the man.

"Not a sound," he hissed.

The Spaniard bolted upward, instantly awake, and he stared at the dagger pressed to his wife's lush bosom. Hard eyes flicked swiftly to the bedside table, noted the absence of weapons, then his gaze narrowed coldly on Will. His hands curled into fists of frustration and impotence atop the quilt.

"The casket!" the woman said, struggling to sit up. Her hands flew to her neck and she jerked the cut riband away then leaned forward to look at the empty table. A harsh sound tore from her throat.

. Logic demanded that Will slice the Spaniards' throats while he could. For he knew this would not be the end of it. Even in the dim light, he judged the Spaniard a formidable enemy. The Spaniard's cold eyes flickered and jumped, measuring odds, calculating the wisdom of attack. Will's sword whispered from the scabbard and he reevaluated his bargain with God, sweat forming on his brow. He itched to protect his flank, to perform the sensible act. But even if he could square welshing on his bargain with God, the Spaniard was unarmed. No man of honor slew an unarmed man in his bed.

"Fernando, for God's sake, do something!" The woman rose to her knees and slapped the man's shoulder.

"If he moves, Señora, you both die."

She spun toward Will and raised her hands in appeal. "Wait! The casket you stole—you're stealing a pewter piece of little value." Dark sultry eyes studied him. "Leave that worthless item and take the purse atop the chest nearest the door. You'll find ten ecus inside."

Jesu, but she was a beauty. She was also quick. In spite of himself, Will admired her ingenuity.

"Señora," he said, smiling, "if I were a thief, I'd be more interested in the thousand ducats concealed in the false bottom of your wig box." She gasped and Fernando stopped edging from the bed to stare. Will reached behind him and pressed the chamber latch. "When next we meet, Fernando—if we meet—you are a dead man." Closing the door, he moved rapidly down the stairs and out the inn door toward the stables, hoping his horse was saddled and ready as he'd commanded.

Fernando jumped from the bed and thrust his feet into his stocks. A torrent of curses flowed from his lips. France was a nation of bastardly thieves. A God-fearing man was no safer in his bed than in his carriage. Blast them all to hell. "Scream, dammit," he snapped to Catlina. "Raise the alarm!"

Catlina watched him throwing clothing, searching for his

sword. She sank back on the bed. "It's useless." Bitterness shrilled her voice. "Do you wish to inform everyone in this filthy inn that an Englishman made a fool of you? And if you send the innkeeper and the potboy after him, do you truly believe they will hand you back the casket? No. They will keep it for themselves. And by the time you get into your pants and saddle a horse to chase him yourself, he'll be long vanished."

"What do you suggest?" He threw aside a velvet cloak, swore, kicked a leather case across the rushes. "That we allow the brigand to steal our future?"

"This isn't like before. That was no common brigand. Didn't you hear him? He's English, Nando, English. Think what that means!"

"English?" He stared at her. "Sweet Mary! Of course he's English! *Sí*, the accent was . . ."

"And he knew we were Spanish. He called me 'Señora.' " Catlina nibbled her thumbnail, thinking it through, her mind racing past Fernando. "This was no accident, no ordinary theft. He wasn't searching for gold or interested in money. He came here for the casket." She looked at him. "The heretic queen knows we have the letters; the Englisher is her agent."

"*Had* the letters."

They stared at each other.

"Holy mother," Catlina whispered. The blood drained from her features. Her fingers scrabbled for her rosary and she pressed the beads to her heart.

Not once had she allowed herself to contemplate fully the terrible consequence of failure, not even when the brigands had surrounded the coach. But she thought about it now, hearing King Philip's spidery voice in her memory. "If you fail," he had said pleasantly, "you will answer to God. And to the Inquisition."

The very word was enough to ice her blood. She had seen the Inquisition's instruments of torture, knew what horrors those tools could work on human flesh. Catlina rubbed furiously at the bumps rising on her skin while recalling long lines of penitents limping through the narrow lanes of Seville. The dread auto da fé. For a terrible moment she visualized herself wearing the tall con-

ical cap, carrying the lighted taper. The remembered stench of
burning flesh pinched her nostrils and a tiny moan swelled from
her throat. She pressed her knuckles hard against her lips.

"We must find him, Nando. And kill him. We must have the
casket!"

"The king did not place Spain's honor in the hands of a half-
wit, my dear. I'll have the casket," he promised grimly. "And the
Englisher's balls." Bending, he found his sword and dagger under
the bed and swore loudly. "We leave at cock's crow."

"No, no. We leave now," Catlina insisted. This was no time
for bravado. She flung back the bedclothes. "Wake the innkeeper
and the coachmen. We'll not send them after the Englisher, we'll
go ourselves." They had to try. And they would succeed. She had
to believe that. After lighting a candle, she began throwing clothing into the chests. Her breath emerged in shallow gasps. "Move!
Every moment puts him further ahead!"

She was magnificent. Fernando watched her breasts beckoning beneath her nightdress as she stormed about the chamber. A
flush warmed her skin, her hair flew about her face like a silken
nimbus. Had she been alone when the Englisher approached her
bed, she would have seduced him and killed him. This he knew.
There had been an incident in Venice a year ago . . . What he
didn't know was when she would have slipped the dagger between the Englisher's ribs. Would she have taken her pleasure
first, as he suspected she had done with the cardinal in Venice?

The thought aroused him even as it heated his blood with hatred. There were moments when he dreamed of clasping his
hands around her slender throat and pressing the secrets out of
her. Times when he threw her to the rushes and enjoyed punishing her with his manhood. He knew himself hopelessly obsessed.
There was no man on earth whom Don Fernando Valencia feared;
yet this woman could reduce him with a glance.

He caught her and cupped her face with one hand, his fingertips raising tiny bruises. "You don't command a Valencia as you
would a servant, my sweet," he said between his teeth. Her lips
pulled back and he felt her soft breasts cushioned against his
chest.

Catlina stared into his dangerous smile and altered her tactics. Instantly she summoned tears and molded her hips against his. Her hands fluttered over his shoulders, his cheeks. "Nando," she whispered, "in the name of God don't let them put us to the rack! Don't let them burn us."

Staring into her eyes, he backed her toward the bed. "You'll not burn, my love. You will be wife to the viceroy, queen of the coast." His gaze ravaged her mouth. "I saw him looking at you."

"Sí," she murmured, tilting her hips against his hardening need. "The Englisher wanted what is yours." The pride of Spain, the king's command, even the dread Inquisition could not motivate him as this would. A savage growl erupted from his throat and he pushed her roughly to the mattress.

"And you, my sweet. Did you want him too?" Staring down at her, he opened his pants, his eyes glittering like glass in the candlelight.

She knew how to play his hatreds. "He was very handsome for an Englisher," she murmured softly, knowing she had just slain the Englishman as surely as if her hand wielded the blade.

Smiling, she lay back and allowed Fernando to take her. The few minutes it cost would make little difference. There were no packets out of Eu or Boulogne; the Englisher would therefore return to Calais and thence to England. They would catch him.

They would travel light, send the bulk of their luggage ahead to Madrid. By changing horses and drivers at each posthouse and by sleeping in the coach, they could travel constantly and make excellent time. If necessary, they would follow the handsome Englisher to England. When Fernando had finished with her, she would plant these ideas and let him think them his own. In a duel between the Englisher and Nando, she had no doubt Nando would emerge victorious. She traced the scar on his shoulder with her fingertip and her smile deepened. She caressed the scar on his naked hip; there were none to best him with a blade.

An hour later as their coach raced through the cloudy night, she reminded herself of King Philip's assurance: "You have God and right on your side." Catlina knew this to be true. She also knew the Englisher was no match for her wit and Nando's sword. They would have their kingdom in New Spain. She leaned her head on Fernando's shoulder and slept, but her slumber was restless and filled with dark visions. Silent men in hooded black robes chanted through the corridors of her dreams.

CHAPTER
～9～

ell paced her chamber, stalked the common room, walked in the mist-shrouded countryside. She tried to read and failed, tried to convince herself all was well and failed. Allowing Steele to proceed without her had proved a grievous error. She'd acted the fool, befuddled by a kiss; she'd behaved in a manner as fling-brained as a village lackwit.

Pushing back her hood with an irritated motion, she entered the posthouse and rubbed the cold from her cheeks before taking a stool before the fire to warm herself with a flagon of mulled wine.

Steele wasn't coming back for her; why should he? He believed her dead, his problems solved. He would ride directly to Calais, or, as he'd been gone five days now, he would more likely bypass Calais and meet the pinnace off Bayonne.

Sucking her lower lip between her teeth, Nell frowned at the blazing logs. Last night she had finally admitted the futility of waiting, furious that she hadn't recognized or accepted it sooner. At first light tomorrow she would embark for Calais and—and what? Return to England and the Tower?

Tilting her head back, she gazed unseeing at the smoke-blackened rafters, absently tapping the wine flagon against her knee. No, she would journey instead to Bayonne and surprise Steele when he arrived.

But what if the pinnace was not waiting in Bayonne? What if Steele had encountered the Spaniards and retrieved the casket an hour after leaving her beside the road? It was possible he had returned to Calais days ago and was even now crossing the Channel waters.

Nell stroked her aching temples. For days she had tormented herself with endless questions. The one consideration preventing her from bolting immediately was the realization that if Steele had taken the casket from the Spaniards, it wouldn't matter if she appeared at Whitehall a few days after him. She would, in fact, be safer doing so.

In balance rose the possibility that Steele had failed. Or that he had confronted the Spaniards but they had killed him. In that event, the instant Nell appeared in London she was ruined. She would have neither the casket nor an adequate explanation for their failure.

She slammed a fist against her knee and wished to God she had some bloody answers. Suppose the carriage axle had not been sawed but had snapped clean, suppose it had been merely an accident. In that event, Steele would expect to find her waiting here when he returned.

But if he intended to return for her, then why in the name of all that was holy hadn't he appeared? Had he found the casket opened by the Spaniards, was that it? And, knowing his fate, he'd decided to escape Elizabeth's wrath by fleeing?

The questions galloped through her mind, circling endlessly.

Worse, what if Steele was wounded? Lying in some off-road village, surrounded by Catholic indifference, dying by inches for lack of care? The thought wrenched Nell though she irritably questioned why it should. She had no cause to be concerned for the Duke of Brampton's eventual fate; her only need was to take possession of the silver casket, her legacy.

She tasted her wine then pushed it aside. Will Steele, damn his northern soul, was the cause of her headache and her predicament. When she saw him again—if she did—she'd claw his eyes out for putting her through this uncertainty.

"Sophie Marie? I'll require a coach at first light."

Until the words passed her lips, Nell hadn't admitted she'd reached a decision. And it wasn't until she paced her chamber folding sleeves and bodices into her chest that she understood where she would go. Only one choice was possible. She should have taken it days ago. She would follow Steele and discover the truth. Eventually the path would lead to the Spaniards and she would learn if Will had preceded her and how he had fared. If necessary she would retrieve the casket herself.

"God's teeth!" she muttered, cursing herself for a fling-brain. Habit died hard. A man told her to stay put and she did so without a qualm. Dammit. Here she was, again doing as she was ordered like a model gentlewoman. She, who burned for independence, had meekly acquiesced to Steele's plan. At least that was how it seemed to her now. Would the time never come when she called the tunes?

Kicking off her boots, she dropped to the edge of the bed and reached for the hooks on her bodice. Not for the first time she found herself envying Elizabeth Tudor. No man dared command the queen. Elizabeth did as she pleased when she pleased. A kingdom responded to her whims. Such power, such command of self, was worth coveting. But, Nell thought as she angrily shoved her hair beneath a linen nightcap, such indulgence was reserved for queens. For everyone else, self-reliance was merely a jest. As she herself had amply proven much to her disgust.

Before she pulled the quilts over her head, Nell touched the locket at her throat and smiled grimly. It was a pity A.B. hadn't been a queen and Nell her heir. The idea was appealing but so outrageous that Nell's tight smile relaxed into genuine amusement. Well, why not, she thought as she curled into a ball and waited for the blankets to warm. She would have made an adequate queen. She understood and enjoyed politics, she grasped the responsibility of power, and she had observed firsthand Elizabeth's uses of temper and guile. Last, but by no means least, she would thoroughly have relished being master of her own destiny.

Laughing softly at such fancies, Nell punched up a thin straw pillow and closed her eyes, anticipating a pleasant dream of crowns and gowns and triumphant plots.

Instead, she awoke at cock's crow with a restless memory of dark eyes and firm lips, of a dream figure catching her up in his arms from a carriage floor. "God's teeth!" Even awake she couldn't quite vanquish the memory of hard muscle beneath her fingertips. The whispery brush of a dark moustache across her lips, softer than she had imagined. Jesu, if only she knew he was safe.

The contrary concern raised a startled laugh. Will Steele's fate was no worry of hers. For all she knew he had attempted to murder her and would again if given the opportunity.

Eager to be gone, Nell dressed quickly and completed the last of her packing before descending to the smoky common room for a breakfast of fish cakes, cheese, heavy dark bread, and juniper-flavored ale.

What if he was injured?

"My man has your coach ready, Madame Gutland."

Did he have the casket?

"Thank you, Sophie Marie."

What if he was dead?

She ducked her head and tore her bread into pieces, absently rolling the bits into tiny balls she tossed to the postman's dog. She bit her lip and remembered Will swinging up the pinnace's ropes, an exuberant shout on his lips. She remembered his lips . . .

"Good morrow, Grandmother. There's more food I hope?"

"Will!" Nell jumped from the table and flew across the rushes, flinging herself into his arms. "Will! Thank God!" Her hands raced over the new growth on his chin, over his shoulders and up his arms. "Are you wounded?" He looked terrible, mud splattered and travel weary. Dark pockets of exhaustion underlay his eyes. "Are you well? What news? Did you find them? Did you have to . . . was there a duel? Do you have the casket?" Tears of relief brimmed in her eyes and she dropped her head against his doublet, suddenly weak. In her secret heart she admitted how desperately glad she was to see him alive. "Thank God. Oh, thank God!"

"Such eagerness gives a man welcome," he said gently, lifting her face. His mouth covered hers with hard warmth. "I'd love to ravage you, Nellie girl, but frankly I haven't eaten in days. If it's all the same to you, m'love, I'll eat first and regain my strength."

"Ravage me? Is that what you think I . . . ?"

Horrified, Nell stepped back from his grin and scrubbed her hand across her lips. "You arrogant northern lout! Your conceit is boundless!"

"Now that sounds more like my Nellie." Striding past her he dropped to the bench and drained her juniper ale. "God's blood, that's vile! Innkeeper! Bring us something stout to drink and more food." In three bites, he consumed her bread and fish cakes.

Scowling, Nell took the seat facing him. In five days she had managed to forget what a black knave he was. She wouldn't commit that mistake again. "Well? Did you get the casket?"

He reached a hand toward her, laughing when she hastily drew backward, then he placed a key on the table and patted his doublet. "Success, m'love. I have the casket." He met her gaze. "And—it's unopened!"

She closed her eyes then opened them and a joyous smile illuminated her face. In a burst of sudden elation, she forgave him the stolen kiss, almost forgave him the broken axle. For one glorious moment, Nell longed to throw her arms around his neck and dance him across the rushes.

"Unopened," he repeated. "Thank God."

Another might have overlooked the significance of repetition, but years of studied experience had taught Nell to sense the presence of layered meanings. She examined his expression, one of triumph and relief, and her smile gradually faded as she recognized dangerous currents flowing beneath the surface.

"Leave us," she said when Sophie Marie had served Will. Then, leaning forward, she tented her fingers beneath her chin. "Tell me," she began, her voice pleasantly conversational, "what would have occurred had the casket been opened?"

A look of discomfort tightened Will's expression. "You know as well as I, m'love. The old girl regards an opened casket the same as no casket at all." He ran a finger around his ruff and shrugged. "What would happen? Hanging for me; the Tower for you."

"Actually, I rather doubt that." She lifted the key from the table, felt its weight in the palm of her hand. "More likely we'd both be sent to the Tower for a time, but I'll wager we'd keep our heads. Elizabeth wants her letters returned, that's her primary concern. Aye, she'd be angered by the possibility that we might have read them, but not angry enough to demand our lives. It's fair to say, I believe, that our lives were never truly at risk so long as we returned her precious casket."

Jesu, he was as transparent as Venetian glass. Nell caught a breath. Her brow rose and the ruff circling her throat seemed suddenly to constrict as she observed Will's mounting discomfort.

"I see," she said slowly. "Our lives *are* at issue." She watched the flicker deep in his eyes and the hesitancy about his mouth. "No," she amended, "not *our* lives . . ." A hand fluttered to her breast as his readable face confessed what she suddenly didn't want to know. Her voice cracked around a whisper of disbelief as she understood. "Holy God!"

"Nell, wait . . ."

"Tell me," she demanded. "Tell me what you were commanded if the casket was opened!" She knew, but she had to hear it from his lips before she could make herself truly believe.

"It doesn't matter now." Reaching inside his doublet, Will produced the casket and shook it from the satin pouch. "Dudley's seals are intact. Examine them for yourself." In a blatantly obvious effort to switch the topic, he noticed the tiny scar near her hairline. "What happened to you? How did you receive that cut?"

"As if you didn't know. Tell me!"

Their eyes met across the table and held. Nell's gaze was hard and unyielding; Will's was troubled and ill at ease. Standing, he kicked at the rushes, sending the innkeeper's dog howling. "Dammit."

"She ordered you to kill me if the casket was opened, didn't she?" Nell wet her lips and stared at him from dulled eyes. "Didn't she?"

"Aye." Will flung his cap on the table. "How did you know?"

"Would you have done it, Will?"

"She commanded it." He spread his hands and frowned unhappily. " 'Tis treason to disobey. But Nell, the casket is sealed."

"You would have killed me."

"Nell, for the love of God!"

"Why does she hate me so?" The hands she flattened against the table trembled. All color had bleached from her skin. "What have I done to offend?" She didn't notice the men at the posthouse door or hear Will's roar that sent them hastening back into the cold. "Why would Elizabeth blame me if the casket were opened?" A look of despair pinched her features and she shook her head. "All I've ever done is love her and try to please her."

"Nell . . ."

"No! Don't touch me!" Gathering her skirts, she spun blindly and rushed up the dark staircase to her chamber, where she fell across the bed and stared at the rafters with burning eyes.

She had known Will Steele wanted her dead, but she hadn't guessed a dual reason. Not for one moment had she suspected the command from the queen. Covering her face with her hands, Nell fought to understand but failed utterly. Elizabeth could be ruthless when events required, but she was also noted for a light hand on the ax. She prided herself on being a merciful prince. Yet she would put Nell to the sword for so minor an infraction, for something outside Nell's control.

This then was Nell's reward for saving Elizabeth's life from the papist assassins. To be slaughtered by Will Steele. Not for an instant did she understand.

Bitter tears slipped silently down her cheeks. A dagger thrust of betrayal pierced her body and she curled around it. Elizabeth had been her idol, the woman Nell most admired and wished to emulate. Everything she'd done in her life she had done in hope of winning Elizabeth's favor. The magnitude of her failure yawned before Nell like a black chasm.

Once again she experienced the pain of Elizabeth's rejection. Remembered the slights and petty slaps, all the occasions when Elizabeth's eye had fallen on her with suspicion and wary disapproval. The queen had never returned her love. Never.

"Nell?"

Rolling over, she pushed her hot face into the pillow. "Leave me!" No one had ever seen her weep; she hated him for witnessing her humiliation.

Will sat on the side of the bed and pulled her gently into his arms, catching her flailing hands and pinning them at her side. "Shhh."

"I don't need you! Leave me and . . ." But his strength closed around her and he pressed her head firmly to his shoulder. "Oh, Will." A world of despair spilled from those two words. She collapsed against him. "Hold me. Just hold me."

He whispered soothing nonsense against her hair and stroked her trembling arms. "It doesn't matter, Nellie love. The casket is sealed and you're safe. It's over now."

But it wasn't over. The betrayal would dim her universe for all her days. Nell pressed her face against his stiff collar, inhaling the scent of cold air, rice starch, and him. "Tell me why. Did she admit why she wishes me dead?"

"No."

"Oh, God." Her voice cracked and she burrowed deeper into his arms, leaning gratefully into the kisses brushing her hair. Her fingers dug into his sleeves and she wished she could melt into his strength until the shock and confusion sorted itself out. "I'm sorry. I just . . . I hoped . . ."

He tasted the salty tears streaking her cheeks, pooling at the corner of her lips. "Nell. Nellie love . . ."

Tears ran into his moustache as she lifted her mouth and parted her lips beneath the gentleness of his kiss. Her arms circled his neck and she clung to his strength, wound her fingers through his thick dark hair. And when his hands slid to the sides of her breasts, when her body ignited and their kisses became wild and frenzied before he bent her down to the bed, she whispered, "Aye, oh aye," against his warm breath and lifted to meet the solid power of his body molded against hers.

Hungry for reassurance, for validation, Nell feverishly gave herself to his kisses. Her body trembled, shivered on the rim of something frightening and exhilarating. When his large palm covered her breast she gasped and for an instant her heart stopped then raced. And she wanted him as she had not wanted Edward or any other man. She wanted his strength and his power, his heat and vitality. She wanted the magic he possessed to blot her mind of all but him, his ability to grant her surcease from the waiting pain.

"The chamber door," he said hoarsely. "A moment, m'love."

A moment was all it required for Nell to regain her senses. Struggling upward she watched him reach for the chamber latch and she shook her head as if emerging from a drugged slumber. God's teeth! Fury stained her cheeks. Kicking at her skirts, she jumped from the bed and rounded on him, fists on her hips, an errant lock of hair swinging against her shoulder.

"You murdering son of a wharfside cur! You insignificant northern vermin!" Grabbing up a crockery pitcher she hurled it at him, enraged when he dodged and turned to stare at her, his mouth dropping. "You would have *killed* me! And been glad for the chance! Only this time it would have been the sword or a dagger in the night instead of an axle." Her hairbrush followed the pitcher, glancing off his shoulder. "You filthy pile of flea offal! How dare you push in here and try to seduce me!" There was murder in her eye. If she'd had a sword at hand, she would gladly have sliced him to bits of grease and bone.

Hastily, Will placed the chamber door between himself and the stream of articles crashing against it. "Dammit, Nell," he shouted. "The bloody casket is sealed! Can't you get that through your stubborn head?" Bits of crockery splintered around his hand.

"You miserable, rotten whoreson! Lower than lice, you are! No better than a laystall gull!"

And he had imagined she lacked passion? "Listen to me. I'm going now. To sleep. We'll leave on the morrow for Calais." He waited a moment then slammed the chamber door. Something solid thumped and bounced off the other side. If he planned to survive his exhaustion, he would do well to post a guard outside his door.

At first light, she descended the staircase, holding her skirts away from him as if he were speckled with pox. Chin high and set, she entered the coach without a word. When they halted for the midday meal, Will frowned down at her. "Are you going to pass this entire journey without speaking?"

"You scorn blather, remember?" When he would have protested, she froze him with an icy glare. "You would have killed me. Not once but twice."

"What are you prattling about?"

"Your wicked mischief with the axle, of course." She tilted her head so the small scar near her hairline could be seen, then she tossed her head, pulled back her skirts, and swept past him into the posthouse.

"God save me from the idiocy that women state as logic!" When they had warmed themselves and had been served, he leaned forward. "Are you claiming I am somehow responsible for an axle that snapped when I was miles away?"

"Feigning innocence does not deceive me and does you no credit."

"You do believe it." He was incredulous.

"Continue this pretense if you will, m'lord. One day you shall explain your evil to a higher judge than I."

They resumed their journey in silence.

"They've arrived," Don Fernando Valencia announced when he returned to the hostelry overlooking Calais's harbor. He poured a tankard of wine from the crockery pitcher near the bed and swallowed. "They're stopping at the Wolverine under the name Gutland. He claims to be a Flemish merchant." Alerted by the man he'd posted at the city gate, Fernando had followed the Englisher's hired coach to the Wolverine.

"They?"

"He's traveling with a woman. The woman in weeds whom we met at Lady Leicester's. Nellanor something."

"Robert Dudley's ward," Catlina mused. Thoughtfully she pulled a dark curl over her breast and brushed the ends. "Lady Amesly, wasn't it? Does it strike you as curious that Dudley's ward is part of the plot to retrieve the queen's letters to Dudley? Perhaps she knows their content." Catlina studied herself in the glass. "Which leads us to the next puzzle. Does Lady Amesly seek the letters for the queen—or for her own use, I wonder."

"They proceeded directly to the wharf as if expecting a ship. If so, it wasn't waiting." The moment had given Fernando pause. Had the English immediately boarded ship, hope would have crumbled to bitter ash. The thought pinched his nostrils. He hadn't disabused Catlina of her plan to follow the casket to London, but the plot was futile. Once safely ensconced in Whitehall the letters were most certainly lost to Spain.

"Naturally you will wish to act quickly," Catlina suggested, guiding him. "They'll not dally in this filthy village. I suppose you're planning to lure the Englisher into a deserted lane . . . ?"

Standing beside the window, Fernando pulled the point of his beard and studied the ships at anchor. "He'll carry the casket on his person, of course," he considered, thinking aloud. "Now that he has the woman settled, he'll return to the docks to arrange passage for tomorrow."

He had recalled the woman immediately. Lady Amesly was a beauty, and he didn't forget beautiful women. Ordinarily Don Fernando didn't think northern women appealing, with their cold eyes and pale skin. But Lady Amesly's fiery hair and the spirited spark in her gaze intrigued him. Not enough to risk his wife's wrath, nor was this the time to pursue a fancy. But he passed a brief thought of envy for the Englisher.

"Then there isn't much time."

"Don't concern yourself, my sweet. I returned only to inform you in the event you wished to accept the task of retrieving the key, which I warrant is in the safekeeping of Lady Amesly."

"The possibility merits investigation." Catlina wound her glossy curls high, exposing the nape of her neck.

Fernando gazed at the tender expanse and knew she would have preferred duping the Englisher rather than the woman. Laughing softly, he saluted her with a low bow then settled his hat and pushed through the dockside traffic until he stood directly across from the Wolverine. Chickens scratched across the inner courtyard, laundresses appeared on the upper balcony and draped kitchen linen over the rails. The signboard above the door creaked in a light breeze.

Don Fernando Valencia had killed fourteen men in the course of his thirty years, the first when he'd reached the tender age of seventeen. No man slurred the honor of the House of Valencia and lived. Honor was all. The honor of God, king, country, and the House of Valencia must be defended and protected above all.

At this moment he had only to cast his glance toward the coastal sands to see the charred hulls of the English fireships and be reminded that Spain lay in shame before the eyes of the world. The heathen English had trampled Spain's honor and spit in the eye of God. They had driven the mightiest king in Christendom to his knees and thence to his bed. Equally important, an Englishman had dared hold a sword to Valencia's throat in his own bedchamber, and there to look upon his wife in her nightdress.

Fernando's lips thinned with rage. When the Englisher emerged from the Wolverine doors, it was all he could do to contain his fury and prevent himself from instantly drawing his blade. But too much lay in balance to indulge impulse. Instead he jerked his hat brim forward to shade his features and fell into step behind the Englisher.

It provided a sour amusement that Gutland, for want of his true name, thought to impersonate a merchant. The pose was laughable. The pants tucked into the Englisher's expensive Spanish leather knee boots were cut from high-grade wool. The gold buttons adorning his dark doublet matched the gold thread weaving through his sleeves. A falling collar and the plain design of his attire failed to minimize the richness of his dress. And the arrogant swing of the cape slung across Gutland's shoulder was not the posture of a simple merchant.

The man was a soldier, Fernando concluded. He observed the men in Gutland's path step aside to make way and he amended his assessment. Not a soldier, a leader of soldiers. One accustomed to being obeyed. Authority carved the lines in his face, glittered behind eyes that missed nothing, proclaimed itself in the jaunty challenge of the feather atop his cap. The swagger in the Englisher's step announced him for what he was: one of England's fighting lords. One who had shamed Spain and the House of Valencia.

While Gutland strode briskly up the plank of a Flemish packet, Fernando leaned against a rotting post and turned his face away from the hulks of the fireboats. As in any port, the wharf swarmed with activity shouted in half a dozen languages. Rope snaked across the boards, walls of barrels rose beneath the bowsprits overhanging the docks. The oyster crones and fishwives bawled their wares, masters shouted, horses reared, and carts collided amid steady cursing and spilled cargo.

Challenging Gutland here would be foolhardy; there was scarcely space to maneuver a sword and no opportunity for escape.

Frowning, Fernando considered. Gutland was larger and more powerfully built than he, but he had skill and agility as balance. Experience offered confidence that he could slay the Englisher in fair battle. But did circumstance merit the risk? Did he wish to wager a brilliant future on the outcome of a duel? A hard smile twisted his mouth as he guessed what Catlina would advise.

He waited until Gutland had passed several paces in front of him then again fell into step, his mind retracing the route to the Wolverine. Pleasure gleamed in the shadows beneath his hat brim as he recalled the dark alleyway Gutland would soon enter.

As they approached the narrow opening between two houses, Fernando closed the distance between himself and the Englisher, moving closer until he was but a step behind. In one fluid motion he tossed back his cape and slipped his dagger from its sheath. The Englisher had lived without honor; he would die without honor. Fernando had killed by such method before. Given a preference he would have enjoyed the exhilaration of blades, but the Englisher did not merit an affair of honor, nor did wisdom advise it.

The Englisher stepped into the shadows between the buildings then spun, his face dark. "Hold . . "

Fernando lunged forward and slid the dagger beneath the English bastard's ribs. Stepping back, he watched with pleasure as

Gutland doubled over then fell, striking his head on the stone rim of the gutter. He waited until a scarlet blossom flowered on the Englisher's doublet, until a red pool collected beneath his head. Then he bent and swiftly transferred the silver casket from Gutland's waistcoat to his own before he slipped out the end of the alleyway into the cold bright sunshine.

The incident had required less than two minutes. Two minutes to avenge God, Spain, and the House of Valencia. Catlina would be pleased. He could visualize the heat in her eyes.

Dona Catlina Valencia paused before the diamond-shaped panes of a trim shop and pretended to admire the skeins of lace displayed behind the glass. Ignoring the attentions of two French fops with painted faces and jeweled earrings, she observed the bathhouse across the lane into which Lady Amesly had stepped. In five more minutes, when she could be certain Lady Amesly had visited the bathhouse to bathe and not to discharge some other errand, Catlina would follow.

Fate had played into her hands, she decided with a small sound that resembled a purr. Lady Amesly's eagerness to remove the stains of travel would facilitate the recovery of the casket's key.

What fools they were, these English. One required no particular wisdom to divine their childish reasoning. By the timing of their arrival in Calais it could be surmised the Englisher had slept or otherwise dallied and had therefore lost what time he'd gained. The English were noted for being frugal to the point of ruin and apparently it was so, for it appeared they had not considered that gold would purchase fresh horses throughout the night and a coach could then run without pause. Simplicity of thought convinced them they were secure in their possession of the casket.

Catlina smiled as she lifted her voluminous skirts and crossed the lane to the bathhouse. As expected, it was an abomination. The primitive Calais bathhouse resembled the marble public houses in Venice as little as a pile of offal resembled its originator.

The thatched roof of the structure no doubt provided a haven for fleas and vermin; the wooden walls stank of mold and age. As Catlina approached, a beefy woman appeared in the doorway and upended a pail of sudsy water over the rushes moldering beside the path. Catlina made herself smile and wish the woman good morrow. She asked the price of a hot tub, nodded acceptance, then followed the woman's damp hem inside.

The interior was more accommodating than she had antici-pated. The rushes smelled pleasantly of rosemary and thyme and appeared to have been freshened in the not too distant past. Commodious clothing baskets lined the walls of the undressing chamber and hooks were provided on which to hang one's far-thingale. A sturdy matron as squat as she was tall leaned stolidly against the archway, guarding the safety of the baskets. Catlina stepped past her with a nod, averting her eyes from the growth of fuzz darkening the woman's upper lip.

Once her eyes adjusted to the dim interior light, she skimmed a rapid glance over the contents of the baskets, easily identifying Lady Amesly's dark mourning weeds. Once she had positioned herself before Lady Amesly's basket, she blinked heav-ily, moaned, and pressed a hand to her bosom before she fell to her knees. In the process she toppled the Englishwoman's basket, spilling the contents over the rushes and into her hands.

It was child's play to recover from her swoon, offer helpless apologies, then insist on aiding the attendant in replacing Lady Amesly's goods in the basket. Quick eyes and nimble fingers swiftly found the valuables pouch and Catlina spilled it open. The contents disappointed. She found a man's signet sized for a woman's finger, a worn gold locket, an ivory-handled dinner knife, a chain of inferior pearls, and, the only item worth covet-ing, a pair of jet earrings. The pouch contained no key.

Was it possible the man carried both the casket and the key? Logic insisted otherwise. Each would claim a piece of the booty. So. Catlina had hoped to avoid the next step but she didn't shy from it.

After repeating apologies for her clumsiness, she pressed a hand to her forehead and murmured, "Regrettably I must forgo bathing—my health . . ." To smooth the way, she didn't ask the return of the coins she had paid the moustachioed attendant. "You won't mind if I step inside to inform my—friend—that I won't be joining her."

The actual bathing chamber was large and cloudy with steam. A wide wooden shelf circled three sides of the chamber upon which sat or reclined a half dozen women, some naked, some more modestly attired in the shapeless shifts provided by the establishment. As Catlina narrowed her gaze against the drifts of milky haze, Lady Amesly removed her shift and stepped a shapely leg into one of the wooden tubs centered in the rushes. Before Lady Amesly lowered herself into the suds and steam, Catlina had leisure to study the Englishwoman's slim ivory body, perfect but for a dark bruise on one hip.

There was naught of moment to envy. It was little wonder the men of Catlina's experience preferred warm Mediterranean tints to the frosty paleness of northern women. Other than her flaming hair and the pink tips of her breasts, Lady Amesly was as white as a salted cod. Most unappealing.

Catlina's scrutiny settled on the silk net catching up Lady Amesly's hair, and a smile of reluctant admiration curved her lips.

Paying no heed to the wet rushes dampening her velvets, Catlina moved quickly to the wooden tubs, positioning herself between Lady Amesly and the women reclining on the shelf. Waving the attendant aside, she seated herself upon the woman's stool and, concealing the action with her body, she pressed a needle-tipped dagger against Lady Amesly's bared breast.

"I'll have the key to the casket, my dear," she said pleasantly. To the Englishwoman's credit, she gave no sign of surprise or alarm. Her cool gray eyes regarded Catlina without expression although Catlina guessed a dozen plans swirled behind the woman's gaze.

Lady Amesly's reply was as icy as her eyes. "You may roast in your papist hell. My dear."

"I would suggest—my dear—that you are in no position to indulge arrogance."

Though the admission annoyed her, Catlina gazed into her adversary's eyes and recognized that she and Lady Amesly were drawn from the same dye lot. Instinct told her each was skilled at dissembling, each resisted yielding, and each made an implacable enemy. While being able to understand one another added to the game's interest, it also increased the danger.

Lady Amesly glanced at the dagger and raised an eyebrow. "What a pity to waste this amusing drama. But I'll wager you're aware the key is not in my basket, nor, as you can see, on my person. So I'll thank you to take yourself away and leave me to my bath."

"Come now, Lady Amesly. Let's not undervalue one another. Take down your hair and give me the key." No flicker of admission passed those gray eyes. "The key by itself is not worth dying for, would you agree?"

Catlina pressed slightly on the dagger and smiled as a red bead appeared beneath the tip as shocking as a rose upon a snow bank.

Lady Amesly regarded the drop of blood then slowly reached pale arms toward her hairnet.

"Ah, a woman of sensibility," Catlina approved.

"You have the casket then." It was not a question.

"We have your handsome Englisher," Catlina lied smoothly. "Should you prove intractable about surrendering the key or should you raise an alarm before I'm safely away—he dies."

"If you have him, he'll die in any event."

"Perhaps. One thing is certain; your refusal to cooperate will hasten the event."

Waist-length hair the color of a fiery sunset cascaded from the net and over the rim of the tub. Lady Amesly held the key a moment, then tossed it into the rushes and permitted herself a thin smile as Catlina grubbed in the wet and mold to retrieve it.

Catlina stood, hatred flashing from her dark eyes. "Remember this," she hissed. "A word from you—a scream—before I'm safely away, and your handsome lover dies!"

She sincerely regretted not slicing Lady Amesly's ivory throat; she ached to dispatch the Englishwoman for making a cardinal's niece grovel in moldy rushes. But to avenge herself would inconvenience her escape. After dropping the key safely into the palm of her glove where she could feel it against her skin, Catlina nodded to the women ringing the tubs and hastened from the bathing chamber.

She was outside and across the dirt lane before she heard Lady Amesly's scream. In the Englishwoman's place, Catlina would have sounded the alarm the instant the dagger pressed her breast. Turning into the alleyway between the trim shop and the apothecary, she emerged into the lane behind and proceeded with studied calm to her waiting coach.

Before climbing inside she instructed the coachman to drive past the Wolverine so she could fully savor the day's triumphs. A smile that only a Castilian could smile warmed her expression with smug content. Ah, the sweetness of victory. Now she could depart this chill vile country where melons and figs and fat olives were as scarce as leaves on the trees. Soon she and Nando would sail to the richness and glory of New Spain, to a life of ease and lavish comfort. Never again would she exhale and watch her breath hang in frosty vapor before her lips. Never again would she find herself without personal attendants and a retinue of admirers. The king himself would praise her and pile rewards at her feet.

As the coach slowed to negotiate the congested lane before the Wolverine, Catlina languidly turned to the window. Then she started and jerked forward, her triumphant smile instantly vanished. "Mother of God!" Dark fury infused her skin and her lips turned white.

CHAPTER 10

It wasn't Nell's nature to retreat to the luxury or frailty of vapors. Therefore she didn't gasp or swoon when she rushed into the Wolverine and stopped short at seeing Will propped half-conscious and bloody just inside the common-room door. "Innkeep!" Her hem whirled around her boots as she veered toward Will.

"What's the meaning of this?" she demanded of the inn-keeper as she stripped off her glove to lift Will's eyelid. A dazed, unblinking vacancy met her inspection. "Why isn't this man be-ing tended?"

The innkeeper spread his hands across a dirty leather apron. "Two stevedores carried him here from the docks, Madame." He shrugged eloquently. "He's dying."

"And you didn't deign to spoil your sheets by letting him die in bed?" Nell leveled a furious glare, ignoring the innkeeper's faint cough. "In the charity of your black heart you preferred to drop him in rushes jumping with fleas and vermin? You gave him a public wall to expire against?" Her lips twisted. "May God re-ward such generosity."

The innkeeper opened his hands and frowned unhappily.

"Well, mayhaps he's dying and mayhaps he isn't. But he hasn't much hope sprawled here in the cold, has he? With clots like you tripping over him." Pulling to her full height, Nell fixed the innkeeper with icy authority and briskly ordered, "Take Herr Gutland to his chamber at once. I'll require warm water, clean cloths, and salt. Dispatch a boy to the chemists immediately for healing unguents and costmary balm." She clapped her hands together. "You heard me. At once!"

She hoped to God the Spaniards hadn't killed him. Though nothing showed in her expression, Nell's heart thudded against her ribs as she watched two sturdy men heft Will between them and half carry, half drag him up the staircase. Blood stained his doublet and matted the back of his hair; he was dazed and unresponsive. She sucked in a breath and held it. She reminded herself that surface wounds could bleed ferociously and she prayed his injuries looked worse than they were.

Once she had received the items she'd demanded, she dismissed the men and the serving wench then seated herself on the bed beside Will and tugged at the loops fastening his doublet.

"Can you speak?"

"Nellie?" His speech was thick and furred, his pupils large and unfocused. "The bastard took me from behind. Even the Scots, devil's spawn that they are, don't sneak about like skirts and stab a man in his bloody back!"

"Sit up." Sliding a hand beneath him, she guided him upward and peeled off his doublet then his waistcoat. With each layer, the size of the blood stain grew. She didn't bother seeking the casket. The Spaniards had it.

"If I hadn't turned at the last instant, the scurvy bastard would have done me."

"Easy now." Nell pulled away his shirt and guided it over his shoulders then pressed him back to the bed as she studied his side wound. At a glance she understood he'd been very lucky. The heavy quilting that padded his doublet had muted the force of the thrust. Turning when he did had deflected the blade from vital organs. "Turn," she commanded in a tone brooking no argument. "Let me see your head."

Blood continued to flow from the gash. Dipping a cloth in the water basin, she cleaned the wound and examined it closely before she released the breath she'd been holding and felt the tension ease from her shoulders. Both wounds were serious, but not life threatening unless he developed a fever.

"You'll have a hellish headache and fire in your side, but you'll live." Anticipating the headache he'd suffer gave her grim pleasure. Justice came full circle, she thought, recalling the welt he'd raised on her head.

Will swore steadily into the pillow, yelping when Nell dusted salt into his head wound then packed it with lint and covered all with the unguent the boy had fetched from the chemist. "In the name of God, woman! What are you doing? Pouring liquid flame on me?"

She ripped a clean cloth into a bandage, soaked it in wine, then commanded him to turn over as she tied the ends beneath the lock of hair dropping over his forehead. "I've tended braver sprouts in a peasant's brood," she said crisply, turning her attention to the wound in his side. "Stop sniveling."

A half dozen ridges crisscrossed his chest, cutting white tracks through curling dark hair. Old wounds that had healed badly, treated hastily in the field unless Nell missed her guess. Suppressing her curiosity, she treated the side wound and ignored the hisses he made and the sharp intakes of breath when she poured salt in the wound.

It was more difficult to ignore the smooth firmness of his skin, the tensed muscle and sinew hot beneath the cool ministrations of her fingers. She hadn't expected the satiny texture. She hadn't expected to notice his skin at all. As he steadily and soundly cursed the Spaniards, Nell's hands slowed. Fascinated by the rise and fall of his belly, by the line of dark hair that tapered into the waist of his stocks, she placed her palm flat against his stomach, sensing his heat and the rapid movement of his breathing. In a sudden rush, she absorbed the intimacy of the scene. Will, half dressed; she hovering above him with gentle touches which, to the eyes of a casual observer, could have been mistaken for caresses.

"Nellie love?"

Hastily she snatched her hand away and bent to wring the cloth over the basin. What was there about this damnable man that stirred her on such a primitive level? Whatever it was, she cursed it.

"I lost the casket."

She didn't like the sound of his voice. Weak, thready. He'd lost too much blood.

"The Spaniards have it."

"I know. And the key. The woman took it from me at the baths."

Catching her hand, he pressed it briefly to his lips. "We didn't acquit ourselves well this day, but don't flog yourself, m'love. I'll recover the casket." Panting with exertion, he pushed himself up and swung his legs over the side of the bed. "If you'll be good enough to pass me my shirt and my sword, I'll be on my way to kill a God-cursed Spanish blight. They're as malignant as the Scots, by Christ. Boils on the backside of England."

"Of course," Nell agreed smoothly. "But first, m'lord, a cup of ale to strengthen your purpose." She had foreseen this possibility and had taken the precaution of preparing a tankard containing enough sleeping draught to drop a stallion.

"God's blood! My damned head feels like it's stuffed with whirling blades!" He drained the tankard in three long swallows and wiped his mouth. Then he blinked heavily. His eyes dilated and crossed slightly. "You scurvy bitch," he roared. "You adulterated my cup! What did you put in that ale?"

"Something to help you rest," Nell answered calmly.

He swayed to his feet. "Damn you! Right now we know where the bastards are. By first light they'll be halfway across France!"

"You're in no condition to fight."

"God's death, woman! Will you allow me to decide my own fate? I'd rather die with a blade in my hand than at the end of a hangman's rope!"

"You'll die in Calais if you don't rest," Nell said as he sat abruptly and scrubbed at his eyes. She pressed him flat with one finger and covered him. "The Spaniards believe you dead. They have no cause for haste." He fought sleep but his eyelids fluttered above a murderous glare then were still. "We'll resume the pursuit when you're mended."

Now there was naught to do but wait. Nell posted guards outside the door in the event the Spaniards should attempt to finish the job. She dumped the basin from the window, tidied the chamber, then stood beside the bed looking down at him.

By morning she would know if he would catch fever. It passed her mind to confront the Spaniards herself and retrieve the casket. But upon reflection she dismissed the idea with bitter reluctance. They wouldn't be easy prey this time. And, in shameful truth, she didn't know if she possessed the boldness to creep into their chamber and slice their throats as they slept, which was doubtless the wisest way to proceed. Her weapon was words, not blades. Plus, if she were wounded in the attempt, Nell guessed the innkeeper would let her and Will die.

Why the possibility of Will's death dismayed her, Nell couldn't fathom. But it did. Against all logic she didn't want him to die.

Sighing, she seated herself on the stool beside his bed and sent for her embroidery to pass the time. Wielding the needle like a sword, she attacked a yarn lily. She didn't want him dead because she still had need of him.

"Live, damn you," she whispered fiercely, leaning to stare into his craggy face. "There will be no fever. Do you hear? No fever!"

If he caught the fever, he wouldn't have one chance in a thousand. She would be on her own. But if he avoided fever—and she'd taken every precaution—then he'd be up and about in a few days.

After a time she tested his temperature as old Mother Jamison had taught her, by brushing her lips across his forehead. Eventually it occurred to her the forehead was not a true indicator and she began pressing her lips to his mouth instead.

As the cold sun sank toward the horizon, she found herself watching the sand trickle through the glass and anticipating the moment of the next test. To assure herself of the absence of fever.

"You were supposed to kill him!" Catlina screamed. "Must I do everything?" Drops flew from the tankard she waved. "Do you think they will give up, you fool? In a matter of days they'll be after us again!" Disgusted, she hurled a cape into the nearest brass-bound chest, packing between outbursts of rage.

"We'll be safely away before Vespers, my dearest," Fernando commented mildly. It was an affront to learn the Englisher lived, but he was not overly agitated. Before they departed Calais, he would pay a visit to the Wolverine and finish the affair.

Catlina rolled her eyes toward heaven. "Fernando, put aside any thought of returning to the Wolverine. I looked in her eyes, remember? She's not to be underestimated. By now she has guards posted at every crack and cranny. You'd be dead before you mounted the stairs!"

His gaze narrowed and his hand tightened on the hilt of his dagger. No other addressed him with such scorn as dripped from his wife's lips. Countless times he had wondered, as he did now, why he didn't thrash her thoroughly and be done with it. Men who sensibly and regularly thrashed their wives enjoyed docile, compliant wives.

"The English don't know we've learned he isn't dead. Lady Amesly has no cause to post guards."

"She will. I promise you she'll chain all the gates!"

"If Lady Amesly is so formidable," he sneered, "then why didn't *you* kill her when you had the opportunity?"

"I didn't realize it was necessary." She glared down the length of her nose. "Because I trusted *you* had finished the man! Without a man, a woman is disarmed and helpless," she added with heavy disgust.

Though Fernando's honor would not admit to error, privately he cursed himself for not having slit the Englisher's throat for insurance. He saw now that pride had deceived him. He'd gloated too soon and had thus left his victory in doubt.

Brooding, he poured more wine into his cup and watched Catlina flinging items into the chests. What had appeared so simple in the beginning had become a wearisome game of cat and rat. True, he had the casket, but his gut told him the Englisher would soon be on his trail again. Gutland would not give up until one of them was dead. Such a man did not forgive a blade in his back.

Until Fernando placed the casket safely in Philip's ink-smeared hands, each time he glanced over his shoulder he would see the Englisher coming. This time the game unfolded in deadly earnest. Whatever innocence or stupidity had stayed the Englisher's sword that night in Eu would not occur again.

"Jesu," he sighed, thinking of the travails and discomforts of steady punishing travel, wondering at what point the Englisher would leap up before him. Or, more likely, behind him.

He tugged his beard and studied Catlina. Whatever else she was, he admitted she possessed many admirable qualities. Another woman would have complained of sleeping in a flying coach and the hardships of travel, would have bemoaned the lack of maids and comforts, the foreign foods and smells. His gaze followed the voluptuous curve of her body and his attitude softened. Her temper would pass and when it did, his retribution would be sweet. "I'll make this up to you," he vowed softly, aroused by the wine and the candlelight and the angry tug of silk across her breasts. "I'll make you queen of Peru."

"Peru?" Catlina halted mid-stride and whirled to stare at him. *"Peru?"* she asked, her voice spiraling into shrillness.

A string of oaths issued from between his teeth. Damn the wine and this miserable, blasted day. There was nothing to do now but bluff. He tilted an eyebrow and effected a look of surprise. "Of course Peru. I told you."

"Never! You *never* said Peru!" Stunned, she sank to the bed and stared at him through blank eyes. "Peru. Mother of God! Naturally I assumed we would be assigned the East coast! Where the treasure fleets put in. Not the West coast where nothing appears for months but mosquitoes and fleas and those stupid flat-faced Indians Don Hernando exhibited at court!"

"You said yourself New Spain offers undreamed opportunity. And none so great, my sweet, as in the untouched West. It's ripe for plucking. We can make of it whatever we wish."

"Make of it? In the East our fortune is already made! Each time the plate fleet drops anchor the local alcalde extracts a harbor fee worth a king's ransom. Of which he pays a generous percentage to the viceroy! The viceroy, need I mention, receives patronage all along the coast from dozens of alcaldes. The *East* coast!"

"And we will arrange such a lucrative system in the West. It will take time, but our children will inherit a vast and immensely rich empire."

"Our children? You'll drag me to a mud hut isolated in some Indian-infested jungle for the sake of children we don't yet have?" And never would if Catlina had a say in the matter. She knew enough to tuck a jasper stone beneath her pillow, and if that failed, there was a witch in Venice who was said to dispense powders powerful enough to purge one of troublesome discomforts.

"And for us, my sweet. The silver . . ."

"What am I expected to do while you load silver on the backs of mules to enrich the viceroys in the East? Oh, yes, I know about the Peruvian mines and they impress me not at all. Because they mine ore, my lord. Because the raw silver is not minted into coin until it reaches the *East*!"

He winked slyly. "Not all silver finds its way East, my dear."

"Oh?" Her lip curled back from her teeth. "And what shall we do with what silver you manage to steal, Fernando? Shall I build a palace for the edification of the Indian whores? Shall I invite them to fetes and masked balls? There's no one else to invite. There are ten, possibly twelve women on the entire West coast and nine of them are whores. Do you ask the niece of a cardinal to tap fans with whores?" She hurled the wine pitcher to the floor, threw her tankard and then his through the chamber window.

Glass showered, crockery shattered. Within minutes every breakable item in the chamber lay in shards.

"For this I gave up the Venice season?" she screamed. "For this I exposed myself to heretics? To bone cold and food that tastes like tallow? To end in *Peru*?"

"Catlina, the king . . ."

"The king isn't rewarding us, you idiot! We're being punished! Exiled!" She hurled his shaving basin out the window, stamped her boot on a fragment of mirror.

"There's opportunity . . ."

"Opportunity to be buried and forgotten! Opportunity to be eaten alive by insects or Indians! Opportunity to die for want of amusement! What good is it to dine off emerald platters or wear silver buckles and diamond tiaras if there's none to see and envy?"

Fernando had known she would be upset but he hadn't anticipated to what depth. Naïvely, he had supposed he could handle and soothe her. But in truth the picture she sketched of hardship and squalor exerted little appeal. He tried to recall the grandiose vistas the king had opened when he spoke of the gilded opportunities awaiting the right man in Peru. At the moment none seemed weighty enough to offer in balance.

But he tried. "It needn't be forever, my dearest. We'll make our fortune in silver, then we'll return in triumph to Madrid or Venice."

Her laugh was ugly. "A fortune? In silver ore? First you must steal the ore." Snatching up the casket, she waved it beneath his nose. "Not quite as simple to conceal as this bit of silver, Don Valencia. Then you must do this and thus before the ore becomes a coin you may hold in your purse and spend. But it's a brilliant plan, my lord," she said, mocking him. "So long as the king's men don't notice the steady disappearance of several tons of ore, and so long as no one takes issue with your heaps of ore and your stoves and dyes, and so long as the king's counters accept your counterfeit coins. If you can manage all that—then you will be rich."

She made it sound insurmountable. Fernando stared at her. "What would you have me do?" he asked finally. "Refuse the post?"

"Do that and you are ruined," she snapped. "Philip deceives himself that his viceroys profit from initiative, not graft. He chooses to believe he is surrounded by honest men. So what would you tell him? 'I'm sorry, Your Majesty, but there isn't enough corruption in Peru to make a post there worth my while?' Refuse his 'reward' and your career falls to ashes."

"Then it appears we have no choice, my sweet. The king

will dispatch us to New Spain directly after we return with the casket."

She stared at him. "But if we don't return with the casket?"

"We'll end on the rack." The conversation disturbed him greatly. Though it pained his honor, he had to admit Catlina had scored some sobering points. "Perhaps we . . ."

"Be quiet and let me think."

Fernando didn't like her tone, but he did respect her cunning. Swallowing his pride, he watched her fling herself across the bed quilts and glare at the curtains. Then, he opened the chamber door and, as expected, discovered the innkeeper and the serving wenches gathered on the staircase staring up at him. Accustomed to Catlina's tempers and their aftermath, Fernando silently upended his purse above the innkeeper's outstretched hand.

"We'll have wine and cheese served in our chamber," he said without expression. "We'll require a fresh pitcher, a tray, goblets, and utensils." He suspected they would not be departing tonight. "Cancel our coach and order it up for first light. Before morn, place the following items outside our chamber door. A hand glass—something ornamented that a woman of quality will admire—a pot of red rouge, a decanter of ambergris, a basin, and a wig stand." His gaze was cool. "These items are not to be salvaged from the courtyard, but replaced anew." The innkeeper nodded, and Fernando stepped back into the chamber, kicking aside fragments of crockery.

"You remembered the ambergris?" Catlina asked. She lay on the bed, turning the silver casket between her hands.

"Have I ever forgotten?" She had fitted the key into the casket lock and was picking idly at the blue sealing wax on either side of the key. Fernando wet his lips. Though he couldn't precisely recall the glories of Peru, he could recall exactly the king's vivid description of the torments in wait should eyes other than his own examine the contents of the casket.

Catlina regarded him above the gleam of silver. "Have you asked yourself what is inside, Nando? What is so important about this casket that you and I risk our lives to secure it?"

"Letters." She was making him nervous as hell. "Letters to restore the honor of God and Spain."

"But do we know that for a fact? Perhaps there is nothing within but a copy of Lady Leicester's household accounts. Have you considered that possibility?" She ran a slender finger across the etched lid.

He watched her finger slide back and forth, hypnotized by the motion, fascinated as a bird is fascinated by the swaying seduction of a viper. "No," he murmured, following the stroke of her fingertip. "We can't. Don't even think about it."

"Perhaps," she murmured, her voice low and seductive, "perhaps if we knew what these letters contained we could perceive a way to better our situation."

"It's the rack if the casket is opened," he reminded her. His voice thinned and he swallowed. "Catlina, give me the casket, I beg you. What you suggest is madness."

"The rack," she mused, wrapping her finger around the key. Her dark lashes lifted, shadowing her cheeks. "*If* we return to Spain."

"If?" He stared into her sparkling eyes and considered. "The Inquisition has long arms," he said finally.

"And a long list of heretics to occupy them."

"They never forget."

"We will be clever." Her gaze dropped to his mouth and her lips formed into a sultry pout. "Would you consign me to mud and mosquitoes, sweet Nando? Would you see me old before my years? With sun-baked skin like leather? With breasts like empty sacks?"

"No," he said roughly.

She turned the key back and forth in the lock, looking from the casket to his face. "Then let us seize the opportunity at hand. What has value for Spain and England will have value elsewhere as well . . ."

Beads of perspiration rose like pearls on his brow. Clenching his jaw, he paced the chamber, heedless of the crunch of glass beneath his boots. She was shrewd and clever, he gave her that. He would not have thought of such a plot. Fernando turned it in his mind. She was correct regarding the casket's value. It could be bartered for untold riches. Something better than the desolation of Peru. He saw now that Philip had insulted him, had thought to sully the House of Valencia by exiling him to a poor and paltry post. Had he flourished his vanity and sailed grandly to western New Spain, the grandees would have laughed behind their hands. They would have dismissed him for a fool. As Philip obviously had done.

"Open it," he said harshly.

The night was bitter cold. Before the town crier sang the midnight hour, a thin crust of frost had formed on the windowpanes. Nell pulled another quilt over Will. He turned in restless dreams and muttered something about a Scottish toad. A moment later he startled her by sitting upright, looking at her, and saying, "Melon-sized breasts, by God," then he fell back on the bed and slept.

Nell looked down at herself. The stiff, flat bodices decreed by fashion pretended women had no breasts. Melon-sized or pebble-sized, it was all the same to fashion. She ranked somewhere in between, she thought with a frown. Not of a size to be compared to melons.

"Kate," he muttered. "Katie girl."

Kate? Who did he dream of? Was it Kate who possessed the melon-sized breasts? Listening, Nell waited to learn more, but was rewarded only by a low snore.

Raising a hand and sighing, she covered her eyes. Long ago the village lights had winked out across Calais. Silence hung heavy and burdensome, clearing a path to unwelcome thoughts. Her mind wandered a night forest peopled by unlikely companions. Elizabeth, who wanted her dead; Robert Dudley, whose ring she wore and who had left a vacancy in her heart; Edward, poor Edward, a man few mourned; A.B., the mother in her locket whom she would ever seek and never know; Lord Thomas, Earl of Mendenshire, whose home and fortune she coveted; and Will Steele, the rogue who had become so important in her life so quickly.

She looked at him, listened to his breathing, then she hitched her stool into the pool of candlelight beside his bed. If there was any ease to be found in her current circumstance, it was the knowledge that Will would not slay her on Elizabeth's command. Had the Spaniards wished to break open the casket, they would have done so at once. But they had not. It was reasonable to assume Philip, like Elizabeth, had commanded the casket be delivered with seals intact.

But this did not resolve Nell's trouble with Will Steele. Lord Thomas's fortune lay like a sword between them. In that regard nothing had changed. In the cold night silence the echo of Will's words sounded in her ear. "You are not entitled to Lord Thomas's fortune. I am." And, "I swore on my sword."

The broken axle rose large in her thoughts.

If she was to protect her life by striking first, she considered, studying his sleeping face, fate could not have offered her a better opportunity. All she need do was to open the window and remove his quilts. By morn he would be wracked with fever. His death would surprise no one; her name would not be sullied by scandal. The innkeep would swear Steele was dying when he returned to the inn. The plot was tidy and simple. At its conclusion, Nell would be safe and Mendenshire House would be hers.

She turned the plot in her mind, seeking a flaw. Then, moving like a sleepwalker, she stood slowly and approached the frost-laced windows. The latch opened easily and the windows blew inward driven by an icy northern wind.

It was so effortless. So smooth and tidy. Turning to look at Will, Nell wrapped her arms around herself and shivered in the cold; her breath formed silvery puffs before her lips. She considered his quilts and told herself to pull them away. A flick of the wrist. One small swift gesture and she won.

But instead of moving, she stood as rooted and a thin patina of perspiration broke over her body. A tremor began at her toes and swept upward. "Dammit, it's Steele or you," she muttered between clenched teeth. "Do it!"

But her feet refused to carry her to his bed. She shivered in the flow of icy wind like a crack-brain, as if it were she courting chilblains and fever. Finally, she spun and slammed the windows shut with an impatient motion, infuriated by her weakness.

Returning to the illusion of warmth provided by the bedside candle, she dropped onto the stool and closed her eyes. The deed was ill timed, thus her hesitation. She still needed Will Steele to assist in the recovery of the casket. When they had the casket, then she would strike. Abandoning the plot had naught to do with weakness, particularly not with affection. It had to do with expediency. Opening her lashes, Nell gazed at his sleeping innocence.

"Sweet enemy," she sighed, gently brushing a lock of hair from his forehead. Sweet? Will Steele, sweet? The sound of her laughter was harsh and overloud in the silence.

"Kate?" he murmured at her touch.

Frowning, she watched him settle back into a restless sleep. Not that it mattered, but she wondered who this Kate might be. A lover? If so, she thought, recalling Mary, Lady Bledsoe, it must be a lover from the far past. Either that or Will Steele played fast and loose with his affection.

After considering what she knew of his character, Nell eventually concluded Steele was unlikely to be frivolous with his affections. A lout he might be, but he took a northern lord's pride in his loyalty and steadfast nature. His affections would be as fierce as his hatreds. Uncomfortable with the thought, Nell decided Will Steele would be a devoted lover. Therefore, Kate must be a shadow from his past. Not that it was of any concern to her. For all Nell cared, Kate could be in Carlisle now, breathlessly awaiting Steele's return.

In view of Lady Bledsoe, Nell didn't think this was the case. But if it was—she didn't care a whit. It was nothing to her. Her only interest in Will Steele focused on the silver casket. True, she had experienced a slight—a very slight—softening toward him, but that was to be expected in view of their enforced proximity. 'Twas only the situation, not an inclination.

After a time she eased his hand from beneath the quilt and measured her own slim palm against his greater expanse. She traced the callouses on the pads beneath his fingers. The night was long and she had little to occupy her time, thus she excused this twiddle of foolishness. But she smiled when his hand instinctively curled around hers.

By clasping his hand in her lap, she felt oddly comforted and eventually was able to sleep.

Catlina's eyes captured the light cast by the branch of candles and flashed excitement. This was undoubtedly the most fortunate night of her life. The letters were priceless, beyond mortal value. Better than she had dared dream.

"Do you realize what this means?" she asked, her voice awed and breathless with elation. "With these three letters, we hold the queen of England in our hands." Stretching out her arm, she slowly curled her fingers into a fist. "You and I, Nando, can decide the future of England!"

"If they mean what it seems . . ."

"Oh, they do, my sweet, they assuredly do." Her dark eyes glowed. "I think Henri, Duc of Guise, will pay dearly, *most* dearly, to crush England in his palm. With these letters, he can expose Elizabeth to world ridicule, he can create chaos in England."

"But Guise, my love? If France is to have this treasure, why not the king?"

"The king is finished, he's fled to Blois." She dismissed the Valois king with Castilian contempt. "Guise holds Paris and if the people have their way—which Guise will see to—the king will soon abdicate in Guise's favor. Henri will be the next king of France; he'll wear the crown before the turn of the year. We sell to the power, Nando, not to the pawn."

Bending over the bed, she collected the scattered pages and read them through again. It wasn't until the third reading that her eyes widened and she stared into space, remembering, thinking it through. Swiftly, she shuffled the pages of the letters until she found what she sought then laughed aloud in triumph sweeter than any she'd experienced.

"Lady Amesly!" she cried, falling back into the pillows and hugging the letters to her breast. "Now I understand. She knows; she must. And that's why she must have the letters, is desperate to have them!" Her excitement was almost too great to contain. Catlina tossed the pillows into the air and laughed with joy as the plot formed. This would double, no triple, the price she could extract from Guise. "Don't you see, Nando? It wasn't a bruise!"

Fernando frowned. "What are you talking about?"

"Listen . . ."

When she finished explaining, he stared into her sparkling eyes and spoke in a stunned whisper. "Holy Mother of God!"

CHAPTER 11

Hens and gamecocks pecked about the cobbled courtyard where Nell stood. Near the innyard stables a glossy black and white cow awaited milking. One of the cookhouse sculls knelt beside barrels of salted cod, scrubbing brass pots with straw and ash. Enough traffic passed in and out of the inn gate, enough carts and coaches crowded the lane, that Nell could conduct her business with confidence that she would not be overheard.

Even so, despite the noise, Will's bellow could be heard from above. Nell grimaced and glanced toward his window then counted the agreed-upon coins into the soiled palm of the man she had hired.

He was wharf tough, scarred, and rank smelling, but she hadn't hired him for his beauty. He was also of a type to melt into the surroundings, and she watched him vanish between the horses and vehicles without regret. Though he'd served her well. Holding her cloak tight against the cold winds blowing in from the Channel, Nell reflected upon the information she had purchased, then she lifted her skirts and entered the common room, pausing to order Will's midday meal.

"Where have you been?" he demanded when she entered his chamber followed by the serving girl bearing his tray. Before she could respond, his brows bristled and his roar rattled the win-dowpanes. "Give me my pants, woman! Now. This instant!"

"In due time," Nell replied. She took the tray and dismissed the serving girl.

"Return my pants or so help me Christ, I'll walk out of here in my skin!"

She set the tray on the quilt above his lap firmly enough to send his eyebrows soaring. "You'll have your hose and your stocks on the morrow. Now eat."

"In the morn?"

"Aye."

"Well, thank God. What happened to finally make you see reason?" Will asked sourly. He bit into a pheasant leg. "Did some inspired person knock you over the head? Have the Spaniards ar-rived safely in Madrid and it's suddenly occurred to you that we may have lost the casket for good and all?"

Nell scowled. There was nothing under heaven more trying than a bedridden man. The past four days had severely strained her good opinion of humanity as a whole and of Will Steele in particular. If she had a shilling for each time she had tripped up and down the staircase at his bidding, she wouldn't need to wed Lord Thomas, she could purchase a kingdom of her own. She stared at him and sincerely regretted not dispatching him when she'd had the opportunity.

"As it happens," she said thinly, "the Spaniards departed Calais only hours ago."

Interest sparked his dark eyes. "How do you know they only just departed?"

Patience, Nell told herself, patience. "The day you were wounded I hired a footpad to find the Spaniards and spy on them. They lingered in Calais. I don't know why." But she could guess. The Spaniards had waited to discover if Will would live or die. No doubt they too had engaged a spy. "They hired a scarlet coach and took the road to Paris. At first light this morn."

"A *scarlet* coach? to *Paris*?" Will stared. "Are you soul certain your man is reliable?"

"Aye."

"Paris? It doesn't credit."

Nell nodded slowly, turning the information in her mind. "Perhaps Paris isn't as passing strange as first appears," she said finally, thinking aloud. "The Duc of Guise controls Paris, and Guise is in Spain's pay. Although there's talk Guise chaffs beneath Philip's rein and would free himself."

"You've had your ear to the ground, haven't you, Grandmother?" For the first time since discovering his nakedness, a spark of admiration warmed Will's gaze.

"Guise is expected to depose the Valois king and seize the crown. At present the duc is king in all but name. Our Spaniards may seek to benefit from Guise's friendship with Philip and request his protection. Mayhaps they hope for a military escort to the Pyrenees."

Absently, Will stroked the stubble on his chin. "If Guise enters the game, the rules change. The man's a fanatic." He bit into the pheasant and chewed thoughtfully. "Nay, Nellie, this tune doesn't play," he said finally. "Nothing you've suggested makes weight against the urgency of getting the casket to the king. The Spaniards should be running along the coast as they did before."

"I know," Nell conceded. The point worried her greatly. She raised a hand, anticipating his next words. "Nay, m'lord, we'll not leap up and pursue this instant. You need one more day of rest. You're still weak."

"Weak? If I'm weak, 'tis only because you have me trussed up like a hare in a bin," he bellowed, instantly affronted. "Return my stocks and you'll see how weak I am! I'm brim as an ox, woman. Strong enough to overtake the scurvy bastards before nightfall!"

"One more day of bedrest. Then you'll be mended for travel." Folding her hands in her lap, Nell calmly ignored the explosion of oaths.

His wounds continued to seep some, but the seep showed no signs of corruption. Healing had begun. Nell would have preferred to keep him abed another day; however, though he refused to credit it, she too was anxious to resume pursuit. The pinnace waiting off Bayonne would wait only six days more. If the pinnace returned to London without them, two unpleasant events would result: Elizabeth would believe they had failed in her charge, and they would be stranded in France carrying expired passes. Even now, Nell couldn't bear to have Elizabeth believe her faith in Nell had been misplaced.

"You needn't argue," she said firmly, the words a greater effort than he could know. "It's decided. I've arranged a coach for cock's crow. The roads are dry; we'll travel hard and fast, we'll eat and sleep in the coach."

"God's blood, woman! Another lunatic coach?" Disgusted, he hurled the pheasant bone across the chamber. "We should leave now. On horseback."

"On the morrow. By coach." She smiled plesantly. "This is a dispute and by the queen's command . . ."

"Where did you hide my bloody stocks? I demand that you fetch them this instant!"

"Let's see, how shall we pass the afternoon? Would you care to throw cards or play chess?" They had played a hundred rounds of cards and she'd beaten him neatly, discovering he played a conservative wager whereas Nell preferred high stakes and skillful bluffs. On the other hand, she had yet to best him at chess, a defeat that annoyed her tremendously.

"I want my clothes." Angry spaces punctuated the words. "Look at the calendar, Grandmother. Examine the date on your port pass. Think of Bayonne. Try to locate a grain of logic somewhere under your hair."

Nell ground her teeth. "This is a dispute," she repeated. "And I am exercising my prerogative. You get your clothes on the morrow, not a moment sooner. The subject is closed, m'lord."

He folded his arms across his chest, the muscles cording and jumping. "You are a damned irritating woman. Stubborn, high tempered, shrewish, and lacking the sense God granted an ant." He glared at her from beneath heavy brows. "I'll wager your sire or your dam was a full-blooded Scots!"

"I don't know if they were or not." Accusing her of possessing Scots blood was the worst insult he could fling. What he didn't realize was that Nell wouldn't have cared a feather if her parents were Scots. "I haven't a notion who my parents were. Uncle Robert purchased my wardship from the master of the wards when I was little more than an infant." Unconsciously, she pressed the locket beneath her bodice then picked up her embroidery hoop and held the needle to the light.

She had stitched the banks of a wide mere before Will made an explosive sound and dropped back against the straw pillows. Finally, resigned, he spoke. "Your parents were wealthy, then?"

Nell lifted her head. "Whatever gave you that idea?"

"Why else would Dudley purchase your wardship unless it included lucrative lands?"

"I came with nothing. Not a shilling. And I resent your implication. Robert Dudley was an honorable and charitable man. He sought no gain from me."

Will's laugh was genuinely amused. "Leicester? Charitable? The Earl of Leicester, your 'Uncle Robert,' was a scheming, greedy scoundrel who never performed a single action in his selfish life unless it benefited him four ways to Sunday."

"I'll not hear that sort of slander," Nell said sharply, her face paling. "Uncle Robert treated me as a daughter. Whether you credit it or not, Robert loved children."

"I can't doubt it. Not when he devoted himself to creating them at every opportunity."

"You prove my point, Sir, though that was not your intent. Uncle Robert loved Lettice's children and myself as his own, and at no profit to himself."

"Nay, the only person Leicester loved was Leicester."

"You deceive yourself. Can you doubt he loved the queen?" Embroidery forgotten, Nell clasped Robert's signet so tightly, when she lifted her hand the ragged staff and bear were stamped upon her palm.

"He loved her favors more. Leicester set his sights on a crown. He would have romanced a gnome if she could have given him the crown of England."

"You don't know what you're saying. Uncle Robert loved the queen from childhood. He was devoted to her! And she loved him."

"You create a mirage because it pleases you, m'love. If Elizabeth loved Leicester, it was the love one bears a predictable and well-trained pup. Dudley flattered her vanity and was well rewarded for possessing a gilded tongue. As he expected to be. As for Elizabeth, the old girl kept her pup docile by dangling the crown and watching his tail wag. Occasionally she tossed him a lucrative sop. But it was the crown Dudley lusted for, not she who wears it."

Nell stared. "Robert Dudley earned his titles and favors through his love and his unquestioning loyalty to the queen. He waged war for her, championed her; he would willingly have died for her. Robert Dudley, Earl of Leicester, was kind, generous, charitable, and loyal. How dare you undermine his motivations!"

"Did he indeed possess those qualities, m'love? Then what of his unfortunate first wife, Amy Robsard? Found dead at the foot of a staircase under mysterious circumstances? At a most convenient time for Leicester, I might add. And what of the bastard he sired on Lady Sheffield, and the sham wedding he contracted with her? Was that admirable? Or the abortion he procured for Lettice when she inconveniently became seeded during her husband's absence? And her husband, Lord Essex, suspiciously deceased when Leicester's eye fell upon Lettice. And what of his many, many military debacles?"

"Stop this!" Nell covered her ears and closed her eyes. "You've bent an ear to malicious gossip put about by those seeking to discredit a great man. It's all lies! Lies!" Opening her eyes, she stared at him and her voice sank. "Whatever else he might have been, Robert Dudley was my only family and I loved him. If you wish to strike out at me, then do so, my lord. But don't seek to wound me by maligning a man you scarcely knew."

In the ensuing silence they heard carts rattling over the cobbles in the lane beneath the window, an oyster wife hawking her wares. Laughter and the clank of tankards rose from the common room below.

"You credit me rightly," Will said finally. "For which I apologize."

"Uncle Robert was a good man!"

"To inspire such loyalty there must have been more to Leicester than met the eye," Will observed cautiously. Plainly he was doubtful. "It's evident you cared greatly for the bast . . . for him. You miss him, aye?"

Nell tilted her head toward the rafters and sighed. "Aye." Occasionally in the rush of events Uncle Robert moved to the back shadows of her mind. Other times, like now, her loss felt as green as when she'd first learned of his death. She turned his ring on her finger and nodded. "Aye."

"Tell me about the Leicester you knew. What was it like—the legendary Kenilworth?"

Will's intent was as obvious as the dark growth stubbling his chin. He sought to extend his apology by inviting her to discharge her resentment in speech.

Because her temper ran high, Nell seized the opportunity and extolled Robert Dudley's virtues, taking a wicked pleasure in the effort it cost Steele to remain silent.

As she spoke, images of childhood skimmed her mind, no less painful for the passage of years. Succumbing to the echoes of memory, she forgot Will, didn't realize the focus of her remembrance had drifted.

She spoke quietly of standing outside the family group unless Uncle Robert were present to draw her within the circle, which hadn't occurred as often as she would have liked as he frequently was summoned away on the queen's business. More often Nell remained apart, watching Lettice pamper and pet and gossip with her own daughters, Penelope and Dorothy, reserving her impatience and irritation for Nell. She remembered seldom having a new gown but wearing Penelope's castoffs. Being excluded when suitors came to call, overlooked when gifts were distributed on New Year's Day. She remembered being ill with no one but old Mother Jamison to sit beside her bed.

No resentment or bitterness disturbed her expression, for long ago Nell had scorned the notion of self-pity. God dealt the cards and one played the hand one was dealt. It availed naught to rail against the luck of the throw. She had examined her cards and been grateful she hadn't drawn worse. There was much for which to be thankful.

She had spent nine years at court at the center of the English universe. At age eighteen she had married Edward, not an exciting man, not a marriage conceived in heaven, but she had been content. Edward hadn't given her children or a stable home, but he hadn't beaten her either, nor had he flaunted his mistress. They had enjoyed two years of marriage pleasantly founded on mutual indifference.

"My only regret," she said in conclusion, "lies in not knowing my mother. I've missed her so." Now she raised her eyes to Will. "I envy you your lady mother. There are no gaps in your history, no blank spaces. You know who you are and from whence you sprang."

Sudden embarrassment flooded her cheeks with high color. Jesu, had she taken leave of her senses? What was she thinking of? She'd laid herself bare before a man who would one day run her through. She, who should have known better, had succumbed to the intimacy of a sick room. She fervently wished she could recall her words and restore her privacy.

"Some say I sprang from an English sot and an Irish whore."

He hadn't spoken in so long his voice startled her. Bending, Nell retrieved her embroidery hoop and pushed the needle through the linen with a short, impatient motion. "So. What was it like for you? Growing up?" One confession merited another.

"Carlisle was created for small lads with big dreams." Will smiled, watching her needle flash in the chill light. "Ships from far lands bob in her harbor, Roman ruins invite imaginative battles. There's a castle on the hill, crumbling now, and fish to catch, stones to throw. And always a nearby Scots to blood a young man's sword."

As he spoke, soon snared by memory as she had been, Nell turned her hoop in her hands and listened quietly.

Through his remembrance she envisioned Will as a lad tilting wooden swords at straw bales, falling out of trees, proudly riding off to his first border raid. She learned of the scars on his chest, struck there by thieving Scots, and of his lady mother's tender concern. In his voice she heard the fiercely protective pride of northern lords for land and family. And she envied him this. Nell began to understand the war he waged against Scotland as she heard the list of kin and friendships torn asunder by Scottish hostilities, heard the roster of dead buried in the Carlisle yard. His service in the low country with Leicester and the weeks camped beside the Thames waiting for the Spaniards seemed incidental. Will Steele's heart and his war focused on the Scottish border.

"I wish to Christ this casket business was finished. The winter stores should be in, the slaughtering done and the smokehouse filled. Old Middlemast needs keep a sharp watch or James Poole will poach my forest clean. If the Scots leave a sheep to breed by, I'll count myself damned fortunate!"

"Well," Nell commented, surprised that she regretted the end of his story. She noticed he had made no mention of Kate. "We'll be riding for Bayonne a few days hence, the casket in hand."

They regarded each other soberly, their expressions reflective, then both became aware of the fading light.

"Jesu! I should have changed your dressings long ago!" Setting aside her embroidery, Nell hastily assembled a basin of water, unguents, and fresh bandages before seating herself at the edge of his bed. "Lie back and let me see your side."

Will crossed his arms behind his head and a smile broadened to a grin as Nell gingerly lowered the quilt to his waist and, carefully, no further. "Was it you who removed my stocks and hose, love?"

" 'Twas the innkeep," she said, not looking at him.

Her fingers brushed his skin, warm in the chill air, as she untied the band circling his lower ribs. She tossed aside the soiled pad beneath. To her annoyance her fingers trembled slightly as she fashioned a fresh pad from the cloth on the tray. She refused to meet his eyes, and she did not cast so much as a glance at the line of crisp hair tapering down beneath the quilt edge. Leaning over him, feeling his hip against her thigh, she pressed the fresh pad over his wound and fumbled to tie the band in place.

"That first night," he said quietly, watching her. "I dreamed you kissed me."

Her fingers jumped and twin circles of pink bloomed on her

cheeks. Nell wet her lips and frowned. "Dreams are passing strange, m'lord."

"I dreamed you touched my face and kissed me many times. Dreamed you took my hand and pressed it to your breast."

" 'Tis a warm night for this time of year." And close. Odd she hadn't noted it earlier. And why couldn't she tie the wretched bandage? Her fingers had turned to sticks of straw.

"Later I dreamed I held you in my arms and loved you. Cupped your breasts in my hands and sucked the tips to hard little buttons."

Nell drew a quick breath. A stirring beneath the quilt caught her attention, so near she had only to shift her hand to press it. The colors of the quilt spun before her vision. Her breath released in a shallow rush and her skin felt suddenly moist and overwarm. She bit her lip and straightened, leaning toward the tray.

"Turn on your stomach," she said too quickly. "I'll change the bandage on the back of your head." Her voice sounded choked.

"I'm too weak, m'love. It seems you were right after all. You'll have to reach around."

If the task was ever to be finished, no profit lay in arguing. Frowning, Nell reached for the knot on his forehead and her fingers stumbled to untie it. "I thought you were brim as an ox," she said, staring fixedly at the scurvy bandage as if intent would melt the stubborn knot.

"You smell of honey and roses."

"My lord, please." Briefly, Nell closed her eyes. But she felt his stare plundering her mouth, traveling slowly over her face and breast. She sensed his nakedness and heat. And her own pulse fluttered wildly at the base of her throat. "Turn over, I beg you. I can't reach around, I . . ."

"Kiss me, Nell."

"My lord . . ."

"Kiss me as you did that first night."

Something strange was happening to her. A moist heat ignited in her secret places, a sweet ache trembled between her thighs. When she opened her lashes and looked down into his dark eyes, sudden weakness robbed her limbs of strength. "Please, Will," she whispered. "No . . . ."

Lightly his fingertips traced the curve of her cheek, followed the line of her throat to the edge of her lace ruff. His mouth lay inches beneath hers. And his eyes, his intent dark eyes, drew her, compelled her. A strange warm lassitude sapped her resistance.

Slowly, as if enchanted by the stroke of his fingertips, by the depth of his gaze, Nell lowered her lips and pressed them to his. And it was right, so right, that a sound midway between a sigh and a sob broke from her throat as his arms encircled her.

"Nell." He spoke against her trembling mouth, his breath warm and scented of wine. "Nell."

His kisses were soft, controlled, and gentle. As light as a whisper across her lips, her temples, her eyelids. And because her curiosity had tormented her throughout the last days, because now curiosity had ignited to urgency, she pressed her palm to his cheek and smiled at the scratch of new beard against her skin. Her shaking hand moved down and she drew a quick breath to discover the hair on his chest was as soft as forest moss, cushioning her palm from his hard heat. She followed the triangle of dark hair until her fingers bumped the edge of the quilt and she heard his sharp intake of breath.

And then she no longer wanted gentle kisses. Her mouth found his and opened beneath his tongue, her fingers dug into his naked shoulders and her breath burned in her throat. When his hand slid to mold her breast, she arched against him and a soft moan issued from her lips.

"Every time I look at you, I want you," he whispered hoarsely. "Day after day I've lain here, wanting to taste you, touch you, feel you under me."

God help her, she wanted him too. Once in her life, Nell wanted to experience the passion she had sensed in others. Wanted, just once, to offer herself without reservation but with urgency and joy. But such an act was lunacy. She was mad to consider it. "No," she whispered, her reluctance genuine. She wet her lips and firmed her resolve then eased from his arms.

"Can you deny that you . . . ?"

Quickly she placed her fingertips across his lips. "I'll not deceive you, Will Steele. I . . . I've passed a fancy in your direction." She looked into his eyes, knowing her own gaze contained a contrary mix of need and regret, desire and dismay. "Will you send me from your bed to that of your grandfather?" she asked quietly. " 'Twould be incest." The law would view it so.

"Nell . . ."

"Nay, my lord. Not Nell—Grandmother."

Swiftly, while her resolve held, Nell stood from his bed and let herself into the corridor, closing his door behind her. Then she leaned against it and closed her eyes. Tears stung her lids and a growing confusion made chaos of her heart.

Once they were away from the coastal shores, the bitter cost of France's wars of religion became increasingly evident. Though the greater part of the fighting occurred to the South, the North had been raided for food and supplies. Occasionally entire villages had been stripped of their menfolk, conscripted as fodder for Catholic or Huguenot ranks. Nell watched through the coach window as they passed through villages populated largely by dispirited women and hungry-eyed children.

Shaken by the poverty, she looked at Will who was seated across from her. "The parson was correct," she said, referring to the parson with whom they had shared the journey to Calais. "France can't bear much more."

"But where does France look for salvation? The Valois king?"

Nell's mouth twisted. "He springs from corrupt seed." She agreed with Elizabeth in scorning de' Medici blood, and the present king was the worst of a bad lot. Henri Valois's degeneracy was legion. It was accepted he would never sire an heir, preferring the beds of his painted mignons to that of his queen or any other woman.

"Guise, then?"

"Guise is strong where Henri Valois is weak. If Guise seizes the French throne and remains allied with Spain . . ." Nell frowned. Such a possibility bode ill for England. "Guise will not be content with France. Soon he would cast his gaze across the Channel."

"Nellie love . . ."

She read in his eyes that his thoughts had shifted from politics. Quickly, before he could speak further, Nell waved a hand and observed, "We're making excellent time, are we not? And this time the roads are dry."

But the journey could hardly be said to pass in comfort. Stony rutted roads cut through the fields, tossing Nell and Will about the coach like dice in a cup. They had passed a fitful night, clinging to the straps and trying to doze between posthouse stops to change horses and coachmen. At each halt, Will asked after the Spaniards' scarlet coach. As punishing a pace as Will and Nell endured, the Spaniards maintained their lead.

"We'll catch them," Will said, but he didn't sound as assured as Nell would have preferred.

Knowing he itched to proceed on horseback, she curbed a sharp reply born of exhaustion and anxiety. But she was worried. As she gazed from the coach window, watching stubbled fields through clouds of cold dust, Nell berated herself for not departing earlier, for not trapping the Spaniards in Calais, for a dozen lapses real and imagined. She suspected that locating the Spaniards in Paris would be like seeking a needle in a forest, but Paris it would be, for hope of overtaking them on the road had begun to wane.

Heedless of crushing her hat, she dropped her head to the back of the seat and longed for a hot bath and a soft bed. Reddish-gray dust churned up by the wheels and hooves powdered their hat brims and collected in the dark folds of Nell's skirts. By the time they stopped briefly for the evening meal, her throat was parched and her skin felt gritty.

The posthouse sat at the edge of a barley field, surrounded by outbuildings showing evidence of neglect and hard times. The interior was dark and smoky and smelled of onions and sour rushes. But the fire crackled hot and cheerful and the local ale, while weak, refreshed Nell's raw throat. When Will joined her for a meal of bread and a thin vegetable stew, she studied the lines drawing his mouth.

"Are you feeling well?"

An oath accompanied his glare. "I'm a soldier, m'love. Not a pup to be fussed and frothed over!"

"You were also recently wounded and bedridden," Nell snapped, her patience drawing tight.

The tart exchange was the first since beginning the race toward Paris. Despite an underlying tension, they had treated one another with excessive politeness. Each had avoided topics known to be disruptive; they had scrupulously respected the limited space, choosing opposite corners on opposite seats. Endeavoring to pass the time as pleasantly as possible had reaped unforeseen rewards. To Nell's surprise they discovered a mutual passion for falconry, a shared pleasure in the hunt, an affection for reading history on a wintry night.

"I apologize," Will said abruptly.

"What you need, I'll warrant, is a Scotsman," Nell observed, tilting her head.

A rush of pleasure softened Will's expression. It wasn't often a woman comprehended a man's need for activity. "Aye." It would settle his thoughts and improve his spirits to beat the bloody hell out of a Scots. A pity one wasn't about.

"I apologize too," Nell added after a moment.

Looking at her across the trenchers, he saw the exhaustion shadowing her eyes and liked her for not complaining. Not once had she scorned the paltry fare when they stopped to sup, nor had she voiced dismay for the cold and dust. She'd been no more able to sleep than he, but she hadn't protested. She wasn't the court dainty he'd first believed himself burdened with, thank God. Like a gamecock, beneath the pretty plumage lay a fighting spirit.

"Had the Spaniards stopped at the posthouse?" Nell asked when they were again jolting through the hazy sunset.

"Aye." It frustrated him no end. The scarlet coach mounted wings in place of wheels.

"You're worried, aren't you?"

"We aren't following, Nellie love. We're being led."

The same discomfiting thought had occurred to her. "But why?"

"At first I suspected we were following a shill. We chase a scarlet coach while the Spaniards escape by another route."

"Aye. The tune plays. Should we turn back?"

He shook his head. "Nay. We're chasing the Spaniards. It's them all right; they've taken pains to confirm it. At the last post-stop our Fernando washed at the rain barrel, making certain the postman observed the scar on his shoulder. The bastard left us a portrait."

"Then the Spaniards want us in Paris."

"Count on it, love." He brushed the dust from his moustache and stretched his legs.

"The question is why."

"If I knew the answer we'd both rest easier."

They crossed the Somme at Amiens, passing in the shadow of Amiens's great Gothic cathedral to reach the gates where Will persuaded the watch to drop the night chains and allow them to pass. Beyond Amiens stretched open fields, occasionally a stand of winter-bared beech or oak, villages dark and shuttered against the night.

Near midnight, cold and bone rattled, Nell silently moved to sit beside Will, lifting her face in mute appeal. He opened his cloak and smiled as she pressed gratefully into his warmth.

"We won't reach Bayonne in time to meet the ship," she murmured against his shoulder.

"Nay." When she said nothing more, he wrapped his arm about her and closed his eyes.

A pale chill sun illuminated the unfortunate cathedral at Beauvais. As Catholic misfortune entertained the English court, Nell was aware the city fathers had attempted to build the largest cathedral in the world, higher than Notre Dame. To Elizabeth's great amusement, Beauvais's labor proved a disaster of miscalculation and collapse. After centuries of dogged determination, Beauvais had finally abandoned hope of completion when the cathedral's famed steeple had toppled to the ground fifteen years earlier. Nell related the story with relish.

South of Beauvais the posthouses offered poorer fare and the talk in the common rooms turned dispirited and sour. Even to a stranger, the absence of young men was all too apparent. Those remaining, too old or too halt to be of use, talked endlessly of politics. Depending on the sympathies of the village, they decried Catholic butchery or Huguenot savagery. They spit at the mention of the Valois king. And they became cautious and silent when Will and Nell entered for a bite and a pint, regarding them with poisonous suspicion.

Near Creil the coach passed two men hanging from a skeletal oak; a crude sign spiked to the trunk demanded: DEATH TO ALL HUGUENOTS. Farther south chalked phrases defaced walls, buildings, and road markers. PIKE THE VALOIS PIG. VIVE GUISE. And occasionally: THE RELIGION LIVES.

"I feel like a hare racing toward a fox's den," Nell murmured, sobered.

"We may have to hear a mass or two if our Paris sojourn proves lengthy," Will said, then grinned at her horrified expression. "Better a mass than a noose," he shrugged.

After a moment Nell nodded uneasily. It was one thing to discuss the French Wars while tipping cups in London. It was quite another to find herself in the scalding midst of it. She pulled back the window flap to stare at the charred remains of a village chapel and the bleached pile of human bones stacked before it. "This is insanity," she whispered. Suddenly she found herself in wholehearted agreement with Elizabeth's oft-stated opinion: "If one believes in God, the rest is of little consequence."

"It wouldn't be amiss, love, to cross yourself within sight of our next innkeep."

She did so at sunset when their coach skidded to a dusty halt at St. Denis and she saw a row of heads rotting atop the gate pikes.

Then they were crossing the plain between St. Denis and Paris, each spin of the wheel carrying them closer to a city in turmoil. What Huguenots remained in Paris did so in peril of their lives. The king had fled the city, barricades lined the streets.

And somewhere within the city walls the Spaniards waited.

CHAPTER

12

$\mathcal{N}$ot knowing what influence or letters of credit the Spaniard wielded caused Will no small concern. The first rule of war required identifying the enemy's strengths and weaknesses. Will hadn't learned nearly enough. At the moment he would have surrendered a quarter of his holdings to know if the Spaniard possessed French connections advantageous enough to influence the gate watch. Or to arrange men-at-arms on brief notice.

Reaching into his waist pouch, he withdrew their passes and showed them to Nell. "These identify us as Swiss." The name Gutland was certainly known to the Spaniard and, if the Spaniard had powerful connections, would most likely be known to the watch.

Nell gave him a thoughtful glance. "Most resourceful. I should have guessed you'd have a plan."

"One of limited value. The dates, unfortunately, are the same as for the Flemish passes." Unless they moved quickly in and out of Paris their passes would expire.

What he didn't tell her was that no plan would save them if the gate watch acted on orders to apprehend. Escape might have been possible had they been mounted on horseback, but not from a blasted coach.

In St. Denis Will had presented a heated argument for horses before exploding in frustration. Nell had flatly refused to abandon her baggage and coolly rejected his sensible suggestion that she wait behind. If she refused to act reasonably, then he had to admit her position possessed validity. A woman of quality traveling without baggage would elicit comment. This insistence ignored the logic that a man traveling alone on horseback would attract little or no attention. The problem, of course, was being burdened with a skirt in the first place.

Leaning from the coach window, he watched the guards approach, studying their halberds and swords in the light of the torches they held above their leather helmets. There were four. Had he not been caged inside the coach, Will could have fought them if necessary with every confidence of winning.

Instead, he gritted his teeth and extended the passes through the coach window, arranging his face in an expression of indifference. "Be quick about it, Monsieur," he said in passable French. "It's late and my wife is exhausted." He didn't know which smelled worse, the damp miasma rising from the swampy ground or the watchman who reeked of garlic and grime.

The odor intensified as the guard leaned to the window and cast an appraising gaze over Nell. "You are Frau Von Halen?"

"Ja."

Moving forward to block Nell from view, Will inquired, "Can you recommend a modest inn?" The shadows near the wall concerned him, but lay too deep to determine if anyone there paid them particular attention. Will scanned the foot traffic nearest the torches.

"There's a housing shortage in Paris. Haven't you heard? The king himself, God rot his painted soul, couldn't rent a bed in Paris."

"Then we'd best begin the search." Will rapped his knuckles on the coach roof. "Drive on, coachman."

Nell released a long, slow breath. "They weren't looking for us."

Perhaps; perhaps not. Will didn't respond. There was no profit in reminding her the Spaniards wanted them in Paris. Nor would it serve to voice his uneasiness at having passed the watch with so little difficulty. Nor did he wonder aloud if their coach was being followed.

He laid a finger against his moustache and examined the towers of the fortification walls that soared a deeper black against the night sky. He identified the distant spires of Notre Dame and torchlight flickering along the river banks. Otherwise little could be observed. Candles glowed behind tightly shuttered windows; Paris at night was blacker even than London but for an occasional street fire surrounded by hard-eyed men and women upon whom few would dare turn their backs.

He glanced at Nell and pressed his knuckles to his lips. He could have slipped into Paris alone, found the scurvy Spaniards, and been out in a day or so. A man alone didn't require an inn or a soft bed or cumbersome baggage. Alone, he could have moved in the shadows, attracted no notice. Alone, he could have accomplished the business. Silently he cursed Elizabeth Tudor for complicating a simple task, cursed Nell Amesly for her intractability, cursed womanhood for all its contrary manifestations.

He directed the coachman to halt before every inn then Will inquired within. After each query Will returned to the coach shaking his head. There were no rooms at the first two inns; men slept on the rushes in the common room. At a third, those gathered before the fire muttered darkly against Huguenot infidels while honing their blades. He found a room at the fourth inn, but no larger than a cell; its window opened over a reeking smallhouse and the pallets on the rushes jumped with fleas.

Wishing to Christ that he'd followed his instincts and trussed Nell up and left her in St. Denis, Will stepped outside yet another crammed inn and drew a breath. The promise of snow sharpened the night air. He watched a solitary flake drift toward the hat brim of the man blocking his path.

"I was reserving the chamber for the Duc de Porteau, but," the man winked and nudged his companion with an elbow, "it seems the duc has suffered a lover's quarrel with his petite amie." His sly look dipped into a scowl. "Now I have an empty room instead of the purse I have unfortunately already promised to my creditors."

Prompted by weariness and frustration, Will's instinct on overhearing the conversation was to interrupt and engage the vacant chamber. But he hesitated. Coincidence roused his suspicions. The Spanish woman impressed him as cunning enough to arrange such an opportune encounter. It could easily have been accomplished. Someone waiting at the city gate to follow them, and then, when the moment ripened, staging a conversation meant to be overheard. Against this weighed the likely possibility that the Spaniards were themselves seeking lodging and hadn't yet the time to instigate a plot.

Glancing across the cobbles, he studied Nell's anxious face peering from the coach window. The flambeaux flanking the inn's entrance illuminated shadows of fatigue bruising her eyes, the weary slope of her shoulders.

The man with the vacant room linked arms with his companion and nodded to Will. *"Pardon."* They stepped forward into the inky night.

"A moment, Monsieur," Will called, making his decision. If the Spanish woman intended to lead him to a particular address, she would not have waited until he'd first tried six inns. As he negotiated with Monsieur Marroux for the vacant chamber, Will grimly hoped he'd guessed correctly.

"Could this be a trap?" Nell asked when he had directed the coachman to the Rue de Bethisy and returned to his seat facing her.

"Aye."

She worried her lower lip between her teeth and regarded him in the passing flickers of torchlight. "But it might not be."

"Aye."

Before they alighted from the coach, she placed her glove on Will's sleeve and spoke in a low voice. "Will, I'm sorry. I should have waited at the posthouse outside Saint Denis. If you'd come alone . . ."

"I do wish you'd reached this conclusion sooner, Grandmother," he said as he swung her from the coach doorway and looked into her eyes. "Could I persuade you to depart for Saint Denis on the morrow?"

For a long moment Nell returned his gaze without speaking, remembering the torment of waiting while he chased the Spaniards to Eu. But he had succeeded without her. And he had returned for her.

"Aye," she said quietly, gripping his arm. "You'll run the course faster alone."

Relief flashed in a brief grin and he pressed her glove. "We'll pay for three nights as if we were staying. And we'll sign as man and wife. I want you where I can keep an eye on you."

"Aye."

"Aye?"

"I'm not a complete fool."

In truth Nell's nerves were scraped raw. Furtive shadows ran through the dark streets. Twice she had started at the wail of a woman's scream. While Nell comprehended she had much to fear from Will Steele, she also conceded her moment of peril would not occur until they had retrieved the casket. But she sensed the ugly mood of Paris and it unnerved her.

The city held its breath, awaiting but a spark to ignite an explosion. The Valois king had fled, Guise was king of Paris; everyone awaited the final clash. Will had repeated what he'd heard in the inns and Nell had seen for herself the chilling slogans chalked on the stones and buildings. Politics and religion made a charnel house of France. She took Will's arm and stayed at his side as they entered Monsieur Marroux's establishment.

The chamber Monsieur Marroux showed them proved a pleasant surprise. A small hot fire popped in the grate, the floor was bare but polished and clean, and the bed, though stuffed with straw, appeared wonderfully inviting to Nell's tired eyes.

"I'll want a tub in the morning," she instructed Monsieur Marroux. Had it not been after midnight and had she not been so bone weary, she would have insisted he fetch her the tub and hot water now. As it was, she doubted she could keep her eyes open long enough for the water to heat.

"Of course, Madame. Will there be anything else tonight?"

"Mulled wine. And something to eat," Will instructed.

"Of course." Monsieur Marroux withdrew.

The straw crackled under her weight as Nell sank to the edge of the bed and stared dully at her trunks. For her life, she couldn't recall in which trunk she'd packed her night-dress and cap. And the mulled wine, when it arrived, didn't clear her thoughts. Instead the sweet mixture shot to her head and she could scarcely prop open her eyes. Her voice had thickened with fatigue when she spoke to Will who stood beside the window. "What do you see?"

"The river. The Louvre, I think. More important, a roof-top below the window. In the event of trouble requiring a hasty exit, remember it."

She passed a hand over her eyes. "If it wasn't for me, you wouldn't be here. You'd bed down in some stable corner."

"Correct, m'love." His fingers brushed her throat and he smiled. "You're falling asleep where you sit."

What had been true a moment before became a lie the instant he touched her. The dullness fled Nell's gaze and an awareness of the chamber's intimacy straightened her spine. The bed upon which she sat suddenly assumed an importance beyond that of a moment past. She caught a breath and held it as he opened his waistcoat and unbuckled his sword, dropping both over the lid of a trunk.

Will poured more wine and raised the cup to his lips, halting as he caught sight of her stare. Jesu, but she had fine eyes. As cold and slate-colored as the North Sea when she was angry, as intractable as granite when she'd set her mind. And now . . . now filled with smoky speculation where he'd expected only fatigue. Those eyes told him something had altered.

Slowly he set aside the wine cup and his stomach tightened as she stood, her eyes holding his, her slender fingers trembling as she unclasped her shoulder rolls and pulled the ties to her sleeves.

"I think I . . ." Instead of finishing what she'd intended to say, she caught her lower lip between her teeth, looked at him with an odd combination of shy defiance, of invitation and challenge.

For a moment he believed she had failed to notice the dressing screen. Then his eyes narrowed. And he sucked in a breath when she stood before him in chemise and underskirt. She raised her lashes and looked at him and he understood this had naught to do with the dressing screen.

Without pausing to question his good fortune, he opened his shirt and dropped it at his feet, not taking his eyes from her. The chemise rounded her breasts to a tantalizing ripe promise, firelight tinted her skin in hues of rose and ivory. She raised her arms and pins scattered over the planks as her hair spilled like living flame to her waist.

"Come to me," he said, his voice thick. He ran his hands lightly up her arms. "You're trembling, love."

Instead of taking her immediately as he desired, Will reminded himself how skittish she was. Stroking her arms and murmuring against her hair, he drew her forward gently and pressed her against the length of his body. Not fully trusting what was happening, he tasted her parted lips and found there the surrender he'd hoped for.

Before she could change her mind, he swung her into his arms and carried her to the bed. And he examined her wide eyes as she turned her head on the pillow. Color burned on her cheeks and she lowered her lashes.

When he studied her again after removing his stocks and hose, she'd pulled the sheet to her breast and was looking up at him with an expression blending anxiety and expectation. Will had seen that look before. Had he not known better, he would have sworn she was a virgin.

But she'd been wed—and in her eyes he read the history of her marriage bed. At a glance he knew she had never been fully aroused, was inexperienced and uneasy. The woman dropping her lashes bore little resemblance to the woman he had first met. This woman, this lovely slender wraith trembling in his bed, was as vulnerable as the public Lady Amesly was not. The discovery surprised him and cast a different light on the matter. He stretched out beside her, feeling her tense, and gentled her as he would a nervous animal.

He kissed her and caressed her hair. "Nell," he said gently, lifting her chin to gaze into her face. "Are you certain this is what you want?"

"Aye. I've made up my mind." Beneath the sheet, she hitched up her underskirt, parted her thighs, then squeezed her eyes tightly shut.

Will stared down at her. Then he silently and soundly cursed the lout who had been her husband. Had Will entered her now as she clearly expected, he wagered he would have found her as dry as winter hay. Grinding his teeth, he tamped his own fires and stroked the tendrils away from her cheek, trailed his fingers down her throat and across her bared shoulders. Her eyes blinked open and she stared up at him when he lowered his mouth to hers. But he didn't kiss her. Instead he flicked his tongue to the corner of her lips, teasing, while he stroked her waist, easing her chemise upward with an agonizing lack of haste.

He slipped his hand beneath the thin material and covered her breast with his palm, brushing the nipple until it rose like a pink stone between his fingers and he heard her soft gasp. His mouth found the hollow at the base of her throat and he circled her skin with his tongue before dropping lower until he could gently suck her nipple through the cover of her chemise.

"What are you . . . ?" He listened to her voice, judging the throaty tone, the catch of surprise.

She bit off the words as he stroked the curve of her hip, followed the soft swell of her belly to the triangle between her thighs. He caressed her there, not hurrying, teasing her with heat and pressure until her hips lifted to him and she pushed against his hand, a gasp of surprise on her lips. His fingers explored her feathery down, trailed along the inside of her thighs until a rush of moist heat wet his fingertips. Still he didn't enter, but covered her mouth with his own, his hands moving over her, pulling her under him. He waited until her head thrashed across the straw pillow, waited until she writhed beneath him and arched upward, until he saw a glaze of passion blank her eyes. He waited until his own body's demands were a powerful ache.

Only then did he enter her and smile against her hair as she gasped his name and her fingernails raked across his shoulders.

Deliberately, he made himself delay still longer, moving in slow rhythmic strokes until a gloss of perspiration gleamed on her brow and her breasts were damp against his chest, until her hands and kisses were frenzied with need.

"Will!" She was panting, her breath emerged in short explosive bursts. "Something strange . . . I feel . . ."

Now he released the force of his passion and thrust into her with the urgency he had constrained. She met thrust for thrust and the honey scent of her consumed his mind, infused his senses. Her skin was like glowing satin beneath his hands, her breasts soft yielding mounds, her body filled with a wildness that matched his own. Her eyes flared wide and her head pressed back into the pillow and she tensed beneath him, expanded and contracted around him. A tiny scream rasped from her throat and her eyes went joyfully vacant. Only then did he satisfy himself.

When he raised his head from her shoulder, she was staring at him, her eyes soft and shining.

"I didn't know," she whispered. "Jesu! I didn't know!"

Will smiled, realizing he'd been a fool to suppose he lacked vanity. There were two accomplishments he high prized: a dead Scot and the look in the eyes of a well-pleasured woman. Pleased, he touched her cheek. "A taste of wine, m'love?"

"Aye." She jumped from the bed and poured cups of Vernage.

The urge to please would pass, he knew. The thought raised a rueful smile. By morning she would regain the sharp crystal edge he admired. But he admired this side of her as well. Tangled skeins of hair tumbled around her shoulders and down her back, drawing the firelight and glowing like silk. Her damp chemise molded perfect small breasts. The skin above the lace edging the chemise was still flushed with rose as delicate as the pink in her cheeks. She was lovely.

"Why did you change your mind?" he asked when she had served him wine and again lay at his side. Immediately he suspected he pressed his luck with such an ill-conceived inquiry. Good fortune was not to be questioned, but accepted with gratitude.

"I don't know." She spoke slowly, looking into her wine. "I just . . . I don't know."

As he'd guessed, it wasn't the answer he had hoped to hear. By now, he reminded himself irritably, he should have known she wasn't the sort to mouth empty flattery. Still, it would have set well to learn she'd been overcome by his charm, or had been moved to lust at sight of his smile. Something had swayed her. If he hoped to tumble her again, and he most fervently did, it would profit him to learn the trick of it.

"I think," she began, frowning. Her brow tightened in concentration. "I think I'm hoping to breed."

"What?" Wine sprayed from his lips and he stared at her. Until this moment he hadn't considered the consequences of their coupling. He should have discreetly asked if she'd placed a jasper stone under the pillow, or had taken the precaution of swallowing a dill seed.

Nell thought aloud. "I've always yearned for a child," she admitted quietly. He continued to look thunderstruck. "But I can't entirely credit the notion of cuckolding Lord Thomas."

"You plan to cuckold my grandfather?"

"I believe we just did. Lord Thomas and I are plight trothed. Still, that isn't the same as being wed, not exactly. Or do you think so?"

"Let me understand this—you want me to get you with child?"

Tilting her head to one side, Nell studied him. "Aye." The plan jelled in her mind and excitement sparkled in her eyes. "Aye! It's the perfect solution." Will stared at her as if she had abandoned her senses, and she laughed aloud. Turning to face him, Nell explained, knowing she had inadvertently outwitted him. "Will, you're the perfect person to sire Lord Thomas's heir. Don't you see? Then, when my child inherits, the fortune won't pass out of the Brampton family."

"I don't credit what my ears hear!"

"You can hardly object to my wedding Lord Thomas if your son or daughter will eventually inherit. This will honor your pledge to your lady mother as your issue will inherit Lord Thomas's fortune. The monument remains a problem, but . . ."

"Nell, do you hear what you're saying? If you breed off me, my son will grow up thinking his great-grandfather is his father." Will blinked and shook his head. "God's death! Legally, my son would be my uncle!"

"I believe it's possible that I can breed," Nell said, gazing at him with speculation in her eye. "I've heard of such things."

"Jesu! Will you stop looking at me like that? I feel like a lamb under a wolf's gaze."

"Barren women don't always remain barren following a second marriage." Nell firmed her chin stubbornly. "This would indicate it isn't always the fault of the woman."

Grabbing up the sheet, Will pulled it to cover his nakedness. "God's teeth!" There was a predatory gleam in her eye, a half-smile on her lips. "Jesu!"

"And," she added softly, playing her trump card, "even the Fighting Duke would not slay a woman carrying his child."

More wine slopped from his cup. "Slay you? For the love of Christ, woman, why would I slay you? We know the Spaniards won't open the casket."

His pretended innocence didn't deceive her. "Just remember this—it's possible I'm carrying your child." She didn't think so. Not yet. In her heart, Nell believed a woman knew when life quickened in her womb. But the suggestion gave her a shield. This she knew. She read it in his angry eyes. Laughing with pleasure and triumph, she slowly drew a fingertip across his shoulder. "Will?" Her gaze followed his long, hard outline beneath the sheet. And she smiled a woman's smile when she saw the stirring between his thighs.

"We're both tired," he protested, staring at her breasts as she bent over him and pressed her lips to his.

Nell breathed into his mouth, touched the tip of her tongue to the corner of his lips. "Do it again," she whispered. "Make it happen again."

"God's balls!" Her hands made shy overtures, pressing then

fluttering away. He couldn't take his eyes from her breasts. "You don't want a man, you want a bloody stud!"

"Do to me what you did before."

The scent of honey and roses blinded his senses. Her fingers followed the line of hair on his chest to the edge of the sheet then dropped lower and his thighs tensed in anticipation. He swore softly, cursing women and his own lamentable weakness. "At least take off that damned chemise thing!" She did, her movements graceful, innocently seductive, and he sucked in a sharp breath. "Jesu!"

"Show me what to do," she murmured, her mouth teasing down his chest.

Will groaned and buried his hands in her hair.

Nell yawned and stretched then smiled at the frost patterns sparkling pink on the diamond-shaped windowpanes. A cold pale sun edged above the horizon. The chamber was cold and Nell's breath hung before her lips as she had forgotten to bank the fire. She pressed against Will's back, absorbing his naked warmth.

Not even the chill dawn could chase the wonder from her heart. Pressing her forehead to the back of his neck, she touched his hip, lightly, not wishing to wake him. The firm smoothness of his skin assured her that she had not dreamed last night. Truly they had lain together. She had indeed tasted the fire and tempest of passion. Now she understood. In the past she had watched, incredulous, as friends cast caution to the wind and involved themselves in dangerous liaisons. She had thought them bereft of sanity. She hadn't comprehended how two brief moments of pain and indignity merited imperiling one's future. Now she knew there was more, much more, to such attachments than she had dared imagine.

Moving against Will's body, she stretched in languorous contentment, pressed her fingertips gently against her stomach. The moment life quickened would be her happiest day. It could happen. She had pinned her future on the belief that it could.

Again her fingers slid to Will, trailing upward to the patch covering his side wound. And she hid a guilty smile against the hem of the quilt; she'd forgotten his injuries. But she doubted it mattered. Obviously, he was well recovered. When she discovered her thoughts heating, Nell made herself slide from the bed and, shivering, she dressed quickly in the chill air. The etiquette of the moment escaped her, but she concluded it might be unseemly to approach Will this early though she was curious to learn if the magic of last eve could be repeated at will.

Looking at him, she experienced a sudden elation of confidence. Last night's discoveries extended beyond the miracles she'd found hidden within her body. She had also witnessed a power of which she hadn't guessed the existence. Raising her mirror, Nell studied herself minutely, seeking evidence of change. For she had surely changed. The last time she had gazed into this mirror, she had recognized the power of a keen mind. Now she also recognized the power of a woman's body. New knowledge glowed in her eyes. Impulsively, she blew Will a kiss, then stepped into the corridor and quietly closed the chamber door behind her.

When she returned, followed by a boy to lay the fire and a wench carrying hot ale, bread, and beef, Will was dressed and standing beside the window.

He scowled. "Don't leave without telling me," he said when the boy and the wench had departed.

All Nell could think of was food. She was ravenous. "I've ordered a bath," she said between bites. "I'll leave for Saint Denis before midday."

"Good!"

He spoke with such conviction that Nell raised her head and looked at him. For the first time it occurred to her that mayhaps last eve had not been as euphoric for Will as it had been for her. Last night had pointedly underscored her in-experience. Until then, she had in fact been unaware of her ignorance. A rush of color stained her cheeks as she reviewed her actions and wondered if she had failed to give as much as she had received.

"Where will you begin?" she asked, her voice stiffened by concealed humiliation. Judging from his surly expression, the experience had not proved as stunning for Steele as it had for her.

"By getting out of here."

The floor creaked as he paced before the fire. When his urgency began to infect Nell, she set aside her dinner knife and stepped to the window. A soft breath caught in her throat. Paris was larger than she had expected. Much larger. A seemingly endless sea of spires and rooftops flowed in every direction. If there were open spaces, she couldn't spot them from this vantage.

"Jesu, it's impossible. You'll never find them," she whispered. The Spaniards could be anywhere. On this side of the river or the far side. One could search a lifetime and still not explore all the narrow lanes twisting through Paris. Nell stared at a fish cart passing below the window and clenched her teeth. It would be miraculous if Will found the casket. If he didn't . . .

"I'll find them." She felt him approach, halting near enough that she sensed his strength and heat. "Someone must have seen them. Or the scarlet coach. I'll hire agents to scour the city."

Turning aside from the window, Nell looked up at his mouth. "Will . . ."

He moved away from her, thrusting his fingers through his hair. "Nell, I want you out of here. I want you to leave now."

"But I've ordered up a bath."

"This situation doesn't feel right." It was like waiting for the call to battle. The same tense expectancy. Plus coincidence—he didn't like it.

"Can an hour make that much difference?"

He didn't know. But he knew he wouldn't relax until he tucked her into the coach and put this place behind him.

They both looked toward the rap at the chamber door and he sighed as Nell admitted two men carrying a wooden tub. Behind them he glimpsed wenches bearing steaming wooden buckets. A string of oaths passed his lips and he kicked at the logs in the grate. Women were not soldiers, were never intended to be. The man who took a woman on a raid deserved to be branded as a lunatic. If he survived the experience.

"Will," Nell said, touching his wrist. "An hour. That's all I ask." Behind her, the wenches poured hot water into the tub.

It grated against his instincts, but he reluctantly admitted his instincts had been wrong before. After pushing his hat over his curls, he clasped his cape and stared down from the window. A light dusting of snow powdered the lane but the day was clear and crisp.

"One hour," he said finally, hoping he didn't live to regret this. "I'll return in one hour. I expect you to be standing on the stoop ready to depart."

"Where are you going?"

"To hire men and spread them across the city."

Before he left he finished his morning ale, watching her over the foam, seeking hints of the woman he'd bedded. Her exquisite breasts had vanished beneath the brocade stiffening her bodice. The soft glow he recalled had retreated to a familiar wariness. There was nothing in her cool expression to remind him of the vulnerability he'd witnessed last night.

But what rankled his pride, what had turned his expression sour, was knowing she saw him not as a man but as a bloody damned stud. A seed packet. That's all he was to her.

"One hour." He tipped the glass and set it heavily beside the tub. "No more." Then he settled his sword belt and stepped into the corridor before he did something foolish like kissing her.

Paris spread before him, glittering in the touch of morning light on frost-tipped roofs. It wasn't his nature to admit defeat, but he thought about the task before him and frowned. What he hoped to do was unearth two ants hiding somewhere within the teeming anthill that was Paris. "Jesu," he muttered.

He thumbed his cap to the back of his head, strode into the cold silvery air, and beckoned to a pile of rags huddled beside the stoop. "Monsieur? How would you like to earn a pint and a joint of beef?"

Heat rose in a drift of steam above the tub. Nell sprinkled fragrant mint leaves across the surface of the water then impulsively dismissed the wench Monsieur Marroux had sent to serve her.

She intended to dally, to use her hour to the fullest, soaking away the grime of the journey. Every muscle ached from bouncing about the coach—and from Will Steele's enthusiastic ministrations.

But she didn't want to think about Will now. Reaching to unclasp her ruff, Nell concentrated on the life she would have when the queen's business had concluded. A home of her own, she thought dreamily, and mayhaps a child. If only she had a child to love.

The chamber door slammed inward with a heavy crash. Men-at-arms crowded the doorway and the passage behind.

"Halt! Don't move, Madame."

Nell stared at the point of a blade positioned inches from her throat. A half dozen men filled the chamber and surrounded her. One of them tossed her cloak at her feet, another covered her mouth and nose with a damp pad.

A thick, sweet odor clouded her senses and Nell crumpled to the floor.

CHAPTER 13

When she regained consciousness, Nell discovered herself propped against the stone outer wall of a chamber that appeared not to be in regular use. Thick dust furred a crude bench and table, heavy cobwebs stitched the rafters. The floor beneath her skirts was fashioned of roughhewn stone, the dust smudged by recent footsteps.

By pushing up on her toes, she was able to glimpse the river and the spires of Notre Dame through the cracked pane of a window set high in the chamber wall. The view confirmed she hadn't been moved far from the Rue de Bethisy, but this revelation seemed of little consequence. If Will instigated a search, he wouldn't know Nell hadn't been spirited out of the city.

Why hadn't she? For that matter, why would anyone wish to kidnap her in the first place? The questions whirling around the astonishment of her abduction would wait, Nell decided briskly. After smoothing down her skirts, she inspected the door, then ran her palms over the heavy arched wood. It was bolted from the outside; a faint rattle of weaponry beyond the latch suggested she was guarded.

There was naught of interest in the chamber itself. The window was her only significant point of reference. Bending, Nell pushed and tugged the heavy bench across the stones and positioned it beneath the window to obtain a better view. By judging the height of the battlements across a courtyard, she guessed she was confined in a third-floor chamber. Unfortunately no convenient rooftop lay below to facilitate escape.

However, by recalling a sketch she'd once observed in Elizabeth's apartments, Nell recognized the Pavillon du Roi. The corner tower was the French king's Paris residence. By pressing her cheek to the pane, she could glimpse the flagpole atop the tower spire. Had the king been in residence, the pole would have flown his colors. Identifying the Pavillon du Roi meant she was being held in the Louvre.

Holding her skirts close, Nell slowly sank to the bench and attempted to sort her circumstances into logical compartments. The French king was in Blois, and her kidnappers had not worn royal insignia. Therefore, it seemed unlikely the Valois king had commanded her abduction. Then who? And who would dare usurp the king's palace?

There was only one such man. Guise. Henri, Duc of Guise, France's lieutenant general and unofficial king. Nell's eyes widened then narrowed. Guise certainly possessed the power and the audacity to engineer an abduction, but how could Guise know of Lady Nellanor Amesly and why in the name of God would he bother to abduct her? After reflection, Nell concluded she surely must be the victim of mistaken identity. Guise must have intended to abduct the woman originally scheduled to occupy Monsieur Marroux's chamber in the Rue de Bethisy.

Whether this conjecture bode well or ill she was about to discover, Nell thought, rising to her feet at the scrape of the bolt. Clasping her hands at her waist, she drew a breath then lifted her head and studied the man stepping through the arched doorway. He was bareheaded, dressed in dazzling white brocade. A black cape swung from his shoulders, held in place by a jeweled clasp.

All doubt vanished as to her abductor's identity. She knew him at once by the famous crescent-shaped scar curving between his right eye and the outer tip of his moustache. Henri Guise had received his famed wound during his victory at Dormans and with it the nickname of Le Balafre. Instead of detracting from his appearance, the scar added dash and élan to his handsome face.

At a glance, Nell could understand why France preferred this man to their sodomite Valois king. Henri de Guise carried himself with soldierly confidence, looked more a king than his rouged, mincing sovereign ever would.

Restraining an impulse to bend her knee, Nell returned Guise's steady scrutiny. "I demand an explanation for this outrage," she said with cold dignity. Guise was a political and religious fanatic, but he also deserved his reputation as a man with an eye for women. If reason failed, femininity would be her next ploy. Though Nell despised women who summoned tears as a weapon, she was not above such expediency if the situation demanded it.

"All in good time, Mademoiselle." Guise snapped his fingers and a man standing near the guards hastened forward to place a silver casket in Guise's outstretched hand.

Nell drew a sharp breath. She had seen that casket in Robert Dudley's library, she had held it in her own hands. There was no possibility the silver casket in Guise's grip could be other then Robert Dudley's.

And it had been opened.

Suddenly dizzy, she swayed on her feet then raised a hand to her forehead and licked her lips. Jesu, the casket was opened. Guise now possessed whatever secrets the letters had contained.

At Guise's impatient gesture, three women wearing Guise livery pushed past the guards and into the chamber. "Undress her," Guise commanded. His cool gaze swept Nell with a flicker of anticipation.

She stumbled backward from the advancing women. Her eyes had turned stone-colored against a chalky face. It was an effort to control the tremor in her voice. "Has France fallen so low, m'lord, that the head of the Catholic League must take his pleasure by force?"

For the first time since entering the chamber, Henri Guise smiled. "My dear Lady Amesly, regrettably this is business not pleasure. Though I admit you tempt me." He leaned against the wall, arms crossed on his chest, and watched as the women peeled back Nell's sleeves and bodice. "And," he added softly, as they removed her chemise and underskirts, "I assure you, sweet lady, you would not long remain unwilling had I time to pay you the attention you merit."

The blunt force of his gaze and that of his men as they stared at her nakedness stunned Nell, but not as greatly as the realization that Guise had addressed her by name. Humiliation, hot and scarlet, heated her skin as she made the futile gesture of clasping one arm across her breasts, attempted to shield the reddish-gold thicket between her thighs. She felt vulnerable as she had never felt before, and filled with helpless loathing.

But by Christ she would see herself damned before she allowed Guise to enjoy her fear. Aware of the heat pulsing in her cheeks, and despising it, she lifted her head defiantly and held Guise's gaze as he approached her.

Twin fires of ambition and ruthlessness burned in the bottom of his eyes. At recognition of that ambition, a powerful man's most dangerous trait, a chill rose on Nell's skin. Whatever charade they played in this chamber, it was designed to serve Guise's ambition. Of that she was certain, though she couldn't immediately grasp how Lady Nellanor Amesly might fuel the flames of his aspirations.

His fingers came as a warm shock against her skin as he lightly traced the star-shaped birthmark marring her right hip. The color intensified in Nell's cheeks and she stared at a point over his shoulder. She clenched her teeth but did not speak as he shook a letter from the casket. Guise trailed a long finger down the page, found the section he sought, then again leaned to study the mark on her hip.

A cold smile twitched his lips. "It's possible," he mused, glancing again at the letter.

"This, Sir, is an outrage," Nell hissed.

"The mark is on the wrong hip—but that could be subterfuge. A caution." His eyes glittered, rising to Nell's face. "What is your birth date?" Her mouth dropped in astonishment before she blurted the answer. "And you were Robert Dudley's ward?"

Nell forgot she stood naked before a dozen staring men. For the first time in her life she was speechless and could only nod.

Speculation tightened Guise's expression. Then a short mirth-
less laugh bounced from the stone walls. Turning on his heel, he
barked a series of commands. "Give her the crimson suite and
clothing suitable to her rank. She is to be treated with every courtesy, but she is not to leave her chambers without permission
from me." He paused at the arch and looked back at Nell. "Ah,
yes, sweet lady, you will serve very well indeed."

The chamber emptied and Nell was left with the women, who
silently began to dress her. Her mind spun. The man whom many
believed would soon wear the crown of France possessed Elizabeth's private letters. The thought horrified her. And now—now
Will, if he found her, was under direct command to slay her. As
for the humiliation she had just endured, she hadn't a notion
what that might intend. Raising shaking fingers, Nell stroked her
temples.

When she was dressed, a contingent of guards led her
through polished corridors to a suite of chambers so sumptuous
they stopped her breath. Crimson velvet draped a view of the
Seine, flocked the wall hangings, upholstered wide chairs and
settles. Even the lid of the garderobe was padded with velvet. A
mammoth bed dominated the main chamber, enameled in gilt
and crimson, curtained with green gauze, topped by a fortune in
dark furs. To her surprise, the tables were draped with lace instead of carpet; the carpets were smoothed over a marble floor.
Elizabeth Tudor herself possessed no finer apartment.

"Jesu," she whispered, extending her hands to the fire. An exquisite porcelain clock ticked on the mantel. Gold-framed por-
traits of the French nobility adorned paneled walls. The women
had opened the doors of a mahogany wardrobe and were laying
gowns across the furs on the bed.

What did this mean?

"Where is she?"

"Where is who, Monsieur?"

Will Steele drew his dagger and grabbed Monsieur Marroux
by the lapels, jerking him off his feet. "Where is Madame Von
Halen?"

Monsieur Marroux spread his hands and wet his lips. "I know nothing, Monsieur Von Halen. Nothing. One moment she was in her chamber—the next moment . . ." He shrugged elaborately.

The tip of Will's dagger indented the skin beneath Monsieur Marroux's ear. "You're lying," he said flatly. A drop of blood welled around the tip of the blade then trickled toward Marroux's collar. "I am not a patient man, Sir. Once more—where is she?"

Madame Marroux shrieked and clapped a hand over her mouth. Her eyes were the color and size of horse droppings. "Tell him!" she said around her knuckles. She stared up at Will. "For God's sake, Enrique! Tell him!"

"Guise," Marroux muttered, slanting his eyes toward the blade. "Guise's men took her."

"Liar!" A fresh gush of blood spilled toward Marroux's collar.

"It's true, Monsieur!" Madame Marroux rushed forward to grip Will's arm. "A dozen men-at-arms—wearing Guise colors— they came and took her away. I swear it on my oldest daughter's grave!"

"It's true." Marroux's Adam's apple bobbed around a swallow. "Where did they take her?"

They stared at him as if he'd sprouted wings before their eyes. When they swore they didn't know, Will didn't believe them. But he knew they would die before they implicated themselves further in Guise's affairs. Cursing steadily, he lowered his dagger and slammed it into the sheath, watching without expression as Madame Marroux dabbed her husband's neck with the hem of her apron.

He considered questioning them about the Spaniards, but there was no need. This he could already guess. Like the greenest recruit, he had walked into a trap. Worse, he'd sensed it from the first. Nell's abduction could be laid squarely before his door, he was to blame. Furious, Will flung his cap against the wall and uttered a string of oaths. How in bloody hell did Guise fit into this game? Why in the name of God would he want Nell?

Brooding, Will paced before the fire, ignoring Marroux and his wife. There were answers; he had only to find them. What he needed to determine first was the gain in the business. Someone gained by Nell's abduction. Guise. But how?

Nell had no family, no powerful connections. There was no interested party to pay ransom should one be demanded. Even if Guise knew about the casket and the letters—and Will deemed this unlikely—Nell possessed neither. And finally, she had no strategic value. So, why had she been abducted?

Dammit, he didn't know.

But he knew who did know.

And he wished to almighty Christ that he had slain the vile, God-cursed, thieving black Spaniards when he'd had the opportunity. May they rot in hell.

He slapped his cap on his head and slung his cape over his shoulder. Madame Marroux looked into eyes as hard and glittering as jet and hastily moved out of his path.

After two days with little to do but ponder her circumstances, Nell had concluded the Spaniards must have betrayed Philip. For reasons unknown to her, the Spaniards had given Elizabeth's letters to Henri Guise. How and why this event should involve her, Nell hadn't yet fathomed. Nor could she credit the lavish result.

Today, as yesterday, she had been given clothing befitting royalty. Delicate gold lace edged her standing collar, her skirts were made of heavy Italian brocade. A multitude of seed pearls adorned her bodice and sleeves and had been pinned into her hair.

Long ago Nell had learned outer finery spoke much, but what lay underneath said more. In this case, her undergarments spoke volumes. Her underskirts were fashioned of creamy satin, her leather corset was lined in soft silk. Her hose were silk and her slippers cork-soled. From the skin out she was dressed more finely than ever before in her life.

Examining herself in an oversized gilt mirror, Nell could scarcely credit the regal image that stared back at her. Gone were the black weeds of mourning, the jet eardrops and pendant. Her underskirt was popinjay blue, her bodice and overskirt fashioned of gleaming ivory. Blue and silver threads wove patterns to frame the pearls stitched onto her sleeves. The only items she recog-

nized were the worn gold locket at her breast and the chipped
signet ring she twisted on her finger.

Why? The question blew like a constant wind through her
thoughts.

Why the rich clothing? Why diamonds at her ears and wrist?
Why the luxurious chambers and the serving women? Why was
she here at all?

Sighing, Nell turned away from the mirror and glanced
toward the women assigned to serve her. By now she had learned
their names, had learned they were instructed to do her bidding,
but she had learned little else. When not occupied by Nell's toi-
lette, the three women retired to an upholstered niche beneath
the window where they bent their heads over embroidery hoops,
lapsing into silence at her approach as they did now.

Having discovered the futility of posing questions, Nell ignored the women. Instead she leaned her forehead against the
frosty windowpane and gazed at the city beyond the river. The
setting sun spread the lanes and rooftops with cold bluish twi-
light.

When Nell had sailed from England, autumn had been in full
mature glory. Now the trees were skeletal. A light dusting of snow
sugared the rooftops and drifted in the shadows at the base of the
battlements. At home, Elizabeth would be thinking ahead to her
Christmas court, beginning to plan the festivities.

A humorless smile curved Nell's mouth. In the past she had
considered home to be a place of wood and stone and glass. Innocently, she had failed to imagine the concept of home could en-
compass an entire country. But of course it did. At this moment
her dispute with Will regarding Mendenshire House impressed
her as vastly narrow in vision.

"Where are you, Will Steele?" The heat of her breath caused
the glass to fog. She rubbed a space clear and looked out at the
city.

Was he searching for her? Or had he murmured, "Good rid-
dance," and continued his pursuit of the Spaniards and the casket? She guessed he had chosen the casket. Steele was a practical
man—he would immediately accept that he needed the casket;

he did not need Nellanor Amesly. And he had no way of knowing Guise now possessed the casket and letters.

No, she could not hope for assistance from Will. She was alone in her predicament. But then, hadn't she always been alone? Her hand drifted upward to cup the locket at her breast.

"Your grace?"

It required an instant for Nell to remember it was she whom Marie addressed. From the first her women had played the game of addressing Nell as "your grace" as if she were royalty. They bowed to her, jumped to anticipate her wishes. Had the situation not been so frustratingly preposterous, Nell would have thoroughly enjoyed emulating royalty. It amused her to think captivity had provided that for which she had longed. The opportunity to call the tunes, to watch someone else dance on a string as she had done most of her life.

"Yes, Marie?"

The women had risen to their feet and curtsied toward the door. Following their gaze Nell discovered the guards had admitted a visitor. A man who bore a faint family resemblance to Henri Guise. However, the family's famed good looks had bypassed this specimen, she decided. He wore an emerald-studded doublet that pouched over a protruding belly. His surprisingly spindly legs were clad in different colored hose—as was the French fashion—and emerged from thickly padded satin stocks. The lumpish body and grayish coloring reminded Nell of a biscuit clad in jewels and brocade.

"Who is he?" she asked behind her hand.

Marie hesitated then darted a quick glance toward Nell. "Francis, Duc of Loire. The Duc of Guise's favorite cousin, your grace."

Though her distaste didn't alter, a gleam of speculation appeared in Nell's gaze. Surely so esteemed a personage as Henri Guise's favorite cousin would have the answers to her questions. Lifting her skirts, Nell stepped forward and arranged a smile on her lips. "My lord."

"Your grace." Bending over her hand, he touched her fingers to thick damp lips.

So. He too played the charade. Very well, Nell thought, if the lunatic French persisted in foisting royalty upon her, she would not disappoint them.

She nodded with regal poise as she had observed Elizabeth do, then flicked a glance toward the wine pitcher and frowned at Thérèse. "Refreshments for our guest, if you please," she said coolly.

As Thérèse colored and hastened toward the pitcher, Nell waved a graceful hand. "You may be seated, m'lord Duc." She, of course, spread her skirts and seated herself first. While she hadn't yet put the label to this game, she knew how to play it. And she knew chat preceded business. " 'Tis cold for this time of year, is it not?" she inquired pleasantly.

While the Duc addressed the bite in the winter chill, Nell noted that his voice was as thin as his hair. No amount of careful grooming could disguise the sparsity of his pointed beard nor conceal the scalp gleaming beneath hopefully arranged strands. His nose canted to the left, pox marks pitted his cheeks. The cloying perfume he wore pinched Nell's nostrils. She thought him entirely repugnant and wondered at his favored position.

When they had exhausted the weather as a topic, a silence elapsed during which Nell suddenly realized the Duc had been studying her as intently as she scrutinized him. She straightened in her chair and her senses sharpened. She had mistakenly dismissed his heavy-lidded glances, had judged him most likely indolent and of little consequence. But now she recognized the shrewd cunning behind his placid expression. He might be unattractive and clumsy at repartee, but the Duc of Loire was no fool.

"May I speak frankly, Madame?"

"Of course." Ah, now they came to it, the purpose for this call.

He waved the serving women back to the window niche with an impatient gesture, then pursed his lips and looked at her. "We are to be married."

"You jest, of course," Nell replied evenly, dropping her gaze from his oddly twisted nose. "May I offer you more wine?"

"It is not in jest, Madame. I beg pardon for speaking bluntly but such is my nature. And time prohibits subtlety." He laced his fingers over his belly and directed his conversation to her breast. "It is Henri's desire that we be wed."

"Has your esteemed cousin shared his reasoning?" Carefully Nell placed her wine cup on the table between them, taking caution not to spill stains across her skirt. She clasped her hands tightly in her lap and tilted an eyebrow. "Surely the king could arrange a more beneficial match for his favorite cousin than to a foreigner with no connections, no name, and no fortune." This was a conversation Will Steele would have admired, she thought irritably, direct and to the point. She would have preferred it otherwise but her customary polish had deserted her in light of the duc's revelations.

"Henri is not yet king," Francis commented with a sly smile. "But perhaps soon."

"Did I say *king*?" A bit of flattery was never amiss.

Francis cocked his head in the direction of his nose and studied her without pretending to do otherwise. "Let us not be coy, *chérie*. Your connections and name trace to the highest. As to fortune—the treasury of England is more than sufficient, I should think."

"I haven't a notion what you refer to, m'lord," Nell said truthfully.

"Come, come," he said with obvious impatience. "Elizabeth Tudor's bastard will inherit England. Or take it by force."

Nell's mouth dropped and she stared at him. "Elizabeth's bastard?"

"Her consort will rule England."

When she'd recovered from her shock enough to speak, Nell leaned forward. "M'lord, the entire world knows Elizabeth Tudor is as virginal now as the day she was born. What nonsense do you speak, Sir? The queen has no child."

"The deceit is exposed, *chérie*. You need pretend no longer. You of all people know Elizabeth birthed a bastard. And now, so do we."

The intensity of his gaze stopped the smile forming on Nell's lips. He meant what he said. Then the implication of what he'd revealed struck her with the force of a blow.

"My God!" The blood rushed from her face and her hands fluttered to her throat. "You can't possibly think that I . . ."

"Come, *chérie*." Smiling, Francis dismissed her protest with a languid wave. "This bit of theatrics, while charming, does you no credit. The time for pretense has ended. You may admit the truth."

"I know nothing of this!"

His shrug wafted clouds of choking scent across the table. "Then why were you chasing the letters if not to prove your claim?"

"My claim?" Stunned, Nell fell backward in the chair and stared at him. Her mind raced. "If you're this certain I have a claim . . . am I mentioned then in Elizabeth's letters?" She couldn't credit what her ears heard. This was simply not possible.

"You're determined to play the innocent?" he asked irritably. "Very well. In the second letter, which is dated and in the queen's hand, there is reason to believe Elizabeth Tudor admits to birthing a daughter."

Elizabeth Tudor a mother? Nell attempted to visualize Elizabeth welcoming a man into her bed—impossible to imagine—and then lifting her nightdress. It couldn't happen. And then, later, straining in the birthing chair. Unthinkable.

"The letter states the babe was marred by a star-shaped mark on her hip."

Nell's gaze focused inward as she remembered Henri Guise's fingers stroking her skin, tracing her birthmark. She wet her lips and shook her head. "No," she whispered. "Nothing of what you suggest is remotely possible."

"You're mistaken, *chérie*. The English Jezebel wasn't as clever as she planned; the letters prove her deceit. A careful reading reveals the truth. I fear Elizabeth Tudor is no more a virgin than you, my dear." Francis Guise smiled. "The English ambassador has, after discreet questioning, admitted the queen suffered a lengthy illness—pretended, of course—at the time you say you were born. Which coincides with the date of her letter."

"Wait, I beg you. This is all . . . I simply can't . . ."

"Additionally, we have learned Robert Dudley, the Earl of Leicester, purchased your wardship and raised you as his own. As well he should."

Think, Nell commanded herself. Frantically she tried to calm her thoughts. There would be time later to sift them. Pressing her hands together to steady them, she bit her lip hard then opened her eyes.

"You are claiming Elizabeth got a child off Robert Dudley and," she could hardly bring herself to speak the words, "I am that child?"

"The star shape on your hip confirms it." He regarded her with a thoughtful expression. "Although . . ."

"Although?"

"The queen's letter states the mark blots the left hip. The mark you bear is on the right hip. However, Elizabeth Tudor's deviousness is well known. And she would show caution in this matter. Henri believes it probable she altered the truth in the event the letters were not destroyed as she had instructed."

A flood of disconnected images overwhelmed Nell. Behind her stare she saw Robert, dear Uncle Robert, pulling her forward as if she were his own . . . the pride in Elizabeth's gaze as Nell recited a Latin oratory for Elizabeth's visit to Kenilworth . . . the casket turned lovingly in Robert's hands . . . "This is your legacy, Nellie" . . . and Elizabeth: "If you knew your mother, you would devour her."

Dropping her hands from her eyes, she cast Francis Guise a look of helpless appeal. "You have grievously erred, m'lord. This interpretation cannot be credited." His expression darkened and his lids dropped lower. "Even were it so," and she couldn't believe it for an instant, "why would Guise wish us to marry?"

Francis laughed. "Isn't it obvious, *chérie*?"

Of course it was obvious. In a flash, Nell read the entire plot. Had she not been numbed by personal implications, she would have grasped it immediately.

"England," she whispered.

"As your husband, I will lead an invasion in your name.

When we're victorious, you and I shall be crowned king and queen of England. France and England will be united under the Guise banner." Pausing, he leaned forward to examine her blood-less face. "You alarm me, *chérie*. Is it indeed possible you were ig-norant of the letters' content?"

"As God is my witness, I didn't know." Her trembling fingers rose to the locket at her breast. If Elizabeth Tudor was . . . but that was utterly unthinkable. She clasped the locket so tightly her fingers ached.

"You are Elizabeth's bastard," Francis stated flatly. Amuse-ment quirked along his brow. "At least there is acceptable proof for men who wish to be convinced—and there are many."

"She will never admit to a bastard. Never." Nell stared at him. "If you wish to install—someone—upon Elizabeth Tudor's throne, you'll do so only at the cost of war. Only by laying her head on the block."

"The prize merits the cost, *chérie*."

They were speaking treason. A chill pebbled Nell's skin. "But if I don't wish to serve as Henri Guise's pawn?" she asked after a moment. "If I don't wish to assassinate the woman you claim is my mother?"

"You have no choice," Francis answered coldly. Standing, he drew on his embroidered gloves with fastidious care. "I should think you would be elated. If you were as innocent of the truth as you claim, *chérie*, then today you have gained a mother and a crown. I think," he added with a brief smile, "the crown will offer greater warmth and value." He bowed over her hand.

When he'd gone, Nell drained her wine in a single gulp then glanced toward the windows, noticing full darkness had de-scended. Her women sewed by branches of candlelight. "Leave me," she said dully.

As they silently filed past her, Marie bent to touch her wrist. There was sympathy in the girl's eyes and Nell wondered how much the women had overheard. "May I bring you something, your grace? Food? Wine? A sleeping draught?"

"Aye. A sleeping powder."

The response came without thinking. In truth Nell doubted

she would employ the powder as sleep lay furthest from her thoughts. When the women had departed, she lay across the bed and curled her fingers into the furs as if they would anchor her. She gazed unseeing at the scrolled canopy above.

God in heaven. Could it be true?

She thought of the long years of detachment, of scanning endless crowds for a hint of familiarity while others watched mummeries or fireworks. She recalled a parade of faces unknown to her and the constant ache to know her own history.

It seemed that all she needed have done was turn her face toward Gloriana, toward the throne. There she would have found her own gray eyes and reddish hair, her slender bones and bold expression.

But if that was true, then who was the woman portrayed in her locket, the locket she had worn and cherished from childhood? Was A.B. a red herring, an invention provided for the sake of appearances?

And what of Uncle Robert? Nell covered her eyes as the questions assaulted her like a torrent rushing over stones. Robert had loved Elizabeth, of this Nell was certain. And he had loved Nell as his own. He had wanted her to inherit the silver casket. He had said it was her "legacy" because . . . because he had wanted her finally to know her heritage? Was that the answer?

But if Elizabeth Tudor truly was her mother, the mother she had longed for, wept for, then . . .

A sudden fierce resentment overwhelmed her. Anger tightened her jaw. Elizabeth Tudor had denied her. Had never offered a jot of the love and affection Nell had sought so desperately. With startling clarity Nell recalled the queen's impatience, her irritated slaps and sneering remarks meant to wound. Elizabeth had repaid devotion with annoyance, love with indifference. She had, in fact, commanded Nell's death if . . .

"Jesu!" Nell bolted upright on the bed and covered her mouth with her fingertips. "Merciful God!" Now she understood.

Once Elizabeth's letters were read and implications drawn— Nellanor Amesly became a threat to the queen. In the span of one page, Nell had become Elizabeth's rival for the throne of England.

This Elizabeth would not, could not, tolerate. Of course she had commanded Nell's death. As she had commanded the death of Mary, Queen of Scots. So long as Elizabeth Tudor drew breath, no other would sit on the throne or lay claim to it.

Good Lord. Nell covered her eyes with the heels of her hands and dug her fingers into her hair. She had wanted a mother, not a sovereign. She had not wished for this mess. She had yearned for gentle touches, for tender smiles and understanding, not for a rivalry that could end only in death.

A strangled sob broke from her lips and she fell forward, burying her face in the pillow. Emotions as sharp as new blades sliced at her heart: rejection, fury, betrayal. Behind her lids Elizabeth's face rose with smug supremacy. The face of a woman who had scorned her and ordered her put to the sword. A face she had loved and honored.

She no longer knew if she loved Elizabeth Tudor or despised her.

CHAPTER 14

Dona Catlina Valencia congratulated herself on how well her plot had unfolded. Better than she had dared dream. Guise, of course, had immediately comprehended the priceless value of Elizabeth Tudor's letters. And when Catlina had given him Lady Amesly, his elation had known no bounds, nor had his gratitude. As Catlina had predicted, Guise had proven generous, very generous indeed.

Preening, she leaned nearer the jeweler's glass and admired the heavy diamonds flashing against her breast. Diamonds suited her, she decided. As did emeralds and rubies and sapphires. One day she would have them all. "We'll take the diamonds," she said, weighing them in her hand. "And the matching eardrops."

Fernando glanced up from a pair of ruby boot buckles he examined with great interest, and she ordered them as well.

"Would it be wiser, my sweet, to delay further purchases until we have our friend's next payment in hand?"

Guise had agreed to an enormous sum to be paid in three installments, the first of which Catlina had nearly exhausted. Their apartment in the Rue des Barres overflowed with gowns and slippers, wigs and trinkets, artwork and sculpture. An ivory and gilt coach upholstered in moss-green satin—newly purchased— waited outside the jeweler's diamond-paned windows.

"Do you doubt our friend's ability to pay?" Catlina asked, amused by the thought.

"Hardly. But the next installment is not due for several weeks. Perhaps a bit of prudence, my dear?"

"Don't trouble yourself, Nando. The situation is well in hand." What Fernando didn't yet realize was that Catlina held Guise in the palm of her hand. She had tapped a money well.

"Will there be anything more, *Madame*?" the jeweler asked hopefully.

"Not today." She adored the manner in which the jeweler bowed and scraped and hastened to attend her every wish. As well he might; the diamond necklace cost more than he would earn in a lifetime. After Fernando signed the bill of credit, she gave him her arm and accepted his assistance into the coach.

The interior displayed evidence of the Italian influence now so prevalent in France, an influence Catlina firmly approved. She ran her glove across the moss-green satin and smiled, planning where she would first wear the diamonds and which gown would display them to best advantage.

Following what had seemed an almost endless discussion, she had eventually convinced Fernando that they should make their residence in France. With Guise as king, France would displace Italy as the world's cultural and social force. Guise's court would offer a glittering and constant array of balls, fetes, masques, grand banquets, and tournaments. And, as one to whom Guise owed much, Dona Catlina Valencia would assume her rightful place at the center of his court. Her political and social acumen would be admired and envied. Soon, very soon, she would prove a power to be reckoned with.

Catlina had ensured this delicious future by wresting precautionary concessions from Henri Guise. By oblique references, she had shrewdly reminded Guise that it was she who had given him England. He was firmly in her debt and always would be. A favored position at court would not be amiss as a token of his gratitude, nor would a château in the lush Loire Valley. Most important, she had secured his solemn pledge, as head of France's Catholic League, that she and Fernando were now under his protection. So long as the Valencias resided in France, Guise guaranteed that the long arm of Philip—and the Inquisition—would not touch them.

There had been some uncertain moments during the negotiations. Pitting Guise against Philip, his benefactor, had provided Catlina an interesting challenge. Though she had guessed Guise grew restive beneath the yoke of Philip's manipulation, she hadn't known until late in the game whether Guise would scruple to betray the Spanish king. But Guise had usurped Philip's interests in a blink once he comprehended what the casket contained. Precisely as Catlina had predicted he would.

Indeed, Dona Catlina was well content as she swept from her coach and mounted the stairs to her receiving chamber in the Rue des Barres. There she surveyed the items she had purchased to adorn her promised château and herself, taking satisfaction in the evidence of her own unquestioned good taste.

"And now, my sweet," Fernando murmured against her hair, "I shall undress you slowly and lay you on the bed wearing nothing but your diamonds, and then . . ." He sucked in a sharp breath.

She turned at the sound and smothered a cry with her glove. "You!"

The Englisher stepped from behind the chamber door. His expression was murderous, his eyes as chill and hard as chips of stone. By way of greeting he flicked the tip of his sword across Fernando's jaw, opening a thin red line.

"Where is she?"

Catlina stared at the blood seeping from Nando's jaw.

"Where you'll never find her, you whore's son!" Fernando gripped the hilt of his sword.

"You'll be dead before the blade clears the scabbard, Valencia. That I can promise you."

"The casket is where you'll never find it," Fernando sneered. "You lose, English."

Will met Catlina's stare over Fernando's shoulder. "Tell me where Guise took Lady Nellanor or this scum dies." His sword pressed Fernando's chest. "And then you."

She studied the Englisher's icy expression and didn't doubt the validity of his threat. Seating herself on the lid of a trunk, Catlina shrugged and drew off her gloves. "You may as well know— though the knowledge won't profit you. Guise is holding Lady Amesly in the Louvre."

"And Guise now has the casket?" when Catlina nodded, Will swore. "Unbuckle your sword belt," he ordered Fernando. "Now."

"I should have killed you in Calais."

"Aye. But you didn't." Will ground his teeth then twisted his wrist and sliced off the tip of Valencia's right ear. The woman emitted a small shriek and he returned his attention to her. "Why is Henri Guise interested in Lady Amesly?"

Catlina stared in horrified fascination as a scarlet stream pooled against Fernando's ruff. Then her lip curled with contempt and she looked at the Englisher. "As if you didn't know." The Englisher lifted his sword to Fernando's throat.

"Why don't you tell me," he said.

Fernando leaned backward from the blade, his eyes dark with fury.

"Lady Amesly is the queen's bastard." Catlina said. "It's in the letters."

"The queen's . . ." He stared at them. "Jesu! So that's the game. You sold the letters—and Nell—to France!" When they said nothing, he shook his head. "God's heavenly balls!" Stunned, he lowered his sword and walked unsteadily to the wine pitcher on the table, where he drained a cup in two hard swallows.

Fernando's laugh was harsh and triumphant. "When the letters are made public, and they most assuredly will be, the Tudor bitch will be exposed as a liar and a laughingstock. When it's learned the harlot has a natural successor, England will erupt in chaos. Civil war will ensue, assisted by France. There isn't a nation on earth that won't throw its weight behind Guise to unseat the Protestant bitch. With her whelp on the throne and controlled by Guise, Guise will own England to do with as he will!"

Steele nodded. It appalled him, but the strategy played. But Nell? As queen of England? "What makes Guise believe Lady Amesly could be Elizabeth's bastard?"

"The mark on her hip and her connection to Robert Dudley, the Earl of Leicester." Not averse to demonstrating her cleverness, Catlina described the path that had led to her own conclusions, beginning with the mark she had observed on Lady Amesly's hip at the Calais baths. At the finish she tilted her head and regarded the Englisher thoughtfully. "Did you truly believe Lady Amesly was ignorant of the casket's contents? It seems unlikely. Or," she added slyly, "did you hope to win her affection and earn yourself a matrimonial crown?"

"I would stake my life that Nell knew nothing of what was in those letters."

"Perhaps." Catlina shrugged.

"None of this lunacy can be credited."

But he remembered alehouse rumors that Dudley had been Elizabeth Tudor's lover. He recalled time-honored whispers that Elizabeth had birthed a child. Speculations enjoyed over a pint on a winter's night, not to be taken seriously. Until now. Until he recalled the queen's command to slay Nell if the letters were read.

A green-sick expression paled his features. Jesu. The letters had been read. Either he put Nell to the sword or put his own head in a noose. He stared at the Spaniards and thought about killing them.

"Your quarrel is no longer with us," Catlina said hastily, reading his expression. "As Nando said, my friend—the game is finished. With us, that is." Her eyes narrowed. "However. We do have certain influence with Henri Guise. Perhaps we might intercede on your behalf. If the price were right."

"For Scots and Spaniards there is no deed too dire if the price is right." His mouth twisted in disgust. "I'd advise you to plead on your own behalf, *Señora*. Not mine."

Catlina glanced at the sword held loosely in his hand. "There's no call for further violence, m'lord, nor cause for pleas. Our differences are settled, are they not? The matter is no longer in our hands or yours."

"What I would most like is to avenge Nell and England by running you scurvy beggars up a pike," Will answered roughly. His dark eyes glittered. "But that would be too quick, too merciful." He smiled as he watched Fernando edge toward his sword belt, but Will made no effort to stop him. Instead he glanced toward the chamber door and the sharp rap he had been expecting. "I think it will interest you to learn I've spoken to Don Mendoza, who, as you will recall, is Philip's French ambassador. Don Mendoza was greatly agitated to learn you've been treating privately with Guise. He was most displeased to learn you betrayed the king's trust."

"You spoke to Mendoza?" Fernando shot Catlina an alarmed glance before he turned toward the sound of another hard rap against the door.

"Indeed."

Will pressed the latch and kicked open the door, savoring Don Fernando Valencia's expression. The Spaniard blanched to the color of curdled milk when he saw the hooded priests and behind them the men-at-arms filling the passageway. The priests wore the insignia and the malevolent expressions of the Holy Inquisition.

"Don Mendoza suggests you explain yourselves to these gentlemen."

Catlina's eyes glazed with horror as she looked into the hollow darkness of the priests' stares. Death would be a mercy compared to what she saw there. The blood in her veins congealed to ice.

"Wait," she cried as the priests advanced. "Guise will not permit this! The head of the Catholic League guarantees our immunity!" She stepped backward from the priests' silent approach. "I tell you—we are safe! We're under Henri Guise's protection!"

"Dona Valencia," Will said softly from the door. "Do you truly imagine Don Mendoza acts without Guise's knowledge and support?"

She gaped at him, then, as the truth penetrated her fear, her eyes rolled upward. Guise had betrayed them. She forced herself to look into the black fires glowing from beneath the hoods closing around her. Then a bleating shriek scraped her dry throat and she fell unconscious to the floor.

Fernando looked away from her. He chewed his lip so savagely that blood ran beneath his teeth. A wet stain spread slowly across the front of his breeches.

Will touched his sword to his forehead and bowed. Smiling, he closed the door behind him.

"Your color is better this evening, *chérie*," Francis observed, his voice husky with approval. "You will make an enchanting queen."

They dined in Nell's chamber as they had each evening throughout the past week. The menu was as sumptuous as the lace and silver and the jeweled candlesticks. Eggs in broth, fresh salmon afloat in lemon sauce, venison enfolded by spiced pastry, quail and oysters, peacock pie and cheese and winter apples followed by Florentine and sweet tarts. For wine they were served sugary concoctions from the Mediterranean, Muscadel and a heavy Bastard, and Vernage from the island of Crete.

Nell tipped the wine within the chalice she shared with Francis. "M'lord—will anyone truly credit this tale?"

"But of course. We have the letters—the facts speak for themselves."

But what exactly were the facts? From what little Nell knew, she judged the "facts" sketchy at best. Or did she resist because acquiescence meant accepting a living mother who had rejected her from birth? The thought cut to her heart and filled her smoky eyes with a mixture of hurt and hatred. "Elizabeth will never acknowledge me."

"To do so would be to admit her deceit. No, *chérie*, we cannot expect Elizabeth to name you her heir. We will seize what is rightfully yours by force." Tossing back his head, Francis dropped an oyster down his throat. He swallowed heavily. "The French army is invincible."

The French army had turned on itself and fought the French wars of religion. And, Nell thought, other armies had also been thought to be invincible—such as the Spanish—but had proved otherwise. She dropped her lashes, as much to conceal her doubt as to avert her gaze from Francis's trencher. Bits of salmon dribbled down his waistcoat. Lemon sauce greased his beard.

"Once we land on English soil, we may expect English support. There are thousands who will welcome a Catholic sovereign. More who will willingly exchange an aging tyrant for a young queen who can ensure the succession."

"I'm not Catholic, Francis."

His heavy-lidded eyes lingered on her breasts. "You shall be, *chérie*."

"And I failed to provide Edward, my first husband, an heir. It appears I am barren."

His shrug disturbed bits of salmon sticking to his clothing. Pink clots tumbled toward the carpets. "Such inconveniences can be overcome, arrangements made. Do not concern yourself."

"A queen may command even a babe?" Nell's eyebrows rose.

Francis laughed then winked shrewdly. "A crown appeals, does it not? And the power it wields?"

Nell closed her eyes. The idea of a crown was seductive, she admitted it. She who had always suffered the mercy and charity of others, who had proved powerless to influence even her own future—now she was offered the opportunity to indulge every whim. The prospect dangled before her like a sweet on a stick, tempting her forward into the plot. As queen she could reward those who had shown her kindness, punish those who had not. Like Elizabeth Tudor. Like the woman who had abandoned her and later commanded her death.

"And revenge," Francis commented, watching her. He smiled as if he'd read her thoughts. "Revenge appeals, does it not, *chérie*?"

She met his gaze and her own eyes were hard. "Aye," she said softly. "It appeals."

"This mother you have so recently discovered—perhaps you wish to punish her for years of neglect? Perhaps you wish to wound her as she has wounded you?"

A veil dropped over Nell's expression and she abruptly shifted the conversation. Her mother was a pain she carried inside, not a topic to be bandied about with strangers. When the duc announced a late appointment and prepared to withdraw, she accompanied him to the door with decided relief. There, as he had dared the previous night, Francis caught her in his arms and roughly pressed her against the swell of his belly. Wet lips grazed the corner of her mouth, his hands groped for her breasts.

Concealing a grimace, Nell wrestled out of his arms and slapped at his hands. "Naughty Francis. Have patience." Prudence restrained the blow she longed to deliver.

"Patience is not my strongest quality, *chérie*," he said, panting. He caught her wrist and pulled it toward his thighs.

"Fortunately, it's one of mine." At the same moment as she rapped him sharply on the knuckles, she managed a playful pout.

"Charming," he gasped. "A charming little vixen, aren't you?"

"Enough to remind you of your appointment, m'lord. Make haste lest you keep the cardinal waiting." To soften the force of her hand pushing firmly on his back, she leaned to the door and wiggled her fingers beneath a weak smile. "*Adieu.*"

Jesu, he was a sweating, belching pig. With eyes like a weasel and breath like a goat. He possessed more tentacles than a squid. Nell shuddered and rubbed her arms where he had touched her.

After dismissing her ladies she paced restlessly before the fire, from window to bed and back again. There were so many unresolved questions. Most important, most desperately important: Was Elizabeth Tudor truly the mother Nell had sought all her life? The possibility was difficult to accept. Would Elizabeth summon her own daughter to court then disdain her? What mother could so coolly contain any suggestion of tenderness or affection? And yet—there were those incriminating letters. Nell longed to read the letters herself.

What she knew of the letters puzzled her greatly. According to Francis, Elizabeth Tudor admitted to a stunning indiscretion yet deceived the reader as to the location of her child's birthmark. But if Elizabeth feared the letters might be preserved—why commit her error to paper and ink? Yet if she believed Robert would burn the letters as she'd instructed, then why play false with the minor detail of the birthmark's placement?

Nell tapped her fan against her forehead and paused before the fire. If—if the letters did indeed misplace the birthmark and if she was indeed Elizabeth's daughter—then the Guise plot fashioned her as the instrument of her mother's murder. For she would never occupy the English throne so long as Elizabeth Tudor drew breath.

Further, she would not occupy the English throne unless wed to Francis and supported by the French army. If—again if—the French triumphed and if England accepted a young queen in Elizabeth's stead, they would demand of that queen what they had demanded of Elizabeth: a husband of the blood. That being the case, Francis, who traced a claim to royal blood back to Charlemagne, would serve better as a consort than, say, a man like Will Steele.

Will. Jesu, but she missed him. At night he invaded her dreams, covered her slumbering body with his lean strength. Though her captivity and its circumstances occupied much of her waking thoughts, Will Steele was never far out of mind. The scent of an apple reminded her of his breath; when she overheard the guard's baritone laughter she thought of him. She wondered if he would have thought her beautiful in her sumptuous clothing, wondered where he was and what he was doing. She had recalled their night of passion a hundred times.

How differently she might have viewed her present circumstance if it had been Will Steele instead of Francis Guise whom she was commanded to wed. But that was not possible. Will Steele was a commoner.

She sat hard on the edge of the bed and dropped her head into her hands, suddenly thinking of Elizabeth.

"Was that why you didn't wed Uncle Robert?" she whispered. "Because he was a commoner? Was the throne that damned important?" Angry, she struck the bed with her fist. "Was a circle of gold important enough to throw away a man who loved you and a child who needed you?" Was Elizabeth Tudor that cold, that unfeeling, that hungry for power? Aye. A hundred times aye.

Later, when her women returned to undress her and turn down the furs covering her bed, Nell accepted her tooth cloth from Marie and scrubbed the coarse Holland linen over her teeth.

"Do you know why the Duc of Loire dines here each eve?" she asked curiously.

Marie smiled. "He is besotted with you, your grace." She cast a glance over her shoulder then lowered her voice to a whisper. "Thérèse says you are to wed the duc. That it will be a grand and important match."

"The duc is not an attractive man," Nell commented, her mouth twisting.

"Ah, but he's powerful and has important connections. And great wealth and many châteaus." Envy added a wistful quality to the girl's tone.

"And love?" Nell asked softly, looking at Marie in the mirror. "Is love unimportant, then?"

"Toward one's husband?" Marie's mouth curved in amusement. She winked. "Love is between lovers, your grace, not spouses. Husbands are chosen for convenience and fortune."

"Aye," Nell said, meeting her own eyes in the glass. "It appears so."

After the candles had been pinched and the women had bowed and departed for the night, Nell seated herself on a low stool before the embers glowing in the hearth. She thought about Francis and tried to imagine sharing his bed for the remainder of her days. A rush of revulsion prickled her skin.

Not even a crown and all it represented would compensate for submitting to Francis Guise. Would she reject a throne, then? Because she rejected the man who came with it? Would she turn her heel on independence and self-realization? The thought was sobering.

Of course there were other husbands and other armies besides the French. *If* she truly wished to pursue her birthright as revealed by Elizabeth's letters.

If she wished to strike back at Elizabeth.

Her shoulders sank in a sigh and she tilted her head to gaze at the murals, watching the shift of light and shadow. Fate had lifted her up and spun her hard around; she hadn't yet fully assimilated the changes in fortune brought about by events. She needed time to regain control and chart her future as she, not others, would have it.

Additionally, if she were completely honest, she needed time to forget Will Steele. He was a commoner. There was no place for him if she decided to pursue a crown. And if she decided against—he was sworn to kill her by the queen's command.

The night was black, the sharp air icy enough to burn the lungs. Light snow slanted between the dark corner where Will stood and the gray stones of the Louvre. White drifts collected on his hat brim and the shoulders of his cape. The Louvre gate was efficiently guarded, he observed, the thick walls seemingly impregnable. Will stamped cold feet and rubbed his hands together then abandoned his vigil and entered the nearest alehouse. He seated himself by a steamy window and shouted for mulled wine, then wrapped his hands around the cup to warm them.

For three wasted days he had studied the comings and goings at the Louvre gate, examined the battlements and barred lower windows. And he was no closer now to discovering a weakness than at the beginning. There was a weakness, a way to get inside, of this he was certain. The trick was to find it.

He stared at the flickering gate torches through snow melting down the window glass. She would be guarded, of course. But he doubted Guise would mistreat her. Guise was not so foolish as to wound the goose that would lay his golden egg.

Once Will had learned from the Spaniards what the letters contained and that Guise had both the letters and Nell, it had been a simple step of logic to figure Guise's strategy. He would use Nell to gain England. As with all military endeavors, timing would be crucial. This point lay in Will's favor. Guise wouldn't move against England until France was firmly in his control. When this might occur was anyone's guess. Not tomorrow or the next day, which was all Will hoped he needed, but soon.

Will drained his cup and shouted above the pub noise for another, his gaze concentrated on the torches blurred behind the veil of snow. There was nothing more he could do tonight. He rolled his shoulders and rubbed a hand across the back of his neck, idly listening to the chat rising around him as the warmth of the fire and packed humanity penetrated his chill. He'd nearly fallen into a doze when he heard Guise's name.

Returning his gaze to the window, he pretended indifference. But he listened in earnest to the conversation at the table behind him.

Eventually the discussion erupted into a brawl of divergent opinions. But before it did, Will learned Henri Guise had departed with a small army for Blois, presumably to overpower the frightened Valois king. Events in France approached denouement. Of more immediate interest in Will's view, Guise had consigned Paris to the care of a skeleton guard composed of inexperienced if zealous Swiss guards. This could work to Will's advantage.

He stared across the snowy lane at the Louvre's darkened stones; Nell was inside. If he was to effect a rescue, there would be no better time than before Guise returned.

But how?

When he departed the alehouse, Will snapped down his hat brim against the blowing snow and frowned at the Louvre gate. How would he do it? Though it neared midnight, traffic in and out of the palace had not ceased. A man on horseback emerged; two figures on foot appeared from the inky night and passed unchallenged through the guardhouse. Will studied them thoughtfully.

There was a way to gain entry. Eventually he would find it.

Nell perfected her plan throughout the morning, examining each detail, polishing and adjusting.

So long as Guise possessed Elizabeth's letters, Nell and England remained at the mercy of his ambition. As Nell had decided not to play pawn to Guise's king, clearly it became imperative to retrieve the letters. Without the letters, Guise's designs on England would collapse. And Nell would be of no use to him. That much was obvious. If Nell possessed the letters, she also possessed her future. When she was prepared, every possibility examined, she summoned Francis.

When he arrived, pleased but surprised by her summons, she dispensed with chat and questioned him directly. "Is it true Henri has departed for Blois?"

He fluffed out a crimson-lined cape, clasped his hands behind him, and leaned to examine a painted vase. "Why should Henri's whereabouts interest you, *chérie*?"

Concern darkened her gray eyes. Her fingers fluttered over her breast in a calculated gesture, calling attention to the deep square cut of her bodice.

"Because of the letters! Naturally I'm anxious about them. If Henri took the letters with him . . ." She wrung her hands. "Travel is so hazardous—brigands or even an ambitious cohort might steal the casket." She lifted a helpless glance. "Then what happens to us, Francis? To our future?"

"You fear for your crown, *chérie*?" Amusement twitched his lips. "Rest assured, Henri would not risk such priceless documents on the road. I can promise you the letters are safe."

"Thank heaven." The letters were in Paris then, perhaps in the Louvre itself. It wasn't necessary to feign her relief. "Wine, m'lord?" Nell let her fingers brush against his as she served him. "Still . . . I can't help worrying. I fear I'll not breathe easily until I've seen the letters myself."

He stiffened and the point of his beard jutted forward. "Do you doubt my word, Madame?"

"Not at all," Nell said quickly. Having learned the power of a woman's body, she stepped near enough to envelop him within the honeyed scent of her perfume. "The truth is," she raised her lashes slowly and gazed into his eyes, "I've not read the letters, *chéri*. Without having seen for myself, it is difficult to fully accept this unexpected good fortune." A light touch on his jeweled sleeve suggested she included the duc as part of her good fortune. "I should like to read them."

"That is not possible," Francis said to her bodice. Lifting a hand, he caressed one of the curls escaping her hair net and watched it twine about his finger.

Nell was too adept at thrust and parry not to have anticipated his response and prepared one of her own. Surprise arched her eyebrows. Then she pretended embarrassment before she glided away from his touch. "Forgive my blunder, m'lord," she said in a flustered voice. "Naturally I . . . I assumed you enjoyed Henri's confidence and trust."

"But of course Henri trusts me. Are you suggesting he does not?"

"*Chéri*, say no more. I admit my error and beg pardon." She gave him a moment to digest the implication. "Had I grasped the nature of the situation, I would have said nothing." Now her voice cooled slightly and she glanced at him from the corner of her eyes. "I simply supposed, mistakenly, of course, that a man who soon will be king of England could command whatever he wished."

Francis stared after her as the whisper of her skirts took her farther away from him. She stopped before the wall mirror and leaned forward. "The letters are guarded," he said when she appeared to forget his presence.

Nell tucked a stray tendril beneath her hair net, adjusted her collar. "I'm sure they are," she said without glancing at him. She smoothed her skirts. "When Henri returns I'll beg permission to read the letters. Unless you can recommend someone to whom I might appeal now?" A hint of contempt tightened her mouth when she turned from the mirror to look at him.

"I tell you, Henri trusts me!"

"Of course," Nell said politely.

"I enjoy my cousin's complete confidence! We've been intimates since childhood." His voice rose; dark color infused his cheeks.

"As you say," she remarked with an indifferent shrug. From beneath her lashes she noted his clenched fists, his narrowed eyes. "There's no call for agitation, Francis," she said, secretly delighted.

"You don't believe me. I can see that you don't! Must I prove my status?"

"Calm yourself, *chéri*. You need prove nothing to me. I merely wished to read Elizabeth's letters." She spread her hands. "I beg pardon if I've alarmed you or wounded your pride by exposing a sensitive subject."

"This is *not* a sensitive issue!" His mouth worked. His belly puffed in and out; his hands tightened at his sides.

"But, my dear Francis, you said yourself that Henri has locked the letters away and not even you may have access to them."

"I said no such thing, Madame! If I wish to remove the letters I may certainly do so."

Nell looked at him and raised an eyebrow. A tiny smile hovered about her lips.

"You wish to read the English harlot's letters?" he shouted, returning her gaze. "Then so you shall! I'll bring them to you."

Now it was time to sweep the footsteps from the path. When he recalled this conversation later, Nell wanted him to remember that it was he who had insisted he bring her the letters.

She hesitated, tapping her fan lightly against her breast. "I thank you, Francis, but . . . would that be wise? I'd not wish you to make a decision Henri would disapprove. Nor would I relish having you incur Henri's wrath on my account."

"I keep telling you—Henri and I are . . ."

"No, Francis." Regret saddened her expression, along with a shadow of contempt. "I can't allow you to place yourself in jeopardy."

"*You* can't *allow* . . . ?" Spittle sprayed from his lips.

"I think it best you not overstep yourself. When Henri returns from Blois you can beg permission then. If your relationship with Henri is as you claim, perhaps he will accede to your plea."

"Overstep? Beg?" He was sputtering. His cheeks had darkened to an alarming burgundy color. Drawing himself up to his full height, he looked down his nose at Nell. "Madame, you forget to whom you speak. The Duc of Loire begs no man, nor am I in danger of 'overstepping.' I am well within my rights to take possession of the letters if I wish." His fleshy lip curled. "And I needn't 'beg' permission! I've said you will read the letters and so you shall."

She bit her lip; she feigned indecision. Then, beaming, Nell rushed into his arms and covered his pitted cheeks with quick kisses.

"If you insist, Francis, I must bow to your will. And it would please me so greatly!"

Nell forced her body to remain supple as his hands squeezed at her breasts. But when his breath turned ragged and he pulled eagerly at her skirts, she spun out of his arms and wiggled a playful finger. "Afterward," she said, her voice a seductive promise. "After I've read the letters."

The moment the door closed upon his crimson cloak, Nell hurried to the bed and lifted the corner of her mattress to retrieve the packets of sleeping powder she had hidden there. After opening the paper twists, she poured the contents into the wine pitcher, stirred it, then burned the paper cones in the grate. This done, she drew a long calming breath and settled herself for a wait that seemed eternal. Long winter shadows had dimmed the windows before he returned.

"Francis?" she said expectantly, rising from beside the table.

"Here are your damned letters," he snapped, tossing the silver casket onto the furs covering her bed. "I hope you appreciate what I had to . . ."

But Nell wasn't listening. The silver casket caught the late afternoon light. It gleamed like a jewel against the dark furs. And the key was in the lock.

For a moment Nell couldn't move. Then she whispered a prayer of gratitude and rushed forward to throw her arms around Francis's neck and suffer his embrace. Eager kisses bruised her lips and dropped to her breast before she danced out of his arms as he clumsily attempted to maneuver her toward the bed.

"A toast," she cried, pouring cups of the drugged wine. "To England!" she lowered her lashes then swept them upward in a provocative tease. "To us!"

Reluctantly Francis accepted the cup and drained it with impatience. Immediately Nell tipped the pitcher and refilled his goblet then raised her own untasted wine to another toast.

"To King Francis and Queen Nellanor!" She pressed her cup to her lips and pretended to drink.

It happened more quickly than she had imagined.

The empty wine cup dropped from Francis's fingers. A surprised frown arched his brows. He staggered toward her before collapsing heavily onto the chair before the table.

Now was the moment to protect herself. Nell flung out a hand and blinked rapidly. Weaving, she swayed toward the table. "Francis! Help me, I beg you! I feel . . . I feel . . ." She looked into space and spread her fingers. "I can't see!" Making her body go limp, she crumpled to the floor in front of his blunted eyes.

Not until she heard him topple from the chair and crash across the carpet did Nell dare move. Then she jumped to her feet and approached the bed, her steps slowing as she neared the casket. Nervously she wet her lips, smoothed her palms over her skirts. Staring at the casket, she drew a long breath and held it. She had waited for this moment for so long. For all of her life. The silver casket was her legacy; the letters inside contained her history.

Finally, she would *know*.

Feeling her heart accelerate, Nell knelt on the bed and took the casket between her trembling hands. Slowly she eased back the lid then opened her eyes. Three yellowing letters were inside, tied in lengths of faded blue silk.

The brittle pages of the first letter rattled like dry leaves as she withdrew it and reverently slipped off the blue silk. But she did not immediately unroll the pages and smooth them against her skirt.

Instead, she bit her lower lip and turned a blind gaze to the window. The gold locket lay heavy at her breast and she reached a hand to clasp it. Oddly, now that she held her history within her grasp, she experienced a dread reluctance to proceed. Whatever the next moments held for her, she sensed her life would be forever altered. There would be no turning back.

She closed her eyes and inhaled deeply. Then she tilted the pages to the candlelight and began to read.

CHAPTER
15

Sweet Robin, my eyes,

If you but comprehended the anguish you deliver those who love you by your continued absence, you would heed the desire of your queen and return to court at once. In your post of Thursday last you state you can not lift your head nor meet your queen's gaze lest your shame be evident to all. How cruel you are, dear Robin, thus to wrest absolution and explanation from us who be as distraught as you but without leisure or liberty to make issue. Has the fever so scalded your brain that you think never to face us again? Is this misfortune to serve finish to a love and acquaintance dating backward to tender years? God's death, but I shall not allow it! We shall heal this pain between us and continue as before.

If to rise whole from your sick bed you must force an admission of shared error then hear the confession of she whose greatest error lies in loving you. 'Twas she who agreed to seek shelter from the storm in the hunt lodge, she who succumbed to curiosity and a desire to learn of fleshly tempest. 'Twas she who surrendered to the honeyed words and skilled touch of him denied too long.

Robin, sweet Robin, cast backward your thoughts to our history. So braced can you not forgive words spoken in pain and disappointment? Can you not comprehend our fear and our frost? Can you not blind yourself to repugnance or disgust when the far source is recalled? 'Tis no reflection upon your manhood that one *winter stalk failed to blossom neath your tender ministration. If humility be demanded, then mayhap the fault lies within the stalk.*

For what some welcome as nourishment we know as abdication. We have seen death from such sweetly poisonous attentions. Would you have us abdicate life for the dry pain of fleeting passion? Nay, not if you love us as you swear. Not again.

She who loves you has tasted of the apple and found it bitter. If the apple from your orchard is poisonous, my Robin, nowhere can sweet be found. You planted deep and sure, 'tis not entirely your blame the fruit proved dry, unyielding.

This letter must be burned. We command it. None must learn you have taken from us that which cannot be restored, if such were learned . . .

The last page of the letter was missing and thus no signature appeared. But the distinctive handwriting was unmistakably Elizabeth Tudor's. By counting backward, Nell confirmed the letter's date to be eight and a half months previous to her own birth.

Stunned by what she had read, Nell lowered the letter to her lap and stared unseeing at the duc's sprawled form.

Elizabeth Tudor had sexually surrendered to Robert Dudley, Earl of Leicester. Rumors had insisted as much, but Nell had dismissed the gossip as slander. In company with most of the world, she accepted without question Elizabeth's much vaunted virginity. She had smiled at the jests positing Elizabeth as the "second most famous virgin in history." She had believed it true. But it was not. Nell held proof in Elizabeth's own hand that she had tasted of passion's fruit.

Carefully Nell reread the pages, drawing the unmistakable conclusion that the incident had failed to give pleasure to either party. Their coupling had faltered despite Uncle Robert's legendary skill as a cocksman and the queen's renown as a flirt and a tease. Though it appeared Elizabeth suffered disappointment to find it so, the letter suggested she had remained rigidly indifferent to Robert's caresses, had proven incapable of response. Then, mayhaps to mask her inadequacy, it appeared she had hurled insult, had faulted Robert's skill because her womanhood slumbered.

Covering her eyes, Nell recalled Elizabeth Tudor's history as the letter requested. Aye, she could comprehend the queen's insurmountable fear. Upon reflection 'twas no marvel that Elizabeth would approach a man's bed with trepidation.

The greatest passion of the present age had flamed between Elizabeth's father and her mother, Anne Boleyn. But the child Elizabeth had borne witness to the eventual result of that passion. It had ended in blood when her father ordered her mother beheaded. Passion killed, that was the lesson to be learned. It was a message reinforced by subsequent events.

Elizabeth would not have had to look far to grasp that passion led to the axman's block, to death on a blood-spattered childbed, or death by divorce, by desertion. Passion made suet of the heart, rendered judgment irrational. Passion was death, emotionally, intellectually, and physically. A young, impressionable Elizabeth had witnessed passion's lethal embrace again and yet again within her own family. Aye. She had observed the tragic fates of mother, stepmothers, sister, cousin. Was it a wonder she froze at the touch of a naked man?

Nay. The winter stalk had roots wound in history, roots later twisted toward ambition, power, autonomy. But mayhaps Elizabeth had once wished it otherwise, Nell thought, stroking the pages with her fingertips. Mayhaps the young queen had longed to sup at love's banquet—just once—to share the cup of kindred womanhood. Mayhaps in those early years she had not cherished her virginity but had thought it a burden. Whatever her reasoning, she had chosen to bestow her gift upon Robert Dudley. Just once.

Saddened, Nell tied the blue silk and replaced the letter in the casket. Before she held the second letter to the candlelight, she inhaled deeply.

Elizabeth's sweeping signature scrawled across the bottom, but this letter was undated. At first reading it was gossipy, meandering, a letter one might write to an acquaintance of long standing, filled with bits of the moment but of scant interest years later. Only after a meticulous second reading did two particular paragraphs spring into focus. Nell's hands tightened on the pages and her heart bumped against her ribs.

> *It will interest you to learn Lady Boleyn rails at fate as she finds herself in the revolting posture of being seeded. She who erred but once and took no pleasure from it. She reviles her lapse, rages against weak flesh, knowing we must suffer the pain and peril of the birthing chamber. God's death! How long must this lady pay for her blunder and in what coin? She who would rather drown a brat then whelp it grows daily larger and must lace tighter to conceal a traitorous body.*
>
> *This matter does not concern you, Robert; nay, not you. No man travails himself with woman's bitter destiny. He sows his seed and abandons his orchard with prideful ease. Such is the unjust arrogance of breeches over skirts. But know you that Lady Boleyn plots cautiously, confident she can deceive those about her by feigning illness when her time comes. Pray God she predicts accurately.*

The paragraphs lay buried among others of like nature addressing scandals and rumors concerning various court members. Had the second letter not been coupled to the first, it would have appeared innocent and attracted no notice. But Robert had preserved it alongside the first. And Elizabeth spoke of Lady Boleyn. To Nell's recollection, no Boleyns of childbearing age had attended court since Anne and her sister.

The letter fluttered from her fingers and Nell's hand rose to press the gold locket against her erratic heart. Anne Boleyn, Elizabeth's mother. The worn edges of the locket seemed to scorch Nell's damp palm.

Was it coincidence that all her life Nell had worn a locket engraved with the initials A.B.? And now found reference to a Lady Boleyn where none should be? It was certain Elizabeth employed a pseudonym for one whose name could not be written.

But if Elizabeth referred to herself—and it was significant she had lapsed from *she* to *we*—if Nell were possibly the result of

Elizabeth's unhappy coupling, then who was the woman portrayed in her locket?

The scrape of boots outside the door startled her, and Nell swiftly retied the blue ribbon and returned the second letter to the casket before she smoothed open the final pages.

Of all the letters, this was the most important and the most difficult to read. After a lifetime of searching and wondering, finally she would know from whence she sprang.

Her palms were moist; her hands shook so badly the yellowing pages rattled. Swallowing hard, Nell clasped the locket in one hand and held it tightly. She glanced at the date of the last letter.

It was dated little more than a week after her birth date. Briefly she closed her lashes and willed her hands to cease their tremble. Then she read. And as before, the pertinent paragraph was hidden within an outpouring of gossip and idle observation. But when she found what she sought, her heart thudded painfully and her skin felt hot and chill at the same moment.

Monday last Lady Boleyn was successfully delivered of a daughter. The infant is marred by a star-shaped mark on the left hip but healthy otherwise. Lady Boleyn has placed the brat with the Master of the Wards. If you are thus inclined you may assume an interest in the child's welfare. It matters not. The unpleasantness is concluded and forgotten.

Nell stared at the paragraph until her eyes ached. Was that all? Leaning nearer the candle, she swiftly scanned the pages of the letter, seeking another reference, another hint, a suggestion of tenderness and caring. The pages slipped from her fingers and she covered her face with her hands.

God in heaven. Her history, if it was her history, consisted of six sentences buried amidst idle gossip. Marred . . . brat . . . matters not . . . unpleasantness . . . forgotten.

Tears blurred her vision, but she could feel Robert Dudley's torn wax signet beneath her fingers. This then, was the legacy he had wished her to have.

A poisonous urge overcame her as she touched the silver casket. She wanted to hurl it and what it contained away from her. Wanted to smash it, destroy it.

"Like mother, like daughter," she murmured bitterly, thinking of Elizabeth's famous rages.

Elizabeth. The name and the sight of the beribboned letters consumed Nell with the fury of betrayal. "She cast me away like an unwanted pup!" Furious tears glittered in her eyes. "To be forgotten and never thought of again." Jesu, but she longed to scream and sob and throw things at the walls. She quivered with the need to strike out and wound.

But there was no time. Flinging back the furs and linens covering her bed, Nell cut a slash in the mattress with her dinner knife, the motion savage. She thrust the casket deep into the feathers and made up the bed.

Then she lifted her skirts and stepped over the duc's prostrate form. Gripping her wine cup, she raised it in a toast. "To you, Mother," she said in a harsh voice she didn't recognize.

After draining the cup of drugged wine, she lay on the floor and awaited blessed stupor. But Elizabeth's voice rose to taunt her. "It matters not. The unpleasantness is concluded and forgotten . . . you are forgotten. And it matters not."

She welcomed the blackness that fell across her thoughts.

Twirling a stick, Will strolled idly past the gatehouse. While appearing to show no interest, he carefully observed those who passed the guard's scrutiny. Some, absorbed by business, murmured a word then hurried into the Louvre courtyard intent on their affairs. Others lingered a moment beside the guard's brazier before stepping past the swords and halberds. Observation had netted the information that the watchword changed with the morning shift, a different signal daily.

Learning the current watchword did not present an insurmountable problem. Will was now confident he could gain access to the Louvre's interior. What vexed him was how to get Nell out.

Presuming the watch had been furnished with her description, and assuming those exited were ticked off against a roster of those who had entered—how could the feat be accomplished?

How did one render invisible a woman rigged out in puffed sleeves and voluminous skirts? A woman, moreover, memorable for her beauty. This was the problem that occupied his thoughts upon waking and before he retired to the warm straw in the stable where he slept.

Pausing at the corner past the gatehouse to purchase a roasted apple, Will listened to the bells pealing from the tower of St. Germain l'Auxerrois. They made no music for him. These same bells had chimed the beginning of the St. Bartholomew's Day massacre not that many years ago, during which three thousand Protestants had been murdered. He frowned up at the gargoyles and the rose window then dropped his attention to three figures emerging from the church's door.

He watched them turn their collars against the cold and bend into the wind.

And a wide grin spread across his lips. The plan forming at the back of his mind was the sort of plan he enjoyed most. Audacious, arrogant, a touch of poetic justice, though Will was the first to admit he was no poet. Poetry was best left to fops and Scots.

Appetite improved, Will bit into the hot apple and wiped the juice from his mouth. Whistling into the frosty air, he strode toward the stables in the next lane to begin making his arrangements. He knew how it could be done.

Someone was slapping her. Brisk blows stung across Nell's cheeks. Moaning and pressing her hands to her head, she pulled dizzily to her feet. The chamber was cold as the fire, untended, had crumbled to ash. A snowy darkness lay against the windowpanes.

The chamber spun before her eyes and her stomach protested violently. Clapping a hand over her mouth, Nell rushed behind the screen and leaned over the garderobe, vomiting until her throat was raw and burning. When she emerged, white-faced and limbs trembling, she saw evidence that Francis had also been sick.

Raising her hems, she avoided the sickly pools upon the carpet and sank onto the chair before the table. Her dulled eyes followed Francis as he paced before her women who huddled together near the window niche. Their faces were pale and frightened.

"What happened?" Her voice emerged thick and slurred. She genuinely could not remember. Dropping her pounding head between her hands, Nell struggled to bring order to the chaos romping through her mind.

"We were drugged," Francis raged. The heavy jewels on his fingers caught the dim light as he raked them through his thinning hair. "And the letters were stolen!"

"Stolen?" Nell's mouth dropped and panic flared in her eyes. "But how? Who . . . who did this?"

Francis spun on his boot heel and shouted to the guards. Spittle erupted from his lips like musket shot and a shaking finger accused the women weeping near the window. "The bribe must have been generous. They claim to know nothing. Guards!" Disgust twisted his lips above yellowing teeth. "Take them away."

Listening to Francis's steady flow of cursing, Nell watched the guards take her women.

Memory returned in a rush, and a veil of caution dropped over her gaze. This was no time to falter or to surrender to the drowsiness blunting her mind. She wiped her lips and blotted her forehead with the square of lace she withdrew from her cuff.

Francis kicked at the dead fire and flung out his hands. "Who paid them?"

"The Valois king?" Though she suspected Francis spoke more to himself than to her, Nell used the question to begin establishing her own innocence. She rubbed her temples and strained to summon acuity from a mind swaddled in wool.

"Don't be a fool!" A fine spray misted Nell's cheek before he resumed his pacing. "How would that idiot know of this matter? You and the queen's letters are a secret not ready to spring. No one knew but Henri and me."

She was relieved to hear it. "The Spaniards know. And possibly agents sent by Elizabeth." Having planted new fields to plow, Nell crossed her arms on the table and cradled her throbbing head. She would have bartered ten years of her life for a strong headache draught.

"And you," Francis added slowly, halting his pacing to stand before her.

Nell's expression revealed only indignation when she raised her head. "I begged you not to fetch the letters, Francis. I advised you to wait until Henri returned."

"Perhaps that was simply your woman's cunning."

"Are you suggesting I would endanger my life by drugging my own wine? And then destroy letters that will make me a queen?" Incredulity sharpened her tone before she narrowed her eyes in suspicion. "Nay, not I. But perhaps it was you, Francis. Mayhaps you staged this incident. Mayhaps you poisoned our wine rather than admit to an empty casket." She regarded him with silent accusation. "Did you truly bring the letters, m'lord? Or did you fear Henri Guise too greatly to risk his displeasure?"

"My God, Henri!" A greenish cast spread over Francis's features. His voice sank to a whisper. "What shall I tell Henri?"

"Then you did fetch the letters? And they are truly stolen?"

"Yes, yes!"

"Forgive me, Francis, I . . ."

"Henri will be in a rage." He wet his lips and looked at her. "Henri's rage is a terrible thing."

"How can you think of Henri at a time like this?" Nell cried. She twisted her hands and closed her eyes. "Sweet Jesu, Francis! Without the letters, we are lost. We'll never be king and queen!" Jumping to her feet, she caught his arm and looked up at him with an imploring expression. "Our crowns! Francis, we're ruined. We've lost England—we've lost each other!" She held on to him and gazed into his eyes. "You must do something. Quickly!"

"Henri—when the business in Blois is finished, he'll return."

"Francis, you must listen to me."

"Yes."

But he stood as if frozen, his eyes opaque with fear. Nell took him by the shoulders and shook him. "Francis? Francis, you must act with haste. First you must disassociate yourself from the casket. Are you listening? Whatever you did to obtain it must now be undone. Henri must not trace this incident to you."

"No!" A shudder rippled through his body. "This must never be traced to me."

"When your participation in this outrage is concealed, we'll discuss how best to discover who is behind this plot. We'll decide how to retrieve the letters and salvage our crowns."

"We must act quickly," he muttered.

"Yes."

"Henri must never know. Never."

She led him toward the door. "There's no reason he will. If you're clever."

"Yes." Distraught, he muttered something incoherent and rushed from the chamber.

The instant the guards pulled the door shut behind him, Nell collapsed on the bed and pressed her hand against the slit in the mattress beneath the linens.

For the moment the letters were safe and so was she. Without the letters, Henri Guise would have no use for Lady Nellanor Amesly. Nor would there be cause to wed Francis.

But so long as the letters existed, so too existed puppet masters eager to use the letters and Nell to advance their own interests. Guise was but the first.

Her eyes strayed toward the fire one of the guards had rekindled in the hearth, and she imagined the letters burning. It lay within her power to conceal forever Elizabeth Tudor's great deceit and thus return herself to obscurity.

Was that what she wanted?

The flames fascinated her. She thought how swiftly the aged parchment would burn. She could envision the pages curling and turning black.

Jesu, what was she thinking? Nell shook her head. The letters were priceless, irreplaceable. They offered her a glittering place in history, offered the opportunity to confront the woman who had abandoned and rejected her. They provided an opportunity to punish in kind.

Turning her face into the pillow, she blanked the flames from sight. She didn't know what she wanted. Too much had happened in too short a span. Until she could sort out the confusion it would be foolish to destroy her option to deprive Elizabeth of the one thing she valued more than a daughter of her blood: the crown of England. At this moment Nell could not have said with certainty that she would seize that option. But it was good to have it available. Nay, her state of mind was such that now was not a fortuitous moment to make irrevocable choices.

This decided, she undressed before the fire and dropped a nightdress over her hair then slipped beneath the furs. Now that she had the casket and the letters, the next step was to effect an escape. But where would she go? It was that question again, she thought with a grim smile.

Elizabeth would be searching for her and so would Henri Guise when he discovered what she'd done. And he would, of this she was certain. So, where would she go?

She worried the problem far into the cold night. It was better than thinking about Elizabeth. Better than thinking about mothers and daughters.

Except for the single bedside candle she had forgotten to pinch, the chamber was dark and silent. Nell sat abruptly on the bed and listened to the chill silence, straining to identify whatever disturbance had awakened her. A log settled in the grate; she heard a distant whistle from the direction of the river. Thinking her nerves played tricks, she eased back on the pillows, then gasped and jerked upright.

A hooded figure stood beside her chamber door. A priest. He advanced silently, his features hidden within the shadows beneath the dark cowl covering his head.

Nell sucked in a breath and gripped the fur coverlet to her breast. What was a priest doing in her chamber in the deep of night? Had she been discovered? Was she to die? Her eyes widened and her heart skimmed her throat as the priest approached her bed.

"Good morrow, Grandmother." Will Steele pushed the cowl to his shoulders and grinned at her. "Impressive dungeon you have here."

"Will? Oh Will, thank God!" Laughing and blinking against

tears of sudden relief, Nell threw back the coverlet and leaped from the bed. She was nearly in his arms before she remembered. Her nightdress billowed around her ankles as she skidded to a halt then dodged behind the table. Quickly she darted a glance across the lace cloth, the mantelpiece, searching for something to use as a weapon. The brass candlesticks? Out of reach. The painted vase? Not lethal. There was nothing suitable.

"Captivity has done little to sweeten your disposition, Nellie love. I expected a semblance of gratitude. Mayhaps a bit of awe that I found you and turned up in your chamber."

Nell's gaze narrowed; she was undeceived by his cheerful manner. "The casket has been opened," she stated bluntly.

For a moment he didn't respond. He studied her across the table surface, his expression thoughtful. "Ah, you think I've come to slay you."

The intimacy of his tone invited discussion, but Nell sensed the time had passed for chat. She was not taken in by the look in his eyes or the tone of his voice. Given the choice between being drawn and quartered or killing her, Nell understood which he must choose. She returned his steady gaze and to her surprise her chin firmed. "The letters have been read."

"I know."

She gripped the edge of the table as he pushed aside the crucifix dangling from his waist and slowly withdrew a knife from the folds of his robe. Her mouth turned to dust. There was no place to run, no escape.

"Will . . ." she whispered. So this was how it ended. She stared at him, mildly surprised to discover death came clothed in beauty. For at this moment Will Steele was beautiful to her, powerful and fearless, confident and strong.

Time appeared as frozen as the night. It seemed to Nell that she gazed into his eyes for an eternity before she saw a dim flash of candlelight race the length of the blade.

Still she continued to stare deeply into his dark eyes. Waiting. She gasped when he thrust the knife toward her.

CHAPTER
～ 16 ～

"ake it."

Will flipped the blade and extended the knife hilt first.

"Jesu!" Her lips were bloodless, her face the color of new parchment.

"Take it, Nell, and use it against me if you truly fear I would slay you."

Her slim hand closed around the shaft then the knife clattered from her nerveless fingers. Closing her eyes, Nell leaned hard on the table and gulped air into her chest.

"God's death!" Affronted, Will tried to decide if he most wanted to turn her over his knee and thrash her or take her into his arms. It hadn't entered his thick head that she would believe he attempted anything other than rescue. He glared at her, angered by her mistrust.

"I thought you were going to kill me."

"Are you daft? I love you, you lackwit dolt." In his innocence, he had supposed women surmised these things. He'd imagined his calf-eyed glances were as embarrassingly evident to her as they seemed to him. Jesu. If he lived to sweat through his hundredth summer, he would never understand women. Alehouse doxies unremarked for delicacy swore they identified signals testifying to a man's affection. Usually to the vast astonishment of the man in question. Yet slumped before him wearing a nightdress as thin as gossamer stood a woman skilled in isolating shades of subtlety but unable to glimpse the obvious. How did a man cope with such contrasts? One might as well tilt at the wind.

"Lackwit dolt? Oh, Will!"

Suddenly she was in his arms, flying around the table to press against him, her fingers racing over his face, his lips, his shoulders. He didn't understand this contrary shift in attitude, but he liked it.

"I thought . . ."

"I know what you thought," he said stiffly. "And it does you no credit, woman." The scent of honey and roses aroused his senses. He could feel the warmth of her through the thin material of her nightdress. "For a canny woman, you can sometimes be an utter crack-brain." He was in the right and knew it, but his impatience began to evaporate as her breasts and hips melted against him.

Her mouth brushed the corner of his lips. "The letters . . ."

" . . . are lost to us, I know." Jesu, but he wanted her. She filled his arms with yielding softness. He cast a glance toward the furs strewn dark and inviting across her bed. But instead of carrying her there as he wanted, he cupped her face between his palms. "What matters is that you're safe."

"Nay, you don't understand." She shook her head and strands of reddish-gold silk spilled over his hands. When she smiled up at him a glow of triumph caused her eyes to shine. "I have them. The letters."

"*You* have Elizabeth's letters?"

"Aye."

Admiration warmed his gaze. How she'd managed this feat of magic he couldn't guess. But clearly he'd underestimated her grasp of strategy. "A right smart piece of work, Grandmother."

"They've been read, Will. Which means . . ."

"We'll draw that bridge later, Nellie love. First, we have to get you out of here. When does the guard change?"

Nell bent to count the unburned ridges on the hour candle beside her bed. "Very soon. Within minutes, I'd guess." Throwing back the bed linens, she dug her fingers into the mattress and produced the casket.

When she tossed it to him, Will turned it in his hands, thinking it small as an instrument to rock nations. After tucking the casket away, he withdrew a second robe from the folds of his own. "Put it on. You'll make a fetching priest, m'love."

Indeed she did. Eyes dark, he watched her throw off her nightdress. For a moment she stood naked, looking at him, then she dropped the priest's robe over her head and bound up her hair. When he could think coherently, he inspected her with a critical eye. She was tall for a woman and the robe was loose and hooded. "Aye," he said, satisfied. "You'll do."

"One priest entered but two depart?"

"That's the plan. If luck rides with us, the fresh watch will suppose the previous shift erred. Unfortunately, such lapses occur more often then generals care to imagine."

Muted noises rustled in the corridor. The sound of muffled greetings, the tinny clank of weaponry, a curse. Not until several minutes of silence had elapsed did Will brush his thumb across her lips and ask, "Ready?"

She looked up at him, touched his moustache with her fingertip. Her fine gray eyes were cool and steady. "Aye. Ready."

"Pull the cowl far forward and keep your head down. Whatever happens—don't speak. Not a word."

Bending, he kissed her swiftly then strode to the door and opened it. Immediately the guards straightened to attention, hands on the hilts of their swords. When they saw Will's robe, their shoulders relaxed.

"Good morrow, gents."

They nodded. One of the guards yawned and muttered something crudely unflattering about the ancestors of the previous watch when he spotted Nell. Both guards slouched against the wall.

Moving without apparent haste, Will and Nell traversed the long torch-lit corridors, keeping to the shadows when possible. At last they emerged into the chill starry night. A rime of frost glistened on the courtyard cobbles, sparkling in the moonlight where hooves had pushed the straw aside. Will touched her sleeve.

"Through the bailey and out the gate," he murmured. "We're nearly there."

Shoulders hunched forward, Nell followed the hem of his robe. They halted before the watchhouse as an armored guard stepped forward to inspect them. His spurs and chains clanked alarmingly in the stillness.

"Bless you, my son," Will chanted cheerfully. He beamed at the approaching guard and at the helmeted man inside the watch-house who extended red hands over the charcoal brazier." 'Tis cold enough to freeze the Devil's buns."

Catholic priests mystified Will. He had no notion if they ad-dressed mundane matters like the weather or made reference to the Devil's anatomy. Perhaps he'd blundered. Mayhaps he should have clacked the beads dangling from his waist and left it at that. Or mayhaps he should have prepared a small bone resembling that from a Protestant baby and used it to pick his teeth as he'd heard Catholic priests did. Damn their eyes.

The guard did not respond. His humorless gaze swept Will and Nell behind him. 'Twas time to seize the initiative, Will de-cided. To dawdle could prove fatal. Nodding pleasantly, he strode forward, passing the guard then the shutters on the watchhouse windows. He moved steadily past sputtering torches, his gaze fixed on the narrow walkway leading to safety.

"Halt!"

Nell bumped into Will's broad back. Her heart skipped then froze. She pressed her lips into a line and darted a sidelong glance toward the guard who strode toward them with rapid, purposeful strides. Don't speak, she reminded herself. Ducking her head, she stood quietly as Will turned back. She saw his hand drop to the knife hidden within the folds of his robe.

"Do you have business with us, my son?"

"You dropped this, father."

The guard extended the silver casket.

"Thank you." The casket vanished into Will's robe and he

tightened the sash at his waist. "For a moment you held history in your hands, boy. Bless you."

The guard smiled and looked pleased and Nell saw how young he was. But it wasn't until they had stepped into the deserted street fronting the Louvre that her heart resumed a normal cadence. "Sweet Jesu!" she breathed. "And you called me a dolt? How could you drop the casket?"

"A man wasn't meant to wear scurvy skirts! This way. Hurry." He hastened her up a dark lane, keeping to the deeper blackness along the shop fronts.

With each step Nell's heart lightened until exhilaration overwhelmed her. She had escaped Guise, Will hadn't slain her, and they had recovered Elizabeth's letters. A bubble of joy formed in her throat and grew, erupting in laughter. Throwing out her arms, she spun in a circle of sheer high spirits, her slippers skidding over the frost-painted cobbles. Cold white mist plumed before her lips. But she thought it a fine night. One of the finest.

"We did it!" she crowed. Impulsively she pulled Will into an ebony alleyway and kissed him soundly on the mouth.

His arms tightened immediately. The kiss he gave her was not of celebration but deep and eager, tasting of urgency and swift, rough passion.

When he released her, Nell stared up at him, shaken by the ferocity of her own response. "I missed you," she whispered.

"This is most unseemly behavior, Nellie love." Will grinned down at her. "It seems you're not cut from priestly cloth."

Beneath the light words, Nell heard the hoarseness of his desire. "Somewhere," she said. "Take me somewhere and . . ."

He took her hand and pulled her forward.

Saddled horses waited in the warm darkness of a nearby stable. Impatient, they held the horses to a walk through the twisting Paris streets. At the city gate, Will rode ahead and conversed in low tones with the alderman who guarded the night chains. At the finish he tucked a fat purse into the man's doublet and the alderman winked and looked aside as Will dropped the chains.

Then they were flying up the north road leading away from Paris. Nell's hood dropped to her shoulders and her hair streamed behind her. Cold wind stung her cheeks like needles and numbed her hands. When she believed she would surely slide from the saddle, dropped by fatigue and cold, Will turned off the main road onto a lane that led eventually to an abandoned barn.

Inside he lit the brazier he'd hidden there the previous day and saw to their horses. Nell sank to the haystack and rubbed her fiery cheeks and hands.

"Hungry?" Will asked when he emerged from the stalls.

"Aye," Nell whispered, looking at him. But she ignored the basket he set near her feet. Instead, weariness vanished, she lay back on the sweet-smelling hay and slowly, shyly, raised the hem of her robe. "Oh, aye."

His eyes blazed and he smiled.

Clasped in each other's arms, they tumbled about the hay, seeking each other with rough, swift urgency. Later they supped on the chicken and pastries in Will's basket. Then they reached for each other again.

This time, urgencies slaked, they took their leisure. This time, they explored with the languid delight of lovers reunited. Will kissed the star-shaped mark on her hip, Nell traced his scars with the tip of her tongue. He tasted of the downy spring between her thighs, she discovered the spot below his navel that made him groan with pleasure. They teased and tantalized, gave and received, laughed softly and murmured endearments. And at the moment of trembling explosive release, Nell gazed up at him with shining eyes and called his name.

When they were once again clad in the warm woolen priests' robes, Nell picked straw from her unbound hair and sipped the hot wine Will had heated above the brazier.

"Where will we go?" she asked quietly. "We can't go home, can we?" The thought damped the glow still lingering on her cheeks.

Dropping back on the straw, Will propped his head in his hand. "Where else, love? France is not safe; Guise will eventually surmise your plot. The watchhouse guard will recall the casket in any case. I'll wager Guise has men-at-arms on the road by midday on the morrow."

Nell nodded and plucked at her robe.

"Spain is out of the question as is Italy. Ireland and Scotland are populated by barbarians and madmen. Elizabeth has troops quartered in Flanders. England is our only choice."

"Isn't that a bit like hiding the lamb in the wolf's cave?"

"Mayhaps. But if Elizabeth thinks we're on the run she won't look for us in her own backyard. At least not for a time."

"She'll have us killed for certain. You for treason, me for . . . for being me." Nell pressed her forehead against her upraised knees.

"You believe it, then?" Will asked softly. "That you are Elizabeth's bastard?"

"Read the letters."

She waited, gazing toward the stalls as Will held the letters to the brazier and read. When he'd scanned them through twice, he closed the casket and lay back on the straw, folding his arms under his head.

"Well?" Nell demanded.

"Mayhaps," he answered cautiously.

"Will, be reasonable. Why else would Uncle Robert have promised me these letters? If it wasn't that he wanted me to know—finally—my parentage? My own history?"

Will shrugged. "Mayhaps Dudley wanted it known he'd tupped the queen. God knows he was vain enough. Mayhaps it was his history, not yours, that mattered most to him."

"He could have stated his claim while he was alive. But he didn't."

"Had he dared tell the world he'd shared the queen's bed, Elizabeth would have had his head on the block quicker than a hare's blink. If Dudley sought to ensure his place in history by making the tale known, it had to be done when he was no longer present to suffer the inevitable consequences."

"He could have done so by bequeathing the letters to more important folk than me if that was his intent."

"And who might that be? If he bequeathed the letters to Elizabeth, it's certain she would have destroyed them. He would have known Lettice would use the letters for personal gain or to indulge her hatred for the queen. The same reasoning would apply to most of the queen's court. But you, Nellie love, Dudley trusted you. Mayhaps he wanted you to have the letters because he believed you would recognize their historic value and preserve and protect them. Mayhaps he hoped you would give the letters to history after the old girl's death when they could no longer damage her image of herself."

Nell turned the suggestion in her mind, eventually rejecting it. "Nay, Will. There's more to this business than that. If not— why would Elizabeth command my death in the event the letters were read?"

"To protect the deceit. She's the virgin queen, Nell. Purest and most venerated among women. Ethereal, mystifying. Coveted. The deceit is the central issue of Elizabeth's existence."

"Ethereal? Pure?" Nell's laugh was harsh. "The queen possesses the tongue of a bawd and the temper of a warthog. Deceit is her second nature; she feeds on it. Speak of tyranny, speak of vanity—then you address Elizabeth Tudor!"

"But speak to whom, m'love? To a handful of court regulars or to England? To England, Elizabeth is what Mary is to the Church. Elizabeth Tudor is the virgin mother and England is her child. Twenty leagues outside London you'd be hard pressed to find a soul to credit Elizabeth as deceitful or tyrannical. In the provinces entire villages light candles to her, Nell, as if she were a patron saint. They pray to her."

She stared at him.

"Elizabeth Tudor would march through hell to preserve that image. She will reject suitors, deny a woman's secret needs. She will protect her virginity with the ferocity of a savage. She must. For without it, she is just another woman. Her crown and her fame rest upon that thin wall between her thighs. England believes it exists and she will not undeceive them."

Nell covered her eyes and bowed her head.

Gently, he touched her hand. "When she commanded your death, she condemned me as well. Had I put you to the sword then returned to England, I too would have died. You know that, don't you? No living person must know the content of these letters. She won't risk it."

"And the star-shaped mark? Can you dismiss that, Will?"

A silence stretched between them. "It's possible the letters don't mean what they seem," Will said finally.

"Is that what you believe? The mark has no significance?"

"I accept there is enough coincidence, if you will, that men who wish to be convinced will be."

"I see."

"Armed with these letters and abundant self-interest, there are those who will advance you as the queen's bastard and raise armies in your name." He looked at her but the shadows flickering across her face obscured her expression. "Is that what you want, Nell?"

The locket felt heavy against her breast. As heavy as the unanswered questions pressing her mind. "I don't know," she said. She beat a fist against her knee. "She's loyal in friendship, loyal in her hatreds. But she spurns the flesh of her flesh? She's tender to those who take ill or suffer the loss of kin. But she casts aside her issue as one scrapes garbage from a plate." Tears brimmed in her eyes. "Why couldn't she love me? What terrible flaw did she see in me?"

Gently, Will drew her into his arms and rested his chin atop her head. "I love you, Nell." Drawing back, he tilted her face up to him. "Do you want to be a queen?"

"I don't know." She didn't mention that to be queen, she would have to take arms against Elizabeth. But it lay between them. She stroked his cheek. "If I did," she said after a moment, "would you support my cause?"

"I love you—but I love England more. The horror of civil war is behind us, may it please God. But if the crown again becomes a battlefield, if Englishmen take arms against Englishmen—my sword is pledged to Elizabeth. I've betrayed my queen once, Nell. I'll not break fealty again."

She closed her eyes and pressed her face against his shoulder. His answer wounded deeply but did not surprise her. Elizabeth had chosen well in the Duke of Brampton.

"There's something else. I won't be another Robert Dudley," he continued, his voice quiet. "I won't bow my knee to you in public and bed you in private. I'll not wag my tail in gratitude for what bits of life you choose to share. I'll not stand in the shadow of a woman's skirt. I want a flesh-and-blood woman, Nellie love, not a royal image. For once a crown is placed, it weighs heavily. It's never removed. The crown would be there always. In work, in play, in bed."

"Then you would bear arms against me."

"Aye. If the road to Whitehall is the path you choose to travel."

The lines were drawn. But she had known it would be so. As Elizabeth's bastard, Will was lost to her. He was lost to her in any case. Biting her lip, she watched him yawn and stretch against the straw.

"Where will we go?"

"Home to Carlisle."

How easily he said the word *home*. "The queen will find us there."

"The lads of Carlisle won't betray us, m'love." Turning, he pillowed his head on his hand.

"But—sooner or later . . ."

"By then it's to be hoped we'll have found a solution that allows us to keep our heads."

"Aye."

Long after Will slept, Nell remained awake, listening to the even sound of his breathing, to the rustle of the horses in the stalls. Although there was much to occupy her mind, her thoughts centered on Elizabeth. Elizabeth Tudor had been the hub around which Nell's life had circled. She saw that now.

From earliest childhood, Nell's happiness had depended upon the whim of the queen. If Elizabeth allowed Uncle Robert time with his family, Nell was happy. More often Elizabeth summoned him to court and she was not.

Elizabeth had pervaded Kenilworth, present always in the form and focus of Lettice's hatred. Later, Elizabeth had determined the tenure of Nell's court sojourn, had overseen Nell's studies, had arranged Nell's marriage to Edward when Dudley suggested the time was ripe. The plight troth with Lord Mendenshire existed because Elizabeth had desired it. The major events in Nell's life, as in the lives of so many others, had been orchestrated by Elizabeth to please Elizabeth.

The queen's tentacles wound through every moment of Nell's existence. Her life had been an endless dance of attendance. A never-ending quest for approval and acceptance.

But now she understood the dance was hopeless. Elizabeth would withhold approval until the end of her days. The queen would view any daughter as a contemptible pale shadow of the mother. Unless the daughter challenged as an equal.

Nell knew with a certainty of fact that she would earn Elizabeth's approval only when she wrested the crown from her mother's grip. Oddly, Elizabeth would understand and admire such bold ambition. Though the hatred would exist also.

Quietly Nell dropped her head into her hands and wept. The truth was too terrible to contemplate. Only by destroying Elizabeth could Nell hope to gain the approval she had craved throughout her lifetime.

They rode hard and fast, skirting the towns and villages in favor of back roads and trails through forests and stubbled fields. They supped on hare and fish and withered vegetables Nell gleaned from winter fields. At night they curled together for warmth and comfort.

Before long the priests' robes were soiled and tattered. Fatigue pinched Nell's lips. The luster in her eyes had faded to weariness.

"There's a village yonder," Will said, pointing to a clutch of cottages. "Wait here. I'll steal us fresh clothing."

"I'm coming with you."

"Nell, remember Paris?"

"I'm coming." Her stubborn tone resisted argument.

By way of explanation she insisted on a voice in selecting the clothing he would steal. But that wasn't the true reason she wished to ride through the village. She wanted to see the straw wreaths and mistletoe tacked to the cottage doors. Wanted to hear the songs of celebration drifting from the windows of the small chapel.

In England the Christmas court would be festive, the rounds of balls and masques beginning now. There would be fireworks against the winter sky, and a night of bells and rejoicing. Bonfires in the street. Pine boughs and holly to adorn the city gates. And gaiety and laughter.

She rode through the village, staring hungrily at the corn shocks placed beside each door, listening to the drift of distant song.

"This will be easiest," Will said, reining before the village bath. He darted inside then ran out with a bundle of clothing tucked beneath his arm.

A red-faced peasant woman chased after him, halting in confusion when she identified the robes Will and Nell wore. As they galloped toward the forest edge, she raised a fist and shook it after them.

"I think we just gave priesthood a bad name," Nell murmured when they had dismounted deep within the forest. Raising an eyebrow, she separated the clothing and they dressed hurriedly.

Her glum expression lifted when she viewed Will in a farmer's crushed cap and coarse shirt. Smiling, she swept a glance over shirt sleeves that ended well above the bones in his wrists, breeches that strained, and sagging woolen hose.

"Laugh if you will," he commented with a sour grin. " 'Tis a hundred times better than the foppery at court. These be honest clothes a man need not feel shame to wear."

"But the fit," Nell laughed.

"Aye," he smiled, looking her up and down.

The hem of Nell's stolen skirt flapped about her ankles while the waist hung loose and her bodice strained at the laces. Her mantle was homespun and scratchy, and her hat large enough to have settled on the tops of her ears.

They studied each other then burst into laughter. "When we reach Calais, at least we won't attract attention."

Attracting notice was the last thing they wanted as neither

doubted Henri Guise had dispatched men to search them out. And it required no particular genius to surmise their destination.

"But we won't find a decent inn dressed like this," Nell pointed out.

"You purchase something more suitable while I arrange our passage."

By midday of the next day they were within an hour's ride of Calais. When the town came into view, Will reined to a walk and looked at Nell thoughtfully. "We have to die, Grandmother."

"Agreed. Dying will buy us time." Without being aware she did so, Nell had followed his line of thought. When she realized what she'd done, she smiled at Will with affection. It hadn't been so long ago that she'd despaired of understanding him.

Though there was a moment of anxiety, a generous bribe persuaded the gatekeep to overlook their expired passports and they rode into Calais.

"For this to be effective, our deaths must be public knowledge," Nell murmured, guiding her mare through the crowded dockside lanes. They chose an inn not far from the wharves.

"Our deaths must be witnessed and recorded by the entire town," Will agreed. When Nell raised an eyebrow, he smiled. "I have a plan."

The plan required two days to arrange. Two nervous days for Nell, who jumped each time hooves clattered into the inn courtyard. She was certain the noise signaled Guise's men had overtaken them. She didn't relax until she peeped through the window and assured herself the riders were not men-at-arms.

"If we don't depart soon, I'll expire from apoplexy," she said to Will at supper.

The generous fire leaping in the common room hearth, fed constantly by the innkeeper's plump wife, had finally soaked away the chill Nell had begun to believe had settled permanently in her bones. The inn catered to a rough-and-tumble clientele, merchants traveling without wives to the winter fair at Lyons, ships' captains who preferred honest ale and an occasional brawl to more formal accommodations, prosperous shopkeepers journeying home for the holidays. The atmosphere was loud and lively.

"We sail on the morrow," Will promised.

"Thank God. I don't think I . . ."

A travel-stained man entered, looked about, then strode to a group of men sitting near the crockery hutch. He spoke in a low voice then a shout rose drowning the noise in the room. One of the men jumped onto the tabletop and knocked two pewter tankards together until every eye turned toward him.

"Attention," he shouted. Blazing dark eyes swept the common room. "Hear this, all true Frenchmen. This day shall go down as a day of infamy! For today I have news that the Valois whoreson has murdered the Guises!"

A gasp silenced the room. Nell gripped Will's hand and leaned forward.

"Henri, Duc of Guise, his brother the cardinal, and his cousin Francis, Duc of Loire, were slain on orders from the king. 'Twas murder, black and foul." The man's mouth twisted. "Our sodomite king thinks to advance the Huguenot cause, it appears. By slaughtering the head of the Catholic League. Our Catholic king murders Catholic subjects. Is this outrage to be borne?"

"No!" the room shouted. "Never!"

"Shall we assist the cowardly Valois by condoning this egregious act?"

"No!"

"Then follow me! To the king's man in Calais. I say we flay his hide and send it to Blois. Show the Valois butcher what Calais thinks of murdering kings!"

Another man stood and waved his fist. "We'll take the hide of a Huguenot or two in payment for the Guises!"

In a flash the room emptied until only Will and Nell and a scattered number of foreigners remained. By silent accord Will and Nell rose hastily and retired to their chamber above the stairs.

"Francis—murdered," Nell said, sinking to the stool beside the chamber fire. "I didn't wish to wed him, but I wished him no harm."

Will stood behind her and stroked the curve of her shoulders. "The secret of the letters is safe," he said quietly. "The Guises are gone. Whatever the Spaniards admit under torture will carry no weight without the letters as proof. Philip's claws have been clipped."

"Now you and I are the only people who know."

"And Elizabeth."

"Aye. Elizabeth." Nell covered her eyes. "She will hound us to the ends of the earth."

"Nay, Nellie love. News of our deaths will soon reach the old girl's ear. There are English aplenty in Calais to carry the tale. And we're listed on the *Bristol's* manifest by our true names. So far as the queen will know, we'll be dead. She'll think our bones are rotting at the bottom of the harbor."

"At least for a time."

"Aye. For a time."

Nell nodded and twisted Robert Dudley's ring upon her finger. Her thoughts drifted to Henri and Francis Guise.

"They wished to be kings," she said softly. "Ambition forged the blade that killed them." Will's hands paused on her shoulders but he ventured no comment. Tilting her head backward to meet his eyes, she looked at him with a troubled gaze. "Make love to me, Will Steele. Make me forget kings and thrones and the force of grand ambitions. For a time."

He pulled the pins from her crown of hair and a glorious spill of red and gold tumbled over his hands.

The day of their departure dawned cold and clear. A brisk wind chuffed off the channel and snapped the flags atop the masts rocking in the Calais harbor.

Today, Nell wished to draw attention and be remembered. She donned the scarlet gown and silver sleeves she had purchased for this purpose. Will wore emerald velvet and satin stocks and sleeves exaggerated by horsehair padding.

"Tricked out like a queen's fancy man," he grumbled under his breath.

Nell concealed her smile by drawing the feather on her hat

across her lips. They walked behind the wagon bearing their new trunks, all of which were empty but for stones to weigh them. Tapestry valises containing the clothing Nell had purchased had been taken aboard the *Elizabeth Ann* yesterday. The *Elizabeth Ann* was anchored in the berth next to the *Bristol*.

When they reached the plank leading upward to the *Bristol*'s deck, Will shouted for the wagon driver to halt. A calculated scene ensued. Will loudly berated the driver for laziness; Nell pretended to discover the loss of her dinner knife and screamed, accusing the driver of thievery. As they had planned, a crowd gathered.

When their trunks had been loaded aboard the *Bristol*, Will ended the scene by drawing to his full height and leveling a haughty sneer at the gathered throng. "You've not heard the last of the Duke of Brampton, by God!"

Nell tossed her head and lifted her scarlet hem. Will followed her up the plank and across the decking. Once on board they hastened directly to the cabin where their trunks had been taken.

Without speaking, they stripped off the brilliant clothing and donned canvas breeches and coarse shirts purchased earlier from the deck hands. Nell stuffed her hair beneath a knit thrum and thrust her feet into shapeless canvas shoes. Will had done the same.

"No one will be injured?" she asked when she was dressed.

"Most of the crew will be off ship before the *Bristol* sails. The captain, the pilot, and the remaining men will depart in the customs tender. She'll be empty when she blows."

They departed the *Bristol* with ease, unnoticed among a hundred others dressed as they were. Men scurried up and down the *Bristol*'s plank loading kegs filled with sand. The provision barrels stacked at the ship's waist were empty.

When the *Bristol*'s anchor wound up and she moved slowly toward the harbor mouth, Will and Nell, still dressed as crewmen, were standing on the loaded deck of the *Elizabeth Ann*.

"Eventually one of the crew will talk," Nell commented. She watched the customs tender approach the *Bristol* and round the hull. After a few moments the tender reappeared and cut through the water toward the docks.

"Aye."

But they would gain a few weeks before the tale became too great to contain and someone whispered the plot over a pint. A few weeks during which Nell would decide the course of her future. She would plot the shape of her revenge, if revenge it would be.

Turning against the rail, she swept a glance across the throng jamming the wharf. For the first time in her memory, she did not search among the faces for the woman portrayed in her locket.

"The charges are set," Will said, his gaze steady on the *Bristol*. "The ship should be empty." The customs tender had almost reached the wharf. "It should happen about—now."

An enormous explosion split the morning air. Bits of flaming mast and decking erupted toward the sky then hissed down into the water; boiling waves rolled toward shore, dipping the ships at anchor. For a moment a stunned silence muffled the wharf then shouts exploded and a surge of people rushed the dock posts.

Two hours later the *Elizabeth Ann* slipped anchor and hoisted sail. The *Bristol* had burned to the waterline. She tilted upward and glided beneath the harbor waves as the *Elizabeth Ann* sailed past.

Will placed his arm around Nell's shoulders and faced toward England as the breeze freshened and the sails cupped full.

"We're going home, Nellie love."

She leaned into the warmth of his body and studied the quiet joy in his eyes. And she felt the shame of envy.

CHAPTER 17

Bounded on two sides by the rivers Eden and Caldew, Carlisle's castle sat atop a mound dominating the walled town. Years before, Mary, Queen of Scots, had gazed from the castle ramparts, had walked along the curving terrace. Perhaps she had contemplated the spires of the nearby Norman cathedral, built of darkened gray stones pried from walls and ruins dating from the Roman occupation. As a precaution against fire, most of the town shops and cottages were fashioned from sandstone; the city walls were granite, the blocks cut from nearby quarries.

"This isn't the original town," Will explained as their coach lifted over the bridge spanning the Eden and turned onto the Scotland Road. "The blasted thieving Scots destroyed Carlisle. But the city fathers rebuilt it, by God." He added the last with a grim smile of satisfaction.

Carlisle lay a scant eight miles from the Scottish border. Throughout history, the Scots periodically swept out of the Cheviot Hills to plunder the town and surrounding fields. Naturally this precipitated retaliatory raids conducted by Carlisle's good brave lads. A feud of long standing smoldered along Cumbria's hilly borders.

"You're eager to reach Willowick, aren't you?" Nell touched

Will's wrist then pushed her hands into a fox muff and adjusted her boots against the charcoal foot warmer.

"Aye."

His restlessness had increased as the *Elizabeth Ann* approached English shores. Nell had observed his increasing anticipation with a combination of amusement and wistful envy. Although Will Steele was famed as the Fighting Duke, Nell sensed he was also a man of the soil, with roots dug deep in Carlisle's black peaty earth. Carlisle was home, the place from which Will Steele gathered strength and sustenance.

Studying him from beneath the velvet brim of her hat, Nell realized suddenly how little she knew of Will's everyday concerns. Did he actively participate in the day-to-day operation of his estates? Did he sit as justice or delegate the task, as did so many of the lords she knew in London? Who acted as his chatelaine? Was there a woman waiting in one of the fortified manors their coach rolled past?

Perhaps the woman whose name he had called out during his illness? The thought gave pause.

"Will . . ."

"Look there," he interrupted. The coach had swung off the Scotland Road and turned into Brampton Road. "That's Baywick."

Nell leaned forward to glimpse a medieval fortress built to guard the entrance to Weyley Valley, the gorge that opened behind it. Thin wisps of smoke wafted from the chimney stacks; a wood cart turned out of the gate. According to Will, the fortress walls bore scars from a century of Scottish raids, but from this distance Baywick seemed undamaged, a bit of history preserved. Frost caught the late afternoon sun and glittered like sugar on the fortress stones.

"Do you mind terribly not winning Baywick?" she asked. Weak winter sunlight slanted through the coach window and illuminated Will's face. She thought he had never looked as handsome.

"Aye, woman. I mind like bloody hell!" Then, seeing her stricken expression, he bent to drop a kiss on her nose. "But don't flog yourself on my account. I'll best the thieving Scots without it, m'love."

She watched Baywick until it passed from sight. Baywick had spared her from making a fool of herself, for which Nell was grateful. She had brushed perilously near asking if Will's eagerness to return home involved a lover. Mayhaps a woman named Kate.

Frowning, she plucked at her fur muff. A few weeks in company with a border lord threatened to undo years of practiced court conditioning. If she didn't temper her recent use of blunt speaking, soon she'd forfeit the capacity for nuance. With disastrous results if fate ordained a crown in her future. The realization sobered her and she didn't speak again until the coach topped a small rise and a snow-clad valley spread before them.

"This is Willowick," Will informed her with quiet pride. "The Brampton lands extend as far as you can see in any direction."

Nell leaned to the window.

Thick stands of beech and oak encroached upon snow-draped fields. A branch of the Eden, famed for its salmon, wound down the valley like a riband, pooled into an ice-capped lake, then continued its meandering course through the meadows. Nell absorbed the snowy beauty with delight, but it was Willowick manor that caught her breath.

The manor grew out of a low hill, set like an exquisite jewel fashioned of pink stone and etched by lacy drifts of winter-green ivy. Once there had been nothing on the site but a granite keep positioned at the base of the Cheviots to defend against the Scots. Generations of Bramptons had modified and rebuilt until now the stone keep lay outside the manor proper, crumbling into scenic decay, surrounded by snug villagers' cottages.

Nell shielded her eyes from the afternoon sun bouncing off the lake ice and reflecting from the diamond-shaped panes of the manor windows.

"Do you like it?" Will asked, watching her expression.

"Aye," Nell said softly. "Oh, aye. It's lovely, Will."

Willowick was everything Nell had dreamed a home should

be. Graceful. Substantial. Sturdy enough to withstand the ages. As she examined the leaded roof and frosty pink stones, she experienced a burst of bittersweet longing. 'Twas no wonder Will seldom could be coaxed to leave Willowick to attend court; she no longer felt surprised by his eagerness to return.

Holding her hat, she leaned from the window and inhaled the woodsmoke overhanging the valley. And the scent of pine and cold clean air, and the tangy odors of the ciderhouse. A warm yeasty fragrance drifted from the cookhouse behind the manor. These were the smells of home.

As the coach wound upward toward the manor gates, Will took her hand in his.

"Nell, there's something I would know."

"Aye?"

"When you come to my bed—is it only because you wish to be seeded?"

Her eyebrows rose toward her hat brim. Jesu. In the rush of events she had forgotten her plot to foist Will's issue onto Lord Mendenshire. Had she actually deceived herself to that extent? A blush warmed her cheeks.

"Nay, m'lord," she whispered.

His smile warmed her and she would have said more, but the coach halted before the gates to a wooden bridge spanning the fortification ditch. A dozen or more people rushed toward the manor from the manor village, shouting greetings. Men in rough clothing dipped their knees then grinned and reached to grip Will's hand. Rosy-cheeked peasant girls curtsied and colored prettily and peeked at Nell behind shy smiles. Someone pressed a bouquet of dried heather and lavender into her arms. More people ran outside from the manor doors. A boy was dispatched on horseback to Carlisle carrying the news of Lord Brampton's return. Then Nell was swept along with the others into the manor's great hall.

Before she had time to form an impression of arched wooden beams and cherry-wood paneling, a large red-coated setter leaped from the hearth and bounded across the hall. Barking joyously, he jumped up and settled huge paws on Will's shoulders and lapped

Will's face. Will roughed the dog's ears affectionately. "Down, boy," he commanded in a voice lacking conviction, and he laughed when the dog immediately leaped on him again.

"You're home!"

A small breathless girl appeared at the staircase landing, her skirts flying behind her. She clapped her hands then ran down the stone stairs and hurled herself into Will's arms. Laughing and crying, she clung to him like a burr, her petticoats billowing when Will swung her in a high circle. Her small arms circled his neck; she wrapped her legs around his waist and smothered his face beneath a hundred kisses.

"Who is this?" Nell inquired, smiling at the child's exuberance.

Will pried her arms from about his neck, kissed her soundly, then placed the child on her slippered feet. "This disheveled imp is my daughter. Mind your manners, Katie darlin'. This lovely lady is Nellanor, Lady Amesly. She merits a dip of the knee and a pretty smile."

Startled, Nell gazed into eyes as dark and warm as Will's. Her smile dissolved into shock. "Your daughter?" she whispered.

Suddenly shy, the child dipped into an awkward curtsy, then peeked at Nell through a fringe of dark lashes.

More villagers appeared. Dignitaries from Carlisle and nearby manors arrived and Nell stepped backward as people she didn't know moved forward to greet Will. The gathering moved deeper into the hall where hot ale awaited to chase the chill. A joint of beef appeared and mutton sully and steaming pastries spread with rum butter. Nell smiled and returned greetings, nodded and nibbled from the round of day-old bread that served as her trencher.

But her gaze continually returned to Kate, Will's daughter. Though Will was immediately engaged in talk of politics and border skirmishes, he seemed not to mind that the setter and his daughter stayed near his side. One hand stroked the dog's massive head, the other caressed his daughter's tousled curls. The child pressed against Will's legs and gazed up at him with adoring eyes.

Torches and dozens of candle branches had been lit against the early winter darkness before Nell's thoughts settled and she was able to see Kate for herself rather than as Will's daughter. The child's hair was lighter than Will's. Red highlights gleamed in the tangled dark curls. She had Will's crisp classic profile but her small features were softer, still childishly rounded yet hinting of the beauty to come.

But what melted Nell's heart was the girl's expression. The child stared up at her father, rapt, the entire focus of her small being centered upon Will.

Time spun backward as Nell examined Kate's jumbled skirts, the none-too-clean bodice and sleeves just this side of too small. So must Nell have looked once, as she pressed herself beside Robert Dudley in her hand-me-down clothing and slippers that pinched. Like Kate with Will, she had hung on Robert's every word, filled with joy by his return. She had anchored her world to his. Because there had been no one else.

By the time the hall finally cleared and young Kate had been carried upstairs to bed, Nell was in a frenzy of impatience to put the questions scalding her tongue.

"Tired?" Will asked, taking her in his arms and kissing the top of her head. "I should have warned you homecoming would be tumultuous." He poured fresh wine cups as Nell seated herself before the fire, then he sat beside her and stretched his legs out before him. Even learning the barbarous Scots had burned his smoke shed and made off with half a dozen of his ewes didn't diminish the contentment he felt at this moment.

"Tell me about her," Nell said.

"About who?"

"About Kate, of course. Your daughter!"

"She's wonderful, isn't she?" He smiled, delighted by Nell's interest. "I nearly lost Kate last year when she was five. To the purples. Thank God she survived and without any scarring."

"Why didn't you tell me about her?"

He looked at her. "You didn't ask." He was genuinely surprised by the anger in her tone. It was controlled but unmistakable.

"I didn't think to ask if you were married either," Nell said thinly. "Are you?"

Will sat up straighter and shifted on the settle so he could see her face. "No. I've never been married."

"Surely Kate has a mother."

A flush of color stained Nell's cheeks. Sarcasm wasn't her usual weapon. But a sudden explosion of jealousy, more painful than she would have imagined, overtook her tongue. Images of the lovemaking they had savored during the ship's passage, long hours of soft laughter and loving, shimmered in her mind then altered to visions of Will kissing another woman, exploring another woman's eager body. The unwanted images sliced through her like a hot blade.

"Celia died of the sweats when Kate was two years old." Will studied her expression and anticipated the question she would not ask. "Nay, we weren't married, Nell, but I loved her. Very much."

"I see." To her shame, Nell experienced a rush of relief. But her jealousy burned as brightly as before. What had Celia been like to earn Will's love? Did he mourn her still? The questions scorched her heart. Forcibly she made herself think of Celia's daughter instead of Celia.

"Why are you angry about this, m'love?" When she made no answer, just glared at him, Will cast a glance toward heaven. Women utterly mystified him. Did she suppose he'd been a saint? Chaste and virginal before he met her? If anyone should be affronted by their situation, it should be him. It was Nell, after all, who was plight trothed, not him. He was free and unencumbered.

"What will happen to Kate if we're betrayed?" Nell asked.

"And I'm hanged for treason? She's been provided for. I've settled a fortune in Kate's name. When the crown confiscates my holdings, Kate won't be affected as she holds land in her own right. Her future is secure."

"You said *when*," Nell whispered, staring at him, "not *if*." She turned her gaze to the fire and bit her lip. "All we've accomplished by coming here is to delay the inevitable. That's true, isn't it? Eventually, Elizabeth will find us."

A wave of despair darkened her eyes and her shoulders dropped. Aside from the inevitability of Elizabeth's vengeance, agreeing to come to Willowick had proved an error. Aye, coming here had stirred emotions she had believed tightly reined. It wasn't so.

Not since Kenilworth had Nell so keenly felt the lack of a home. No child waited to fling her arms about the neck of Nellanor Amesly, no dog bounded to lick her cheeks, no servants hovered with faces alight at sight of her. She had no home—no place to go or call her own. She had nothing. No fortune, no family, no true history. Slowly, she scanned the hall, thinking Will had been a complete fling-brain to risk all this.

"Why am I here?" she murmured, spreading her hands. "For what possible purpose?"

"To buy time. Time in which to decide if you want to be a queen."

Irritation thinned her lips. "You do have a way of reducing problems to base elements, Will Steele. But there's more to it than that." Wine spilled from her cup and dripped over her shaking fingers. "Who I am is tangled within the queen's letters. This isn't merely a matter of choosing what I want or don't want. It's discovering who and what I am."

"Who are you, m'love?"

"That's what I must decide." Standing, she paced before him then halted and passed a hand across her eyes. "If I'm truly Elizabeth's daughter—then I have a right to the succession." Her expression challenged him to disagree. She didn't speak again until it was evident he would not respond. "But if I decide to . . . to pretend I don't know of Elizabeth's treachery, then I must face her with the opened casket and convince her I'm too daft to connect myself with her letters. If I do that, Will—whether or not she believes me—you and I will die."

The latter choice was unthinkable. In no manner or form did Nell believe she could convincingly persuade Elizabeth that she did not understand what the letters admitted.

A hundred times Nell had imagined confronting the mother who had abandoned her. While standing at the rail of the *Eliza-*

beth Ann, she had stared at the horizon but had seen only Elizabeth Tudor's canny eyes. She had relived the rootlessness of her
childhood, had recalled her first flux, her first love, had agonized
through memories of the countless times she had wept for a
mother's loss. It was unimaginable that she could stand before
Elizabeth and not scream: *Why? Why did you abandon me? Where
were you when I needed you?*

"The choice," she said finally, "is between spilling your blood
and mine or that of thousands through civil war."

"Nay, Nellie love." Firelight glowed in her hair, shimmered
along the folds of her skirts. Ablaze with light and emotion, she
looked every inch a young queen. "The choice is between forgiveness or revenge."

She stared hard at him then placed her wine cup on the
Turkey carpet draping the nearest table. "I'm weary," she said
abruptly. "I beg permission to withdraw, m'lord. Please summon
someone to show me to my chamber."

Will watched her go. She would not welcome him into her
bed tonight.

The contentment he'd experienced earlier left him, and lines
of concern drew his brow. Leaning forward he rested his elbows
upon his knees and idly stroked the setter's head.

Not for the first time, Will pondered the future, his own and
England's.

There would be those to embrace a Protestant queen of an
age to ensure the succession. This he did not doubt. When Mary's
head had rolled off the axman's blade, her son, James, became
Elizabeth's most likely successor. But Will believed the border
lords would never accept a Catholic Scotsman as their sovereign.
They would pledge their swords to Nell rather than risk James as
Elizabeth's heir. But English Catholics would defend James. As if
this were not enough, Protestant England would split between
those who currently enjoyed Elizabeth's favor and largess and
those who would fashion their ambitions on Nell.

Will could identify four major factions which, human avarice
being what it was, would split again into factions within the factions. The result would be a long and bloody war.

Whoever won—Elizabeth or Nell—England would end bank-rupt. At that point, Will thought, projecting his worst fears, England would fall prey to foreign scavengers. If not through war, then by marriage. A French or Spanish king would sit England's throne. Whichever woman triumphed, the counsel would insist on marriage, for the succession lay at the heart of the issue.

The private cause was another matter. He understood Nell's conflict tracked back to the conversation he'd had with her in Calais. Staring into the fire, he recalled the words of a motherless daughter and the pain and bewilderment underlying Nell's soft voice. He'd heard rejection there, and a hurt that ran too deep to plumb.

When the village crier passed outside the ditch, Will yawned and stood. His own future had passed outside his control, a situation that filled him with frustration and impatience. But there was naught to do about it. If Nell announced for the crown, his sword was pledged against her to a woman who wanted to stretch his neck. If Nell decided to forgo the throne—and he didn't fore-see this occurring—then he and Nell were as good as dead the moment Elizabeth's agents located them. Which they eventually would. Of this he was soul certain.

The setter followed at his heels as he mounted the stone staircase to his bedchamber. There was naught to do but savor the time remaining to him. He would enjoy Willowick and Nell and Kate as long as was possible.

'Twas how you lived, not how long. At least that's what he told himself. No man lived forever.

Nell stretched and yawned and blinked against the pale win-try sunshine penetrating the gauzy material of the bed curtains. For a moment she didn't recall where she was, then she remem-bered and regretted the absence of Will beside her. She'd behaved badly last night; she would make it up to him today.

She rested her cheek on the pillow that should have been Will's. But after a moment she sensed she was not alone. Pulling back the curtains she peered into the chamber and discovered

Kate standing quietly beside the bed, her hands folded against
her skirts.

"Good morrow," Nell said, startled.

"Good morrow." Kate studied her solemnly. "You're very
beautiful. Everyone says so. I think so too."

"Well, I'm pleased you think so."

They looked at each other. Then Nell impulsively patted the
bed beside her. Kate's face lit. She hesitated only a moment, then
scrambled up the bed steps and snuggled against Nell's side. Nell
smiled, reminded of a small warm puppy.

"You smell good, like roses I think," Kate said. "I have a kitten, you know. Did Papa tell you? His name is Wiggins. I got him
from Alfred, the stable boy. Mary—that's the cook's girl—she
gives me milk for him."

"Whoa," Nell laughed. "Talk slower, you're going too fast
for me."

Kate drew a breath then looked up at Nell; her large dark eyes
were sober. "I don't have a mama. I wish I had a mama more than
anything."

Jesu. Nell released a breath then lifted a strand of Kate's tousled hair. "If you had a mama," she said, struggling to keep her
voice light, "she would ask you to wash your hair."

"Mary says mamas make you do things you don't want to do.
Mary says I'm lucky not to have a mama." Kate bowed her head
then cast Nell a swift troubled glance. "Do you think that's true?"

God in heaven. Lettice's daughters had told Nell the same
thing when she was Kate's age. The cook's daughter was as stu-
pidly cruel as Penelope and Dorothy had been. Her arm tightened
around Kate's small body.

"No," Nell said softly. "I don't think Mary is correct."

"Neither do I." The child smoothed a palm over the quilt
edge. "If I had a mama I'd do everything she said. I wouldn't com-
plain at all."

Elizabeth's face appeared so sharply in Nell's mind that she
could see the queen's rouge and rice powder. She shook the image loose with difficulty and returned her attention to Kate's waif-
like face. Good Lord. Had Nell looked this vulnerable when she

was six? So trusting? So eager to love and be loved? She brushed a strand of hair from Kate's soft cheek, sensing the child's need to be touched.

"Where is your father this fine morn?"

"He rode out with Mr. Masterson to inspect the village for repairs."

"Ah, then it appears you and I are on our own today. And I have an idea." Nell smiled as if the thought had just occurred. "Let's pretend, just for today, that you have a mama and she has told us to wash your hair."

The child considered, then her eyes sparkled and she nodded enthusiastically. "I like pretend games."

"In fact, I think we'll begin with baths for us both."

Doubt dimmed Kate's exuberance. "Mary says folks catch their death if they wash in winter."

"Not if we order the tub placed before the fire and insist on plenty of hot water and dry linens."

The sparkle returned to Kate's eyes. "Can we have the rose-scented soap?"

"We can."

Kate pressed her face against Nell's shoulder. "I like you, Lady Nellanor," she said quickly before she jumped from the bed.

Nell was waiting when Will returned before the evening meal.

"I missed you, love." He placed a kiss on her hair and removed his cap and cloak.

Face flushed, she followed him into the great hall and waved aside the wine he offered.

"Did you know Kate's tutor is totally inadequate? He'll have to be replaced immediately." When Will moved to warm his hands before the fire, she followed at his heels. "Kate can scarcely read. She doesn't know a single Latin phrase and she's terrible at ciphers! I ask you—how will she be able to figure her household accounts when the time comes?" Nell looked at him, her mouth pursed as she fumbled for the list she'd written. "I can recommend these tutors . . ."

Will raised a hand. "Give me a moment to catch my breath, woman."

"Her clothes are simply outrageous, completely unsuitable for a duke's daughter. She's wearing gowns years out of fashion, Will, and most are too small. You'll have to send to London for material. I've made a list of the goods we need and the amounts. Mr. Masterson should see to this first thing on the morrow. As for boots and adornments . . ."

"Lord preserve me!" Will rolled his eyes then grinned at her. "You've been at Willowick less than a day, Grandmother. And already you're reorganizing my daughter, my household, and me." A movement caught his attention, and he looked over Nell's shoulder. "Well, well, well. What have we here? Who is this beautiful young princess? And why wasn't I told Willowick was being visited by royalty?"

Blushing with pleasure, Kate darted a shy smile at Nell, then curtsied before her father. Her hair, curled and glossy, shone in the candlelight. She wore a freshly brushed and laundered gown, the seams of which Nell had let out following their midday meal. Her dark eyes danced as she looked up at Will.

Standing aside, Nell watched Will make a flourish and bow low before his delighted daughter. Absorbed in each other, they seemed to have forgotten her. After a moment, feeling that she intruded upon a family intimacy, Nell slipped into the corridor. She pressed her forehead to the wall and blinked against the heat stinging her eyes.

Later, when Will entered her chamber and parted the bed curtains, Nell opened her arms and held him tightly, wanting to melt into him. As if sensing her mood, he made love to her with exquisite tenderness, and kissed the tears from her cheeks without asking explanation.

Within a matter of days, Nell felt as if she had always lived at Willowick. Without conscious thought she stepped naturally and happily into the role of chatelaine, taking charge of a household too long without a woman's guiding hand. With Kate following at her side, watching and learning, Nell turned the manor inside out.

"We usually sweep out the rushes come spring, m'lady."

"Nay," Nell said, frowning at the girl standing before her. "We'll do it twice a month from now on."

Next she ordered the long process of washing and bleaching the linens despite the low hum of grumbling.

"Aye," she conceded grimly, "the sun is hotter in summer. But the linens need washing now."

The sheets would be washed with lye soap, boiled, then draped over drying racks behind the manor before they were spread with fresh sheep manure, baked, then washed again with lye. Last, they would be soaked in pine water then dried in the winter sun.

"Does it matter what kind of urine?" Kate asked when they turned their attention to the tarnish dulling silver trays and tankards.

"That of a healthy male is best, but any will do. So long as it's mixed properly with the right amount of vine ash." Nell stood over the round-faced servant girl mixing urine and ash, watching with a critical eye. "When you're finished scrubbing the tarnish, Meg, the pieces are to be soaked in vinegar suds for six hours." The girl sighed heavily and nodded.

Under Nell's careful stewardship, the manor began to gleam. Although the servants had begun to glance at Nell less kindly. The work satisfied her and kept her mind occupied.

"At last," Will said the next day. "I didn't think I'd be able to coax you away from your keys and apron," he teased, guiding his horse next to hers.

Nell smiled, lifting her face toward the mist overhanging the Cheviots on the far horizon. Plumes of frosty vapor spouted from the horses' nostrils. The cold crisp air imparted a healthy glow to her cheeks.

"You're right," she admitted, surprising him by agreeing. "This is wonderful. I should ride with you every morning."

" 'Tis a more fitting pastime for a queen than chasing brooms, m'love."

The words were intended lightly, she knew. But they raised issues Nell had avoided since arriving at Willowick. In truth, she had seldom been happier. Caring for Will and Kate—believing herself needed—fulfilled longings dating back to her distant past. Now her days were full, her nights replete with joy and soft laughter.

"This can't last, can it? I'm only deceiving myself." She reined at the edge of the forest and cast a wistful look back at Willowick. Frost sparkled over the pink stones and rimed the heavy shutters at the windows. Drifts of smoke curled from the chimneys promising warmth and welcome. In a short time she had formed an attachment for Willowick, had grown to love it as Will did.

"Nay, Nellie love."

Elizabeth would intrude. Elizabeth would demand her pound of flesh. Nell dropped her lashes, looking away from Will's dark gaze. "I won't let her slay you, Will Steele. I won't do that to you. Or to Kate." She spoke slowly, in a low tone, giving voice to a decision she hadn't realized she'd made until she heard herself speak the words. "Even if you take arms against me, Will, I won't give you up to the hangman's noose. I would rather England ran red with blood than meekly surrender our lives to Elizabeth Tudor's deceit."

"Jesu. So it begins. Nell, listen . . ."

But she could speak of it no more. She dug her spurs into the horse's flanks and galloped back to Willowick, leaving Will to stare after her.

At the manor door she skidded to a halt and tossed her reins to the waiting boy before she rushed up the steps.

"Kate?"

"She's in the solar, m'lady."

Kate was the key to her decision. As Nell's love for Kate had blossomed, her feelings for Elizabeth had hardened into hatred. It was so easy to love a child, so easy. Only a woman with heart of ice and stone could turn her back on a child's unquestioning love. Such infamy was unforgivable. It had to be punished.

"Ah, there you are." Nell stepped into the solar and seated herself on the sunny window ledge. Immediately the calming effects of the bright chamber and Kate's warm greeting eased the tension from her shoulders. Smiling, she reached to unpin her hat. "What are you doing?"

"I'm playing queens," Kate explained, pointing to two dolls made of straw and yarn seated before a miniature wooden table.

"Queens?"

"Aye. This is Elizabeth. She's the English queen." The English queen sprouted vivid red hair beneath a circlet of gold yarn. "And this is Mary. She's the thieving Scots queen."

Concealing a smile, Nell thought how like her father Kate sounded. She knelt to examine the Scottish queen's sour expression, painted on the straw by a childish hand. "Hmmm. Tell me about your queens."

"Well, the English queen hates men and babies. She won't marry and she won't have babies, you see. The Scots queen hates men and babies too but she pretends not to; she murders her husbands and she gives away her baby because she doesn't want him." Kate bent over the dolls to straighten their gowns.

Shocked, Nell stared at Kate's hair riband.

Unaware of Nell's stunned expression, Kate chattered on. "Queens don't like children; none of them do. Mary says they don't have time for children because they're too busy making rules and making wars and murdering other queens. They murder each other, you know." She looked up when Nell gasped. "Do you want to play?"

"No." Oh, my God. "No, Kate. Not today."

Standing abruptly, Nell stared down at the two dolls threatening each other across the tiny wooden table.

She clapped a hand over her mouth and ran from the solar.

"We have to talk, Nell."

"Please, Will, not tonight."

Her gray eyes implored him not to put the questions that needed asking. Undressing silently, he pulled back the quilts and slipped in beside her, gathering her close when she scurried into his arms.

Patience, Will admitted with a sigh, was not his strongest armor. Yet he knew her stubbornness; it would avail him little to press. "When?" he asked, not bothering to conceal his irritation.

"Soon," she said, her voice muffled against his shoulder. Her naked breasts warmed his side and the scent of her hair muddled his thoughts. "I envy you Willowick, Will. It's so peaceful here."

"But for how long, m'love?" Beneath the linens her fingers found him and stroked along his length. He groaned and caressed her breast, rolling the nipple into a sweet hard bud.

She moved on top of him and looked down into his eyes, her own gaze troubled. "Do you love me, Will Steele?"

"You know I do."

"Then speak no more tonight." Lightly, her fingertips covered his lips. "Make love to me. I need you so much right now." Removing her fingers, she leaned to kiss him, her hair falling to enclose them within a silken curtain.

Later, he pillowed her head on his shoulder and listened to the soft murmur of her breath. She made a sound in her sleep and pressed against him as if seeking comfort. He held her until she relaxed in his arms, then he turned his face toward the lemony dawn spreading beyond the bed curtains.

Trust a woman to announce she would plunge a country into blood and war then refuse to say another damned word. The lines framing his mouth deepened. Fate had tipped the glass and he imagined he could hear the grains of sand falling toward destruction.

After reflection, he conceded the futility of attempting to alter Nell's decision. First, it was not his right. Second, a part of him understood the seduction of power. Provided the same opportunity, he might have taken the same decision. Who could say? 'Twas a heady challenge to control the fate of men and nations.

Still, he deeply regretted the maelstrom to come. He'd spent much of his life riding to battle and, like most soldiers, his dreams were haunted by corpse-littered fields. Despite the bravado of war camps, he knew of no man who rode into battle with a glad heart.

What propelled men into the field was ambition, honor, and loyalty. The slim woman he held in his arms would elicit such emotions.

That Nell would excel as a leader, he didn't question. She was wise enough to surround herself with sage men, canny enough to tread safely the marshy ground of politics. With prudent counseling and the experience granted by time, he was confident she would prove a worthy daughter of her mother.

He hadn't led men into battle without becoming a keen judge of character. Survival depended upon it. The readiness of his weapons was a man's first priority. But equally important, if not more so, was the choice of who rode beside him and behind. This decision was never taken lightly, but made after considerable thought and meticulous winnowing. Battle companions could and did mean the difference between life and death. One trusted one's life to the swiftness and sure sword of the man riding behind.

Will believed in the swiftness and sure sword of the woman sleeping in his arms. Throughout their weeks together, she had proven herself time and again. He had observed her at her best and at her worst. And he would choose her as his flank man any day. Had fate cast them differently, he would have been proud to raise his standard in her service.

She groaned and moved against him, then opened her eyes and sat up, instantly awake. "I had a dream," she said, gripping his wrist. "A terrible dream! There were two queens . . . made of straw and red ice . . . and a child, bleeding from the heart . . . and I . . ." Nell covered her eyes and shook her head violently. "I looked at the tall queen and I loved her and I hated her!"

"Nell . . ."

"She pointed at me and she said: 'It matters not! The unpleasantness is forgotten!' "

"Put it away, m'love. 'Twas just a dream." Holding her tightly he kissed the tears hanging on her lashes, soothed her until her trembling abated.

"Will." She clutched his arms, stared into his eyes. "I don't

want to be like her! I don't ever, not ever, want to be like Elizabeth Tudor!"

" 'Twas just a dream, love."

"But I am like her, aren't I?" Despair filled her eyes and she
pressed her face into the pillow.

CHAPTER
18

*D*isturbed by the dream, Nell lingered in bed after Will had departed. Today he planned to review the estate account ledgers with Mr. Masterson. Though he hadn't said so, Nell guessed Will was putting his affairs in final order. Mayhaps this was wise. In truth, Will's future didn't flicker bright.

By retaining the silver casket for her own use instead of returning it to London, Nell delayed Will's execution—but she didn't negate it. The moment Nell challenged the crown, Elizabeth would set a price on Will's head—if she hadn't already—for Will had disobeyed a direct royal command, and, more important, he could corroborate Nell's claim.

Aye, Nell thought, Will Steele's future was dim indeed. Regardless of the path she chose. But he could keep his head a little longer if he declared for Nell. Yet he refused to betray his oath to Elizabeth.

"Damned stubborn northern lords," she muttered.

The silver casket lay nested in her lap and she ran a finger across the etched lid. How much simpler everything would be if the Spaniards had not broken the seals. Then she wouldn't now be plotting how best to set history in motion, wouldn't ache inside whenever she thought of Will Steele.

Kate peeked through the bed curtains, then, as had become

her habit, she climbed the steps and snuggled beside Nell. "What's that?" she asked, touching the lid of the casket.

"This?" Nell tilted the silver casket in the morning light and sighed. "This, Katie darling, is a dilemma."

This morning Kate had brought Wiggins and the kitten chased across the bottom of the bed batting at dust motes.

"What's a dilemma?"

"It's when one wants two opposing things at once. Like your game of queens." Nell watched as Kate stroked the silver lid and traced Robert Dudley's broken wax seals with her fingertips. "Your queens can't have husbands and babies *and* a crown. It seems a queen may have power, but not love. While ordinary women may have love, but not power. When one wishes for both—it's a dilemma."

"Aye." Kate nodded wisely. "Queens are afraid of loving. They don't do it. Even I know that." She bent forward to rub Wiggins's stomach and didn't see Nell cover her eyes.

"Is it so wrong to want power over one's own life?" Nell whispered. "To revenge old wounds?"

Kate looked up, thinking Nell addressed her. She frowned, trying to understand. "Do you want to be a queen?" Her frown deepened. "I think you have to be born to it."

"It's all very confusing, Katie."

"Nay, m'lady." Kate placed her small hand in Nell's. "I wouldn't want to be a queen. Would you?" She pressed against Nell's side. "When I grow up I want a home and babies of my own. 'Twould be kingdom enough for me."

Jesu. From the mouths of babes . . .

"M'lord?"

Will looked at the ink blot spreading beneath the tip of his quill. He realized he had been staring at it for several moments. "Forgive me, Mr. Masterson. My mind wanders."

"Shall I fetch some ale, m'lord?"

"Nay." He sanded the blot and pushed from the table. "Tell the boy to bring my horse around. We'll finish this on the morrow."

The accounts were in order, his review merely a matter of

form. Though it pained him to think of Brampton lands passing to
the crown, as they would when Elizabeth declared him a traitor, at
least he had done what he could to protect Kate. Her dower would
be high enough to attract a comfortable match when the time
came.

The cold air and prancing stallion didn't settle his thoughts as
he had hoped. He rode through the manor village, returning greetings, nodding approval when he noticed the repairs he'd ordered
had been completed. It occurred to him there were people in the
village whose great-grandfathers had served Brampton lords as
they did. And it shamed him to know he would be the last Brampton, the one who lost Willowick.

Digging in his spurs, he galloped toward the Cheviots. If God
chose to smile, he would encounter a Scots raiding party. Never
had he felt so great a need to smash and fight. If he couldn't do
battle with events, he could, by God, bash a few Scottish heads.

But the Scots were tucked into their winter dens, conserving
their energy for spring plunder. Will knew this. But still he raced
the stallion toward the hills, plunging through chest-deep drifts
until both he and the horse were panting with exhaustion.

It helped some, but not enough. The problem was, he loved
her. God curse him, he loved her.

He'd always known women would be the death of him.

"God's balls!" he swore. Then he laughed out loud.

Nell's silence throughout supper wasn't as obvious as it might
have been as Kate chattered happily about the day, which they
had spent hawking in the west field. Nonetheless, she was aware
that Will's eyes lingered on her face. And she knew he would not
long be put off. There were questions that demanded answers.

"What?" Will asked Kate. Like Nell his thoughts had strayed.

Kate looked at them both then shyly repeated her question.
"Is Lady Nellanor going to be my mother?" The hope in her expression faded to confusion as a silence lengthened.

Will reached for the quail and cracked the bird in his hands.
Half he served to Nell, half he dropped on his own trencher.

"Lady Nellanor is our guest, Kate. She'll stay with us a while longer, then she must depart."

"Oh." Quick tears brimmed in Kate's eyes. She dropped her head and wadded her napery into a ball.

Sweet Jesu. Nell stared at the child and felt as if a yoke of granite had descended about her shoulders. As certainly as if she saw into Kate's mind, she knew what the girl was thinking. And her heart twisted. Gently, she touched Kate's shoulder.

"I didn't have a mother either." She drew a breath and met Will's gaze across the table. "Until very recently I didn't even know my mother's name."

"Truly?"

"Truly." Without thinking, Nell cupped the locket lying between her breasts. "All I had was a false image." She didn't know why she continued to wear the locket. It no longer meant anything. It never had, but she hadn't known that. The locket had been nothing more than a red herring given her by Robert Dudley to conceal the truth. Anger darkened her expression and she pulled the locket from her throat and dropped it beside the wine cup she shared with Will.

"Did it hurt your neck?" Kate asked.

"It does now."

"I . . . may I have it? To remember you by?"

"Aye, if you like. You could place a portrait of your father inside."

Pleased, Kate pushed from the bench and took the worn gold in her hand. She examined the locket carefully then pressed the latch and looked at the portrait inside. Surprise rounded her mouth.

"Papa, Lady Nellanor has a likeness of Lady Carlisle."

Wine spilled over Nell's fingers. Her heart banged against her chest and the blood rushed from her face. "Kate! You recognize the portrait?"

"Nell? Are you well?"

She was not. The hall spun before her eyes. Her breath seemed to stick in her throat. She didn't resist when Will's strong hand supported her back and he guided the wine cup to her lips.

"Katie darlin', let me have the locket." Will studied the portrait then frowned at Nell. "You continue to surprise me, m'love. Why on earth would you carry a portrait of Anne Baywick? Was she kin?"

Nell gripped the edge of the table and lowered her head. When the dizziness receded, she gazed up at Will. "God in heaven, tell me! Who is she? Do you know her? Is she alive?"

"Lady Nell is shaking, Papa!" Kate ran around the table and placed her arm around Nell's shoulders.

Kneeling before her, Will framed her bloodless face between his hands. "Anne Baywick died twenty years ago, Nell."

"When I was two." She wet her lips. "How did she die? How do you know her?" A hundred questions—nay, more—burned her tongue. A sense of unreality made her feel suddenly weightless, as if she would float from the bench if she relaxed her grip on the table edge.

"A larger version of the locket miniature hangs above the mantelpiece in Baywick hall. Kate and I have seen it many times," Will said. Kate nodded solemnly. "I don't know the entire tale, but I believe Anne Baywick was slain in a Scottish raid."

"Oh, God. Sweet Jesu." One of Nell's hands left the table edge and closed around the locket. "Until I read Elizabeth's letters, I thought this woman—Anne Baywick—was my mother. But I knew nothing about her; I didn't know if she was alive or dead. Not even her name." She gripped Will's arm and lifted pleading eyes. "Who was she? What was she like?"

" 'Tis said Anne Baywick was a beautiful woman, much loved in the town." Concern knit his brow. "Nell, you're trembling like a lamb at shearing."

"Was Lady Anne your mama?"

Nell pressed her hands together hard and bit the inside of her cheek. "I don't know. Uncle Robert told me this locket was tucked into my swaddling bands when I was left with the master of the wards." Had Robert said that? Or did she remember it so because she had wanted it to be true? "I always assumed . . ." She touched a shaking hand to her forehead. How odd the tricks of fate. She who had never had a mother now had two. "I have to go there, Will," she said, looking at him. "I have to go to Baywick."

"Aye." He brushed a fingertip over her lips. "Tread softly, Nellie love. History hangs in the balance."

"I have to know the truth."

"Mayhaps 'tis not the truth you want, m'love."

She closed her eyes. "I have to know."

Snow fell through the night, draping rooftops and blanketing the fields. Clasping Will's hand beneath a spread of fur robes, Nell listened to the whisper of sleigh runners gliding over the crust. Though she hadn't slept, she felt vividly alive to the ice-blue sky, to the cold morning sunshine that transformed the snow crystals into glittering jewels. A flow of chill air ruffled the feathers on her hat and cooled her hot cheeks.

Whether or not Anne Baywick had been Nell's mother, a life-long mystery was about to be solved. Finally she would know the woman in her locket. She approached the moment with fear and longing.

At the door to Baywick manor, Will lifted her from the sleigh and clasped her shoulders. Wordlessly he embraced her then led her inside.

The interior was dim. Heavy dark woods. Stone walls. Large faded tapestries. The great hall was strewn with rushes that smelled of dust and disuse.

Will presented her to Baywick's aging bailiff and his wife, but Nell heard their names as if from a far distance. She stood as though rooted, staring upward at the portrait over the mantelpiece.

A shaft of light falling from the high narrow windows near the roof arches illuminated the likeness of Anne Baywick. The same likeness Nell carried in the locket she had worn all her life.

But unlike the miniature in her locket, the Baywick portrait had not faded with time. Now Nell knew that Anne's laughing eyes had been as clear and gray as her own; Anne's hair was a fiery reddish gold as were the curls pinned above Nell's ruff, as brilliantly colored as Elizabeth Tudor's tresses once had been. Immediately Nell noted the resemblance between Elizabeth and Anne Baywick. But Elizabeth's features were thin and sharp, softer and more rounded on Anne. Where Elizabeth Tudor was handsome, Anne Baywick had been beautiful.

Somewhere behind her, Nell heard Will speaking to the bailiff and his wife; she heard him call her name. But she could not tear her gaze from the portrait. She had confided her childhood secrets to this woman, had longed for her, had dreamed of her and had loved her. Anne Baywick had played as large a role in Nell's life as—as had Elizabeth Tudor.

A persistent hand plucked at her sleeve. Reluctantly Nell turned from the portrait.

"M'lady?" The bailiff's wife coughed into a wrinkled hand. A shapeless black gown hung from her thin frame. "Lord Brampton, he says you have need to know of Lady Anne." Nell nodded dumbly as Dame Haldon inspected her with eyes the years had robbed of luster but not of sharpness. The old woman bobbed her cap. "Aye," she said finally. "You look like her."

"I . . . I'd like to sit down."

Dame Haldon led Nell to the settle before a small fire dwarfed within the mammoth hearth. She seated herself on a stool facing Nell and folded her hands against her skirts.

"She were distant kin to the queen, you know. She used to say she and Bess Tudor looked enough alike to be sisters. Like acorns from the same tree. But my Lady Anne were more beautiful than Bess Tudor."

"Dame Haldon, I need to know . . ."

"I know what 'tis you want to know. Lord Brampton, he told me." The old woman gazed into the fire before making up her mind. Finally she shrugged. "Mayhaps it's time the tale be told. Mayhaps she would have wanted someone to know."

"Please—I must know if Lady Anne gave birth to a child."

"If I'm to tell it, Ladyship, I'll be telling it me own way. From the start, lest you err and think my Lady Anne did less than right and proper."

Will came to stand behind her. He placed his hands upon Nell's shoulders.

"Lady Anne wed young as they did in them days. Still do if they's enough fortune to be gained. She were nine on her marriage day, and Lord Carlisle, he were twenty and five. I weren't there, you understand, not for the match. I came to Lady Anne's service where she were twenty and judged ripe to run a household and do her duty by Lord Carlisle. Lawrd, I'll ne'r forget the day she came to Baywick."

The old woman stared into the flames as if the past flickered there, and her face softened.

"Laughing and skittish and so vibrant alive, she were. 'Twas plain to all Lord Carlisle were besotted with her—and just as plain that she were not. But she wanted to be, and that be the God's truth. Lawrd, how she tried to please that man, tried to love him."

"But she couldn't?" Nell lifted her face toward the portrait, toward softly laughing eyes.

Dame Haldon shrugged and smoothed her bodice. "He weren't a cruel man, Ladyship. He were just a dull man. Goutylegged and bookish, he were." Her faded eyes caressed the portrait. "While she, my Lady Anne, she took life in gulps. Riding and dancing, hawking and hunting, taking each moment and making it sing. Whatever she did, she put her heart behind it. 'Tweren't no deception in her, not a mickle ounce. Lord Carlisle, he knew he had her body but he dint have her. Do ye know what I be saying?"

Nell nodded.

"Well. One day when my Lady Anne were taking bread and cheese to old Alderson—he were took sick and feverish—the Scots came. Swooped out'en the hills like devils, they did. And Jamie Gordon took her. Woulda killed her sure, but he saw her first so he took her instead. Carlisle, he went crack-brained when he returned and found her gone. Went to war against the thieving Scots, he did. Vowed to kill ever last one until he had her back."

Bobbing her cap, Dame Haldon looked into the flames, remembering. "Then one winter morn the Gordon brought her back. 'Twas the only way to end the war. She were riding pillion, her arms around his waist and her head on his shoulder, her hair blowing free. The Gordon kissed her good-bye and it broke the hearts of those of us what seen it."

"She was with child," Nell whispered. She gripped Will's hand so tightly he winced.

"Aye. Lord Carlisle, he said he'd dash the babe's brains against the stones. Said he wouldn't have no Scots bastard at Baywick manor." The old woman met Nell's gaze. "She wanted the Gordon's babe, Ladyship. Wanted that babe like she wanted air in her lungs. When her time came, she invented a message from Bess and sent Lord Carlisle off to court at London. Then she got up from her bed, torn and bleeding she was, and she carried that babe to Carlisle Town. Wouldn't trust the deed to none but herself."

"A daughter."

"Aye. A girl child." The fire popped and settled in the silence. "The life went out of her then. My Lady Anne, she did grieve terrible for that babe. And Carlisle, he tried everything to make her tell where she'd hid the infant. Beat her bad, he did. Turned ugly mean. But she wouldn't speak. Not a word."

Nell covered her eyes.

When Dame Haldon resumed, her voice was strained and thin. "Then one Maying, the elders set the pole near the forest edge and the whole town was there. The Scots rode out of the woods, not whooping and warring, but silentlike. And Jamie Gordon rode toward my Anne, looking like a young God, he did, fierce and tall and riding that white stallion." She closed her eyes and her hands tightened in her lap. "He stopped not ten feet from where she stood. And he held out his hand and said he'd come for her if she would have him. My Anne looked at the Gordon, her eyes shining fire, fair ablaze she were. And then Carlisle killed him. Shot the Gordon with a crossbow before my Anne could reach him."

"And Anne?" Nell spoke but no sound emerged.

"The Scots went mad like they do, but it was fair battle. When 'twas finished, my Anne was dead like so many others."

It was Will who broke the silence. "Tell her about Carlisle."

"Carlisle were wounded but 'tweren't nothing. Lord Carlisle lived twenty years more, searching for Anne's babe, he was. He never give it up. He were still searching last harvest when he died."

Nell dashed the moisture from her eyes with the back of her hand. "The babe," she whispered. "Did the babe have a mark? A star-shaped mark on one hip?"

Shock pleated the wrinkles folding Dame Haldon's cheeks. "Nay! That babe were perfect in every way!"

"Did you see for yourself?" Will asked.

A struggle ensued behind the old woman's eyes. "I dint see the babe naked," she admitted finally. " 'Twere swaddled when I seen it. But that babe were perfect! My Lady Anne, she told everyone how perfect were the Gordon's babe! 'Tweren't nary a blemish. If that babe had borne a mark, my Anne would have told me so. The midwife would have spoken. Nay, Ladyship. The babe were unmarked and perfect!"

Nell stared upward at Anne Baywick's portrait. There must have been a mark. She wanted Anne Baywick's babe to have borne a star-shaped mark. Withdrawing the locket from her bodice, Nell held it to her cheek then cupped it in her palm as she had done so many, many times before.

Dame Haldon stared. "That's hers! The Gordon give it to her and she wore it always! Where did ye find it?"

Nell explained, but Dame Haldon shook her cap in disbelief.

"Nay, Ladyship. 'Tisn't possible. Ye couldn't have had this locket tucked in your swaddling. My Anne were wearing it when she died. Two years after ye say ye were swaddled."

Nell was speechless. Will stroked her shoulder and leaned to the bailiff's wife. "Can you tell us what happened to the locket after Lady Anne's death?"

"Aye, m'lord. The locket were bequeathed to Lady Anne's kin cousin. I know 'tis a fact for I placed the locket in his hands meself. And I said the words she'd vowed me to say."

"Robert." Nell's voice cracked around a whisper. "You gave the locket to Robert Dudley, the Earl of Leicester."

Dame Haldon's eyebrows rose toward her cap. "Aye, Ladyship. 'Twere Dudley I give it to."

"What—what did you say to him?"

"What she vowed me to say. That he were to do with the locket what he deemed best and wise. My Anne said Dudley, he would know what were meant. If 'twere not possible, then the locket were to be dealt as Dudley thought fit."

"That's all?"

"My Anne thought 'twere enough," Dame Haldon said primly. " 'Twas the safest course."

Nell dropped her head and covered her face with her hands. Robert Dudley had known of Anne Baywick's tragedy, that much was certain. The rest remained shrouded in mystery.

Had Robert given Nell the locket that had belonged to her mother as he had claimed? Or had he witnessed her deep need and filled that need by giving her an illusion to cling to? In his fashion Robert had been a generous man. Nell could imagine him believing no harm would come if he gave Nell a locket that more rightly should have gone to another child. If he knew Anne's child was lost or dead. Had he known? One layer of truth peeled back only to reveal another layer, still murky and unknown.

Dropping her hands, Nell stared up at Anne's portrait, seeing her own eyes, her own hair and mouth. But those features could also have belonged to Elizabeth Tudor. Nell resembled them both.

Dame Haldon studied the despair pinching Nell's face. "Ye say ye've worn this locket all your days?" When Nell nodded, she tilted her cap and squeezed her eyes shut. Then she sighed. "Well, then. Do ye ken the secret of the locket?" she asked finally.

"The secret? I know of no secret."

"Give it over." Dame Haldon turned the worn gold in her hand, then pressed the latch that opened the lid to Anne's portrait. She gazed upon the portrait for a moment, then beckoned Nell closer. "Once 'tis opened, ye press the latch thrice more like this." A second compartment opened and Nell gasped. Dame Haldon hesitated, then extended the locket to Nell's shaking hands.

A man's portrait backed the portrait of Anne. Blazing dark eyes stared at Nell from beneath heavy brows. The man was proud and fiercely handsome.

Nell wet her lips before she could speak. "Bruce Gordon?"

"Aye. 'Tis the Gordon himself."

Later Nell would stare at the portrait of the Gordon until her eyes stung, but now her attention centered on a folded yellowing paper that had conformed to the shape of the locket over the years. She touched it with shaking hands. "Jesu. I didn't know. All these years, and I didn't know."

Carefully she pried the paper free and smoothed it against her skirts. The tiny square shimmered behind a curtain of tears. Sweet, sweet heaven. If only she had known of the message. If only . . .

"Nell? Nellie love?"

"I . . . I can't." Her fingers quivered too violently to steady the paper. She couldn't see past the tears welling in her eyes. "Please, Will. Read it to me."

He accepted the square of parchment and walked nearer the light flickering in the hearth. Before he read, Will glanced at Nell who rested her head against the settle back. Her face was as white as her lace ruff, turned upward toward Anne Baywick's portrait.

He cleared his throat.

"*My dearest child. If you are reading this, I am dead. But death has not dimmed my love for you. Wherever fate takes you, my spirit shall follow. Live your life fully, my heart, my beautiful daughter. Don't be afraid to live and to love, for love is all that matters. All else is illusion.*"

Will looked at the tears streaming from beneath Nell's lashes. "It's signed, *Your loving mother, Anne Baywick.*"

And then it was finished. There was naught more to say. Moving as if her feet were wooden, Nell walked outside to the sleigh and waited there while Will pressed a purse into Dame Haldon's hands.

An early darkness cast long blue shadows across the snow as the sleigh carried them home to Willowick. Silent tears slipped from Nell's eyes, and she felt too drained to halt them. She buried her face against Will's fur collar and clasped the locket as if it were the most precious jewel in history.

At the gate, Will lifted her from the sleigh and carried her inside and up the stairs. After undressing her trembling body, he laid her gently between the bed linens and stroked her until the warmth slowly returned to her limbs. Gently, gently, he caressed her breasts and hips, lingered above the star-shaped mark, then ran his hands along her calves and thighs. Her lips parted beneath his. And she came to him with a passion as fierce as the night winds.

When finally she fell back into the pillows, sated and exhausted, he called for hot wine and sausage, and when they had eaten, he took her again, this time with slow tenderness. He didn't enter her until his body and hers trembled with need and urgency, and he read her subtle signals, followed where she led until they were drenched and their passion feverish and explosive.

Stroking the damp hair from her temples, he gazed into her eyes. "I love you, Nell."

She kissed his palm then closed her brimming eyes and turned her face away.

When Will finally slept and the manor had quieted into chill darkness, Nell stared upward unable to sleep.

"Who am I?"

The question had plagued her throughout her life.

Slipping quietly from the bed, she tied on a thick velvet wrapper and paced before the embers dying in the fire. She pressed a hand to her forehead and followed the circles in her mind.

She began with Elizabeth's letters. The letters suggested she was the queen's bastard. But the star-shaped mark had been identified on the wrong hip.

Next her thoughts jumped to Dudley. Robert had told her the locket contained a portrait of her mother. Had he played false to protect Elizabeth? Regardless of Robert Dudley's words or intent, Anne Baywick had made no mention of a star-shaped mark. She had, in fact, belabored her babe's perfection, had made issue of it.

Thrusting a hand through her hair, Nell paused before the bedside table containing her small collection of belongings. The silver casket, the gold locket, and Robert Dudley's chipped signet. A paltry collection for all her years. And all she would ever have of herself. What answers were to be gleaned lay in the items before her. Her heart told her so.

Returning to the hearth, Nell sank to a stool before the embers and closed her lashes. Carefully, meticulously, she recalled each word of Elizabeth's letters, then she reviewed what she had learned of Anne Baywick's story. Two such very different women. And one of them was her mother, this also her heart insisted. But which?

Was she the daughter of a coldly calculating woman who deliberately chose power and ambition above the love of a man and child? Or was she the daughter of a woman whose passion for life and love had eventually killed her?

Unable to sit quietly, Nell rose and restlessly wandered the chamber. She lifted a wine pitcher, replaced it. Lit a candle and extinguished it. She slipped Robert's ring upon her finger and stared at the worn surface.

"Sweet Christ, I wish you were alive," she whispered.

But would Robert have unraveled the mystery if he were alive today? Nay, she thought, scrubbing a hand across her eyes. Nay. He had not done so when he'd had the opportunity. Why? Because—Nell was Elizabeth's whelp, the brat Elizabeth would rather have drowned than acknowledge. Robert Dudley had taken his queen's secret to the grave.

But he had wanted Nell to have the casket and the letters. Why?

Because Nell was his daughter and Elizabeth's? This question led her back to the central enigma: Why would Elizabeth place the mark on the wrong hip?

She wouldn't. Therefore, Nell must be Lady Anne's daughter. But if she was Lady Anne's daughter—why had no one noticed the star-shaped mark? Without the mark, Nell could not be Lady Anne's daughter.

The mystery circled round and round until Nell's head ached with it. Pausing in her aimless pace, she eased back the bed curtain and her eyes softened as she gazed at Will's dark curls against the pillow. If Elizabeth was her mother, Will was forever lost to her.

A cramp pained her stomach and she turned aside, letting the curtain drop. She loved him. She hadn't wished it, hadn't sought it, but she loved him.

Could she cast Will Steele aside as Elizabeth had cast off Robert Dudley? Nell's lip twisted. Was she as vain and capricious as Elizabeth Tudor, a woman who chose power above passion, a crown instead of love? A woman who, if the letters could be believed, abandoned the flesh of her flesh saying: It matters not?

Nay, never. A shudder passed through Nell's body. Elizabeth Tudor was not the woman she wished to emulate. Never. Her heart yearned toward Anne Baywick of the laughing eyes and passionate spirit.

But there was no star-shaped mark on Anne's perfect babe.

Again and again Nell's thoughts returned to the missing mark. Sinking to the stool before the embers, she buried her face in her hands. If only she could be certain Anne's message had been written to her. If Anne had but mentioned a mark, a hint of a mark. If she hadn't made such issue of her babe's perfection . . .

"My God!"

Nell sat upright and blinked at a point in space. "Oh, my God!" Her hands flew to her mouth, smothering a sudden cry. "Of course. Aye. Oh, aye." Tears sparkled on her lashes. "I would have done the same!"

Laughing and crying, she dashed the tears from her eyes and ran to the bed and threw back the curtain.

"Will! Wake up, Will." Sitting on the bedside, she shook him until he frowned and pushed up on his elbows. "I know who I am!" Her face was radiant. Her eyes were shining. "After all these years—I finally *know*!"

CHAPTER
19

'Tis the birthmark, isn't it?" Will asked. "The mark's the key to it."

"Aye." She pulled her legs up on the bed beside him. Excitement glistened in her eyes.

"Well, then. 'Tis as I feared. It's war," he said dully. "Mother against daughter. Englishman against Englishman."

"Nay, Will. Nay. Lady Anne was my mother!" She dropped a kiss on his surprised mouth and caught his hands between her own. "Don't you see? Anne *had* to claim the babe was perfect. If she'd admitted to a birthmark, she would have made it easy for Lord Carlisle to find the child and kill her."

"Aye," Will agreed slowly. "I see where this road leads."

"Lady Anne protected her babe the only way she could. By insisting it was perfect and without blemish, she set Lord Carlisle a false scent. She made certain he would never find and harm her babe." Tears of happiness streaked her cheeks. She tossed back her hair and clasped Will's hands to her breast. "She loved me, Will. She loved me enough to give me up because it was the only way she knew to save my life. She did everything possible to protect her babe . . ."

"Aye," Will said. "It had to be that way. The mark would have flagged the child for Carlisle's vengeance." He caught her face and held it. "Then there isn't to be a civil war?"

"Nay! If we haven't misread the letters—if Elizabeth Tudor truly birthed a child—it wasn't me. It can't have been me, Will. Lady Anne Baywick was my mother!"

"You don't want a crown?"

"I don't need a crown anymore to know who I am."

They regarded each other a moment, then Will gave a shout and grabbed her, tumbling her in the linens. "I love you, woman. I don't care who the hell your mother was. I love you!"

Nell's eyes twinkled up at him as she wound her arms around his neck. "Even if I'm part Scot?"

"I've always suspected it," he murmured, kissing her throat. "No woman could be as maddeningly stubborn without a generous dose of Scots blood. 'Tis a shame for you, woman, but somehow we'll live with it."

"I love you, Will Steele." It was the first time she had spoken the words aloud and she marveled at how wonderful they sounded. "I love you."

"It vexes me greatly that it took you this long to admit it."

"You knew?"

Pulling back, he placed a hand on his heart and pretended astonishment. "How could you not love me?"

"Shhh. You'll wake the manor." Laughing, she placed a finger across his lips.

"I'm landed, wealthy, and my sheep are fat and healthy—those your kin haven't stolen, blast their eyes. My wool is the finest in the entire North. I'm told I'm not unpleasant to look upon. I can drink any man under a table and love a woman to distraction. And—I'm as mad as a March wind for you."

"Oh, Will. I do love you."

He laughed then his expression grew serious. "Marry me, Nellie love. Kate and I need you."

"You'd wed a lass who's part Scot?" Her eyes twinkled up at him.

" 'Tis against my better judgment, and I'll be a laughingstock, but . . . aye, m'love. If you'll have me. And if you don't invite your thieving kin to the wedding."

She kissed the corner of his mouth. "I'll want to visit court on occasion . . ."

"Once a year. No more." His lips brushed across her eyelids.

"Mayhaps twice a year." Slipping her hands beneath the linens she trailed her fingers between his thighs.

"Jesu," he groaned. When his lips released hers, he pushed up and gazed into her eyes. "One thing—this business about your opinion prevailing—we've finished with that nonsense, agreed? Or are you planning to order me about for the rest of our lives like you've been doing the past few weeks?"

"I'm certainly going to try, m'lord." Laughing, Nell twined her arms around his neck and molded her body to his. "But I'll be clever. You won't notice."

"In that case . . ."

Their lovemaking was full and satisfying. No barriers lay between them now. As dawn spread the snowy fields with pink and blue, Nell rested in his arms and smiled, comforted by the sweetness of knowing she had finally come home. To a family of her own.

"Are you awake?" Will asked, stroking her hair.

"Hmmm."

"It seems we've overlooked a few major items, Grand-mother."

Grandmother. Nell's eyes flew open and she pushed up on an elbow to stare down at him. "Lord Mendenshire!"

"Aye. Not to mention the casket and the letters. And the Tower for you and a noose for me."

"God's teeth!"

Anyone not seeing the speaker would have judged from the voice and the inflection that Elizabeth Tudor had entered the room. Nell cleared her throat and swore softly.

For an instant doubt clouded her expression. Then resolution firmed her mouth and her gray eyes steadied. She had made her choice, and she had not chosen Elizabeth. She had chosen Anne Baywick and a life filled with love. She would not look back, nor, she knew, would she suffer a moment's regret.

"This requires some thought," she said, lying back in his arms.

"Mayhaps," Will agreed dryly.

"I think the queen will release me from my plight troth—if the matter is presented cleverly." She tapped her teeth with a fingernail. "Which leaves us the casket and the letters . . ."

Day after day, she turned the problem in her mind. She held the casket on her lap and ran her fingertips across the torn wax seals. A hundred times she cursed the Spaniards for their greed. A hundred times she wished the seals were whole and undisturbed.

"We could tell Elizabeth we didn't read the letters."

Will lifted an eyebrow and shook his head.

"We could destroy the letters and tell her . . ."

"Nay, Nellie," he said quietly.

"Dammit!" Her chin firmed stubbornly. "I won't give up. There's an answer and I'll find it."

She did. And the answer was so simple. It had been there all the while.

Sitting up in bed, she looked at Will's shoulder and laughed out loud. There, where his shoulder had rested against her hand, was a fading imprint of Robert Dudley's signet. The ragged staff and bear.

She held out her hand and examined the ring. Aye. With a bit of blue wax and a rubbing of gingerroot to give an appearance of age . . .

"Lady Nell?" Kate appeared at the bed curtains, Wiggins under her arm. "Is Papa awake yet?"

"He is now," Will said, yawning.

Kate and the kitten bounced onto the bed and settled between them. Nell gazed at Will over Kate's dark curls and a shining radiance illuminated her smile.

"I know how to do it," she said. And she told Will her plan.

Kate looked at them. "Does this mean Lady Nell can stay with us?"

"Aye," Will said softly, looking at her over Kate's shout of joy.

"I love you both," Nell said, reaching to embrace them.

No crown on earth was more precious than the love she saw in their eyes.

They stood close, Elizabeth noticed, almost touching but not. Looking away from them, she held the silver casket up to the wintry light and examined Robert's wax seals. The seals were intact. She studied them carefully then narrowed a cool gaze on Will Steele and Nellanor Amesly. The moment stretched long before she inserted the key into the casket's lock and broke the seals. Her long finger touched the yellowing letters inside. She knew at a glance the letters were hers, the originals. Dropping the lid, she lowered the casket to her lap where it caught the firelight and glowed against her jeweled hands.

"Very well," she said finally. Did they think she failed to notice the quick glance they exchanged? "You are released from your pledge to Lord Mendenshire, Lady Nellanor. You have our permission to wed Lord Brampton."

Human nature never failed to surprise. She had judged them as compatible as fire and water. Nodding to Will, she added, "Baywick is yours, m'lord. Cecil will have the documents for you by midday."

They bowed, curtsied, and blathered flattery at her until she dismissed them with a flick of her fingertips. Before the door closed, she saw Steele pull Nellanor into his arms and, laughing, swing her up and then against his body.

Turning in her chair, Elizabeth watched the snow whirling out of a gray sky, melting down the windowpanes. A log shifted and popped in the grate, the sound loud in the empty room.

Would she see Nellanor again? Mayhaps once or twice a year. The thought caused her a momentary pang, uncharacteristic and unexpected. It didn't matter.

Watching the snow raised a chill to her hands and she edged her chair nearer the fire. The silver casket slipped across her brocade skirts and she caught it before it fell. She touched the broken wax seals.

"Did you think we wouldn't know?" she said aloud. Had they truly believed she wouldn't recall Nellanor wore Robert's old signet, she who remembered every detail regarding her sweet Robin? Or that she wouldn't guess how easily a pattern could be cast and aged with a rubbing of herbs?

"The bear's ear is missing." Time had chipped the piece from Dudley's signet. She remembered teasing him about it, urging him to commission a new ring. Shaking her head, carefully, so as not to disarrange her wig, she made a sound partly derision, partly grudging admiration.

Then, slowly, she opened the casket and withdrew the first letter, slipping the blue ribbon with fingers that trembled slightly. She read it through twice, remembering. The color of Robert's eyes that day, the soft urgency of his kiss against her mouth. The touch of his skin. Then she deliberately dropped the pages on the fire and watched them burn.

"The girl is a fool." She stared at the snow dying down the windowpanes. Frost had begun to form at the corners.

She read and reread the last two letters before she fed them to the fire and watched the pages blacken and curl.

"Only a fool would exchange a kingdom for love." Snowy light cast long chill shadows across her breast. "Only a fool," she whispered, watching as the last letter fell to ashes.

But there were tears in the old queen's eyes.